DRESSED TO KILL

DRESSED TO KILL

BOOK 1

Crown Fall

Podium

Podium

DRESSED TO KILL

CHAPTER 1

My mother was a sewing machine. Not a mechanical one, though she may as well have been. Her hands blurred at incomprehensible speeds, her needle buzzing as she worked; the system imbued her with speed and accuracy that veered past the realms of the mechanical and into the realms of magic.

Her needle wove through cloth with supernatural precision, bending to align itself or twisting in midair to perfect a stitch, the sound louder than a sewing machine. Our house was a sewing machine, too, though it no longer worked. Like all things in our town, it had fallen into a state of disrepair. It was not through a lack of effort on our part. Warped glass in the ceiling let just enough light into the workshop to work by. Wallpaper hung in huge, decaying sections, like sloughing flesh on a desiccated animal.

I was just happy we didn't have any flies.

Time and wear had chipped away tiles, sections missing from the workshop floor. Few remained pristine. Scabbed-over scars decorated the surviving furniture; marks of repairs that fought against the march of entropy. We couldn't afford proper carpentry this far out in the sticks.

The wrecks of old furniture stacked against the wall like a bone pile; the old chairs and tables that weren't worth repairing leaned on each other for support, legs missing and surfaces worn down through the wooden lacquer. Despite our best efforts to keep the place clean and dry, it still smelled like mold.

Mom's current table creaked under the pressure of her work as she stitched together leather at superhuman speed. Then she stopped. It was always weird when she [Canceled]—looking at the action hurt. One moment, her hands were down, needle stabbing into the leather work, and the next she was inches away; though she hadn't moved at all. Magic was weird.

She looked at me with tired eyes and an even more tired smile. The work was done for the day. A pile of clothing stitched from cloth and leather was piled on the table nearly to the point of toppling.

"My light." She stood. The chair screeched as it moved over the tile. "He should be here soon. Are you excited?"

"Yes." I swallowed and looked at the door. Today was the day her power would be mine.

I nearly jumped when I felt my mother's hand land on my shoulder. Nervous energy filled me today, making me distracted. It was only fair. Today was the day I found out if I inherited my mother's class.

I didn't have her hair or her face. Mom looked almost nothing like me; her hair was brown and frizzy and locked into tight curls. Her facial features were soft. Round. The only thing I got from her was her eyes. Bright blue.

"My light," she said. I turned to her. She searched my eyes. "I know you don't want to." She paused, figuring out what she was going to say. "I know you like what we have here, in our little workshop in our little village. But this village won't last much longer."

"Unless a Noble starts actually clearing the dungeon," I said. She searched my eyes again.

"If you do get your—his class…" *Your father's class.* She left the words unsaid. "You shouldn't limit yourself to this village. If the world is open to you, Gwendolyn," she said, using my full name to let me know she was serious. My father the Noble.

"I know, Mom," I said. She had had this talk with me more than once. Dozens of times, since I turned fourteen and approached the age when I would gain access to the system. Even so, she had also been teaching me to be a seamstress for years. I didn't have the system-enhanced powers she did, but I was still alright at it without them. I bit back the frustration. She was just trying to help.

"Think Noble thoughts. Think monster slayer." She gripped my shoulders tight.

"I will."

"Now help me carry these."

Mom pressed leather padding into my arms. It was all I could do to keep the piled stack from toppling, leaning to look around as I stepped out of the workshop and into the living room.

"Esmeralda," Maritha said from the couch, nodding at my mother. "The priest is already here. Hurry, so he leaves. He's making the entire town stink." She was knitting something together. Everyone in this house was always working. Patched-together upholstery strained to contain the worn padding of the room's furniture. The fireplace crackled. I smelled someone making food in the kitchen, which meant I would probably have to do dishes later. As with every other structure left in the village, a half-dozen people lived inside. The field around the dungeon sustained the buildings, and since no one had cleared it in years, it continuously shrunk, taking the buildings of the village with it. Soon, there wouldn't be any left. And the Noble who owned the village would take a fee for every villager he relocated.

The priest was already here. He rode in on a wagon half the size of our house with no animal to pull it. It snuck over our dirt roads to sit pressed between two rows of houses. Outside, a small line massed; the children in the village who had reached eighteen this year would be meeting the priest to unlock their system.

My mom led me past the wagon and the starry-eyed children staring up at the priest's wagon waiting for their turn. The church soldiers standing around it looked bored. I didn't get to look long as Mom led me away and down a different street, near the core of the city.

At the center of our town was the entrance to the dungeon. It was a dilapidated ruin, made of cut white bricks overgrown with moss and creeping vines. A hollow archway held a rippling image of stretching farmland interspersed with copses of trees. It was not dissimilar from our town. I turned away, rushing to catch up with Mom.

The sound of metal pounding metal overwhelmed every other noise in the calm of the streets. The forge's heat and sound dominated the central street of the town. The workshop of the town's only blacksmith was built into the house, like our own, though the working area was kept outdoors. Smoke billowed out of an ever-burning furnace.

"Bob," Esmeralda said. I wasn't sure if he heard her.

He was standing over an anvil, bringing down a hammer bigger than his head on a steel rod, a rolled cigarette burning in his mouth. The bang, bang, bang of metal on metal continued.

Bob towered over me; he was easily over six feet, bald, shirtless, and scar free. When using a blacksmith's tools, he possessed a superhuman ability to manipulate them. No normal human would be able to lift a hammer that large. The torque would break their wrist. It was an ignoble class, an unchosen blacksmith, able to wield a hammer and swing it fast enough that it could crush a car. Yet for some reason, people insisted that the noncombat classes could not fight monsters. They couldn't clear the dungeons that kept the cities alive and pumping.

"Bob!" Esmeralda said, louder.

"Just a second," he said, his voice audible over the ringing despite not raising it.

After a final hit, he dropped his hammer. It crashed so hard it shook the ground, dust coming loose from the roof. Bob grabbed the burning piece of flattened metal and rounded it out, bending the shape, handling white-hot metal bare-handed without so much as wincing. His hands didn't burn. With an irreverent toss, he dropped it into a bucket of water, liquid splashing out and hissing with heat when it hit the ground. I only noticed Gerald all but hiding behind his father when he made a noise at the boiling water splashing out, stepping backward.

He looked nothing like his father. Messy brown hair hung over his face. He met my eyes with an excited smile.

"Aren't you getting your class today?" I asked Gerald.

"What do you need?" Bob asked, voice booming.

"The padding. For your last order." Mom held up the leather in her hands.

"I already got my class," Gerald said. He looked around conspiratorially. He looked like he was going to be sick.

Bob's eyes lit up as he reached for the leather.

"Thanks, Esme. Come in."

Mom tried to wave him back, but he insisted. I followed her, Gerald walking alongside me.

"What about you?" Gerald asked me.

I dumped the leather padding onto a grease-covered shelf, picking up a piece that fell. Mom followed Bob into the kitchen.

"Not yet. I'm going after this," I said.

"Gwen!" my mom shouted. "Do you want tea?" She leaned out of the kitchen, looking down at me.

"Yes!" I replied to Mom before turning back to Gerald.

"I want you to know. Our classes won't change anything between us. I'm going to make it regardless. Your first weapon." Gerald held out a pinky to me. With a nervous smile, I returned the gesture, looping my pinky around his. We shook on it.

"You'll have to make something that will still work when I end up as a seamstress," I said, bitter, smiling.

"I still have the schematic." He nodded seriously.

"Schematic?" I laughed. It was too serious a word for our plans. I stepped past him and into the kitchen.

Bob delicately poured from a tea kettle into metal cups. The water steamed and frothed, condensing on the warped glass window above the sink.

After pouring out five cups, Bob took his own, swished it around, and drank it, still steaming. He let out a contented sigh.

Mom looked at the remaining cups dubiously. Gerald fetched a metal coaster, throwing it down onto the counter and reaching for an oven mitt. He stopped halfway, hand hovering in midair, and looked up at his dad.

Bob nodded.

Gerald touched one of the cups tentatively, as if afraid it would bite him. He poked it with the edge of two fingers before yanking them back as if the cup burned him. Then he reached out, pressing a palm to the cup, before finally closing his hand around it and putting it on the coaster. He'd inherited his father's class and his resistance to heat.

"Sorry about that," Bob said.

"He forgets sometimes," Marielle said from the dining room. Bob's wife was visible through the open floorplan of the house. She was leaned over the table, carving complex patterns in a piece of metal.

Gerald touched the cup to the engraved piece of metal he had set on the counter. It flashed blue. The cup stopped boiling.

He turned around, handing it to me with a smile. I took it in turn, taking a sip and nearly gagging at how bitter the tea was.

"Gerald…your elders first," Bob said, scolding his son.

"It's fine," Esmeralda said with a smile.

Gerald rushed to cool Mom's cup before handing it to her. She took a sip.

"I'd kill for one of these coolers," Mom said.

"You'd have to. They cost a gold," Marielle said from the dining room. "We just have it until we find a buyer. Then it's shipping out."

I took another sip. The tea was still bad. I set it down on the counter.

Mom drank the entire cup down. Then she drank mine.

"We'd better get going," she said, stretching. "The priest won't be here forever."

"Gwen. Good luck," Gerald said, serious. He reached forward for a hug, squeezing me, before pushing me back. "We need it," he whispered.

I swallowed nervously. Mom led me out the door, and I followed behind her to the priest's wagon in the middle of the street. The line around it had cleared.

Guards in armor of pristine white stood at attendance. Silver light radiated off them like a heat haze, bending the air. One guard had her helmet off. She glowed with prestige and strength that shattered when she took a drink from a flask. She nodded at me.

"Think Noble thoughts," Mom said to me. I looked up at her. We hugged.

The door to the wagon swung open, one of the village's children stumbling out. He looked up at me, excited, then shot off at a run. A pungent smell rolled out of the wagon. It was closer to a bus in size, pristine white and engraved with silver filigree. It looked like something from my old life. Something from Earth.

I stepped toward the wagon, sparing one last look back to my mom before throwing myself up the steps, several feet off the ground.

The wagon was bigger on the inside than the outside, and it wasn't just a trick of perspective. It had to have been as wide as the street inside. Smoke poured out from behind the priest, who himself was lowered into a plush, reclining couch that stretched across a wall.

Soot piled into the corners and edges against the white-painted wall. Cushions and blankets covered couches; storage containers were sunk into the floor. The priest was old. Older than anyone from the village; his hair was snow white. His robes matched it. His eyes were glued to the ceiling. I followed them, tracing the complex patterns decorating the ceiling.

I had seen no evidence of gods. But people weren't any less convinced of them in this life than the last.

"Gwen," the man said. He wasn't looking at me.

Think Noble thoughts. It was an old tradition. Maybe a bit of ancient superstition. People believed that if you thought about the class you wanted, you were more likely to be assigned to it. I didn't believe in it. I thought Noble thoughts anyway.

I hadn't told him my name. But priests had weird access to the system in a way that others did not. His eyes were irritated; pink. I didn't know if it was from his eyes being exposed to the smoke or from him inhaling it. His eyebrows furrowed as he raised a hand toward me, stopping in midair, looking increasingly confused as he scrutinized me. It became harder to maintain the facsimile of a smile. He was a dozen feet away, but I still felt so uncomfortable in this room.

He leaned forward.

[Awaken]

I shuddered as I felt power roll through me. There was a singular moment when I felt a presence of incomprehensible size turn and focus on me. I felt as if my soul was being weighed, judged, and measured. Time stood still. It was like I was in a river, power battering me from all sides. I was falling down and down. *Think Noble thoughts. Helping people. Killing monsters. Owning land.*

I felt it look away. It was as if all the light had gone out and I was hovering in perfect darkness. The world was so beautifully empty without its presence looking down at me. A bright blue box hovered in my vision.

CHAPTER 2

My father was a Noble. He left my mother behind in a border town with a large payment and a magically enforced vow of silence.

Half the village was hopping that I would be a Noble too.

Everyone in this world had a class; a preconceived place in society where you belonged. They were passed from parent to child. Rarely, just rarely, the gods would see fit to change the place of a single person, adjusting their class and raising them into Nobility. They were the Chosen.

I wasn't born a Noble. And I wasn't Chosen, either.

[Seamstress class unlocked: +5 to SPEED and DEXTERITY. +(10%+2%/Lvl) to all stats gained from crafted items.]

[Gwendolyn Tailor][Human, Lv1][Seamstress]

[Health: 10/10][Mana: 10/10][XP: 0/10]

[ATTRIBUTES]

▶SPD: 10

▶WIL: 5

▶STR: 5

▶DEX: 10

▶CON: 5

▶PER: 5

[SKILLS]

▶Crafting I

▶Running Stitch I

[PATTERNS]

▶NONE

My breath came back haphazardly. The blurred image of the room confronted me, and I struggled to blink it away, only to see the face of the priest inches away, leaning over me, eyes bloodshot. I recoiled, falling backward.

The priest stepped back.

"I thought you would be Chosen." The priest said, voice dripping with disappointment.

"Why would I be Chosen?"

"You have…" The priest sighed, falling backward into his chair. "So many threads attached to you."

I stared at him, waiting for more. He stared at the ceiling. Then he waved in a rather rude, dismissive gesture, the long sleeves of his robes falling back as he did so.

"Go."

I moved to stand but lurched, falling sideways, my body moving faster than I expected. My doubled speed was unkind to my coordination.

I stumbled out of the wagon and looked up at my mom. Her eyes were full of hope, and anything I could say would disappoint her. She wanted the best for me—to have a better life, to have been born with power, to be a Noble like my father. I was going to disappoint her.

"Are you—" she started to ask.

"I want to go home." I interrupted her, pushing past her, stumbling up the road. I didn't feel faster or more dexterous. My body felt wrong. I was going to disappoint the entire village. Deep in my heart I had always known I wouldn't inherit my mother's class. I was going to end up a Noble like my father. I had made plans. Dozens of plans for what to do when I became a Noble, to take over and buy this village so I could keep it alive. It would be simple. Easy. Why would the world give me something I wanted?

My plans had to go on anyway. My memory shot to my mother's supernatural ability to sew, the way her needle carved through tanned leather like paper. It could carve through living flesh, too, I knew.

I pushed open the door to our house and workshop, shot up the stairs, and pushed into my bedroom. I only had to share it with two other people. But the room was separated by hung curtains, giving an illusion of privacy. Complex patterns were weaved into the hanging cloth, tapestries decorated with images of a disorderly sky and verdant greens of forests, leftover thread from a hundred commissions interwoven in collages of color.

I collapsed into my bed and stared at them, emotion overwhelming me.

This was wrong.

I had mentally prepared myself for this outcome, all of my surface thoughts agreeing this was natural. But it was wrong. It wasn't what I really expected. Two lives full of failure. I curled up into a ball.

When my mom called me for dinner, I ignored her. She talked softly into the room, letting me know it would be down there when I was ready. I drifted in and out of sleep, waking up to find quiet shuffling in the room around me and a blanket over me.

I curled back up in the dark.

I don't know how long I sat before I heard the tinking noise on the window. One. Two.

God damnit, Gerald. Someone shuffled next to me in the dark.

I grabbed my backpack as I shot to my feet, trying my best to brush the wrinkles off my clothes, and rushed out the door before anyone could beat me to it. The creaking of the door made me cringe. Even trying my best to be quiet, the stairs protested loudly, old wood clinging desperately to life. I touched the knob on the front door.

My stomach growled.

I turned back and looted a wooden bowl. It smelled good; it was stacked full of soggy vegetables and meat, but I was sure it was fantastic when it was made. I heard the door creak open behind me and ran outside, awkwardly carrying the food.

Gerald was throwing rocks from the street.

"What are you doing?" I asked in stage whisper.

"Waking you up!" he said.

The door creaked open on the other side of the house.

"You're waking the whole house up," I hissed, looking back at the house even as I started speed walking down the street. I grabbed his arm and led him away.

"You said you'd meet me an hour ago," he said, cradling the wooden box in his arms as he struggled to keep up with me.

"That was before I got my class." I realized I had run ahead of him without trying. He was nearly jogging to keep up. Being a forger didn't necessitate speed. I slowed to let him match me, turning into the quiet street. The village was nearly dead quiet, save for the sound of wind whistling through the streets and shaking the trees.

I ended up following behind Gerald as he led the way to the dungeon at the center of the city.

"So you didn't…" Gerald started again, looking over at me. I looked up from the ground, meeting his eyes as he trailed off. "Sorry," he said.

"Swords won't do me any good, if you're asking," I said, nodding at the box he held. I tried to keep the bitterness out of my voice. Judging by Gerald's expression souring, I failed.

"Sorry," he whispered again.

We reached the dungeon, standing outside for a quiet moment, just us and rustling leaves.

Gerald popped the box open and presented it to me without meeting my eyes. He stood a full head over me.

I stared down into the box. Two polished metal needles as long as my arm were pressed into silk cushioning.

"They're not swords," I said, letting out a breath and grabbing one. It was cold in my hand.

"It's just like we talked about," he said. "I figured…either way, they count as swords, for the system. Which means they have weapon stats. But…" he trailed off again.

It was a gigantic sewing needle, wrapped with leather for a handle, a hole at one end for thread, big enough to accommodate rope. It was black and polished to a finish, sucking the heat from my hand.

I held it out in my hand. The weight strained my wrist. For the first time, I reached out to the system-enchanted magic inside of me, imagining the air as a cloth to stitch. A notification hovered in midair, already fading as quickly as it appeared.

[Running Stitch I] [FAILED CAST]

Magic grabbed my arm like an iron vice grip closing on it, locking it in place. Then it dissipated.

I frowned.

"Didn't work," I said.

"Oh, here. Maybe…" Gerald grabbed the box from the ground, pulling out the padding to reveal a rope supporting the cloth. He held it out to me. I looked at it in mute disbelief for a moment before tying the rope to the hole.

[Running Stitch I] [Mana: 9/10]

The iron vice grip of the system locked on my arms again. I gripped the needle with both hands, stabbing forward with a speed that whistled as it split the air, my arms automatically moving as if to thread the rope.

[Cancel]

I staggered forward as the magic released itself all at once.

Then I stood in awe, regulating my breathing. It would work. I could use the magic of sewing to fight.

"So?" Gerald asked.

"It could work. But…only to clear the lowest level of the dungeon. The seamstress class just doesn't have the stats necessary to kill monsters," I said. "Unless we…"

The words trailed off, dead on my tongue. I wanted to be the hero who saved the village. I didn't want to be a seamstress. Yes, I wanted to be like my mother. But I always thought that, with me being reincarnated on this world, I would be a hero of some kind.

Main character syndrome.

"Unless you make clothing out of the monsters. For the stats."

"Stupid," I said.

"Crazy," Gerald replied. "But it was your idea. That's the plan, right?"

I sat down, picking up the bowl of food and scooping it into my mouth bite by bite. Gerald sat on the muddy flagstones beside me. His eyes glanced from me to the giant sword to the dungeon. He was nervous, too. His fingers bounced on his knee.

"We're doing it," I said, taking the final bite of my food.

"We?" Gerald asked.

"I'm doing it. You stay out here. You're too young."

"Right," he said.

I pulled my backpack free and went through its contents. Bandages, check. The single potion our household owned, looted from our locked cabinet, check. It didn't glow as brightly as I remembered. Pain-numbing leaves for chewing, check. Bottles of water to clean a wound, check. I tied the rope around the second needle and looped it to my backpack, then strapped it onto my back. I held the other needle with both hands.

Gerald hugged me, then stepped back.

"Be safe," he said.

"It's just wolves, right? If it looks dangerous, I'll run." I nodded. "Don't worry."

The dungeon entrance loomed over me, made of stacked white stones covered in plants trying desperately to reclaim it. The portal surface was rippling, the world on the other side hard to make out. I sucked in a final, steadying breath, clutching the needle with two hands, knuckles white with tension.

Then I stepped into a world full of monsters.

CHAPTER 3

I slammed into a wall outside of reality, diving into an ocean of unreal, breaking the surface of the water to see something alien. My ears popped as reality shifted and unmade itself around me, an overwhelming feeling of vertigo sending me stumbling forward. I gripped onto the needle in my hand as reality shifted from wrong to right in an instant.

It was still daytime inside the dungeon, the sun low to the horizon and cutting the landscape in colors of burning orange and red. I checked my surroundings, alert, but there was no monster this close to the entrance. Despite their name and reputation, dungeons were relatively safe, so much so that the resources at their edges were harvested by the villagers.

Fields of grains waved in an invisible breeze, an ocean of farms expanding outward to the edge of the dungeon where the world grew hazy. A dirt road led upward to the center of the dungeon, a pile of boulders pinning the entire world together.

I looked back at the dungeon entrance. On this side, it was pristine, maintained by magic. Alabaster stones reflected the sun's light, polished to a reflective sheen.

The muddled image of Gerald was visible through the archway, barely identifiable through the rippling haze between us.

I steadied myself, turned around, and started walking toward the pile of boulders at the center of the dungeon.

I could do this.

I could kill the monsters. And I could still be a seamstress.

All I had to do was hunt a few animals. I had done that before. Granted, it was with a gun and an entire lifetime ago. And they weren't wolves. I kept telling myself I had no reason to be nervous, pressing on despite the floaty feeling urging me to turn around and lie down for the night.

It was just some wolves. Wolf-shaped things. Hardly even unworldly monsters. Probably under that pile of rocks. Or on top of it.

With a steadying breath, I strode forward into a den of monsters.

Every time I cleared the dungeon, it would slow down the town's decay. Eventually, with daily clears, I could reverse the decay and expand our village. I could prevent my family from being shipped off and sold as serf labor to another Noble or clipped onto an infrastructure project a world away from the life we've built.

The small pile of rocks loomed over me when I got close, boulders stacked haphazardly, filled with openings that led downward into a wolf den. I heard scratching on the stone as I approached, slowly, step by step, holding the needle between me and any danger as I followed the road around. The stones compressed against each other, forming an archway that opened down into the dark. The sun's light at my back cast my shadow long into the cave.

This was the Dungeonheart, the core of this floor that held the monsters or bosses.

I squinted to see inside.

Rumors from the town told me that it was full of wolves—just normal wolves. But no one knew how many there were. I stepped forward toward the entrance.

A wall of fur and flesh and teeth leapt toward me the moment I took the step, its form resolving in the dark, my eyes seeing its legs flash as it threw itself off the ground and rushed toward me. It let out a noise halfway between a bark and a growl.

[Running Stitch I] [Mana: 8/10] [Cancel]

[+4 XP]

I heard the crunch of bone, flesh giving way with a dull wet noise. My arms sagged at the weight as I tried to reconcile what I was looking at, the magic that had grabbed my arms and forced them to move confusing my sight.

There was a dead wolf on my sewing needle. It hung limp, blood oozing from the point of contact in its skull. I gasped, kicking the monster repeatedly to try to free it from my needle. With the third kick, it struck the ground. I panted from the effort, crouching low, holding the needle, looking for more monsters. Adrenaline pumped through my limbs. I was a coiled spring, ready to jump forward.

Nothing came.

I crept over the body, walking deeper into the cave, my eyes adjusting to the dark, following the sound of scratching. A wolf dug at the stone wall and the ground, freeing dirt. It stuck its nose down, sniffing at whatever it was trying to free from the earth.

I buried my sewing needle into its skull.

[Running Stitch I] [Mana: 7/10] [Cancel]

[+4 XP]

Exhilaration washed over me, releasing the fear of confronting a cave full of monsters. My eyes scanned every shadow. I was happy to be short for once; I barely had to duck to fit into the home of the wolves.

One of the shadows moved. Its eyes flashed in the dark. How had I not seen it?

I threw myself at the ground, feeling my leg scrape on the dull stone, my ankle resisting bending farther with a spike of pain. The wolf landed with a thump, dashing forward and turning around. Its form blended with the shadows filling the cave, and even as I watched it became less corporeal, harder to track with my eyes.

[Health: 9/10]

I waved the pop-up away.

The wolf had a fucking stealth skill. Give me a break.

[Running Stitch I] [Mana: 6/10] [Cancel]

[+4 XP] [Level up] [Excess discarded]

My hands shook from the adrenaline. I put a foot down and forced the wolf off my needle, dropping the body on the floor. Turning to look deeper into the cave, I weighed my options.

What would this wolf give me? I could make a cloak from its pelt, deep black. Would it raise my dex? My speed? Or, could it grant me a skill of its own?

I didn't need any more kills. I was already level 2. I grabbed the leaking corpse of the wolf and dragged it out of the cave, careful and quiet, moving far from the wolf den. The world was plunging into shadow, nighttime encroaching in the dungeon world. When I'd dragged the wolf far enough, I fell back to sit and pulled up the leg of my pants.

Falling against the stones had broken open my skin, leaving me bleeding, and this world didn't have antibiotics. It was ironic that I was injured by the environment rather than the monsters. I reached into my bag for a canteen of water and cloth to clean and dress the wound before packing up and dragging the wolf body to the exit.

I should have brought a wagon—the other bodies were going to go to waste. The dungeon would erase them tomorrow. Stretching, I finished dragging the monster out, nearly falling to the ground as I stepped through the portal back to town.

Exhilaration warred with my nerves, extra shocks from the adrenaline fading. There was a dull ache in my leg. All I wanted to do was scream with joy. Being a seamstress didn't change any of my plans. I could still protect the town from the encroaching eviction and I could still inherit my mother's shop and will. My earlier worry was foolish.

I dragged the corpse through the dungeon entrance and into the city.

"What are you going to do with that?"

I nearly jumped out of my skin, turning to look at Sandy. Staring down from her height, a full head over mine, she made Gerald look small. She walked toward me, looking me up and down, her eyes hovering on the blood that had soaked through my pants. She sighed with disappointment.

"I'm going to make…" I trailed off. What was I going to make out of it? I looked back at the wolf's body. "…a cloak out of it."

"Yeah, you're gonna kill the wolf, butcher it, strip the body, and tan the leather by yourself? In your tailoring workshop?" Sandy asked, gesturing to my backpack. I took a step back. "With a seamstress class?"

"I didn't—no one said I had a seamstress class," I replied, looking over at Gerald.

"I didn't tell her," he said.

"If you had a Noble class, you wouldn't be sneaking around to clear the dungeon in the middle of the night," Sandy replied. "It would've been an event with the whole town invited to party."

Shit, was I that obvious? I stared wide-eyed at Sandy.

"No, but I know for sure now," Sandy said, as if I'd asked the question aloud. "So I'm going to assume you haven't told your mom."

"She wouldn't approve," I said.

"Alright. I'll let you know when the leather is ready for you. Do you want the bones?"

"What?" I asked, caught off guard. Sandy was a year older than me—she had always been abrasive. I assumed she would rush to her father or my mother and tell on them tonight. Instead she was here. "You're offering to…what? Butcher it for me?"

"Yes," Sandy said, clearly irritated she had to explain. "My father never comes into the butchering workshop. We can drag it there and no one will ever see it."

"Why?" I asked.

"Because I don't want to move. Yet. Stupid as your plan is, if you can keep clearing the dungeon, I can keep living here," Sandy said, stepping past me and grabbing the wolf. She picked it up by the scruff of its neck, moving it with ease. Another bonus of her class, probably. "Are you coming?" Sandy stopped and turned around to ask.

I looked to Gerald. He shrugged.

Sandy led us to her workshop on the other edge of town from my house. The streets were dark, everyone packed inside and asleep for the night. Sandy led us to a side door barely hanging on its hinges. The smell of blood and wood poured out as she pushed it open, the hinges creaking protest.

"Mind the step," she said.

I followed her carefully over the uneven ground, taking in the room. An oil lamp burned in a corner, providing enough light to work in. Sandy threw the wolf to the side, blood pooling where it landed. Hooks hung from the ceiling, mostly empty. One of them had what looked like a deer hanging from it. It wasn't really a deer, just something close to it. I always mentally translated the words for animals to their English equivalents.

A table in the corner was covered in polished knives, a bucket of water sitting on the side.

"You sleep in here?" Gerald asked. I looked back at him.

He was staring around in a daze. Indeed, pressed into one corner of the room were a bed and a dresser, clothing hanging from the hooks. The other workshop furniture had been pushed to the side or sat in disrepair.

"Better than having to talk to my dad," Sandy said. "Or share a room with five people."

Without pause, she reached up and pulled an apron from its hook on the ceiling, tying it behind her back. Then, she lifted the wolf with one hand, turning it around appraisingly. The monster was almost as large as I was—it was disquieting to see it handled so easily. Sandy mumbled to herself.

"Probably will only take a day or two," she said. "I'll take most of the meat as payment. You never answered. You want the bones? There's not much fat on it."

"No!" I said. "Why would I?"

Sandy shrugged.

"I could take some of them. I think I might be able to make something with them." Gerald said.

"Alright. Whatever I don't feed to the dog, then," Sandy said.

"When did you get a dog?" Gerald asked.

"Yesterday. Still a pup. One of the Templar Guards found it in the forest, traded it to us. I'll let you know when I'm done." Sandy looked over the tools on her table, eventually settling on a very, very large knife, before turning back to the wolf.

"I'll uh, talk to you then," I said, stepping back before Sandy started carving it open. She grunted an affirmation and I pushed my way out of the door.

"So…how did it go?" Gerald asked. I grunted.

"Well enough. Nothing but a few wolves inside. That one I brought…is something special, I think."

"You level up?"

"To two." I replied.

"What are you going to spend the points on?"

I pulled open the system.

[Gwendolyn Tailor][Human, Lv2][Seamstress]

[Health: 9/10][Mana: 6/10][XP: 0/10]

[Points available: 1]

[ATTRIBUTES]

▶SPD: 10

▶WIL: 5

▶STR: 5

▶DEX: 10
▶CON: 5
▶PER: 5
[SKILLS]
▶Crafting I
▶Running Stitch I
[PATTERNS]
▶NONE

▶DEX: 10
▶CON: 5
▶PER: 5
[SKILLS]
▶Crafting I
▶Running Stitch I

CHAPTER 4

I didn't open the shop to see what I could spend my point on until I was back in bed. A single point to choose my direction for the next days or weeks. I had hidden my bag in the workshop's pile of disused furniture, the needles and health potion shoved into a sagging cabinet that barely held itself together.

And now that I was finally under the blanket lying in bed in a room I shared with five people, I mentally invoked my single point and the shop.

[Tutorial: Skills are pulled from the skill deck 3 at a time, based on available materials, resources, and levels.]

[Skill Shop]

▶Wardrobe I

[RARE] Seamstress Inventory skill. Grants users access to a single outfit storage inventory. Additional levels allow additional storage.

▶Cross Stitching I

[COMMON] Enables system assistance with a new stitch type. Additional levels increase proficiency.

▶Quick Change I

[UNCOMMON] Allows user to instantly exchange a single piece of clothing with any article they are in physical contact with or that is stored in their Inventory. Additional levels allow user to change up to an entire outfit.

[Seamstress Inventory skill: Wardrobe]

My eyes glazed right over the skill shop. I had all the combat skills I needed to keep killing wolves. What I really needed were defenses, stats and skills that I couldn't achieve by being a seamstress.

The skills would be useful in the far future.

[Pattern Shop]

▶Lumberjack Pattern (Basic)

[COMMON] Grants minuscule bonuses to Strength and Constitution dependent on craft quality and materials used. Grants bonus point to Lumberjack skills depending on craft quality and materials used.

▶Peasant Pattern (Basic)

[COMMON] Grants minor bonus to Constitution dependent on craft quality and materials used. Grants bonus point to first skill in status.

▶Hunter Pattern (Basic)

[UNCOMMON] Grants minor bonus to Perception and Dexterity dependent on craft quality and materials used. Grants bonus to hunting skills depending on craft quality and materials used.

I needed a pattern that could help me fight. Granting bonuses to skills meant a point or more gained—which, if you had no points, meant that you would achieve that skill, even if it would only last as long as the clothing did. A Lumberjack pattern, for example, might give me proficiency with an axe—useful, if I didn't already have two giant needle swords.

A Peasant pattern would raise my constitution and health, letting me survive longer.

But there was only one thing in this shop that I needed right now: the Hunter pattern. I purchased it and felt the information flow into my mind. It was more like remembering than learning, old thoughts stuffing themselves into a dusty corner of my mind but coming to the surface like I had always known them, memories of cutting and crafting this particular pattern.

Like a memory from another life.

I closed my eyes and sighed contentedly, filled with the knowledge that I had magic. I had the power to protect the town, and I had the power to carry forward my mother's legacy.

When I awoke, the sun was already falling on my eyes, my skin warm from the heat.

"Gwen!" Esmeralda shouted again.

My body ached, and I groaned and curled up instead of replying.

"Wake up! We have breakfast downstairs."

I threw the blanket over my head, but then my stomach growled, and I pushed the blanket off and grumbled some affirmative at her to get her to close the door.

My mother waited for me at the table. She had clearly already eaten, but my plate was loaded with food, and she sat and stared in silence. We rarely ate this well—fresh bread, eggs, and meat—and I shoveled it down. Mom stared at me appraisingly.

"So…" she started. I looked up at her without swallowing, mouth full, scanning her eyes. "I took on a big work order. I was thinking…you could help me complete it. It will help keep you occupied."

I set my fork down and swallowed, still scanning her. She fidgeted.

"It's too much for me to do by myself, I mean." She rephrased the statement in a way that made me feel needed instead of saying that she got a huge work load to distract me from the fact that I was not a Noble. I was not destined for greatness. But more sewing wouldn't distract me. She must have seen the look on my face, because she continued.

"I could always cancel it if you…if you don't want to?" she said. There was a spark of hope in her eyes. I had not actually told her that I did not inherit my father's Noble class. She just guessed as much from me collapsing into my bed. Like Sandy said, if I was a Noble or Chosen, the entire town would've known.

"No, it's okay. I want to," I said, pushing the plate of food away. I wasn't hungry anymore. "But I don't have any patterns."

"That's great! No, I mean, it's okay! You can help stitch and as long as I finish the product, its quality will be mine. And you will still get XP!" Mom said, spitting out the words quickly, course correcting halfway through.

I ate the rest of my cold breakfast much more slowly.

There was a pounding at the door. I held my fork in my hand and looked to my mom, who in turn looked over my shoulder.

"Coming!" Teretha shouted; as much as Teretha could shout. Her voice was like a songbird's. She rushed out of the living room. As always, her arms were covered in stains from poultices, paints, and pigments made and collected from whatever she could find, grow, or buy around the town. She was probably my second favorite person in the house, after my mom. I always called her Terry.

I kept eating as the door swung open.

Valjean was looming in the doorway. He wore a jacket finely inlaid with gold filigree and played with a pocket watch between his fingers, brown curls falling in a wave over his head. His eyes scanned the inside of the living room before he turned back to Teretha. A well-manufactured smile took over his face.

"Hello, Teretha." The voice was sincere. At least it sounded sincere, but who knew how many levels he had in charisma?

"My lord," Terry said, half in jest, making a mock bow.

"Still just a mayor, I'm afraid. I'm here about the…" He turned and looked over Teretha's shoulder, down the hall that led to the front door. The dining room was at the back of it, and I leaned to get a look at him. For just a moment, I saw his manufactured charisma drop as his eyes locked on mine. They were cold, calculating, and scanning, all behind a mask of cordiality.

"For the order!" Mom said with a smile. "Terry, could you show him to the workshop? We will be out in a moment."

He smiled again. Terry led him away, the door slamming shut behind them.

I finished eating, pushed the plate back, and stood up.

He was alone in the workshop when we got there, spinning in circles and looking around. A second noble pushed the door to outside open a moment later, carrying a bolt of woven denim and crates of leather stacked high, dressed in armor that lacked the filigree and decor of Mayor Valjean's. He nearly threw the boxes to the floor. I cringed at the action. Another tile was probably broken under that stack of goods.

"Will this be enough?" the mayor asked, looking down at me, though the question was directed to my mom. She looked through the boxes.

"It'll be plenty," she said, turning to address him. "End of the week?"

"Yes. I'll be back then. Don't be late." Mayor Valjean's eyes never left me. I stared back up at him defiantly. There was more to this. He wasn't just here to place an order. He was evaluating me, scoping me out. Seeing if I was a threat. Seeing if I was a Noble. His eyes broke away. "This workshop isn't much. You know, you are quite talented. It's a waste of your skills. You could do more at Foundry."

"I'd hate to part with my workshop," Mom replied, crossing her hands and staring back at him. A tense moment of silence passed between them as he stared at her.

"I see," he said. "Well, I can't guarantee that you'll be relocated to Foundry if you wait until the town collapses."

"I understand," Mom replied with a smile. Another tense moment passed.

"Good luck," he said, sparing another glance my way. Then he left.

"He's such a dick," I said the moment the door closed behind him.

"He never had a life like ours," Mom replied after a pause.

"Still a dick."

She pulled free a bolt of denim fabric, laying it out on one of the workshop tables, then pulled one of her tiny sets of scissors. They were meticulously polished, a fine sheen of handcrafted silver that fit my mom's hands perfectly. Her eyes scanned the cloth, seeing things I couldn't. She activated some invisible skill and then dove into the work, cutting a pattern into the cloth.

She cut at the corner of the denim, but the cloth also cut in three other places, the magic tripling her efficiency by replicating the pattern across the entire section. Her scissors shot across the cloth, her hands moving at superhuman speed. She finished the patterning in moments, passing the cut cloth to me, then returned to work.

I watched for a moment.

She pushed the cloth flat and together, activating some kind of skill that made the holes in the cloth stitch themselves back together, creating more usable fabric for patterning instead of scrapping the misshapen sections between the cuts.

I needed skills like those. How far could thread-control and -mastery skills go? They could eventually add to my repertoire of offensive abilities. My mom looked up from her scissors, smiling as she looked at me.

"I just need you to stitch here, my light," she said, tracing with her finger part of the cut I was holding,

I looked down. Added together, the pieces of denim formed the top of overalls—some kind of laborer outfit to boost labor skills, most likely. I would've figured that out in a moment.

"I was just watching you work," I said, stepping back and putting the material down on my own table before taking a seat. I threaded my needle, lined up the two pieces of work, and prepared to stitch, before realizing I had a faster way, now. The iron grip of magic took control of my arms as I activated [Running Stitch I], the needle shooting through the fabric and attaching the two pieces together. I smiled as it finished minutes of work in seconds, completing an entire stitch.

[Running Stitch I] [Mana: 9/10]

Shit.

Using the skill cost mana whether or not I was using it to kill a monster. That meant that I had to conserve it over the day. If I used it all to craft sewing goods, I wouldn't be able to clear the dungeon.

"You get the experience when you finish the piece. It's alright," Mom said. She must have noticed my frown. "Well, when I finish the piece, you will get experience. You will be leveling in no time, little light."

"How far can we level just from sewing?" I asked, staring at the fading notification.

"I'm in the thirties. One of the highest in the town." Mom puffed up her chest and spoke with pride before she stepped around the table. "We only really level up from work that challenges us. Once you've done enough of this, you'll get less experience. Don't worry about your mana." She placed her hands on my shoulders.

"Do Nobles have that, too? Are monsters worth less the more they kill them?"

"I'm not sure." My mom frowned. "Your stitching looks great, though."

"What if I sew without using skills? Will I still gain experience?"

"Yes." Mom frowned. "Though we might not finish in time like that. You'll be out of mana and sewing by hand by the end of the day, don't worry."

I picked up the cloth and needle and started sewing without the use of my skill. Mom stepped back out of my shadow and toward her own table. My leg still ached. We worked for hours, stopping briefly for breaks and lunch, and then continued until the sun set. Each set we were crafting consisted of at least five pieces—a set of overalls, a hat with a fixture for some kind of lantern, a denim shirt and pants, and a set of shoes for rough terrain.

Because I was only assisting, I only gained experience when mom finished the complete set.

We only finished two by the time the sun set.

When exhaustion crept in I found myself stabbing my hands, blood dropping onto the leather and denim as I worked. I bandaged them and continued to work.

"At this rate, we won't be able to finish twenty-four in a week." I said.

CHAPTER 5

Don't worry, my light. You'll be gaining new skills and levels before the week is over. And as you learn the patterns, we can work faster. How did you feel about your first day?" She smiled.

"I liked it," I said honestly, smiling back. It felt good to be creative, to make things with my hands. It also felt good to destroy things. I could help my mom in her shop and I could keep the town from collapsing.

There was a pounding on the workshop door, three harsh knocks. I wasn't sure if they were knocking or trying to bust the door down. I looked back to my mom. She shrugged, bewildered.

The knocking came again.

I swung the door open. Sandy looked down at me. A stain-covered leather apron clung to her still. Dried blood covered her hands.

"Gwen, it's done—" she started, then stopped, looking up at my mom and making an annoyed face. She schooled it. "Esmeralda."

"Sands."

"I'm taking your daughter," Sandy said. She locked a hand around my arm and practically yanked me off my feet and toward the door.

"Will you be back for dinner?"

"We have extra! I'll feed her!" Sandy shouted, throwing the door shut behind her and dragging me out into the night. The sky was darkening. Sandy let me in an unexpected direction, looping far around her workshop.

"Where are we going?" I asked, pushing Sandy off me. She turned around with a scowl on her face.

"To the edge of the town. I have to show you." She whipped back around and continued stomping through the night over the foliage that lined the space between houses.

I followed.

The town provided a curtain of safety. Ours was too small to provide much arable land, but the effects of the system kept out the world's monsters. It kept the weather tenable and the environment friendly, and every day, we lost a little bit of the town to the monster-infested wilderness beyond it.

I had been to the town's end before, I had seen its constant shrinking. It was a bright shimmer in midair, an incorporeal world boundary; you could walk through it, but there might be consequences on the other side. Sandy led me through copses of trees to the very edge of it. She fumbled around in the dark for a second before lighting an oil lantern with a spark.

The ground here was stomped flat, like she visited it every day, her own shrine to a personal apocalypse. A wooden plank lay on the ground, stretching out beyond the boundary of the world. The slow and subtle decay of the town's protection was visible on it; inch by inch, beyond the wall, the wooden plank decayed. Nothing from our world survived the Wild.

At the farthest edge of the wooden plank, the wood had rotted away into dust. Each day was clearly marked by perfectly even sections of decay. Sandy pulled out a knife from inside her apron and carved a gouge into the ground with a curse.

"It still rotted last night. Look. The town's decay was halved but not *stopped*. Isn't the point to stop the decay?" Sandy asked.

I crouched down beside her, observing the gouges in the ground that stretched far, far outside the barrier to where the light fell away into opaque and sticky black. How long had Sandy been watching this? Counting away the days?

"Rome wasn't built in a day," I said.

"What?" Sandy snapped her head to face me. She looked at me like I was crazy. Maybe I was. I had lived here so long that sometimes I wondered if I had simply imagined my last life.

"Sorry. Dumb saying. We need time, is the point."

"We're running out of time. We have to—before the dungeon collapses," Sandy said. She cursed again. "We have to go faster. We don't need to waste time sewing clothes."

"We?" I asked.

Sandy huffed out a breath.

"Sorry. It's just—my dad—do you want the wolf pelt now?" Sandy asked, veering away from the conversation. She stood abruptly. I studied her for a moment.

"Show it to me," I replied.

Sandy calmed on the walk back to the workshop. She paused outside the door. A lamp burned inside. With a grunt, she swung the door open and stepped inside quickly, eyes darting around the room. Then she sighed in relief.

"Fighting again?" I asked, following behind her.

"Yeah," she said, walking up to her workshop table.

I walked beside her to the racks hanging with already tanned leather before leaning down and running my hands through the wolf's fur. I wondered if tanning was actually this fast and easy without magic before deciding it didn't matter. I didn't live on Earth anymore. There was one large piece of hide and dozens of smaller strips.

"I'm going to go get dinner," Sandy said. "Dad insisted on cooking the entire wolf."

"You gave it to him?" I asked, my head whipping toward her.

"Don't worry. He thinks I killed it."

"What?" I asked.

"Yeah. I—I've done it before. So he just assumed that I did it again when he stumbled into my workshop."

I was stunned for a moment. She had done it before? She was clearing the dungeon at some point? And—

"That's why you fought with your dad? He thought you were clearing the dungeon...again?"

Sandy nodded. I looked back down at the furs, trying to figure out a reply. I wanted to scold her for going and doing something so dangerous, but then, I was the one killing monsters now.

"I'll be right back," she said, avoiding the conversation and walking through the door that led deeper into the house—after removing the furniture she had placed to barricade it.

I held a strip of wolf leather in my hands and grimaced. If I had my mom's ability to easily sew pieces together, this would be more valuable. I would have to stitch all these pieces together, bit by bit, before I could cut them and pattern them.

The smell of the food Sandy carried preceding her, somehow filling the room through the crack below the door. She shoved the door open with a shoulder and stumbled into the room. She set the plates down on her work table, leaned over, and grabbed a piece of sauce-covered wolf meat with her bare hands and ate it.

"What's wrong? Will it not work?" Sandy asked, worried.

"It'll work." I finally stood. "Just...I need to kill more of these."

My stomach rumbled. I flopped into the chair at the desk. It creaked in protest, leaning slightly, and I grabbed at the table to stabilize myself. The food supply of the village was lean. I was familiar enough with wolf meat.

Sandy watched me expectantly as I took a bite of the food. The meat nearly melted in my mouth, far more tender than a grown wolf should be, the flavors exploding in a range so complex I flinched. Sandy nodded.

"Dad's cooking. Why he's trying to move to a proper city. Nothing for him here," she said.

"Why have I never had this before?" I asked.

"Doesn't cook for free. Turns almost all our meat into preserves to store them long enough between shipments. Merchant shipments only come monthly. Not at all during winter. Barely make enough back to buy the meat for the next batch," Sandy said.

"He'd probably get everything he needs and more around the village if he traded his cooking for it."

"Tell him that." Sandy grabbed her plate and sat with her back to the wall, shoveling the food down.

I took my time, only to be caught off guard by the system alert when I finished.

[STR +2] [DURATION: Until next long rest]

"What?" I stared at the notification.

"It's monster meat." Sandy said. "Means stats. That's why the jerky sells."

The possibilities of food-based stat bonuses were endless. I wondered what the peak of the cooking class looked like—would it be enough to elevate someone to superhuman level on food alone? Did chefs receive more points from their own cooking in the same way that I gained a bonus on stats from my own clothes? I side-eyed Sandy.

"I didn't get his class. Plus, he has dozens of levels. My class gets cooking skills, but I'd need dozens of levels more to do anything like that," Sandy said. Her hands fidgeted. "You're clearing the dungeon tonight, right?"

"Yes." I wiped the sauce off my fingers onto an already blood-stained cloth.

Sandy moved to my side of the table. She rested her hand on the knife stabbed into its surface.

"Wasn't an invite," I said, frowning.

"If I'm going to get yelled at for clearing the dungeon, I might as well actually clear it. Besides, you didn't make it to the end yesterday." Sandy ripped the knife free with a popping noise. She sheathed it somewhere in the apron she was still wearing, then wiped her hands on the leather and stepped to her bed, lifting up the frame to reveal a hidden bag. She turned back to me. "You need to grab your things, right? I'll meet you outside the dungeon."

I assessed her. She wasn't taking no for an answer.

"Alright," I said before sighing. I guess I was gaining a plus one.

Circling back to my house, I found the workshop empty. Mom must have turned in for the night already. My backpack was just where I'd left it, shoved into a dilapidated cabinet. I took a moment to throw a sewing kit into it.

Sandy was not outside the dungeon when I arrived. I only looked around for a moment before stepping in. The world lurched like the dungeon had sucked me up and spit me out on the other side, but it had grown late enough that it was dark even here, none of the disorientation of switching from day to night. The moon hung huge in the sky, far larger than any moon could possibly be without ripping the planet apart.

It took up a third of the sky, a giant white eye staring down at me.

I wondered if the dungeon was a planet at all, if it was a real place or just a fictitious piece of flat land rendered in some simulated void.

"It's not that impressive," Sandy said from behind me. I nearly jumped out of my skin.

"The moon shouldn't be that big," I said.

"It's not our moon. Not our world."

I turned to regard her. Despite her insistence that it was ordinary, she was looking up too. She seemed to chew on her thoughts, moving slowly and intentionally.

It took me a moment to notice what was different about her: she was wearing armor. It was old and battered. She wore metal shin guards with spots where rust had been scraped away, and gauntlets with missing fingers on both of her hands. She still wore an apron over the rest of her.

"Increases my skills," she said. "Your mom made it, actually."

"Oh," I said. "And that helps you…"

"Kill monsters. Yeah. My butcher class lets me see the easiest way to cut them to pieces. My activated skills automate it." She started walking toward the center of the dungeon. I trailed behind, holding one of my sewing needles.

If Sandy was going to start clearing the dungeon with me, she would need new armor. We would be able to kill double as many of the wolves. But we could also carry double as many out.

"What does it look like?" I asked, as we approached the entrance to the wolf den.

"I see red. Glowing lines to bisect things."

"Like, all the time?"

"No," Sandy said, eying me. "Only while holding a knife."

"Oh," I said. Sandy was currently holding a knife. I saw the way she looked while holding it. Cold and calculating. I wondered if her ability worked on humans, too.

CHAPTER 6

The wolf den fell away into blackness. Outside, the moon was bright enough to light up the fields. But unlike the sun, it couldn't penetrate deep into the monster's home. The entrance to the den was a black mouth speckled with jagged stones like hungry teeth.

"You got a lamp in there, right?" Sandy asked as she eyed my backpack.

"Figures." Sandy said, stepping toward me. I flinched back at her extended hand. "I'm going to use an aura skill—I'll loan you my sight. Won't give you night vision, but…"

"I'll be able to see the outlines of where to dissect the monsters." I said. Of course the skill worked like that. This world's entire system seemed broken in so many fundamental ways. The way it created a de facto ruling class through blood-line-inherited power was just one of them.

[Sandy Butcher is offering to share buff (Butcher Vision) with you. Accept?] [Y\N]

I accepted the prompt and it disappeared. Sandy pulled out a tiny knife from the pockets lining the inside of her apron and extended it to me.

"Thank you?" I said. The blade was only the length of one of my fingers, a tiny paring knife with a decaying wooden handle. Disturbingly, a red cross section spread in a crawl across Sandy. I frowned at it.

"Have to be holding a knife," she said.

I now had the giant sewing needle in one hand and the tiny knife in the other, though I had no thoughts about using the knife to fight. Sandy led the way into the mouth of the cave, staying low and with the wall on her left. She pushed into the Dungeonheart, creeping through the caverns until we came across the first of the wolves.

They didn't act like real wolves. This was the same wolf that had been scratching at the rock the last time I was here, and it was scratching at the rock now, like a static NPC stuck in place, an object in the world for us to kill. I couldn't see it in the dark, but I heard its scratching grow louder.

I saw the long red line that flowed down its back, showing where to best bisect it. Blood red lines floated in the darkness. They spread the longer I looked at them, a red ring circling its neck and each of its legs, and then Sandy dove into it.

When I had killed the monsters the night before, they had died instantly. My needles stabbed directly into their brain, crunching through skull and obliterating soft tissue.

This time, the monster didn't die instantly. It howled and mewled and protested. Sandy's knife flashed in the dark, running the red line and bisecting the wolf in a move so precise it must have been controlled by the system.

"Kill it," she said, stepping over its body. I could see from the position of the lines and circles highlighting it that the wolf had collapsed to the ground. It was paralyzed. And it wouldn't stop making noise.

I did my best to guess where the head was and crunched down with the needle. It survived. Wasting my mana to kill a paralyzed wolf wasn't an option; after all of this was done, I still needed to spend time crafting the gear from the monsters. So I stabbed again.

[+2 XP]

"Fuck," I said.

"You alright?" Sandy said. I could hear her move back toward me in the dark.

"Yeah, just got half the XP. Didn't think it'd drop so fast."

"C'mon, I'm moving forward," Sandy said, continuing into the cave.

I followed her footsteps as we walked deeper into the cave than I had been previously. At the center of the Dungeonheart, the ceiling opened, letting moonlight pour into a wide, circular room. Vines hung down from outside, perfectly still.

A wolf lay sideways under the light, red lines crawling across its skin as I observed it. I fiddled with the paring knife in my hand as it rose to its feet and shook its head. Then it howled. Two more howls answered it from inside the tunnel.

"Shit," Sandy said as she dashed forward, already stabbing downward. The wolf dodged to the side. The system-enhanced butcher skill she used didn't care. It nearly yanked Sandy off her feet as it ripped her forward. She stabbed the knife down with a blatant disregard for her physical limits. Blood spurted as the wolf was carved open. Sandy didn't look back as it collapsed to the ground.

She held a knife out to the tunnel entrance that fell away in darkness on the other side of the room. I rushed up to her, scanning the edges of the room.

"How many of them are there?" Sandy asked, her voice filling with tension.

"I only killed three last night. So at least four?" I said, my head flicking between the two tunnels. "That means there's at least two left."

One of them jumped out of the dark toward Sandy. She ducked forward, her hand flicking unnaturally as she cut into its leg. The wolf mewled as it crashed into the ground, now missing a leg. I caught a flicker of red in the dark behind Sandy, squinting for a moment as the lines of the [Butcher Vision] started to crawl up the fourth wolf.

"What are you doing? Kill it!" Sandy said, looking at me.

The invisible wolf jumped at her from behind. I dropped the paring knife, activating [Running Stitch] with both hands. Sandy jumped backward as my needle shot toward her.

[Running Stitch I] [Mana: 8/10] [Cancel]

The wolf's jaw just barely grazed her arm. Sandy made a noise of pain and shock. My sewing needle hit its head. Sandy jerked back, scoring her arm on the wolf's teeth.

[+2 XP]

Sandy dashed past me, stabbing again. A second wolf collapsed in front of me, now missing both of its front legs.

[Running Stitch I] [Mana: 7/10] [Cancel]

[+2 XP]

The weight of the two wolves on my needle sent me to the ground. I put a boot to one of them, pulling the needle out of one of their heads before staggering back. Then I worked on working it out of the second.

"Is that a sewing needle?" Sandy asked, leaning over me. "That works?"

"Yeah," I said between grunts.

"You think Gerald will make me a sword?" Sandy looked down at her knife.

The needle popped out of the wolf's head.

I finished off the third wolf that had been left paralyzed between us. It didn't die without effort.

[+2 XP]

"If you can find the metal for it," I said, before pointing off to the side. "Your paring knife is in here somewhere."

Sandy walked over and picked it up off the floor instantly. I wondered if she had some kind of skill to find her tools. I sat down and put the sewing needle in my backpack, pulling out the water and cloth.

"Let me see your arm." I said.

She sat across from me, presenting her arm. I winced. The wolf's tooth had dug furrows into her, breaking the skin and trailing blood.

"It's not that bad." Sandy said.

I poured water over the cuts before applying one of Terry's magical poultices. That was no hyperbole—they were literally magical poultices. I wrapped the cloth around her arm over the poultice.

"Which ones are we taking home?" Sandy asked. I looked up to find her staring at me with peculiar intensity.

"That one." I pointed to the wolf with the ability to turn invisible. I was hoping—praying—that I would successfully graft that skill onto the outfit I created out of it.

"We can bring home at least two. If not three." Sandy looked around.

"What would we need them for?"

"It's free meat. And levels for my butcher class. You know, I cleared the dungeon, but I never butchered the monsters. I can level twice off of them." Sandy stood, walking to one of the wolves and inspecting the body before hefting it up and dragging it toward the exit.

"I'm surprised they're worth anything to you." I grabbed the stealthy wolf's corpse and followed her out of the den.

"Regular animals stopped giving XP," she grunted as we exited into the wide-open fields of the dungeon, "But monster's still do, apparently. Going to abuse that for however long it lasts."At the exit of the dungeon, Sandy said,

"Alright, wait here."

"Wait—" Sandy jumped through the dungeon gate and out into the town. Wait here? She didn't tell me she was planning on doing anything. The distorted image of the town gave me no answers as she disappeared into the street. I looked down at the wolves and sighed. I wasn't going to leave these here either, so I would have to wait until she returned.

I tapped my fingers against my arm, looking around warily. It felt like an hour before Sandy came back.

"Okay," she said, hands on her hips.

A wooden cart followed behind her.

"What took so long?' I asked.

"Had to convince him," she said.

Gerald followed behind the cart, pushing it in. He was pale as a ghost, staring up at the moon in mute horror. My mouth widened a little.

"Gerald? Why did you…"

"You know why my dad walked into my workshop the other day?" Sandy asked.

"Because you gave him wolf meat to cook," I replied.

"No. Because you left a trail of blood going right to my workshop. We dragged the body there, remember? So I got us a cart. Now…let's go grab the rest of the bodies."

"Uh…you guys take it. I'll stay here," Gerald said.

"Alone in the dungeon?" I asked.

"Good point, we do need a lookout. I'll look out. From the town," Gerald said, jumping back out through the gate.

Sandy shrugged at me.

We rushed the cart up the hill and to the Dungeonheart, loading up the two wolves we had left behind, legs and all, and then loaded the wolves at the exit. Gerald met us outside the dungeon. We rushed back to Sandy's butcher shop.

Gerald looked around nervously, rubbing his arms as he stared up at the hooks on the ceiling. He let his eyes linger on the knives Sandy was setting on the table. She seemed to have an endless supply of them inside her apron. I sat with my back to the wall, taking the sewing supplies from my backpack.

Gerald winced as Sandy stabbed into the black wolf's corpse.

"So, Gerald," Sandy said, carving down the side of the wolf. "How much would it cost for you to make me something?"

"Like what?" Gerald asked.

"Like her needles," Sandy said, not turning around. She stabbed back down, carving away.

"Like a—like a knife?" Gerald asked. He was still standing nervously.

Sandy paused. She stabbed her knife down into the table then grabbed a cleaver, whipping around to face Gerald. Her face was practically aglow with excitement.

"How about a cleaver? A giant cleaver?" she said, holding the knife out to Gerald for demonstration. He flinched back.

"Dad will wonder what it's for," he said, looking away.

"But you made her needles," Sandy said.

"Everyone thought she would be a Noble."

I tuned them out, starting work on my sewing project. The Hunter pattern had been ingrained into my memory. I moved with someone else's muscle memory, the pieces coming to me with practiced ease as if I had done it a dozen times. I started with the fur cloak, my hands guiding me to cut open a hole in the center for my head before splitting it down the middle.

After a few stitches, the system recognized my progress, rewarding me with a status of the work.

[Tacca I]

▶3% complete

[PROJECTED SKILLS]

▶Shadow Cloak I

▶Random Hunter Proficiency I

The system had given the set a random name—Tacca I. I dove right back into working.

[Running Stitch I] [Mana: 6/10]

The world around me fell away into nothing as I began to flow with my sewing. The sections I cut away wouldn't be wasted. They would be repurposed, stitched back together into the collar and the hood. I didn't have my mom's skill to recombine fabric; instead, I had to stitch it together piece by piece.

[Running Stitch I] [Mana: 5/10]

I sighed contentedly. The hood and collar were starting to come together. The workshop door opening shook me out of my reverie; Sandy returned to the workshop. I didn't know she had left. She held a box that clinked and shook with every step. Gerald was sitting nervously on her bed, staring at me.

Sandy set the box down in front of him. It was full of chipped blades and broken chunks of metal, some claimed by rust and eaten away.

"This enough?"

CHAPTER 7

He assessed the box, his expression showing a rare focused seriousness. He seemed to count in his head, then grimaced.

"Maybe. Fine. I can try to make you a cleaver. It's going to take a couple days. And it's going to be unwieldy," he warned. "The weight's going to be totally unbalanced."

"It's fine. Just make it," Sandy said.

[Running Stitch I] [Mana: 4/10]

[+2 XP] [Level up]

[Hunter's Cloak (Common, Darkness) completed!]

I sewed the last of the hood together, earning another level-up as I did so. Level 3, reached in a day and a half of work. How many more levels would the wolves provide me before I had to switch to other methods to level up?

[Quality Assessment: (Ragged)]

Hey…system! The quality of this was way beyond just ragged; the fur and leather of the wolf was plush and handsomely dark like a robe made of shadows. The fact I had to stitch multiple pieces back together and cut them apart, as well as the quality of thread I was using, must have reduced the total quality. But if this was ragged, I didn't know what the system considered high tier. I would have to ask.

As for it being a [Darkness] cloak…I could only assume that was because of the elemental aspect of the wolf monster I killed. It must've possessed a darkness-related stealth skill.

Sandy had her arms far apart to demonstrate the prolific size of the blade she wanted Gerald to craft. He rapidly shook his head in disagreement.

"When does the next floor of the dungeon open?" I asked aloud, interrupting Sandy and Gerald arguing over the design of the cleaver. Sandy side-eyed me, her arms dropping.

"Dunno. Took a week or two last time. Wasn't clearing it daily, though. Couldn't keep up." Her eyes scanned the pile of wolf carcasses as she said that last part.

"Can you keep up now?" I asked her.

"What are you going to do with the bones?" Gerald asked.

"What?" Sandy turned back to Gerald.

"The bones. I think I can use them," Gerald said. "No, just the teeth. Can you give me the teeth?"

"I guess so. You're not putting them on the cleaver are you?" Sandy made a disgusted face; as if cutting apart the monsters and sorting their insides was completely normal but pulling out their teeth was gross.

"Not on the handle," he said, staring intently at the wolf sprawled across her workshop desk.

I packed up my cloak into my rapidly filling backpack. At this point, I was going to have to make a bigger one, and it wasn't included in the Hunter pattern.

"Deal," Gerald said. He had a look of hunger in his eyes.

"I'm heading back to my workshop," I said, standing.

"You can crash here if you want," Sandy said, looking over.

"No; I still have four mana left. I need to finish more of our order."

"What?" Sandy asked. "You're still doing regular sewing work on top of all of this?"

Gerald stared at me intently.

"I have to keep my mom's shop running," I said. "Besides, it's still good for levels."

Sandy nodded at that.

"I'll bring more food by tomorrow morning."

"Isn't it going to cause a yelling match with your dad if you show him all these corpses?" I asked.

Sandy only shrugged. Gerald loaded his box of old knives and tools onto the cart and followed me out, sounding like a rolling cart of thunder.

"How are you going to pass that off to your dad?" I asked Gerald.

"I'll just be honest." He shrugged. "Dad doesn't care what we get commissioned. He makes weapons all the time."

"Huh. Okay," I said. "I'll see you tomorrow?" I asked.

"Might take me a couple days to finish the cleaver. I have to help with other orders in the shop, too," he replied. His eyes didn't leave the metal on his cart. "Soon though!" he called out as we split off.

I rushed back to the workshop, moving the door quietly to avoid its creaking protests waking anyone. Stuffing my backpack into the cabinet, I got to work, picking up some already-cut patterns from the crate mom had left them in as well as a sewing kit from a desk.

[Running Stitch I] [Mana: 3/10]

[Running Stitch I] [Mana: 2/10]

[Running Stitch I] [Mana: 1/10]

[Running Stitch I] [Mana: 0/10]

I had almost finished the patterns as I ran out of mana. There was just one left. Exhaustion set in, making me bleary eyed. I tried to rub the tiredness away. None of these would give me any experience until mom put the finishing touches on.

When I had exhausted my mana, I worked by hand, leaning over my chair and onto the desk for support. The exhaustion made me prick my fingers more than I would've liked, but I finished every precut piece that had been left behind. I set the needle down and sat down at the desk, appreciating my work.

Content and exhaustion warred through me. In the end, I couldn't even work up the willpower to walk upstairs to my bed, passing out then and there in the workshop.

My mom whispered me awake. I winced as I felt my back ache from sleeping in such a contorted position, then shot up as I smelled the food.

"Good morning, my light," she said, sliding a plate of food to me on the desk. "When did you sneak down to the workshop?"

"Last night," I mumbled, and then I was shoveling food. Sandy had been by already, because breakfast was strips of meat.

My eyes scanned the workshop. I had always seen the place as beaten and worn down. How long would it be before I had the resources to improve it? To make it better? To replace the tiles and the furniture and the windows?

Mom worked on finishing an item, glancing up at me when her hands moved supernaturally fast as I finished eating.

I lay back down on the desk.

[+2 XP]

[Miner's Shirt (Uncommon, Null) completed!]

[Quality Assessment: (Fine)]

Mom looked between what she worked on and me, eyebrows raised in a question. I sighed. I should climb back up the stairs and throw myself into bed, but I wasn't sure if I really had the time. We would need to do more work in the workshop.

"What time is it?" I asked, looking out the window. The sun was already well into the sky.

"Oh, I don't know, afternoon sometime," Mom said.

I must have worked late into the night.

[+2 XP]

[Miner's Shirt (Uncommon, Null) completed!]

[Quality Assessment: (Fine)]

Mom stopped this time, staring at me. After a pause, she spoke.

"I thought that would be enough for a level up," she said, walking over to me and dragging a chair across the tile. The scraping noise filled the room. I looked up at her as she sat.

"Oh. Oh!" Right, the XP for crafting would probably be worth a level…if I was still level 1, and not level 3 already! "You know, I think I did get a level up," I said.

Mom grimaced, as if my lack of excitement was a condemnation. Of course anyone who had just gained access to the system, who had just gained access to magic would be excited beyond belief. I pulled my system open with a thought.

[Gwendolyn Tailor][Human, Lv3][Seamstress]

[Health: 10/10][Mana: 10/10][XP: 4/10]

[Points available: 1]

[ATTRIBUTES]

▶SPD: 10

▶WIL: 5

▶STR: 5

▶DEX: 10

▶CON: 5

▶PER: 5

[SKILLS]

▶Crafting I

▶Running Stitch I

[PATTERNS]

▶Hunter Pattern

My eyes flicked to my mom and my mouth dried up at the look on her face; pained compassion mixed with grief.

"You know," she started, "it's not too bad being a seamstress. There are worse professions. It's not bad even in a city. We can find jobs almost anywhere, once the town shuts down, we can get a job in a big workshop. The pay will be…enough to live on. Maybe we could find a town by the ocean."

"Mom. I'm not upset about being a seamstress! I promise! I was just awake all night," I said.

She leaned back. The grief in her eyes didn't lessen.

Out of the corner of my eye I noticed the wolf pelt cloak I had made hanging out of the bottom of a cabinet door. Shit, did I leave it like that last night? Or did she notice it and stuff it back in? I did my best not to look at it, pulling open my skill options.

[Skill Shop]

▶Hand Spinning I

[UNCOMMON] Allows user to rapidly thread together fibers by hand. Also grants one point in Thread Mastery I. Additional levels will increase speed of user and quality of final product, but will not increase Thread Mastery.

I started reading them aloud to my mom, but she interrupted right after the first skill.

"That one," Mom interrupted.

"What?" I asked. "Why? We can buy all the thread we need."

"Not for the skill—no, for Thread Mastery! It's a passive skill you can't even put points into. The only way to gain the full skill is to grab all ten of its subskills. Thread Mastery is a legendary skill. It's vanishingly rare, especially at level one," she continued.

"At least let me read the rest," I replied, continuing down the list.

▶Quick Change I

[UNCOMMON] Allows user to instantly exchange a piece of clothing with any article they are in physical contact with, or is stored in their Inventory. Additional levels allow changing up to an entire outfit. [Seamstress inventory skill: Wardrobe]

▶Mending I

[COMMON] Allows user to repair clothing from patterns they are unfamiliar with. Additional levels increase quality of final product.

Mending would be perfect for if I damaged my clothing fighting monsters. I took a look at my mom.

"Hand Spinning. Please, my light," she said.

"What can Thread Mastery do?" I asked.

"Free control of threads! My ability to merge two pieces of work together is just a subskill of Thread Mastery three! Seamstresses with Thread Mastery above five are coveted. There are myths of seamstresses who can use them like a spider webs, even to—" Mom cut herself off, looking away awkwardly. My eyes flicked to the cloak hanging out of the cabinet. I wasn't sure if I was imagining it falling further.

"To what?" I asked, mostly just to distract her. I pushed my plate toward her, standing and walking past her.

"Kill monsters," she said.

I staggered forward, stopping before I reached the cabinet.

"What?" I asked, turning around. Mom was still looking away, fumbling with the plate. I shoved my backpack upright inside the cabinet and closed it.

"Well, it's… The story ends with him dying, so."

"*Who* dying?" I pressed.

"Sorry, I don't want to give you any stupid ideas." She turned around. "Alex was a tailor who was rumored to have Thread Mastery seven. There is a story, a fanciful story, of him beheading a monster that set on a caravan he was traveling in."

"With string?" I asked, incredulous. He used thread to garrote monsters? Why hadn't I thought of that?

"It sounds…fantastical." She sighed, taking my plate with her toward the house. "A fantasy story. An escape from reality. Stupid, too. No seamstress will be killing monsters."

"No stories are stupid."

I selected the Hand Spinning skill.

CHAPTER 8

I dreamt I was a human-shaped spider; from a ball of yarn in my hands, threads spread out in all directions. They wrapped around my mom, around Sandy, around Gerald, and even around the priest. Out of all of them, he was the only one who didn't struggle. He leaned forward, bound in a cocoon of web, and then his face changed to my father's from my old life.

"I thought you would be—"

"Gwen?" My mother's voice interrupted me.

The dream flickered away in the way dreams do, like memories that had overstayed their welcome, dissolving into dust. I groaned and opened my eyes. It was already light out, the light filtering through the patterned curtains that segmented the room.

"I slept in again," I said, forcing myself up out of bed.

"Are you up?" Mom asked.

"I'm coming," I said. She shut the door, and I made my way to already-cold breakfast.

Mom sat across from me again, her face set in a frown. I avoided her gaze while I ate. She put her hand to my forehead unprompted.

"Are you feeling alright, love?"

"Do I have a fever?" I asked.

"No," she said, pulling her hand away.

I chewed on my food, thinking of a response to ward off the incoming inquiries. She couldn't know I was hunting monsters. It wouldn't do to hurt her by having her think I'm in danger; not until I'm strong enough to prove that there is no danger to me.

"I'm just tired. I've been hanging out with Sandy a lot."

"You can invite her over, you know."

"The house is crowded enough."

"We will have more space when we move to a city," she said.

I put my fork down. She wrung her hands.

"I'm almost at my next level."

"Good! Good, my light."

The tension between me and my mom never resolved throughout the day. We worked for hours until lunch, only talking occasionally in awkward back-and-forths spat in a few words. But she didn't understand—couldn't understand. I couldn't explain to her that I had no plans to move and was risking my life killing monsters every day for minimal reward.

Every few minutes, I looked to the door, waiting for Sandy to knock.

I used more of my mana today. The first floor had held only four wolves, so I used five of my total mana. I used more of my mana today on the work order. I had to get levels somehow. By the time the sun set and we exhausted our stack of supplies, my experience was already at nine. We completed a total of nine outfits out of an order of twenty-four; we still needed to speed up if we wanted to meet our Noble's deadline.

I leveled up again after the third outfit, debating over my choices. The Inventory skill for the seamstress class reappeared—Wardrobe I. I grabbed it, thinking of my cloak spilling out of the cabinet the other day.

To my dismay, the experience gained for completing the patterns dropped immediately after; I only gained a single experience for each completed pattern after that. It felt like too little for the amount of labor involved; each pattern involved a complete set of five pieces.

Maybe I had just been spoiled by how much experience was granted from killing wolves. A single clearing of the dungeon pushed me at least forty percent to my next level; how was that actually less effort than crafting a complete set of clothes? Not to mention the risk of death and dismemberment.

I played with Thread Mastery while thinking about my future upgrades. A loose bit of yarn followed my hand sluggishly, as if it was being pulled by a magnet. I played with it back and forth on the table during a much-needed break from constant working.

"Maybe we could use the money from this commission to take a trip to the city," Mom said, still sewing something together as she talked. Despite her currently looking away from her work, it was still coming together perfectly, hands blurring with movement.

I looked up at her, still propping my hand up with a fist.

"Why don't we upgrade the workshop instead?"

Mom bit her lip.

"No sense in fixing things we can't keep," she said.

I looked around. The chipped tile and warped windows showed decades of age.

"What about stuff we can bring with us? Equipment?"

Mom measured me carefully, staring down at me. I met her gaze.

"If you're sure that's what you want," she said. "Maybe we can order more clothes for you."

"Do we have a new catalog?" I asked, leaning forward. Mom smiled at my excitement.

Pounding came from the door. I shot up to get it. Mom raised her eyebrows.

"I'll get it."

The door swung open before I reached it. Sandy looked to me, then looked to my mom, then raised her eyebrows.

"You ready?" she asked.

"Just a sec," I replied, turning back and walking over to the cabinet. I pulled out my backpack. My mom's eyebrows rose even higher.

"I'll see you in the morning?" she asked. "Sandy, tell your father I said thanks for the food."

"Will do, Miss Tailor," Sandy said.

"Your place first?" I asked.

"Yeah," she said. I shut the door behind us.

We speed walked through the town toward her house. Sandy was filled with energy; this was the least abrasive I had ever seen her.

"Get your new cleaver already?" I asked in a low tone.

"No." She frowned. "Gerald said it'd take a day to smelt and refine all the metal into higher-grade steel before he can even start crafting it. Going to be a few days. What about you, how's your cloak?"

"I...haven't tried it on yet," I said.

"Why not?" Sandy asked.

"I just show up stomping around my house with a Darkness-imbued cloak? No. My mom would ask so many questions."

"Should just tell her." Sandy shrugged. "My dad already knows."

"About you! Not about me," I said. We walked into Sandy's workshop. "Not about me, right?" I asked this time.

"Nah." Sandy waved my concerns away. "Okay, put it on!" she said, reaching down and donning her own mismatched armor.

I pulled the cloak out. It was soft and fine; the work on it was high quality, despite the system describing it as Ragged. I tied my hair back before putting the cloak on, reaching up and pulling my pony tail out of the collar.

"Moment of truth?" Sandy said.

I pulled open my system with a shiver of anticipation.

[Gwendolyn Tailor][Human, Lv4][Seamstress]
[Health: 10/10][Mana: 5/10][XP: 3/10]
[ATTRIBUTES]
▶SPD: 10
▶WIL: 5
▶STR: 5
▶DEX: 12
▶CON: 5
▶PER: 7
[SKILLS]
▶Crafting I
▶Running Stitch I
▶Hand Spinning I
▶Thread Mastery I
▶Wardrobe I
[PATTERNS]
▶Hunter Pattern
[RESISTANCES]
▶Shadow: 1

"I think I'll need the full set to get any skills," I said.

"And the stats?" Sandy asked, touching the cloak and feeling the fabric.

"Plus two," I replied.

"Two what?"

"Dex…and per."

"Impressive," Sandy said.

The cloak felt heavy on my shoulders. I twirled in it once. It spun around me, heavy and strong. Then I raised a hand and touched it, invoking my new skill with a thought.

[Wardrobe I]

"Woah!" Sandy said. "Shit, is that the stealth skill?"

"No." I laughed. "It wouldn't be much of a stealth skill if it just turned the cloak invisible."

The feeling of suddenly losing two dex was much more noticeable than gaining it. I felt like I had just drunk an entire pitcher of coffee, all my moments uneven and twitchy. It was distinctly uncomfortable.

With a strain of mental thought, I invoked the skill again. The cloak reappeared around me.

"How long do you really think you're going to be able to hide that from your mom?" Sandy asked, quirking an eyebrow.

"As long as it takes," I replied.

She rolled her eyes before leading the way to the dungeon. We crept more carefully this time, Sandy carving apart and dropping a monster before I stabbed into it, conserving mana for making more Hunter pattern tonight.

"What?" I asked aloud, shocked. There was no experience, no pop-up, no reward.

"Finally stop giving experience?" Sandy asked.

"Let me take the next one," I said, tracking the pattern of glowing lines in the dark. I dashed forward.

[Running Stitch I] [Mana: 4/10] [Cancel]

The wolf went limp without a noise, collapsing on the floor of the wolf den.

I sat over the body in silence.

No experience.

I closed my eyes. This meant the only way I had to level up currently was crafting.

Something slammed into my side, sending me tumbling in the dark.

I rolled on the floor, grabbing the needle, but the tiny paring knife I used to share Sandy's buff fell out of my hand, bouncing on the floor with a clinking noise.

"Don't close your eyes in a dungeon!" Sandy said.

There was a snarl, then a whimper as a knife parted flesh. Sandy was barely visible in the moonlight that managed to claw its way through the piled stones that made the wolf den. I fumbled in the dark for the knife, cursing as I found the blade before the handle. A tiny cut was opened on my finger, but I'd have to deal with it later. We had another two wolves to kill.

"Sorry," I said. "You okay?"

"Not a scratch on me. You?"

"I think you might've knocked a health point out of me," I said, stabbing down to end the wolf's suffering. This was the stealth wolf—and still, no experience. "I need experience faster," I said, though I kept my eyes open this time.

"Then we have to open the next floor of the dungeon," Sandy said, eyes staring down the corridor.

"What will it take?" I asked.

"First, finish your outfit. Then make me one."

"We need this second floor to open," I said. After seeing what the first floor could offer me in power and stats, I was already itching for the next.

"Shouldn't be long. A few more days to fully clear this one, and the next floor will open here." I stood and started down the den. The rest of the monsters died without incident; we dragged two out and started our new routine.

Clearing the first floor of the dungeon couldn't push the city outwards; it couldn't reclaim The Wild for use to build. But it meant no more houses collapsed as the Wild closed in. It meant the Noble who owned the town couldn't force us all to leave for profit. And it meant we were progressing forward.

Sandy carved apart a new wolf. Tonight, I would stitch an old one back together, working on the jacket that fit under the wolf pattern cloak. The dexterity afforded to me by what I had crafted would allow me to craft faster. To kill better.

"Have you been to the second floor?" Sandy's knife stopped mid-cut. Standing over the sliced-open wolf, she turned to regard me.

"Yes."

"What's down there?"

CHAPTER 9

It's full of fucking monsters," Sandy said. "Changes every few weeks. But it's always fuckin' bugs."

She lurched forward and finished off another wolf. Its mewls were pitiful, echoing in the dark.

"Bugs," I said, nodding. "I can work with bugs. Chitin armor…giant silkworms."

"You'd better not make me any clothes out of bugs," Sandy said, stepping forward into the dungeon.

We cleared out the last of the wolves, standing in the large chamber that was open to the moon's light.

"There," Sandy grunted, half pointing to the ground.

"What's there?" I asked.

"'S where the entrance to the next floor would open if the dungeon was clear," Sandy said, wiping her blade with her apron.

We dragged the wolves back and got to work, life falling into a sublime and dangerous routine.

Piece by piece, I worked on completing the hunter set, excited to raise my stats and gain a Stealth skill. Something completely outside of my class.

By day, through the week, I worked with my mom to complete the work order. Even without the use of mana, I was slowly becoming more proficient at the pattern. On the third day, we completed six pieces of the outfit, leaving me just shy of a level.

At night, after killing the wolves, I completed another piece of the Hunter pattern. Without mom to finish most of the work using her enhanced skills, it took me much longer to make each piece, though I approached the most difficult one first.

The outer piece of the outfit's top came together. Sandy's dad bought the butchered wolf meat. The money circled right back to fabric used to continue making the Hunter pattern.

I finished the top.

[+2 XP] [Level up] [Excess discarded]

"Done?" Sandy asked, leaning over my shoulder.

"Yes," I said. Then I groaned. "Discarded an XP."

"Just one?" Sandy asked.

"Hours of effort. Gone. Poof," I complained, gesturing with my hands as if I was blowing away dust.

"Don't be so dramatic. The next floor of the dungeon should be opening soon."

[Skill Shop]

▶Cross Stitching I

[COMMON] Enables system assistance with a new stitch type. Additional levels increase proficiency.

▶Quick Change I

[UNCOMMON] Allows user to instantly exchange a piece of clothing with any article they are in physical contact with, or is stored in their Inventory. Additional levels allow changing up to an entire outfit. [Seamstress Inventory skill: Wardrobe]

▶Pattern Projection I

[COMMON] Seamstress Vision skill. Grants user access to a pattern overlay on fabric.

Pattern projection sounded similar to Sandy's Butcher Vision; I wondered how many equivalent skills there were across classes. It would be useless for teaching me to cut the pattern; that was already deeply ingrained in my mind. However, it could let me tell whether or not there was enough fabric for a pattern with nothing more than a glance.

I grabbed Quick Change and activated it. The pattern in my hand disappeared in a flash of a hundred thousand motes of rainbow-colored immaterial light, reappearing over me.

[Gwendolyn Tailor][Human, Lv5][Seamstress]

[Health: 10/10][Mana: 0/10][XP: 0/10]

[ATTRIBUTES]

▶SPD: 10

▶WIL: 5

▶STR: 5

▶DEX: 14

▶CON: 5

▶PER: 9

[SKILLS]

▶Crafting I

▶Running Stitch I

▶Hand Spinning I

▶Thread Mastery I
▶Wardrobe I
▶Quick Change I
[PATTERNS]
▶Hunter Pattern
[RESISTANCES]
▶Shadow: 2

I continued trudging through the week, each day much the same, pushing me to the brink of what I could tolerate in exhaustion. We had more than enough material from killing the wolves, but we still couldn't take a break; the next floor of the dungeon wouldn't open.

The finished clothing did nothing to help me craft during the day, but my increasing skill meant we had almost caught up with the full work order. There were two sets left to craft Friday night, the sunlight shifting from daylight-white to a burnished orange where it filtered through the warped glass windows of the workshop. The Noble would arrive tomorrow.

I sighed as I finished another pattern. The sets had grown routine, mundane. At first they presented a few challenges in learning each individual cut and how it was sewed back together.

"Will I stop getting experience for this eventually?" I asked Mom.

"Yes," she said with a frown, looking over at me. "But you can take your time. There's no rush, my dear. If you start making your own pattern, you'll probably get more experience for each piece."

"How does it work? Do you stop getting experience when it stops challenging you?"

"I'm unsure." Mom shrugged. "I have plenty of patterns that give me no experience despite still being a pain in the neck. Perhaps it's simply when you craft something new."

I nodded setting down the piece of fabric I was working with.

"At this rate, we won't be done by tomorrow morning." I frowned.

"It's alright." Mom waved it off. "Valjean will be here all tomorrow. We can finish in the morning."

I frowned at that, but kept working. By the end of the night, there were two unfinished sets.

But I didn't have the time or mana to spare. That night, I completed the wolf set. It hung heavily on me, layers of leather, fur, and cloth. Despite being four, even five layers thick in some places, it felt abnormally cool. I stood after equipping the last piece. Sandy sat on her bed, looking up at me.

[Tacca I]

▶100% complete
[Generating skills…]
▶Shadow Cloak I
▶Bow Proficiency I
I did a twirl in the cloak.
"Is that it?" Sandy asked.
I pressed a hand under my chin, tilting my head and opening the system.
[Gwendolyn Tailor][Human, Lv6][Seamstress]
[Health: 10/10][Mana: 1/10][XP: 2/10]
[ATTRIBUTES]
▶SPD: 10
▶WIL: 5
▶STR: 5
▶DEX: 22
▶CON: 5
▶PER: 16
[SKILLS]
▶Crafting I
▶Running Stitch I
▶Hand Spinning I
▶Thread Mastery I
▶Wardrobe II
▶Quick Change I
[PATTERNS]
▶Hunter Pattern
[RESISTANCES]
▶Shadow: 5
[TEMPORARY SKILLS]
▶Bow Proficiency I
▶Shadow Cloak I

With a satisfied smile, I mentally reached out and activated the Shadow Cloak skill. The lamps in the room guttered, their flames blowing in an invisible wind as the room's shadows stretched out from the wall to creep up my body, blanketing me in a sticky cloak of black.

Sandy blinked for a second, then squinted, like she couldn't quite see me. She tried to look directly at me, but her eyes passed over me.

"Gwen?" Sandy asked, leaning up out of the bed.

I waved a hand in front of her face, not replying. She blinked when my hand came close, then stepped forward, stretching out an arm to where I had been.

I dodged behind her, smiling all the while. Gwen turned around, looking between her bed and the door. With a grin, I dismissed the skill, feeling my last drop of mana dissipate. The shadows vanished with an audible pop.

"Woah," Sandy said. "And you got that from clothes? That's almost, like, a Noble skill."

"I think it's because the materials are from that particular wolf," I said. The wolf itself had a stealth skill; I was just borrowing it.

Sandy contemplated it for a second before stepping forward and falling back onto her bed.

"Makes enough sense. Wonder if my dad can make invisible food out of it."

"I gotta go," I said seriously. Sandy shrugged.

I crept back to the house, entering through the side of the workshop before stuffing my backpack away in my favorite hiding cabinet. I sparked an oil lamp on, bringing it to the desk, still wearing the complete wolf outfit. With my dexterity all the way at twenty, it was a completely different world of skill.

During the day, I felt like a fumbling child trying to work with just my baseline stats. With a dex of twenty, it was like my hands could perfectly match my thoughts. I fell into a fugue as I worked, stitching together the last pieces of the two sets. The final stitch would still have to be done by Mom; I didn't have the pattern unlocked. But she could do it in seconds now instead of hours. I smiled as I finished another piece.

Then the door creaked open.

I panicked, standing, then sitting, then throwing myself under the desk.

"Gwen?" Mom asked, holding out a lamp to see.

I was still wearing my wolf cloak and monster killing clothes! I grabbed at the cloak before realizing how stupid I was being, then used Wardrobe to store it.

Standing up, I looked nervously at my mom, then smiled. I was trying my best to hide the worry in my eyes.

"Is this what you've been up to late at night?" Mom said, walking over to me.

"Ye—yes!" I said. "I want to get all the patterns done. For our work order."

"Oh?" Mom blinked, looking between me and the desk. Stupid. She wasn't talking about me staying up and doing the work order. I was still wearing the rest of the wolf pelt outfit. "So that's the pattern you picked?" she said, gesturing at me.

"I…yes."

"Where'd you get the materials for it?" she asked. Her voice was soft, not accusatory.

"Sandy gave them to me," I said. It was technically true. Not even a lie. Mom put a hand on my shoulder.

"No work for you tomorrow. You need to go get some sleep," she said, then smiled. "Come on."

I sighed in relief. How would Mom react if she knew I was spending the night killing monsters? Sewing clothes was much more reasonable. It was an alright cover.

Sleep took me instantly; I all but collapsed into bed. Without anything to work on the next morning, I did feel a little lost. I joined Terry after breakfast.

One of the house's bedrooms had been converted into her workshop. She was an alchemist whose class specialized in healing potions; something extremely expensive to cultivate levels in. Out here in the sticks, she could hardly gain any resources to help her progress in levels; the healing herbs simply couldn't create anything to help her level.

Normally, if you had a rarer or more specialized class, a company might hire you and raise your levels. Terry had no such luck.

The shelves of her room were covered in containers full of plants; metal tins, glass jars, and wooden barrels. She stood at her workbench grinding flowers with a mortar and pestle. None of those were the reason I enjoyed spending time with her.

She ground the flowers down into a purple powder, picking up a pinch between her fingers and rubbing it on a canvas.

"How's that?" she asked.

"It's a good purple," I said.

The other wall of Terry's room was lined with paintings, jars of pigments and colors. She made some healing pastes for the village, but most of her time was spent painting. Paintings of beautiful, surreal landscapes warred against paintings of glowing potions and city skylines for my attention.

"It's too dark," Terry said, grabbing some other pigment and mixing it into the powder.

I turned around, working on a painting of my own. It was crude, nowhere near as good as Terry's, but I'd have years to practice it in this world. There were no cellphones or civilization, so not much else to do.

The door to Terry's painting room swung open.

"Noble's here," Maritha said.

CHAPTER 10

I rushed down to the workshop. Mom was already packing the crates full of the finished articles. She only took a second to look at me. Joining her, I folded the assembled mining outfits together and shoved them into the crates.

We were done in only a moment, shuffling out of the workshop. I slammed the crate into the door to open it, sending it creaking on its hinges.

There was no one outside.

I turned around.

"Town hall," she said, gesturing with her head toward the town center.

I led the way. The walk was only a few blocks, but it felt so long. My eyes didn't leave the dungeon when we entered the town square. The structure hadn't changed at all, but I still couldn't look at it the same.

"Gwen." Mom said. She had already walked past me and was standing outside the door to the meeting hall.

I nodded in acknowledgment, stepping up. I could already hear the not-shouting match on the other side.

The door creaked open with a rush of hot air. The sound of crackling wood under-toned the serious and angry discussion at the table.

"—Again, because we should be moving now, not waiting for the town to collapse." Sandy's dad, Henri, gestured wildly across the table as he spoke.

Gerald's mom and dad sat near the Noble on the other side. Gerald stood behind them, wringing his hands. He looked panicked when he made eye contact with me. I smiled at him.

In total, there were six people at the table before we sat.

"Valjean," Mom said, nodding at the Noble.

He nodded back. He was leaning back in the chair, arms folded, face bored. He wore a blue suit filigreed with silver. Another Noble stood behind him, wearing light armor.

"You ask this every time. Wasting all of our time," our town's baker replied. "Time better spent determining our next shipment. I want to push for a higher allocation of flour. I'll pay for more."

"Aye, and I'd put in an order for more barrels," the town's winemaker said.

"These problems," Valjean said, unfolding his arms, "would be fixed by moving to Foundry."

I slammed the crate down on the table. Valjean's eyes pivoted to me slowly. I smiled.

"We can wait," Mom said. Valjean nodded.

"I'd like to move now, rather than sit around here," Henri said.

"You're the only chef class in the town. It can't survive without you. And I can't force anyone to move," Valjean said, eyeing Henri. "Not unless the town collapses."

I took a seat at the table, rubbing at the splotches of paint on my arms.

"We need the dungeon maintained," the baker interjected again.

"I have to clear the dungeons in Foundry and Ironside," Valjean said, his head snapping to attention. "Even this dalliance of a day here is going to cost them progress. Not to mention guarding the trade wagons that run between the villages. You won't be able to get more maintenance without hiring mercenaries."

"The full council is here," Henri said, nodding at Mom. "I motion to move the town to Foundry."

"Seconded."

"Approved," Valjean replied.

There were groans in the room. Valjean remained impassive.

Gerald's parents raised their hands. Henri's did the same. There were three votes for the motion in an instant. I felt like the floor dropped out from under me as I looked around the room. The baker and winemaker, elected officials of the town, kept their hands down.

I looked at Mom. She was already staring back at me. I felt the blood rush out of my face, the chill of panic run up my spine. Everything I had been doing for the past week—the late nights working, the monsters I killed, the days spent covering my arms with blood instead of paint—everything could be gone in an instant.

"Motion defeated," Valjean said.

"It's not defeated. It's three and three," Henri said. "Esmeralda, vote. Your daughter's not Chosen. She's not going to be."

"Shut your mouth," Mom said, her voice poisonous.

"Break the tie!" Henri spat, looking angrily at Valjean. "Before we all die in this nothing town."

"Point of order," Valjean said.

Henri leaned back in his chair, the movement slow and controlled, basically gnashing his teeth as he folded his arms.

"You call that motion every month, Henri. Just give it up."

"Legally, no one here can move without someone replacing their critical duties. Anyone leaves and the town won't function," Valjean said. "Eventually, the town will collapse due to the dungeon's decay. We do not have the resources to keep all three of my towns maintained."

Gerald gripped the table. I looked over to him. There was something like shame in his eyes. But there was nothing to be ashamed of; we were already doing all we could.

"Next order: the distribution of the space available in the trade wagon. Three crates are already reserved for my order." Valjean gestured at Mom.

"Five crates for food," Henri spat.

Most of the table looked at him appraisingly. Gerald paled. Valjean stared.

"Alright. Anyone else?" he said, turning and looking at the rest of the table.

"Two barrels," the winemaker said.

Eventually, the entire space of the wagon was filled, using crates and barrels as standard sizes. Near the end, there was a back and forth of who would get to ship their product first.

With the dangers the Wild presented, the only way goods could be shipped in or out of the town was with Noble guards, and the only Noble guards that worked around here were Valjean and his men. Near the end of the meeting, Valjean motioned forward.

His bodyguard checked the contents of the crates, then fished out a bag of coins and counted a few out, pressing them into Mom's hand. Her chair scraped as she stood to leave. I followed. The main point of the meeting ended, the full council was no longer needed.

Instead, Henri pestered Valjean with questions about finding a person who could replace his position in the village.

"Well, how did you feel about your first big job?" Mom asked, bumping into me.

"It was…good," I said. "I wish there were more opportunities to be, I don't know, creative."

"You could pursue improvisation skills. Eventually maybe even make your own patterns," Mom said. "But those jobs aren't the ones that pay the bills. It's a balancing act. We will get some new potential orders to choose from next month at the council meeting. You should work on your own pattern more. You can improvise all you want on it."

I nodded. We walked for a while in comfortable silence.

"Why does Henri want to move so bad?" I asked.

"Well." Mom coughed, startled at the question. "He hasn't had the best time here. He was from a city, originally—tier two or three—and moved here with his wife, years ago. Before we changed mayors and the town really started to decline."

I chewed on that. His wife wasn't around anymore. Why did Sandy want to keep the town alive so bad? It wasn't like she hung out with the other young adults of the town or could take over her father's job.

"What happened to her?" I asked. Now that she mentioned it, I had the memory of her funeral. It was probably half a decade ago. No one mentioned how she died.

"Henri said she went out to the Wild and never came back."

"Is that true?" I asked. "Why would she…"

"I don't know. She was a butcher. Maybe she was…hunting?" Mom said.

Many things clicked into place at once.

"When did the town start shrinking so fast?" I asked without thinking.

Mom stopped walking, turning to me.

"My light…" she said.

"I'm happy being a seamstress," I said, lying through my teeth. I swallowed hard.

"Alright." My mom sighed, walking forward. "It's probably what you're thinking. About five years ago."

Mom stepped into the workshop, the door whining in complaint.

"I'm going to go see Sandy," I said.

She stopped and stared at me.

"Just don't pick at any old wounds."

I let the door swing closed.

When I found Sandy, she was hard at work, a dozen stinking corpses hanging from her bedroom-workshop. The trade wagon must have brought them in. They weren't all shapes I was familiar with.

They hung from the hooks on the ceiling while Sandy worked at her workstation, grunting with visible effort as she tried to pry apart a chitin carapace. The monster corpses hanging from the ceiling didn't have chitin; or if they did, it had already been peeled away. It piled in a corner.

"Dad still at the meeting?" Sandy asked with another grunt, pulling off a plate of chitin. She sent it clattering against the wall, joining a pile of cut and broken plates.

"Last I saw." I replied, stepping through the bodies and looking down at the pile of chitin, thinking about how to approach the question I wanted to ask Sandy.

"Dick," she said, working a tool under the chitin covering a monster. "Sends me all of this and tells me to work on it."

What strained the relationship between them so badly that she cursed her own dad?

"This would make good armor," I said, picking up a piece of the chitin and knocking on it with a fist. It wasn't what I wanted to say.

Sandy grunted noncommittally.

"So," I said. "Why do you want to clear the dungeon?"

Sandy looked up at me, eyes sharp as knives, staring down in a moment of tense silence that hung between us.

"To keep the town alive," Sandy said, resting her hands on the cold, red chitin of the monster she was cutting apart.

"You were clearing the dungeon a year ago?" I asked, searching her eyes. "I heard the town started shrinking faster five years ago."

Sandy sighed and looked away from me, leaning forward over her table.

"It didn't take you this long to figure it out, did you?" Sandy asked. "I thought you knew."

"Knew what?"

Sandy looked back at me, eyes a little softer this time. Then she grabbed the monster she was tearing apart, lifted it, and slammed it onto a hook hanging from the ceiling. She peeled off her apron—this was one of the first times I had seen her without it—and threw it onto the table. It made a wet noise. Sandy leaned against the wall, eyes hardening as she looked down at me.

"Don't do that. Don't probe for it like it hurts me for you to say it. Say it."

"She was clearing the dungeon."

"My mom died in the dungeon," Sandy said.

"But then—why?" I asked, stepping forward. Unexpectedly, Sandy flinched. I retreated a little. "Why would you follow her down to clear the dungeon yourself?"

"Because. She's still down there."

CHAPTER 11

She's…still down there?" I asked. "You don't mean—"

"She's not alive." Sandy said, leaning forward. The hanging carcasses in her workshop cast shadows on the room that crawled up the wall.

A silence stretched between us. I looked down at the floor, caked in dried blood that crusted the texture carved into the stone bricks. The iron smell of blood warred with the scent of spices that escaped the door to the house. Sandy's dad was cooking.

"Okay," I said.

"Okay?"

"I'll help you. We have to clear the floors to be able to get—to get farther down, right?"

Sandy stared.

I jumped at a knock at the door. It swung out on its hinges. Gerald stepped in, holding a huge cloth bundle, his eyes wide as an owl's as he scanned the hanging bodies.

"Sandy!" Gerald said. "Your dad is a dick."

"You can't just say that," I said.

Sandy laughed.

"You go to your first town meeting?" she asked, reaching out to help Gerald with the bundle.

He had to stand his cloth package upright to be able to navigate through the carcasses before pushing it into Sandy's arms.

"Yes!" Gerald said, exasperated. "He's so…so…"

"Assertive," I suggested.

"Arrogant," Sandy replied. "Demanding. Patronizing."

"Yeah. That," Gerald said.

Sandy unbundled the cloth, letting it fall loosely to the floor. She smiled viciously at the tool she held in her hand; it was not quite a sword.

The blade was square from tip to handle, the sharpened edge gleaming in the lamplight. Bones decorated the blunt edge, wolf teeth pointed inward. The only thing sharper in the room was Sandy's smile.

"Today's the day," Sandy said. "I can feel it."

Sandy played with her new cleaver, cutting directly through the chitin covering the corpse she had been working on. Her eyes widened.

"Do you have to get your patterns for smithing one at a time?" I asked. "You must be leveling fast."

"I…no, I started with some," Gerald said. He looked away from me, not meeting my eyes, staring at the blade in Sandy's hand. "It's fun, though. There's always a ton of work orders. My dad had been behind on them for years. We're catching up."

Gerald pressed his back to the wall, sliding down to the floor.

There was a knock at the other door this time. Gerald and I both jumped, but Sandy just scowled, turning around and kicking away the chair that blockaded the door to her house. It swung outward, revealing the tired face of Sandy's dad.

In the softer light of Sandy's lamps and the fleeting afternoon, he looked beaten and exhausted rather than hateful. His eyes scanned the room, lingering on the huge cleaver Sandy held.

"What?" she asked.

"Food?" he said, pushing the plate in his hands forward. It was stacked to the point that it looked like it would fall off. "For you and your…friends."

He stared at Gerald.

"We don't need your…"

"I'll take it!" I interrupted, snatching the plate out of Henri's outstretched arms. He frowned, stepping back. Sandy slammed the door in his face.

Gerald looked nervous, picking at pieces from the plate and considering them carefully before eating bite by bite. I sat down next to him as I waited for night to fall. We definitely weren't traipsing to the dungeon in the daylight for anyone to see us, especially since the town was extra active today with Valjean's presence.

"So what kind of work orders do you guys have?" I asked Gerald.

"Huh?" he asked, looking up. "Oh. Boring stuff, mostly. Occasionally weapons and armor but mostly smaller metal stuff. Candle holders. Parts of lamps. Nails. Gears. Bolts."

"Crossbow bolts or machine bolts?"

"Machine bolts. They're a pain because after each one we have to resmelt all the filings," he said.

Then he dove into the intricacies of smithing.

We whittled away the last hours of daylight until the sun set and then kept each other company until it was dark outside. Gerald went home after eating.

"He's so nervous lately," I said, leading the way out into the street.

Sandy grunted. She was carrying her giant cleaver like a baby, still wrapped in cloth.

"Probably just because Valjean is here. Who isn't nervous around Nobles?"

The wagons the Nobles led into town were in the central square, the horses tied to a post nearby. They were giant silhouettes in the streetlight; burly, monstrous things, their presence setting me ill at ease. It felt like a monster was staring me down from the alleys, even though I knew they were most likely asleep.

We crept around the wagons arranged in a half circle. They were still only half loaded with goods; the rest would be shoved on tomorrow morning. This close to them, I noticed there was dried blood crusted on the side of the wagons. I stopped in my tracks and stared at it.

The Wild was a dangerous place; the safe zone of the dungeon made sure that no monsters accosted us inside the city, but the animals that roamed it survived by virtue of strength alone, which meant almost everything out there could and would eat you. Only the Nobles had the capacity to defend transports through the Wild. In a border town, that meant only the mayor and whatever unlanded Nobles he had enlisted.

One day I would be able to travel the Wild by myself. Already I felt the effects of reaching twenty-one dex; I might not have reached superhuman, but I felt as if I was already near the human limit.

We stepped into the dungeon, the lurching sensation washing over me. I staggered forward when solid ground came back under my feet. Sandy followed behind.

"Today's the day. I can feel it," Sandy said, dropping the cloth from her cleaver. Then she pulled out a lamp from her own bag, sparking it to light. It was brighter than the ones in her room, featuring a metal base and thick glass.

"When did you get that?" I asked.

"Got it just for the dungeon. It's hardened. Delivered today."

I blinked at that, confused.

"If you got it today, doesn't that mean you ordered it last month with the last shipment?"

"Yes," Sandy said. "I figured either you became a Noble or I went back to clearing the dungeon."

She looped the lantern on her belt and stepped forward, her cleaver menacing as it glinted in the light. Our nightly dungeon clears had become routine. I barely even paid attention to the heavy fatigue that hung over me night after night.

I felt what Sandy was talking about as we stepped into the Dungeonheart. The air felt like it was full of static electricity, making my hair stand on end.

We found the first wolf quickly. It charged us with a growl. I trusted Sandy to deal with it, watching her back. The blade cut the air with a rushing noise. The squeal of the wolf joined the wet noise of torn flesh, then a crack, and then two thumps.

Two halves of the wolf hit the floor, already dead.

I turned to look at Sandy. She was staring at the blade in her hand with a frown. "This isn't normal, Gwen."

"What do you mean? It's a better knife, right? Better performance is…" I stared at the two halves of the wolf corpse "Could you try to keep them in one piece? Maybe a clean cut at the neck. That's going to be a pain to stitch together."

Sandy's eyes read invisible text in the air as she pulled open her system.

"This blade is raising my speed and strength by five each. That's…good, right?"

"A new blacksmith shouldn't be able to…it doesn't make sense."

"Maybe his dad helped." I shrugged. "We can check after we're done here."

We moved deeper into the dungeon. Each time Sandy swung, she carved directly through the monsters, the blade tearing them apart like wet paper. The messier fighting style also left pools of blood as we mushed through the cave. I activated [Shadow Cloak] as we entered the final room.

There was only one wolf left. The stealthy wolf posed no threat to us anymore; Sandy killed it with no more effort than the previous monsters. I paced around the room as the static buzz in the air rose to an uncomfortable level.

It felt like magic in the air, static electricity building and pulsing inward. The edges of the wolf glowed and then fell dim, all the static in the air disappearing at once.

"No," Sandy said. "Shit."

She walked to the center of the room, touching the ground with her fingers.

"What is it?" I asked, breaking out of stealth to step forward. "Is it opening?"

"It's not. But you felt it, right? It can't be more than a day away," Sandy said, staring down at the floor.

"Then let's get ready for tomorrow," I replied.

Sandy dragged the shadow wolf—the only one we kept. The others weren't even worth selling, according to Sandy, and we had an excessive supply of basic leather.

With my mana full, I was able to sew together Sandy's cloak with superhuman speed.

[+2 XP]

I stood with a yawn and a stretch, holding out her cloak. Sandy was at her desk, paging through a book. I flicked my wrists, making a flapping noise with the cloak to grab Sandy's attention. She looked up from where her head rested on her hand.

"Finished?" she said, stepping forward and grabbing a handful of the fur. She ran a hand through it. "It's…nice."

The book on her desk folded itself shut, tired and wrinkled paper reforming to its memory. The cover was colorful; pink with an image of a flower imprinted on it.

"Try it on," I said.

She spun the cloak onto her shoulders, pushing an arm through it before staggering over, blinking wide-eyed.

"Woah," she said.

"That's the attribute bonuses," I said with a grin. "To think Nobles just get to raise their attributes with their levels."

"Who needs Nobles when you have this?" Sandy laughed, sitting back in her chair. She squinted forward. The cloak raised dexterity and perception by two points each; a quantifiable difference in ability.

"Tomorrow. We'll be ready," I said, nodding seriously. I touched a hand to my chest, and, with a thought, the cloak disappeared from over me and into the wardrobe. I switched shirts, too. A handy feature of the skill was that it pulled out the clothes perfectly clean and wrinkle free.

"What are you doing tomorrow?" Sandy asked suddenly, leaning back in her chair and basking in the glory of her new cloak.

"Sleeping in," I said. I could finally relax after a week of staying up late to sew to keep up with the work order the mayor had assigned us. Maybe mom would pick up another one tomorrow. But I could deal with it later. For now, I needed to relax.

"Maybe doing some painting," I followed up.

When I made it home, my bed practically sucked me in.

I didn't expect to wake up to shouting.

CHAPTER 12

The town—my house—was a flurry of activity. People were yelling in the hall. "Gwen!" Terry shouted, throwing the door open to our room. "The Noble," she said.

"What?" I asked, still waking up. It was noon. Or afternoon. I wasn't kidding about sleeping in.

"It's—there's a meeting."

"A council meeting?" I asked with a stretch. Then I rose to peek out the window.

There were people running down the street.

"What's going on?" I asked, spinning.

"Someone's clearing the dungeon!"

"What? Right now?"

"No! But the town stopped decaying. So someone has to be..." Terry wrung her hands.

Shit, did we get found out this fast? I basically sprinted out of my room before turning around to get pants. My heart was racing. Clearing the dungeon always came with some complications, like the very small issue of it being *technically* illegal and property theft, since the contents of the dungeon belonged to the Noble.

"Is my mom out at the meeting?" I asked.

"He gave the whole town a summons! Everyone who's able is there," Terry replied.

We shuffled out the door to find the Noble in the town center, surrounded by dozens of people. Parents held fidgeting children still. The mayor held his face in his hands, pinching his nose and sitting on a barrel. The wagons had moved farther from the center of the town.

Council members shouted on either side of him. One of his two unlanded Nobles looked like he was about to doze off, leaning against the wagon behind him.

I approached the meeting slowly, eyes jumping around. Strangely enough, Sandy's dad was quiet, his face stuck in a frown. Sandy stood behind him. Mom stared at Sandy with a frown.

"—clearly the consequence of YOUR daughter," the winemaker spat at my mom. She continued to stare at Sandy. "Well, aren't you going to say something? She has bastard's blood."

Mom moved in a flash, slapping him across the face. The winemaker stumbled back, looking up at her.

"That's enough," Valjean said, stepping forward off his crate and rubbing his head like he had a headache.

"It's probably just a one-off freak accident," Henri suddenly interjected.

"The shrinking of the town—this has to have been going on for a week," Valjean replied.

I stepped up behind Mom, who was rubbing her hand. She reached out and threw an arm around me.

"The only thing my daughter has done is work late to finish our work orders. Valjean can attest," she said.

He looked down at me. I nodded.

"If there is any Noble in the town—" Valjean stepped forward, eyes sweeping the crowd. "—let me reiterate once more that you are *obligated* to report your status. Our nation *needs* you."

I caught Gerald standing behind his dad. He was pale, and when he met my eyes, they were full of fear. I smiled at him. It would be fine. Everything would be okay.

"We have a few more days before Foundry's dungeon must be cleared again. Until then I'll be here. We will investigate the dungeon," Valjean said. "All of you, go home. The council will meet again today."

Barely anyone left the crowd; only the oldest members wandered away. There was an instant change in atmosphere as dozens of conversations stirred in the crowd. The paranoia of being stared at chilled my spine.

I stepped through the crowd to Sandy.

"Hey," I said, looking between Sandy and her dad.

"Lunch?" she asked.

We walked back to her house in silence, packed a basket of food, and then rushed away from the town into the woods where Sandy measured the town's decay.

We ate in silence. The bread was fresh from the city, with chunks of fruit in it. We didn't grow any fruit in our town, which meant for half the month the fruit would be weeks old.

"They caught on so fucking fast," Sandy said, finally breaking the silence that hung over us.

"How did they even…" I trailed off, staring out at the lightly shimmering air at the border of the Wild.

"Cobblestones. Gotta be. Mayor was probably watching the town's decay, too. I miss the old mayor. He didn't give a shit either way. Valjean is…so invested in the town collapsing."

"What now?"

"We just keep clearing the dungeon. The mayor can't stay here forever." Sandy made a tsking noise. "He won't even dedicate the time to clear the dungeon himself. You think he has the time to sit here and guard it? No. Same plan as always."

"Then we just have to wait for him to leave."

"No!" Sandy said. "No. We can't do that. It'll push back our progress."

"You think we're going to be able to go in at night?" I asked.

"We have to."

We fiddled away the daylight hours in Sandy's workshop. I still had more materials to work on, though I saved all my mana, finishing another piece of Sandy's set.

[+2 XP]

[Gwendolyn Tailor][Human, Lv6][Seamstress]

[Health: 10/10][Mana: 1/10][XP: 6/10]

[ATTRIBUTES]

▶SPD: 10

▶WIL: 5

▶STR: 5

▶DEX: 22

▶CON: 5

▶PER: 16

[SKILLS]

▶Crafting I

▶Running Stitch I

▶Hand Spinning I

▶Thread Mastery I

▶Wardrobe II

▶Quick Change I

[PATTERNS]

▶Hunter Pattern

[RESISTANCES]

▶Shadow: 5

[TEMPORARY SKILLS]

▶Bow Proficiency I

▶Shadow Cloak I

I threw the finished pants onto her bed, where they landed in a pile. The sun was only just falling. Sandy's wolf-fur cloak was hanging beside the door. I kept working, starting on the shirt. Sandy had more butcher work to do. After a few hours, she looked up and out the warped window panes to outside.

"Let's go," she said.

This time, we approached the center of the town more quietly. We crept around behind the houses, staying in the shadows of alleys and backyards and under trees full of falling leaves that crunched under our step.

Without a word, we circled far around, approaching the entrance. We stopped dozens of feet away, staring at where one of the unlanded Nobles sat outside the dungeon, arms crossed and awake. A campfire set into the center of the cobble road burned brightly.

"Shit," Sandy whispered.

We backed away, heading out.

"He can't stay there all night, right? He's gotta sleep," I said. "We just need to wait more."

Sandy bit a nail. I had never seen her so nervous.

"Yeah. Yeah, you're right. As long as he moves before the dungeon resets."

We moved farther away, out of people's yards but in view of the man through a gap between the houses, and waited in the dark. The ground was wet, fall approaching fast, and silence and tension hovered between us.

"Even if he comes once a month, it won't be enough to set back our dungeon clear," I said.

"He could start rotating families out of town until the dungeon stops being cleared," Sandy said. "He could hire a guard just to sit outside the dungeon. And the more floors we clear, the worse the dungeon will decay when it goes a day without being emptied."

We really had to do this. Every day. Forever.

"Let's give it another hour," I said, stepping away and turning back toward Sandy's house.

She followed me after throwing a last look over her shoulder. We took a direct path to the workshop, creeping inside.

"The hell?" Sandy asked as she stepped in. "Dad."

The door to the house was thrown open, the chair that had been used as a makeshift barricade tipped over on the floor.

"What happened?" I asked, scanning the room. There was little else out of place.

"He probably wanted to yell at me again," Sandy tsked, throwing her door shut.

"He took the cloak," I said, looking at the bare wall that the door had revealed.

"What?" Sandy spat. "That son of a…"

Sandy slapped the wall before turning away from it in a huff.

"Do you think he knows?" I asked Sandy.

"He has no reason to guess we're killing monsters. He definitely knows you're crafting things now," Sandy said, leaning over her table. "Shit. I don't—we can't stay here. Let's go back."

I just nodded.

We watched the town square through a crack between the houses, waiting patiently. Sandy tore apart the grass below her, rolling it in her fingers.

There was finally movement in the town square, but it dashed every hope we had. The second unlanded Noble joined the first before he left. They sat and talked for a moment before they changed shifts without leaving the dungeon open.

Sandy said nothing.

"We have to clear it," I said.

Sandy nodded. Without a word, she dug in her bag, then held out the tiny lantern. I grabbed it.

Then I activated [Shadow Cloak], feeling the darkness creep up around me.

My boots didn't make a noise as I stomped through the dried fall leaves, blackness sticking to me like tar. The closer I got to the campfire, the more I felt the skill strain, as if it couldn't find enough shadow to conceal me. I crept around the outer periphery of it. The guard's eyes flew up to where I was a moment ago. In a panic, I froze.

He slowly looked back away into the night, huffing and rubbing his arms. I kept creeping around the side until I was pressed against the dungeon entrance. Sliding behind him, I slipped into the dungeon. The embrace of shadows felt much safer here where the campfire's light could hardly reach. I crept up to the dungeon slowly and carefully. I was alone this time.

[Shadow Cloak] dropped from my shoulders silently as I lit Sandy's lantern. I held it in my left hand and my sewing needle in my right.

[Running Stitch I] [Mana: 8/10] [Cancel]

The first of four wolves fell without a struggle. I looped through the den. The buzzing in the air pressed against my skin; it was warmer than yesterday, the air humid in the cave, rich with the scent of earth and iron from the blood clinging to my needle.

The second wolf I killed made my hair stand on end like the room was full of static electricity. Killing them was routine. Easy. The third died. The fourth crept out of the shadows as if it knew its death was inevitable.

It wasn't wrong.

[Running Stitch I] [Mana: 5/10] [Cancel]

When its body hit the floor there was a thrum of mana, a pulse roaring through the floor like a heartbeat. I staggered backward when it hit me, stabbing my sewing needle down to recover my footing. A second pulse came a moment later, the beating heart of a living dungeon. Then the floor deformed and broke; a twisted archway of stone grew from a wound in the floor. Mana sparked and crackled between in it like it was unstable, the rippling image of a jungle hovering on the other side.

Of course the second floor to the dungeon opened now that I was alone.

CHAPTER 13

Was it worth it to take the risk? To dive into the next floor of the dungeon, alone? I should—

I should stop kidding myself. I decided to face off against a pack of wolves with nothing but a big metal rod. I decided a long time ago—years ago—that I was going to clear the dungeon, to keep this new life of mine alive. For myself. For my mom. Of course I was going to clear the next floor. Every kill means more experience. More experience means more opportunities. A new type of monster just meant a fancy new dress to me.

Sure, I didn't end up a Noble. But I wasn't just a seamstress anymore.

[Shadow Cloak I] [Mana: 4/10]

A cloak of darkness hugged me tight, blocking the lantern's light from escaping. Darkness filled the cave, save for the golden orange-light of the portal. I stepped into it as a walking shadow.

The change in environment assaulted my senses once again. Though it was deep night on the first floor, on the second it was golden twilight; soft light filtered through the leaves of a dancing canopy. This floor of the dungeon was the forest; it was huge and alive and everything moved and smelled of rich earth and life.

Insects, mushrooms, and vines covered the trees. Birds chirped. There was an open path before me, the trees thinnest along a road of rough earth and tree root and what foliage could survive this far below the canopy.

The shadows between the trees were deep.

I stepped off the road, walking carefully over uneven terrain, blending in with the shadows. Sandy said the second floor contained bug monsters. There could be anything in a forest. I kept my eyes open as I crept forward inch by inch.

I only had enough mana to kill four more.

My imagination went wild with what I would face. What if there were millipedes the size of horses? Would they die instantly? Butterflies that could fly away from me? No, that would be ridiculous. Butterflies weren't monsters. The more I scanned the floor of the forest the more cramped it felt.

Though it appeared open, it was far more restrictive than the first floor. Beyond the sparse trees was a wall of warped bark. The floor was only an illusion of a forest. It was a cage full of monsters.

The forest road twisted and turned, the wall winding at the edges. I followed it for minutes without seeing a monster. Ahead, the canopy fell away into shadow, the shape of leaves dancing in the trees. My paranoia grew.

Something moved beneath me, the ground giving way. I jumped backward as I scanned the ground. The shadows of the canopy distracted me from the terrain below. I wasn't sure whether I'd see that I'd stepped on a snake or that there was a sinkhole opening beneath me.

Instead I saw a web sliding across the ground.

A monster slammed into the ground where I had been. It had eight legs, a shining carapace striped in hot pink and metallic red. It chittered as it spun about, eight eyes glinting with the golden light of late afternoon, fangs dripping a purple liquid so bright it seemed to glow.

Of course it was spiders. Why wouldn't it have been spiders?

[Running Stitch I] [Mana: 3/10] [Cancel]

[+6 XP] [Level up] [Excess discarded]

Chitin broke almost as easily as muscle and flesh, my needle stabbing directly through the side of the monster. The needle struggled to break through the hard armor, but only for a moment, then it cracked through the carapace and into the gooey flesh, and the monster fell dead.

[Shadow Cloak] fell away and bug juice splattered onto me.

"Spiders." I cursed.

Then I assessed the side of the bug again. All told…it was rather pretty, the way the light reflected off its carapace. If I cut the side into pieces, I wondered if it could make passable armor. I wondered what element and skills it would grant. The ability to manipulate spiderweb? A higher level of Thread Mastery? The power to climb walls?

I would find out later. For now I needed to clear as much of the dungeon as I could. I watched the ground more carefully now, stepping over roots and into areas I could clearly see.

The shadows around me now seemed to take the form of all kinds of bugs. My gaze jumped around, scanning the shadows for lurking monsters. Occasional breezes sent a rustling noise through the canopy, leaves fluttering to the ground.

I screamed as something grabbed my foot and threw me to the forest floor. The world turned upside down. It closed around my ankle and ripped me off the ground. Only an instinctive response kept me holding onto my needle. My vision was mottled black, shadows dancing as branches moved.

A spider hovered in front of me.

It chittered, curious, reaching out with its fangs; I swung backward, throwing my body weight into the motion. The spider skittered back. The ever-burning lamp at my side fell from my belt and hit the ground with the sound of shattering glass and the rush of fire that found new fuel.

I tried to stab the sewing needle toward the spider, but it jumped away, dodging from me. Finally, I activated my skill.

[Running Stitch I] [Mana: 2/10] [Cancel]

The grip of magic pulled my arms in a vice, forcing my body to bend upward until the needle stabbed into the spider. I only had a moment to wonder how much I could abuse the movement of this magic before the smell of smoke overtook my other senses. My eyes started to burn.

[+4 XP]

The spider's body dropped with a crunch. But that still left me dangling upside down as smoke poured off the dead leaves at the bottom of the forest.

"Shit, shit, shit."

My momentum left me dangling helplessly, swinging back and forth. There were at least thirty feet between me and the ground, enough to break a leg if I was lucky. Luck wouldn't help me survive the fire. Would a healing potion heal burns? Would it heal a broken leg?

I had a feeling the answer to that last question was no.

I swung to reach the nearest branch, building up speed as I made myself into a living pendulum. I reached out with my free hand, brushing the side of the nearest branch, before swinging back with a thunk and slamming into the tree behind me.

[Health: 9/10]

My momentum was gone in an instant, a stark reminder of the weight of my failure. The fire licked up at me from below, hungry and angry and spreading with the sound of crackling wood and leaves, steam and smoke sputtering up to sting my eyes and choke me. I started swinging again, this time mindful of the tree behind me, and when I got as close as I dared, I activated my skill.

[Running Stitch I] [Mana: 1/10] [Cancel]

Magic ripped me forward, straining my arms and slamming me into the tree. The needle split the bark…and I swung backward as the force disbursed. [Running Stitch] canceled, taking the mana and one of my sewing needles with it. I coughed as fire built in my lungs, the smoke unavoidable. I was almost out of mana.

[Health: 8/10]

I couldn't afford to die here; how stupid would I have to be to die here? I wasn't even going to die to the monsters. I was going to die to a damned lamp. I needed to get out of here. The pain in my lungs intensified instead of weakening, my lungs full of fire. I was coughing ash, heat stinging my skin as the fire tried to alight the roots of the trees below me. The smallest saplings went up.

[Health: 7/10]

I swung for the rope and missed it. With shaking hands, I pulled out the second sewing needle from my bag, doing my best to cling onto it. All I had was stealth and stitching. I needed more. This is what Nobles were born with; the power to survive. They would have mobility skills to escape or survival skills to absorb the fall into the fire below. All I had was a stupid outfit and stupid sewing skills.

[Health: 6/10]

There was still a rope hanging from the end of the sewing needle stuck in the tree. I pulled on [Thread Mastery] as hard as I could. The rope inched toward me, swinging with me as I neared it like my hand was a magnet.

I felt the bonds around my ankles loosen.

I wasn't close enough to grab the rope. I was going to fall if the threads loosened. I tried to pull myself up to grab them instead—maybe if I pulled myself above the canopy I could crawl away. Instead, I found the web holding me aloft inching toward me just like the rope. Thread Mastery worked on spiderweb, too, apparently.

If Thread Mastery worked here, what else would respond to it? Exhausted and out of options, I pulled myself to the tiny end of the web, reaching out for the needle. With careful application of [Thread Mastery] I pulled the web through the eye of the needle.

[Health: 5/10]

With my last bit of my mana, I activated my skill.

[Running Stitch I] [Mana: 0/10]

I stabbed forward into another tree. This time, I kept going, stitching a pattern into the bark. The web burned as it spun around my ankles. The magic unraveled the spiderweb hidden in the canopy above, forcing it forward and into the bark.

[Health: 4/10]

I stitched patterns into the bark until the web ran out, my ankles burning and bleeding, my lungs gasping for air. When the last of the web above unraveled, I simply dropped, grabbing for the tree and finding a handhold in the web I had stabbed into its side. Great stitches of messy spiderweb adorned the bark in a pattern down its side.

I hugged the tree, inching down step by step before falling a few feet at the bottom. My lungs protested, gasping for air.

[Health: 3/10]

Pressing myself low, I sprinted onto the forest path and back toward the exit, fighting the ever-present smoke. Fire and ash gave way to birdsong and small animal calls, now raised into a massive alarm. I kept jogging forward.

One of my two needles was stabbed into a tree on the second floor of the dungeon. If anyone found it…there would only be one answer as to who was clearing the dungeon with a giant needle.

I gasped for air like a drowning woman, staggering to all fours before turning back and looking at the fire. It was spreading. Slowly. Blood stained the inside of my pants where the snare burned my skin and pulled me into the spiderweb. Ash clung to me.

I pushed myself to my feet and ran until I slammed through the portal back to the first floor. I didn't think I could run anymore, but I had anyway. I pressed my hands to the cold stone, feeling the heat drain from my body, relishing in the dirty floor. Wolf corpses lay in pooled blood nearby. Relief was an unexpected emotion upon seeing a corpse.

Gasping and hacking, I unbuttoned my backpack with shaking hands and found the healing potion inside.

Then I stopped myself, still choking on the taste of smoke. I wasn't in any danger. I looked back at the portal to the next stage of the dungeon. The monsters didn't follow. I was as safe as I could be.

Except my [Shadow Cloak] was gone and so was my mana. I had no way to get out without the guard seeing me.

CHAPTER 14

I couldn't just walk past the guard. There was no story I could use to talk my way out of it. I was out of health, mana, and options, pinned in the dungeon. I desperately wanted a shower and my bed, covered in sticky ash, my lungs heaving and desperate for air. I wanted to see my mom again.

Could I even survive in here?

I started walking out of the Dungeonheart, my ankles and lungs aching, occasionally coughing as I walked. Once the dungeon closed, as it did every night, days would pass inside. The farmers who lived in our village used that to their advantage, cultivating the wide-open ranges of the first floor of the dungeon to grow crops year-round.

Fields stretched out before me in a dead-quiet night. I had never focused on the land before to see how unnatural it was. There were no small animals or insects stirring in the dark, which let the sound of the distant river and irrigation canals wash over the landscape.

I walked toward the water until I saw the moonlight's reflection in its surface. Then I sunk to my knees and grabbed at it, drinking water as fast as I could, trying to wash away the ache in my throat. Finally, I collapsed by the shore. At least I wouldn't freeze. I closed my eyes and reached out to open my system, praying that I would get some kind of skill or level to get me out of the dungeon unseen.

[Skill Shop]

▶Mending I

[COMMON] Allows user to repair clothing from patterns they are unfamiliar with. Additional levels increase quality of final product.

▶Unweaving I

[UNCOMMON] Grants user the ability recycle items into base materials.

▶Thread Sensing I

[RARE] Grants user a metaphysical sense of threads they are connected to, allowing them to see where they are through walls and what is in contact with them. Additional levels allow farther sensing. Grants Thread Mastery I.

Nothing. There was nothing that could help me. I groaned. Was it too much to ask for bonus mana? If I were a Noble I would've had a free attribute point to dump into my willpower and increase my pool. I kept reading.

[PATTERNS]

▸Factory Worker Coverall Pattern (Intermediate)

[RARE] Grants large bonus to Constitution. Inflicts penalty to Perception. Grants set bonus based on craft quality and materials used.

▸Miner Pattern (Basic)

[UNCOMMON]

Grants minor bonus to Perception and Constitution. Grants bonus to mining skills depending on craft quality and materials used.

▸Shell Dress Pattern (Advanced)

[RARE] Grants bonus to Speed and Dexterity. Grants minor bonus to Perception. Inflicts minor penalty to Constitution and Strength. Grants set bonus skill based on craft quality and materials used.

My eyes stopped on the last option. It wouldn't solve any of my immediate problems, but from my understanding, the system wouldn't offer patterns you couldn't get the material for. So what did it mean by shell?

We didn't have crabs here. There was no ocean on any floor of the dungeon that I knew of. So this must have been a spider shell dress that granted a set bonus. It was far stronger than anything else I had seen, and a logical next step. It wouldn't help me escape, though. I selected it and stood back up, examining the fields. There were rows of growing wheat swaying in a soft wind.

It wasn't as if I could just magic up a loaf of bread. And I didn't have a knife to make wolf meat. Farther down the path were root plants. I dropped to my knees and pulled one out. They were like carrots but baby blue. I brushed the dirt from them.

They were half-grown and stumpy. Normally they had a soft, sweet flavor. I bit into one. My teeth didn't carve all the way through. It was rock hard. I groaned. Maybe I could order some mana potions from the next round of merchants. Come to think of it, I never asked how much money we earned from our work order. Maybe I could've bought a mana potion earlier. I groaned.

All I needed was a long rest to recover my mana. I propped myself against a tree and closed my eyes.

Sleep refused to find me. The sun rose in the dungeon while I was still wandering the floor. In deeper floors or higher-level dungeons, there would be the kinds of herbs that were needed to make potions or rarer materials. I'd heard that instead of farmland, the dungeon of Foundry contained mines. Here there was almost nothing.

The gigantic moon fell and the sun rose in its place, perfectly opposite. Despite the illusion of being real, this dungeon was fake, propped up by magic and forced into existence. Out of curiosity and boredom I walked to the exit. The dungeon gate that normally showed a wavy image of the village instead showed a flickering image. One moment I saw a forest on fire. Then a town made of black rock and filled with purple fog. It didn't seem closed. It seemed like it was a portal flickering through a hundred locations instead of a safe passage back to the village.

I ground down the baby blue carrots as I explored every inch of this level of the dungeon. The wolves had yet to respawn, though the dead ones were melting away. I didn't want to sleep anywhere near the Dungeonheart. The deeper portal was open, showing that the floor had reset. A canopy of leaves danced in the wind. The deeper portal would reset three times before I left, not that I would risk clearing that floor alone again.

I almost died.

There was nothing much else to do. I sat in a field, feeling the soft warmth of the artificial sunlight pouring down on me, and slept. I blinked myself awake to find the sun low, still exhausted and now covered in dirt.

My system snapped open before I had the fully conscious thought that I wanted to see it.

[Gwendolyn Tailor][Human, Lv7][Seamstress]
[Health: 8/10][Mana: 10/10][XP: 0/10]
[ATTRIBUTES]
▶SPD: 10
▶WIL: 5
▶STR: 5
▶DEX: 22
▶CON: 5
▶PER: 16
[SKILLS]
▶Crafting I
▶Running Stitch I
▶Hand Spinning I
▶Thread Mastery I
▶Wardrobe II
▶Quick Change I
[PATTERNS]
▶Hunter Pattern

▶Factory Worker Coverall Pattern
▶Miner Pattern
▶Shell Dress Pattern
[RESISTANCES]
▶Shadow: 5
[TEMPORARY SKILLS]
▶Bow Proficiency I
▶Shadow Cloak I

My lungs ached less. A long rest restored half my health and worked at restoring my aching ankles, too. I would still need to do some work to bring my clothing set all the way to max.

Still, I couldn't leave yet. I waited until the exit opened before finally activating [Shadow Cloak] and slipping past the guard. Days had passed in the dungeon, but outside, it had only been an hour. I wasn't eager to repeat the camping experience. Mud and ash warred for positions on my clothes and skin. I placed my clothes into my Wardrobe and retrieved them one at a time until they were all clean before rushing home and collapsing into bed.

I woke to someone violently shaking my shoulder. Smacking at the hand, I blinked away my sleepiness.

"Gwen?" Sandy asked, looming over me. Mom was in the doorway, wringing her hands.

"Yeah," I said, blinking away sleepiness.

Sandy threw a look back to Mom, face full of concern, then she looked back at me.

"I didn't see you today," Sandy said.

Bleary eyed, I looked out the window. It was evening already.

"I slept in," I replied.

Sandy ate a meal with us. The conversation at the table was stiff and quiet. Mom left as soon as we finished eating. Then we headed to Sandy's workshop.

We had piles of leather from the earlier clears. I reached to grab a piece to work on. I needed to get Sandy's stealth skill. My hands still shook thinking about the second floor.

"So? Did it open?"

"Yeah. And I almost died," I said with a grimace.

"What?" Sandy asked with a scoff. "The monsters there can't be that much of a threat, can they?"

"No. I uh, dropped the lantern."

"Oh. Are you alright?" Sandy asked.

I grimaced again. She changed the subject.

"What's the second floor?"

"A forest with giant spiders."

"How giant?" she asked.

"I don't know. Dog sized?" I stopped and stared at the piece of leather in my hand. There was a mental pull for which direction I wanted to move on Sandy's set, now that I had two patterns. The pattern of the Shell Dress pushed at me. Memories of viable materials for it washed over my mind. It needed leather and cloth still. String. I had been borrowing much of the material from Mom's workshop to complete the previous patterns, but there was a limit on how much I could steal before we needed to start buying things. And then shell. I saw a few different types used.

Crab. Turtle. Giant, monstrous armadillo shell. Or chitin. The spider's exoskeleton would work.

"Not too bad then," Sandy said, chewing her lip. "Be careful, Gwen. Don't push yourself."

"What?" I asked, shocked. I looked up from the piece of work I had in hand. Between the two of us, Sandy had been the more aggressive on pushing more floors and clearing more of the dungeon. But today she suddenly stepped back.

"I just mean—don't die," she said, looking at me sincerely.

"I won't. I can't yet."

I worked into the night. There was no mana to spend, which meant every stitch had to be done by hand. Step by step, I continued work on Sandy's clothing set.

[Tacca II]

▶60% complete

▶Quality +0

[PROJECTED SKILLS]

▶Shadow Cloak I

▶Random Hunter Proficiency I

I paused and looked up at Sandy.

"If I brought my equipment in, I could probably use the accelerated time in the dungeon to finish the rest of your outfit in a night."

Sandy looked up from a book she was reading on her bed, considering it seriously.

"No. The mayor will leave in a few days." Sandy kicked her legs off the side of her bed and stood up. "How much experience were the spiders worth?"

"Four for the one I killed," I replied. "But I leveled up right away."

Sandy nodded like she expected that.

"How…" I asked, then paused, trying to figure out how to phrase the question. "How deep do you need to go?"

Sandy grimaced.

"I'm not sure. It's not like she took me with her. It's dangerous no matter how skilled you get. You can clear the dungeon perfectly a thousand times. You only have to mess up once. A tiny trip. A slip. Health points protect you. But it's not like we can raise our constitution much. My dad did what he could." Sandy's face soured. "Specialized meals to raise stats. Took him entire days to cook sets of the stuff."

Sandy grabbed a bag from the workshop table and headed outside. I put down my work and followed her.

Around back was a huge dilapidated pen she had started repairing, a wooden fence that used to house animals for her mom to butcher. Now it just held Cinnamon.

Sandy pushed the door open and the dog ran out, jumping up to her.

"Who's a good boy?" Sandy asked, scratching the dog behind the ears.

What felt like months ago the priest's caravan guards had found the dog in the woods and given it to Sandy. It was huge, its body covered in cinnamon-orange fur with white swirls through it. The dog licked Sandy's face and she laughed.

"He's growing kinda fast," I said, bending down and petting him. He turned his affections to me. My eyes lingered on his claws. They were huge and ivory white. The dog already rose to my knees—it had been a puppy so recently.

"He probably has a little bit of wolf in him," Sandy said with a shrug. "He's friendly. It's okay."

CHAPTER 15

You named your wolf-dog Cinnamon," I said.

"Does he not look like a Cinnamon?" Sandy looked offended.

I evaluated the dog closely. He was panting with excitement, curled tail wagging behind him. Mud clung to his paws. Sandy stood behind him, holding a leather leash she had clipped on.

Sandy pulled on Cinnamon's leash and he walked astride her, staring at me as he did. We took a walk around the village to kill the time, moving along the very edge. Sandy stepped with measure, staring out into the Wild beyond. Cinnamon sniffed and looked out curiously, but he was well-behaved. Far too well-behaved, as if he was intelligent. I couldn't help but stare at him.

When he panted, his fangs were visible, huge and so pure white they almost glowed. He seemed to be constantly smiling. He caught me staring, his eyes widening as he stared up at me. I scratched between his ears.

We crossed back through the center of town, staring at one of the unlanded Nobles Valjean employed as a guard. He stared back with suspicion, eyeing Cinnamon. Cinnamon growled as he passed.

The guard rested his hand on the sword at his side.

We crossed back toward Sandy's house.

Her dad was sitting on the porch outside, smoking. Shadows covered his face, his eyebrows dark and furled, and the smell of alcohol hung off him.

"Come in," he said, staring hard at me, and then at Sandy. He ashed his cigarette, stood, and walked inside.

Sandy bristled. Cinnamon barked once. She scratched his ears.

I had never been in Sandy's house proper. Maybe once at some point as a kid while her mom was still alive, but the memory was a blur. The house smelled of food.

It was a graveyard of dead memories. Dust hung on the framed portraits on the wall. Lamplight snuck down the hallway, painting them a burnished red-orange. Sandy looked distinctly uncomfortable as she followed behind me.

Cinnamon left a track of muddy pawprints, head swiveling to look down the hallway. His eyes glowed golden-brown in the dim light.

We stepped from the hall into an open workshop that must have filled half the house.

The center of the room held a table long enough to seat eight. Most of the chairs and table were in disuse, piles of clutter filling up half the table. Sandy's cloak was spread over the other half. Cabinets and counters pressed into the walls, shelves lined with spices over sinks full of dishes.

The room was hot and filled with the sound of crackling wood. I found the source of the sound in a bank of smokers, their chimneys stretched up to the roof.

Henri sat at the end of the table and gestured at us to join him. I sat down, curious what he had to say.

"You made this?" he asked me before Sandy even sat.

I ran my hands over the cloak. The fur was cold and fine to the touch. I turned it over to stare at the stitch work. It wasn't my finest. My inability to recombine the leather meant that I had to cut the pattern and then stitch more pieces back together. Inside, the cloak was a motley quilt.

"Yes," I said.

Henri folded his hands. They were wrinkled and calloused. He still wore his wedding ring. His folded back sleeves left his arms showing, tattoos of animals creeping down one side. He rubbed his eyes.

"It's fine work. Let me pay you for it, at least," he said.

"What is this about?" Sandy asked pointedly.

"You have to stop," Henri said authoritatively, his voice not taking no for an answer. Cinnamon bumped his nose into Sandy's hand, staring up at her dad.

"No." Sandy's tone was venomous.

"You—" Henri started, raising his voice, then stopped. He covered his eyes with his hand again. "Valjean will be clearing the dungeon tonight. He is hoping to catch whoever is clearing the gate unprepared. *Since they snuck by the guard.*" Henri said the last bit pointedly at Sandy.

At least he had no idea it was actually me clearing the gate.

"What is your obsession with stopping me? Do you just want to abandon Mom so quickly?"

"I just want my daughter alive," Henri said, standing suddenly. His chair scraped the tile.

Cinnamon growled, hackles rising.

"Do not get caught. Do not get injured." Henri left the house. Sandy and I sat as the front door creaked open then slammed.

"He isn't going to go tell someone, is he?" I asked, concerned.

"If he was, he wouldn't have warned us about Valjean tonight," Sandy said, chewing her lip. "Maybe you should stay back tonight."

"No," I replied after a moment of thought, pressing my hands over the cloak. "I lost one of my sewing needles inside when I…if he finds it, I'll be found out."

Sandy tapped her fingernails on the table. Then she grabbed the cloak and stood. I followed.

As we moved toward the workshop, the smell of food grew stronger. Henri had prepared an entire meal and left it on the worktable. For both of us. So maybe he did suspect me.

[CON +6]

The meal left me filled with energy and strength. It made me feel more real and complete. My health doubled.

With a content sigh, I stood, gathered my backpack and supplies, and changed into my cloak.

"I'm going to try to bring home one of the spiders today," I said.

"Make sure it's dead," Sandy said between bites, still eating.

I pushed open the door to outside, pausing for just a moment.

[Shadow Cloak] [Mana: 9/10]

The clock ticked on my mana. But I wondered, did I really even have to clear the first floor of wolves again? Could I just skip the floor and move straight to the spiders?

I slunk through the town, lurking in the shadows of buildings as I crept around the square. When I came into view of the dungeon, I was shocked to see Valjean himself there, strapped in armor and mounting his horse. He spoke tersely to the guard who waited outside.

The guard departed.

Valjean entered.

He had to duck to ride the horse inside the dungeon. The horse itself was a monstrous thing, bulging with muscle, larger than any horse I had seen in my last life. I wondered what kind of classes and skills horses gained. As far as I knew, every living thing here, even insects, had access to the system.

Valjean had a shield the size of a man strapped to his back and a long halberd in hand, both dark black with bright white filigree. The horse trotted through the portal. I waited for a few minutes before following, slinking along the border of the open square before diving into the portal. Valjean trotted forward far ahead of me, through the plains, up the road, and directly into the Dungeonheart without stopping. I had to run to keep up. He didn't seem to notice me. I didn't know what kind of skills Nobles had, but his didn't seem to include stealth detection. I wondered if he would notice the shadow wolf inside. He walked casually, whispering something to his horse as he went.

"Good boy. That's the way…" he said, patting the horse's side.

His halberd flashed in the moonlight trailing into the cave. There was a thumping noise as a wolf died. He didn't even look up.

Was that a skill? Or just his stats? Was his perception so high he saw it and reacted instantly? I crept behind him.

I could do that. My skill wasn't so different.

Valjean looped around the dungeon. Twice more, his blade flashed, instantly killing the wolves. Not just killing them—mangling them. I looked down at one. His blade hadn't cleanly parted them like Sandy's, nor pierced them like my needles. He swung the curved blade of the hatchet with enough force to shatter their bones, leaving the monsters in piles and splatters.

They weren't worth recovering. Hopefully he wouldn't mangle the spiders as badly as the wolves.

I watched tensely as he trotted his horse around the Dungeonheart. His expression was bored, looking through the shadows. The gate to the next floor was closed.

The shadow wolf leapt at his back. He didn't see it.

Its mouth clamped on his arm, tearing viciously, flopping about and digging its claws into the horse's side. The horse didn't seem to be in any pain; it made a noise of discontent.

"Shadow monster? A first-floor miniboss…" Valjean was almost whispering, though it echoed in the cave. It was barely audible over the growling of the wolf. As if bored, he reached out with his open hand and grabbed the wolf by its fur.

There was a crunch.

The body flopped to the floor.

He stared at the wolf for a second before trotting through to the next floor.

I waited a minute before following behind again.

Valjean's experience showed. He stared upward at the canopy, patting the side of his horse again. I wondered if now was the moment to rush forward and look for my sewing needle before he found it.

"I hate ambush floors," he said, holding up his halberd. I wondered if now was the moment to rush forward and look for my sewing needle before he found it.

It glowed with mana as he began to activate a skill. It seemed like one that took a moment to charge.

After a second, his blade flashed left to right. A wave of light passed through the trees. The forest shook.

The trees began to fall, the closest ones first. Painfully bright light began to pour in from the open canopy as dozens of trees collapsed like dominos.

Valjean began to casually saunter into the trees, his horse crushing the wood where it stomped on the fallen logs.

I shouldn't have been worried about Valjean finding my needle. He didn't even look. He just stomped his way down the twisting floor of the dungeon. His singular attack had cleared the monsters. Broken spider corpses sat beneath tree branches. I carefully counted them all; there were six in total. Enough to expend the whole of my mana.

Unless I found a way to expand my mana, my dungeoneering would end at this floor.

Valjean walked to the end of the second floor; a place I hadn't reached when I was first here. The floor ended in a wall of trees blocked by hanging vines. It seemed as though his skill hadn't cut through the vines.

"Only the second floor," he said. Then he turned around. His eyes swept the floor behind him.

And he waited.

I watched for a few minutes to see where he would go or what would happen. But nothing did. Assured he was staying still, I crept back toward the exit. I saw Valjean's head turn, but his eyes passed right over me, as if he could see the impression of motion but not the motion itself.

I walked back to where I suspected the needle was, finding it half buried in tree limbs. A spider corpse sat on the floor next to it, crushed inward like a broken candy shell. I pulled the needle free with a crunching noise. The [Shadow Cloak] stretched around it, hiding it from view. It was covered in grime and ash, pressed into the earth. Nine days had passed on the second floor.

I clung to the shadows of the foliage that remained, reaching out and grabbing the spider body as well. I felt the [Shadow Cloak] stretch, struggling as it spread out, thinner and thinner.

Then it snapped, disappearing without a sound. I felt Valjean's eyes land squarely on me.

CHAPTER 16

I dropped the spider and ran.

Stupid move. I didn't have the speed to outrun Valjean's horse.

The sound of the horse's hooves tearing apart the crumpled underbrush came closer and closer, a cacophony behind me.

I reactivated [Shadow Cloak] and did something stupid.

[Mana: 8/10]

I dropped to the ground, lying flat. Wind caught the stray hairs on my face. He leapt over me, slamming into the portal. Had he seen my face? The cloak covered most of it. My hair was tied back in the hood, though my clothing would stand out. But it wasn't like I had worn the hood in public.

I propped myself up on my elbows in the muddy earth, the ground squelching as I stared at the portal. He knew I could use invisibility and had presumed I kept running for the exit. Maybe a real Noble would've had a mobility skill that would let them reach the portal before him. Whatever his leap of logic was, it saved me from being caught today.

I scrambled forward, staying low and at the dark edge of the dungeons walls, pausing for a moment to inspect the dungeon floor on the other side of the portal. My eyes were adjusted to the twilight of the second floor, while the first was in dusk. I could see nothing on the other side.

When I crossed the threshold, I did so with paranoia, eyes wide to see what I would find.

There was a flash of golden light. Behind me, Valjean whipped his horse about, pointing it toward the dungeon entrance. It was a trap. Some kind of magic trip-wire must have revealed as I crossed the gate. I jumped, ready to dodge a furious attack from Valjean.

None came.

"Show yourself," he said, horse trotting forward slowly. His weapon was laid across the horse. "Why are you doing this? You have nothing to fear from revealing your class as a Noble."

Valjean looked at the portal, rather than at me to the side. Slowly, carefully, I crawled to the edge of the room.

"Being Chosen isn't that bad. I was Chosen, too."

Bad? Being Chosen? I didn't know what the hell he was talking about. How could being elevated into the highest class of society possibly be bad?

I tripped over one of the decaying wolf corpses, smearing my hands in the pooling blood.

Valjean crossed the room in an instant, hand outstretched to catch me. I kicked off the stone ground, blood slick and wet beneath my feet, and slammed into the wall, still covered in the cloak of shadow. Valjean's hand grabbed dead air.

When he turned, the expression on his face was furious.

"Stop this! You're not helping the people of this town. Why keep it alive? Just so they can live in squalor?"

Why was he trying to let it collapse? So that they could live in poverty in a city? I had to bite my tongue, keeping slow and low to the wall, navigating around the room.

"I'll sponsor you into the Academy. You can gain the skills you need. Conscription isn't so bad." Valjean's horse padded around the room. I crept along the wall.

The horse turned, its head swiveling on a gigantic neck until it hovered inches from me. It sniffed.

Valjean pulled the head away, circling the room,

"You can't just hide in here forever," he said.

He was right. I also couldn't leave without a spider corpse. I got no experience today. I had to get something. So I did another stupid thing. I jumped back into the second floor of the dungeon.

The quiet of the dead forest greeted me. Some small bugs chirped where they survived in the brush. I sat and waited for Valjean to detect me entering somehow, for him to rush back in. After a few minutes of nothing happening, I felt my muscles relax.

With the canopy of trees destroyed, the wind that would normally shake the branches instead whistled as it crossed over the gap. I walked back to the discarded spider corpse. Valjean would be on the first floor for a while; there was no way he would suspect that I would go deeper into the dungeon instead.

I judged the size of the spider's body. It was about the size of my torso; too large to fit in my bag. I put a foot on it, grabbed one of its limbs with both hands, and pulled.

The leg came off surprisingly easily, with a crunch and a pop. I staggered backward with surprise at just how easy it was. I repeated the process eight times, stuffing the legs into my backpack. It probably hadn't taken enough time for Valjean to have given up his search on the first floor.

I dug through the logs, pulling out globs of sticky web covered in leaves. I added them to my backpack, too, then slung it back over my shoulder and crept toward the portal. I stepped through slowly.

No magic tripwire went off. Valjean was gone. I crossed slowly to the exit, walking out into the town center.

One of the two unlanded Nobles pounded on the blacksmith's door. I heard distant shouting from another part of the town. They carried bright lamps that shone like spotlights, possibly some artifact of magical origin. The town center was alight as if it were daytime.

I felt the [Shadow Cloak] strain before I ducked away to a different street. Creeping through someone's backyard, I saw the way back to my workshop was blocked by another light plodding down the street. The Noble pounded on another door.

I crept to the town's edge, slinking around the backs of houses, pushing through bushes, and hiding in the shadows of fences. The workshop finally came into view.

Valjean and my mom were at the front door. My stomach dropped.

Had he seen me? Was his perception so high he recognized me despite the cloak and my face being blocked? They talked quietly but urgently. The Nobles were checking every house to see who was missing.

I quickly rushed around the town's edge again, dodging the burning lights to move toward Sandy's house. I pushed the door open without knocking; it creaked on its hinges.

Sandy looked up from another book, blinking rapidly.

"Gwen?" Sandy whispered.

I dismissed the [Shadow Cloak], coming into full view, still panting. She must have seen the panic in my eyes, because hers widened. Without replying, I stripped my backpack off, shoved it under the bed, and used my skills to rapidly change.

"What's happening?" Sandy asked, standing up now.

"Surprise census," I replied. "Valjean saw me."

"He—he saw you? Does he know?"

"I don't know—I had the cloak on. I don't think he saw my face. He was at the workshop—at Mom's."

"Shit," Sandy said. She was pacing now. "Town's going to be pissed tomorrow." She walked to the desk, grabbing her giant cleaver sword, before running back to her bed and throwing it under the mattress. "Town's going to be pissed tomorrow."

"So what now?" Sandy asked.

"I—I don't know!" I said. "He cleared the entire second floor with a single swing."

"Love to see him do it with a sewing needle," Sandy said.

"There's no way we can fight him."

"Then let's not get caught," Sandy said.

The shouting up the street grew closer, the Nobles dipping into each home and checking the rooms, comparing them with who they knew lived there. We were still panicking when they reached Sandy's house. I nearly jumped as the first knock fell on the front door. Sandy and I stared at each other.

"Dad still isn't home," she said finally.

The knocking came again. Wordlessly, we rushed out of the workshop and to the front door. That harsh light they held spilled in through the windows, bouncing off the walls, casting the room in a terrible glow.

The door swung inward with a rush of cold night air and we stared up at Valjean. The light in his hand made him almost a silhouette.

"Ah—girls. Is…Henri home?" he asked, then, under his breath, "Too tall to be him."

"No," Sandy said, slamming the door shut.

Valjean caught it with one hand. He wasn't carrying his halberd anymore, but he was still covered in his armor. Dust and dirt that he had flung up on the forest floor of the dungeon clung to parts of it. He smiled, eyes creased with stress.

Then he pushed the door open and stepped inside.

"I'm sorry to be impolite. We have a census of the town to take tonight, you see."

"Why?" Sandy asked. "Should wait 'til tomorrow."

"I received an unfortunate letter. I'll be leaving tomorrow to deal with a situation in Foundry." Even as he replied, his eyes scanned the hallway. Then they landed on me like a weight.

Why? I jumped through a mental checklist. I had changed out of the clothes I was hunting in. I put my backpack away. I wasn't holding a sewing needle. I followed his gaze down to my hands.

They were covered in wolf blood.

"Are you alright?" Valjean asked, looking up at me. There was no worry in his eyes. Just suspicion.

"We were…" Sandy started.

"Butchering," I said. "I was looking at the leather Sandy was working on, haha," I said nervously.

"Ah, right," Valjean said, swiveling to Sandy. "You're a butcher. And you… inherited your mother's class." He said the last part to me.

"Yep." I smiled.

Valjean smiled back, then stepped back into the night. The door shut.

Sandy and I sat in silence in the cold hallway as the light slowly grew distant. Valjean pounded on the next door.

"Shit," Sandy whispered.

"Safe for another day," I said. "He can't come back for another month, right?"

I left the hallway without looking back. I pushed back into Sandy's workshop and yanked the spider legs out from under the bed. Then I displayed them proudly to Sandy.

She flinched back.

"This is what you have to show for all this?" she asked, pulling one of the spider legs free but holding it at arm's length.

"Tried bringing a whole corpse. That's what started the mess. The [Shadow Cloak] gave out trying to hide the whole thing."

I dumped out the legs and the web, grabbing the globs of it myself while Sandy walked the leg over to the table.

"Alright. How do you want it?" she asked, lifting up the piece and holding it into the lamp light. Orange light glittered off the ivory and metallic red pattern on the leg.

I pulled from the memories impressed on me by the Shell Dress pattern for an answer.

"Can you cut some diamond shapes out of it?" I asked.

Sandy snorted before pulling up the leg and stabbing into it. As she worked, more shell than should've been possible was extracted, bending itself into diamond shapes. She worked carefully to make sure each diamond was composed of only one of the leg's two colors. A pile of fist-sized, diamond-shaped tiles littered her desk in moments.

"I may have mostly collected skills to cut through hard shells or help me kill monsters," Sandy said. She must have seen the look on my face.

"Now we need to get you one of those for leather."

I pulled on my own skills of [Thread Mastery] and [Hand Spinning], using one of my needles and magic in place of a spindle. The spiderweb spun round it. I pulled a fine piece of thread through.

Sandy worked on the next leg, then turned back and looked at me.

"Have you even finished my stealth set yet?" she asked.

I dropped the spiderweb and dug under the bed for the final pattern pieces of her set with a flushed smile.

CHAPTER 17

With eight mana left in the bank, I could finish Sandy's set in a single night. My increasing practice with Thread Mastery and using the magically enhanced stitching made it quick and easy, the articles coming together at magical speed.

[Tacca II]

▶100% complete

▶Quality +0

[Generating Skills…][10 Skill Shards]

▶Shadow Cloak I

▶Tracking Proficiency I

I finished the set before the night was out. Sandy wore it proudly.

"It has pockets," she said.

"Can't cheap out on the pockets," I replied, not looking away from the pile of spider scales that had built up on her desk.

Sandy gave the legs to Cinnamon, unwilling to waste any meat. Spider legs or chicken legs; it didn't make a difference to him. He chewed and crunched happily through the hard bits that remained.

I crashed for the night. In the morning, I ate breakfast with everyone who lived in the Tailor house. In loud conversations, the women of the house guessed at the reasons for Valjean's midnight census. They debated if someone had gone missing or been lost in the dungeon. I just quietly ate my breakfast, enjoying the opportunity to take my time eating.

The Noblemen had left in the morning.

"Weeding?" Terry asked, looking over the kitchen table at me. I was still shoving down second helpings, but I nodded yes anyway.

We worked in the neglected garden for probably an hour, tearing out green invaders. It was tedious labor that left me covered in dirt and with plenty of time to think.

The garden was a tiny raised bed in a square lot behind the house surrounded by overgrown berry bushes. Terry grew those for pigments in paints. Flowers and herbs competed for space in her limited poultices, though they took ages to grow.

"Why don't you grow these in the dungeon?" I asked, looking at the herbs.

"They match the energy of their environment," Terry said with a wave. "They come out of our dungeon dark black. Great for pigments. We have a few. Or they become clear. I made a poultice with those once." She sounded like she was going to continue, but trailed off and kept grabbing plants.

"What happened to it?" I asked.

"It made wounds disappear," Terry said, staring into space.

"Isn't that...good?"

"Oh. No. It didn't heal them. Just made them…" She gestured with her hands.

"Invisible?" I asked.

She nodded.

Terry was trapped at her level. To level up, she would need reagents she couldn't get her hands on. Alchemical reagents were expensive, often given by priority to the potionmasters trained by colleges or who ran conglomerates. To level up, she would need expensive reagents she couldn't get her hands on.

It sounded like our dungeon had a shadow element throughout all the floors. It filled me with grim anticipation for what we would find lurking at the deeper levels.

The shade provided by the house gradually slipped away as the sun rose in the sky, my hands raw and covered in dirt from pulling free every last weed we could find in the garden. When there was none left, I went to the workshop.

There I found a pile of barrels full of supplies. Mom was working on repairing her own sewing gloves.

"Did we get a new work order?" I asked, looking over the barrels.

"No!" Mom said, excited. "I—we—I figured you could work on your own patterns! Then we can send these out to be stock in a shop somewhere. Foundry."

"My own patterns," I repeated, looking at the barrels of leather, fabric, and thread. The raw resources made me reach out for my mental link to the Shell Dress pattern. Collated experiences of dozens of seamstresses and tailors constructing the pattern flowed through my mind like dreamy memories.

How many Hunter patterns was she expecting me to make? And how much of the leftover resources could I appropriate for myself? Every pattern required cloth and thread of some kind on top of the monster materials. Eventually, Mom would notice the goods missing from her workshop. I placed a hand on the rim of one of the barrels, staring down inside it.

"Yes! Aren't you excited to make your own? You got a pattern, right? Your first one!" she said, happily.

I smiled.

With no rush on the job, we had all day to work on the materials.

We worked on the set for a few hours. Mom gave me pointers on the various cuts and stitches. She rejoined the material smoothly so I wouldn't have to kludge the scraps back together.

She didn't make a single comment on me avoiding using my mana.

"Did Valjean find you last night?"

"What?" I blurted, stabbing myself in the finger. I shook my wrist to ward away the prick of pain.

Mom blinked.

"At Sandy's house? I told him that's where you went. He was interested in where you were last night," Mom said. Her tone was slightly more serious now.

"Oh! Oh. Yeah. He stopped by."

"Good," she said, continuing work on a set of her own.

She had brought out dusty mannequins that normally lay in the furniture pile. Years of wear and tear marked them. Some leaned at a bend. Some were missing heads or arms.

A few sported pieces of the multiple garments mom had made just today.

There was a knock on the door.

"Esmeralda," Henri said as Mom pushed the door aside.

"Henri."

He pushed out a wooden crate. Mom took it, popping it open.

"What is this? A peace offering?"

"No. I still think we should leave this damned town. Just…have more than I can sell this month. Thank your daughter for me," Henri said, sweeping his gaze to me.

"What?" Mom asked. "Oh. We must've taken up too much space on the wagon with our last work order," She tsked.

"Sure," Henri said. Then he reached inside and shut the door.

Mom set the crate down. It was full of cuts of meat, spiced and wrapped in paper.

"Good time for lunch?" she said.

Sandy twirled. The loose cloak spun out around her. It was only afternoon, and we were still in her workshop. I was scarfing down leftover sandwiches while we procrastinated heading to clear the dungeon.

Valjean left in the morning. The only thing between us and the dungeon was time, or being seen.

"How does it work?" Sandy asked, grabbing the bottom of her cloak and running her fingers over it. "Is there a button, or…"

"You should have the skill on your sheet. Just like your normal skills," I said.

Sandy nodded, her eyes glazing over as she opened her system interface.

Then she disappeared.

It was hard to look at the space she was standing in—like trying to focus on a blind spot. Rather than her being invisible, it was like everything around her collapsed inwards and my mind made out a blurred image. I reached out and felt my hand run into her. I watched my forearm disappear in midair, like it was being dissolved, panic filling me despite the logical understanding that this was how the skill worked.

There was a whooshing noise as Sandy's [Shadow Cloak] fell away, revealing her standing right in front of me, gripping my arm and staring down at me. "Are you ready?"

I double checked my backpack. Both sewing needles hung from it. I had also spun threads of spiderweb—one now slightly older than the other, thanks to being left in the dungeon. It had lost some of its luster that no amount of polishing could return to it.

"Race you there!" Sandy said. Then she disappeared.

"Wait! I won't even know…" The door swung open. "…When you're there."

[Shadow Cloak][Mana: 9/10]

I shut the door carefully behind me before walking toward the dungeon. I didn't bother running. The shadows strained in the afternoon light, but managed to remain in one piece if I stayed near the long shadow cast by the village's buildings.

It was still twilight inside the dungeon, the golden-orange light of the sun painting the empty farmland. My [Shadow Cloak] strained under the light.

I jogged up the path to the Dungeonheart just to find Sandy already there, smiling dumbly and swinging her legs from the rock she sat on. I was about to cancel my [Shadow Cloak] when I got a better idea. Instead, I climbed up the rocks behind her as quietly as I could, then dismissed it.

"About time you showed up." I said, swinging my legs to match hers. She scrambled forward, shocked.

"What?" she asked. "No way!" She frowned.

"Yeah, I've been here for a while now, just waiting for you to notice," I said, faking a yawn. "You know. Seamstress speed."

Sandy opened her mouth to speak. Then she laughed instead. I smiled and dropped down from the rock. She folded her arms.

"Maybe we can bring back a whole spider today," I said, looking to the cave. "We're going to have to conserve mana…I don't have enough to kill all ten of the wolves."

"I'm right here, you know," Sandy said, throwing an arm around me with a smile. "You don't gotta kill all ten. You take care of the spiders."

"You're right." I said. "Go kill all the wolves for me."

Sandy laughed, but she reached to her waist and pulled free the gigantic cleaver-sword Gerald had made for her. She was still wearing a butcher apron under the cloak.

"Is that a sheath?" I asked, looking down at the leather scabbard she decorated her waist with.

"Made it myself," she said by way of reply.

We stepped into the Dungeonheart.

The light leaking into the Dungeonheart made the wolf hunt easy. Sandy activated [Shadow Cloak] again, disappearing. The static wolf clawed at the wall, sniffing under the stone.

Then its head rolled across the ground. Watching gave me a headache. Its head had disappeared for a second as [Shadow Cloak]'s invisibility poured over the sword.

"Was that a skill?" I asked.

"Just a heavy swing," Sandy replied. When she spoke, the invisibility of the cloak faltered, splitting open to show her upper body floating in midair before collapsing around her again. The rules of the ability seemed poorly defined. A skill broke the ability, but regular attacks didn't.

Two more wolves died just as easily. I followed behind as we entered the final room. My eyes jumped back and forth, scanning. I didn't bother wasting my mana by activating [Shadow Cloak]. I already had to use it to get into the dungeon.

The last room of the dungeon was eerily quiet without Sandy's usual grunting or conversation and the last wolf prowling in stealth. I held my needle out in front of me.

There was a scrape of stone behind me. I whipped around to meet the wolf.

It hit the ground in two pieces behind me, Sandy's stealth disappearing as she swung with a grunt.

She smiled wickedly, panting as she stood over the corpse.

"If this is even a tenth of how good it feels to be a Noble, it's no wonder the bastards are so cocky," Sandy said. "What other skills can you make? I'll give you all the wolves you want if you can give me magic."

"Magic? Our classes are already magic," I said, leaning down over the wolf. The clean cut in the middle would add a ton of work to make the leather usable.

"Not crafting magic! Real magic. I want a fireball."

"A fireball?" I asked, turning and frowning at Sandy.

"Or lightning. Like in the stories. The Noble always has some crazy magic."

"Probably need something a lot bigger than a wolf to craft something like that," I replied.

Sandy paused, putting a hand on her chin. Then her eyes lit up.

"Floor three."

"What?" I asked.

"Floor three is going to have a boss! It's farther than I've managed to clear on my own. The boss will give us some kind of magic. Definitely. And then you can craft it for me," Sandy said.

"Alright," I agreed with a smile. That was always the plan, after all. But... "First, we need to clear floor two." I stared into the open archway that led deeper inside. The warped image of the forest showed on the other side.

Unlike the golden-orange sunset of this floor, it looked like it was dawn inside. The bottom of the forest was cloaked in black with crimson red painting the tops of the leaves.

"I'm ready," Sandy said, nodding at the gateway.

"After you," I replied.

She stepped through.

CHAPTER 18

The second floor opened up before us. Sandy paused feet away from the glowing archway, the light of dawn dancing through the trees. The wind carried the scent of the forest, pushing about loose strands of my hair to tickle my face.

Sandy breathed heavily, closing her eyes and drinking in air. Then she laughed.

"Are you alright?" I asked, glancing at her. I dipped my hands into my pockets and stared out at the forest sprawling out away from us. It was much less welcoming now that I knew what lurked in the shadows.

"It's just so much easier," she said. "So much easier when I'm not…alone."

Her eyes scanned the forest's shadows above.

"Yeah," I said, looking up. "I probably wouldn't be back here so soon without you."

"I don't see anything from the tracking skill yet," Sandy said, still scanning. One of her hands was on her oversized cleaver. "Whole floor is different."

"It's different? You're the one who told me it was bugs."

"The type of floor never changes. But the layout can. It was a big muddy cavern last time I made it to the second floor. Full of monsters covered in legs," Sandy said. She stepped forward into the path that wove between the dungeon's walls, leading the way into the dark.

I stayed closed behind her, watching the ground while she watched the trees.

"Found one," Sandy said, staring up at the trees.

The monster seemed to notice.

There was a rush as the spider descended with spiderweb behind it, dropping straight toward Sandy. She started to pull her cleaver free.

She wouldn't manage it fast enough.

[Running Stitch I] [Mana: 8/10] [Cancel]

[+4 XP]

My needle caught the spider in midair before it could land on Sandy. Green bug juice splattered on both of us.

"Nice save," Sandy said, resting a hand on my shoulder.

I was panting, the spider dangling off my needle.

Slowly, I lowered the needle, letting the spider's body fall off the edge. It crumpled to the ground. I sighed in relief.

Sandy held her blade out in front of herself, its menacing form gleaming in the dawn's light. We stepped deeper into the shadowy area of the forest.

"Another one," Sandy said after a few minutes. A hiss and a rush of air answered her as the spider descended, though she was ready this time. Her blade rang out as the metal hit chitin, the spider's hiss rising in volume. The two halves of its body rolled through the forest floor in separate directions.

The web behind one half pulled taught and it started to climb upward with only a few of its legs, the other half sloughing out monster flesh and seeping viscous green.

I stabbed it through the face.

[Running Stitch I] [Mana: 7/10] [Cancel]

[+4 XP]

The needle slammed into the tree behind the monster, embedded in the bark. I put a boot to the spider's shell and yanked to pull the needle free, splattering more spider blood onto myself.

My hands were covered in the gunk. I looked down at it, rubbing it between my fingers.

"What are you doing?" Sandy asked.

"Do you think this would make a good pigment?" I asked.

"The hell, Gwen?" Sandy said.

"For Terry to paint with. She's always looking for more pigments." I turned back to see her face screwed up. "What? It's just monster blood."

"Only you would be thinking about making paint out of monster corpses." She shook her head.

"What does that mean?" I asked. "I mean, we might as well not waste it, right?" Sandy laughed.

"Yeah. Why not. Sure. I'll bottle some blood when I cut it up."

The third spider was practically routine when we fought it. Sandy hit it like a batter, sending it flying. By the time we killed the fourth, she had figured out how to swing at the falling monsters, using their weight against them. It hit the ground in two pieces.

"How many on this floor you think?" I asked.

"More than four," Sandy replied.

We were nearing the end of the wooded trail that led to the last room of the dungeon. The sun was rising—or whatever magical source passed as the dungeon's sun was growing brighter, the red light giving way to bright white light, peeling back the shadows of the forest.

There were no landmarks.

The forest seemed to change each time I passed through it. Though that might have been because each journey through it seemed to destroy the entire tree line. First the fire, then Valjean single-handedly cutting down every tree inside.

There was a rush of air above me. I looked up in time to invoke my skill, the magic rectifying my aim and stabbing the needle forward with a crunch.

[Running Stitch I] [Mana: 5/10] [Cancel]

[XP +4] [Level up] [Excess discarded]

"Move!" Sandy shouted, her hand slamming into my back and sending me tumbling forward.

Sandy screamed. I looked back to see a sixth spider on her back. She had thrown herself between me and the monster.

Nausea rolled through my stomach. Legs shaking, I forced myself forward, activating my skill.

[Running Stitch I] [Mana: 4/10] [Cancel]

[XP +3]

Sandy staggered forward. The monster's corpse was still on her back. I reached out and grabbed it, wrapping my hands around the cool chitin of its legs and throwing it away.

"Sandy?" I asked. She staggered forward to the tree, laid a hand on it, and vomited.

"S'good," she said. "Fine. I'm fine."

She turned to face me. A black line streaked up from under her cloak and onto her face.

It pulsed.

She doubled over and wretched.

I threw my backpack to the ground with shaking hands and pulled free the potion. Sandy slunk to the ground. She closed her eyes, pushing a hand up through her hair.

"Hurts like a bitch," she said.

"Keep your eyes open," I said. "Stay awake. What's your health at?"

Sandy blinked as I held the potion up to her. Then she slapped a hand down on top of it.

"Not that bad," she said. "Just need a sec. Poison won't—"

She twitched as the black streak running up her face pulsed.

I pushed the potion up to her mouth. She shoved it back weakly.

"Got more than ten left. Hold on," Sandy said.

The black line streaking up her face pulsed one more time and then faded, leaving behind a patch of only slightly discolored skin.

Sandy groaned.

"Hurts like a bitch. Seventeen left," Sandy said.

"Seventeen?" I asked, still holding the potion but not forcing it on her.

"Health." Sandy barked a laugh, before pushing herself up to her feet. She winced at moving her back. "Not my first. Won't be my last. Not the worst I've had."

"What do you mean it's not the worst you had? You just got bit by a monster!" I was shouting now. "Sit down!"

Sandy rolled her eyes, but sat back down.

There was a rumble through the ground, a quiet pulse that I was familiar with now. We'd cleared the floor, and the next was opening.

"Poison hurts," Sandy said with a shrug. She winced at the movement.

I frowned and pushed myself all the way to my feet.

"Let me see."

I pulled free cloth strips for makeshift bandages and pain numbing poultices from Terry and sat down behind Sandy. The cloth strips had to be wrapped all the way around, tight to her back. The discoloration was worse at the location of the bite, still black but no longer pulsing.

"It's bad," I said, staring at the bandages.

"It's nothing a long rest won't fix," Sandy said.

She wasn't wrong. A long rest fixed damage to my lungs and restored my mana.

"Why?" I asked, thinking aloud.

"Because the potion's damn expensive. I don't want to waste it. What if there's an actual emergency, like—"

"No, I mean why does a long rest heal us like this? At first I just thought, you know, it's magic. Like the rest of this world. Didn't question it."

"Magic? It's just the way things work." Sandy turned around and frowned.

"Yeah. I mean, it's almost like how the dungeons reset themselves overnight," I said, looking up at the trees. The forest looked like old growth, like it had existed for years and decades, not been regrown only a night ago.

"It's how things are," Sandy said, shrugging. She didn't wince as badly this time.

"Feel better?" I asked.

"Yeah," she said before standing. "Which ones do we want?"

I looked out over the spiders. Almost every one had a different color, shining shells with metallic reds and blues and purples striped with ivory white.

"The red ones, I think," I said, packing my backpack.

We ended up managing to drag four out. I filled my backpack with handfuls of knotted web. The sun had fallen outside the dungeon by the time we left, and we carried the bodies in the dark.

I kept taking sneaking looks over at Sandy. Besides grunting a little more than normal, she seemed fine.

She even started working when we got into the workshop.

"You can't wait a day to butcher those?" I asked.

Sandy had a spider on the table, lining up its legs with a gloved hand while another brought her butcher sword down to chop them off.

"Time's wasting. What do you think happens when Valjean comes back?"

"We have a month," I replied, looking around the room before taking a seat on Sandy's bed.

She turned to look at me.

"We only have a month. He's not going to come back empty-handed. He'll be bringing an investigator, or…" Sandy trailed off, turning back around and flipping the spider over. She grunted as she cut off another set of legs and pushed them into a bucket. "A priest or a tracker," she finished.

"Couldn't we just leave it for a few days at that point?" I asked. "With a month of progress?"

"The farther the dungeon is cleared, the faster it'll decline," Sandy said with a turn. "We have to kill the boss of the third floor before Valjean returns. If we can do that, we can open the next dungeon entrance."

"Another dungeon entrance?" I asked.

Sandy grunted in reply, setting her gigantic butcher knife aside in favor of a different one. She split the shell of the spider, pulling it to pieces and throwing the chitin chunks onto the floor. The smoothed surfaces rolled around, glittering in the lamp light.

"Four more dungeon entrances. The secondary dungeons are supposed to open at the edge of the town's walls…wherever those would be if they were still standing. Were you serious about the bug blood?" she asked suddenly, turning around.

"I… Four? Then…we have thirty days to kill the first boss," I said. "Bug blood. Sure. Why not."

She pulled another bucket free from under the desk, placing it on the floor beneath a hook behind her. Then she stabbed into the spider and sliced it in half with a terrible tearing noise. Blood dripped onto the table.

She slammed the spider onto the hook and turned to the next corpse.

"How fast do you think you can finish our next set of armor?"

I mentally pulled at the Shell Dress pattern and the pieces I would need to assemble.

"We'll need leather. We can use the wolves for that, but we'll need fabric too. I'm not sure how much I can steal before Mom notices. But maybe I'll get a skill that can help."

"Forgot how nice it is to level up constantly," Sandy said, grumbling.

I pulled open the skill shop.

[Skill Shop]

▶Mending I

[COMMON] Allows user to repair clothing from patterns they are unfamiliar with. Additional levels increase quality of final product.

▶Pattern Projection I

[COMMON] Seamstress Vision skill. Grants user access to a pattern overlay on fabric.

▶Embellishment I

[COMMON] Allows user to generate embellishments that raise clothing's quality level and change its properties. Additional levels increase the available embellishments and their properties. Grants Thread Mastery I.

CHAPTER 19

I wasn't going to give up another chance at Thread Mastery this early, especially not after sacrificing the last one. I grabbed Embellishment.

[Gwendolyn Tailor][Human, Lv8][Seamstress]
[Health: 10/10][Mana: 4/10][XP: 3/10]
[ATTRIBUTES]
▶SPD: 10
▶WIL: 5
▶STR: 5
▶DEX: 22
▶CON: 5
▶PER: 16
[SKILLS]
▶Crafting I
▶Running Stitch I
▶Hand Spinning I
▶Thread Mastery II
▶Wardrobe II
▶Quick Change I
▶Embellishment I
[PATTERNS]
▶Hunter Pattern
▶Shell Dress Pattern
[RESISTANCES]
▶Shadow: 5
[TEMPORARY SKILLS]
▶Bow Proficiency I
▶Shadow Cloak I

A pile of shining spider parts in a mix of shining, metallic colors sat in the corner of Sandy's workshop. Even the white pieces showed a slight iridescence when bent in the light.

Before I could assemble the scales, I had to create the bodice of the dress. I cut the pattern from wolf leather, stitching scraps back together to fit the design. I decided it wasn't worth the effort to remove the fur after a few minutes of effort.

Instead I just sewed the cloth layer over the fur, creating a layer of insulation. The pattern memories overlaying my own made it feel like something I had done a hundred times.

"I don't know if this will work," I said, holding a scale up.

"Wrong size?" Sandy asked, looking up from her book on her bed.

"Yeah. A little smaller, I think. Like this shape," I said, illustrating by drawing my finger along the section of scale to cut out.

Sandy cut apart the scales into smaller pieces like it was nothing. Amazingly, each diamond scale cut apart into three complete scales, warping to perfectly fit.

Then I tried to stab my needle into one. With my heightened dexterity, it was easy to avoid the needle bending back and stabbing myself as it scraped the side of the scale.

My strength, on the other hand, wasn't enough to cut through it.

I frowned, realizing for the first time that I needed stronger needles.

I could use [Running Stitch], but it would be a waste to use it one scale at a time. I created a pile of them next to me, activating the skill and feeding the scales to it. Both of my arms operated at superhuman speeds as I stitched the scales in, completing the first row around the shirt easily.

I stopped when I noticed something amiss: the farthest left scale was loose. The thread stabbed through the chitin was fraying.

[Running Stitch I] [Mana: 3/10]

"The thread isn't durable enough," I said, inspecting the scale. Stitching the rest tore the thread apart as it moved through the chitin. I pulled it apart scale by scale, plucking them free and setting them on the table.

Then I reached under the table and grabbed the spiderweb cloth I had spent my spare time and mana spinning.

I stitched the already-pierced pieces in by hand, conserving mana as I reattached them to the dress's bodice, then used the rest of my mana to complete most of the work on the bodice.

There were still scales left over, but the night was growing late. I took a step back to admire my work.

The dress was mostly colored scales, iridescent reds and purples fighting for the dominant color of the dress.

Sandy yawned.

I yawned in turn.

Then I headed home, leaving the dress standing on her desk. Tomorrow we had to clear the dungeon again, hopefully without getting bitten. Maybe on my own if Sandy wasn't fully recovered.

I fell asleep easily and woke softly to the midday light, ambient noise filling the house.

No one was home when I went downstairs, breakfast going cold on the counter. The table was missing. I ate my fill and then followed the source of the noise to the workshop.

There, all the house's tables were grouped into one large table in the center. Half of the village's adults must have been gathered. Goosebumps ran up my neck for a moment as I stared through the open door to the workshop. No one looked my way.

Then I remembered what day today was; Mom hosted a tea tasting.

I stepped into the workshop. The scent of baked goods overwhelmed the normal scents of the dusty workshop, pitchers and teacups warring for space on leaning tables and creaking furniture.

"Gwen!" Mom yelled for me from across the room.

I waved halfheartedly, but she waved me over.

"Come here!" she said.

Mom pushed a cup of tea and a kettle into my hand. Behind her, Gerald's mom fussed over a magical hot plate, boiling another kettle.

"How are you doing? Did you sleep well?" she asked.

I sniffed the tea. It smelled spicy; I took a drink.

"Well enough," I said. "Is this cinnamon?"

"It is! We got some new to try with the last shipment." Mom smiled, fussing over my hair. I still had bedhead, my hair untied and fraying in every direction.

"Go say hi to everyone!"

The next hour was a blur. I must have said hi to every villager twice, pouring out more tea, hosting the party. I was still half in pajamas. At some point I lost my cinnamon tea, switching to a floral one I didn't care for at all, which made the kettle last longer.

I finally found my own spot to take up residence, sitting down across from Gerald. He looked at me with a nervous smile.

"Hey—"

"Hey!" he said. We both talked at once. He was full of energy and I was out of it. "How's it—" He paused. "How is it going? How are you doing?" He smiled.

I took his tea. It was cold. I swapped it for an empty cup and refilled it.

"Thanks," he said, drinking. "God, that's so much better."

"It's going well," I said, eyes jumping over to the cabinet where parts of my wolf outfit were stored. It stood out more with so much of the furniture removed from the walls. I tried not to let my eyes linger on it, focusing instead on the pile of goods mom had acquired to help me facilitate my crafting. I felt a pang of guilt for not being awake to help, but I had stayed up too late.

Everything was going well. Too well, even.

"You?" I asked.

"So good! We can almost keep up with all the work orders. You should see all the crazy things we craft. Armor and weapons are just the beginning. The really weird stuff comes from Valjean—machinery. Big gears, steam engines—they use regular fire and water to make things move!" Gerald went off, gesturing wildly with his hands. "I…love being a blacksmith." He said the last bit sadly, retreating back into himself a little.

"I'm glad," I said with a smile. "I love being a seamstress."

He drank from his tea again.

The rest of the day was mundane. I helped mom clean up, gorging myself on the leftover baked goods while they were still fresh. I felt full from all the bread before the day was over. Neither Henri nor Sandy showed up.

When evening came, I walked to Sandy's house.

She was out back playing fetch with Cinnamon and a spider leg.

"Good boy. Who's a good boy?" Sandy said, patting him on the head while his tail wagged. The spider's leg ended in a jagged, pointed tip.

"Are you crazy?" I asked, leaning my arms over her fence to stare inside. "What if someone sees that?"

"I'll just say it's something Dad had imported in." Sandy shrugged. "We get weirder shit all the time."

Sandy whipped her arm out, the spider leg flying until it slammed into the side of the house. Cinnamon tore up mud and barked as he chased it before grabbing the leg and thrashing with it. He growled as he chewed on the leg, huge teeth visible as he slammed it into the ground over and over.

Then he turned about, plodding daintily toward Sandy and spitting the leg out at her feet. His tail wagged.

Sandy turned to me. Cinnamon picked up the leg and walked behind her as they joined me at the fence.

"Dad said he liked your scale dress," Sandy said.

"Where were you guys? You normally come to the tea tasting," I replied.

"I stayed home to avoid Dad so it wouldn't be awkward."

"And let me guess, Henri stayed home to avoid you."

"Yeah! And then he walked into my workshop anyway!"

"Tell him I said thanks. Was he bringing you food?" I asked.

Cinnamon dropped the spider leg in front of me and barked. I picked it up and threw it. It didn't go nearly as far as Sandy's toss.

"That's not the point! He could at least knock or leave it in the kitchen!" Sandy said.

"I haven't eaten anything but pastries all day," I replied, looking toward her workshop.

"There's leftovers inside," she said.

"You should ask him to make us something to raise our will," I said, walking toward the door.

Sandy threw herself over the fence, following behind.

"Yeah right. Like he'd do that. Just food to raise constitution 'cause he thinks I'll die."

"You literally got bitten by a giant spider last night," I replied, pulling the door open.

There was a woofing noise as Cinnamon jumped over the fence. He sprinted toward me and dropped the spider leg. I flinched, stepping back.

"Cinnamon! Bad dog!" Sandy said. Some of the mud had gotten on her clothes—more than usual. She groaned.

I scratched the dog behind the ears and stepped inside. He barked again. Sandy dragged him back to the fenced-in section of the backyard, pushed the dog inside, then found a way to sneak back. We pushed aside Sandy's makeshift barricade and stepped into the kitchen.

The worktable was covered in food.

"I need to start stashing my stuff here," I said, dropping my backpack.

"Good idea," Sandy replied. She stepped past me to cut apart more spider shell.

I worked on hand spinning more thread from spiderweb using a borrowed spindle, conserving my mana for dungeoning as we waited for night to fall. This time, we conserved every last bit of mana, not activating stealth until we were deeper in.

"If your dad can't make us food to enhance our will…" I said, holding out hope that he would make us food. Sandy stared at me incredulously. "We need to save even more mana. Like use none at all on the first and most of the second floor."

"Our stats should be enough to fight with," Sandy said.

"Tonight we try to clear the dungeon without skills," I decided.

CHAPTER 20

Sandy grunted as she swung her blade. The wolf landed in two pieces.

"Easy," Sandy said, letting the blade drop. The metal clinked against the stone floor.

"Easy for you," I said, lifting my sewing needle and creeping around the Dungeonheart. Sandy would have no problem killing the monsters without skills. "Not fair. You have a sword."

"You've got...needles," Sandy said.

"I need a proper weapon. A giant pair of scissors or something," I said as we rounded on the next wolf. It was my turn.

I swallowed hard as I approached. Killing a wolf shouldn't be a problem. I had superhuman dexterity. Dozens of them died at the end of my needle. It would be easy.

The wolf scratched against the wall, sniffing the dirt as if it were actually alive. But every time the dungeon reset, this same wolf would be here, scratching away at the stone.

When I stepped to within arm's length, it stopped, looking up at me. I forced myself through the motion; the superhuman dexterity assisted me as I stabbed forward, as if I was under the mechanical control of Running Stitch even though I hadn't activated a skill.

Flesh parted under the force of my needle until I hit something solid. The needle was rough against my hand as I scraped along the wolf's skull, blood pouring out of the open wound as it howled and jumped backward.

I staggered forward. I hadn't taken the time to aim. Without the mechanical strength of the magical sewing skill, my strength wasn't enough to punch directly through bone.

Moving with the fall, I stabbed forward, aiming for the creature's eye this time. The needle stuck hard into the wolf's head as it went limp, falling to the floor.

"Easy," I said, grabbing the needle with both hands to try to free it. I failed. It was stuck in the bone, blood seeping around the edge of the needle.

Doing the work without the use of magic was messier. More brutal. Running Stitch made killing monsters so clean and efficient.

I pressed a boot to the wolf's head, pushing it into the floor until I could feel it deform against me, and pulled. The needle came free with enough force that I staggered backward.

"Let's go," Sandy said, patting my shoulder and stepping in front of me. She dispatched the next two wolves with ease. Even the wolf that hid in the shadow was an easy kill for her. She approached it so casually that I didn't realize it was happening; I wasn't holding a knife to see its outline in the dark.

Sandy just walked forward in the room and then swung, seemingly without reason. The blood was visible first, a line gushing up into the air where she cut it. Then the wolf became visible as it died, its [Shadow Cloak] dissipating.

"Good to let loose now?" Sandy asked as she rolled her shoulders, stretching out.

"No," I replied, stepping up and looking over the wolf.

"We killed them all," she said.

"We should conserve all the mana we can," I replied.

Sandy shrugged and stepped through the portal.

Midday light greeted us, filtering through the canopy of leaves above. Sandy tested the weight of her blade in her hand. We dove into the shadows of the trees without another word between us.

The first spider came after only a few minutes. We were ready this time, jumping back as soon as it began its dive, Sandy already mid-swing.

The chop sent legs flying, the spider's body tumbling end over end with a hissing noise. Then it retracted its web, shooting back up the tree. I ran forward to stab it, but it was already gone, back up into the dark.

"Shit," Sandy said.

The spider dove again.

[Running Stitch I] [Mana: 9/10] [Cancel]

[+3 XP]

This time it was instantly impaled on my needle, splitting chitin and spilling hot spider blood onto my hands.

"Gross," I said, kicking the spider off the needle. The cleaner cut provided by the magic made it easy.

"I thought we were practicing?" Sandy said.

"There's a place for practice," I replied, looking up at the canopy, then back down at the corpse.

The spider was covered in segmented plates of chitin. There were sections where the plates disconnected, soft sinew binding the body parts together where the armor parted.

I pushed my needle into one, releasing gore down the side of the spider's leg.

"Going to be less to use if you keep that up."

I waved Sandy away, experimenting with my dexterity. With a flick, I aimed at a joint along the spider's body and stabbed, instantly cutting into the spider corpse, and started to smile.

"Gwen? You're weirding me out."

"I can kill the spiders," I said.

"Uh yes, you can," Sandy replied.

"No I mean—without skills. Next one, you cut the string! I got this. You can kill the wolves and I can kill the spiders."

"Oh," Sandy said, still staring down at my hands. I ripped the needle out of the spider.

We continued through the forest, ready and waiting for the next ambush. When it came, Sandy jumped out of the way, the spider landing on the ground. She swung to cut the rope.

The web bent and grew taught, but didn't split.

"Gwen!" Sandy said, voice rising in pitch.

I stabbed down between the spider's plates, goring it. It hissed, spinning toward me, the needle ripping free with the motion. Sandy brought down her blade in a chop that cut through the first layer of the monster's exoskeleton before bouncing against the second.

The monster staggered toward me. I deftly stabbed into its face, finally killing it.

[+3 XP]

"Four more."

"Easy," Sandy said.

"Not good enough. I need to kill them in one hit," I said, looking down at the mutilated spider corpse. We were wasting good resources.

We got better with each kill. I practiced stabbing down into the segmented bodies of the spiders, succeeding in quick kills on two of them. Their eyes weren't empty sockets that allowed easy access to the brain; there was no fast and easy kill.

Sandy proved unable to cut the web threads that the spiders propelled on. We worked on combining our attacks to kill them quickly, accruing a total of eighteen experience points. The last two spiders dove together again. The second floor's pseudo boss was the monsters' teamwork, rather than another ability.

We were ready this time. Sandy used a skill to cut one of the spiders into pieces that silently rolled across the forest floor, while I used the momentum of the other ambusher to stab deep into it, tearing apart its flesh.

I left the dungeon with nine mana; more than I ever had before. We even managed to carry out more of the spider bodies, jumping right to work in Sandy's workshop.

"We need to get another table in here," I said I as leaned over Sandy's workbench, using [Running Stitch] to feed scales onto the leather bodice of the Scale Dress pattern.

"You really think we can fit more furniture in here?" Sandy asked.

I often had to turn my shoulders sideways to step between the hanging corpses, and now the buckets that collected pigmented spider blood as well. I still hadn't asked if Terry wanted it—but it was messy to let it pool on the floor.

"No," I said, holding up one of the glass bottles of green spider blood. It was viscous, sticking to the walls of the glass bottle as I shifted it back and forth. I sighed and set it down, turning back to my dress.

One of the scales had cracked.

I squinted, leaning forward to examine it. The crack had spread from where I had pierced it. Though the cut was clean, the dress was already wearing down.

[Cleome I]

▶[5% complete]

[PROJECTED SKILLS]

▶Blue Skill II

I turned the scales over in my hand, looking for some better way to stitch them together. I couldn't find one. In my system-imprinted memories, the seamstresses and tailors who worked on these pieces were able to stitch them on without them falling apart. I sighed and resolved to ask my mom tomorrow. I applied my mana to beginning the workings of the set's boots. The pattern called for leather boots covered in sweeping plates of chitin. I made the boots out of the ivory-white spider scales. The boots had to be constructed of several different plates; they rose so high they went above my knee, which meant they needed to bend.

I packed a bottle of spider blood into my backpack and headed home, my mana exhausted for the night. Shoving my backpack into a disused cabinet, I headed to bed.

Breakfast was calm. No one was even talking about Valjean anymore, the event little more than another passing oddity to occupy the townsfolk's time.

I rushed into the workshop and pulled the spider blood from the cabinet and brought it to Terry, who was already setting up in her workshop. In a pestle, she was making a poultice from leaves. She smiled at me as I stepped into her workroom, holding the glass bottle behind my back.

"Whatcha making?" I asked, leaning near her.

"Something for pains," she said before transferring the leaves into an open ceramic jar and shoving it to the shelves that surrounded the room. I had no idea how she remembered what was what; probably a system-generated skill. There were hundreds of bottles of different shapes and sizes along every wall except the one that hosted canvases for painting.

"Brought you a present," I said, still holding the bottle behind my back.

"Plants?" she guessed, leaning her head to the side as if she could see behind me.

"Nope. Try again," I said, stepping slightly to the right to better conceal the bottle.

"A painting."

"It would have to be a small one for me to carry it here," I said.

"Good point." She hummed as she slid the mortar to the side. "Food," she guessed again.

"Nope," I said, putting the bottle down between us. Even with the yellow and brown staining of the glass, the green inside was such a vibrant, lively color.

Teretha lifted it without comment, holding it up into the beam of sunlight that crossed through the window and lit up the bottle.

"Pigment," she said, staring at it in the light. "Where did this come from?"

CHAPTER 21

It's spider blood! Sandy got it," I said, not missing a beat. It wasn't the least bit unbelievable that Sandy could collect some. She had weirder corpses shipped out here. "You mentioned you…"

"Spider blood," Terry said, swirling the bottle. "I have used something like it before."

She fumbled over her table, pulling out a brush and trying to apply it directly. It was basically a thick paste, smearing the page rather than spreading.

"I could dry it out and extract the pigment…" she said, trailing off and flipping through her paperwork.

"You'll have to show me what you make with it," I said.

I went to the workshop to continue the crawling work I'd been doing on a generic Hunter pattern. Mom crafted a pattern across from me, a thick padded outfit that I couldn't discern the purpose of.

I kept trying to think of ways to fix the breaking chitin of the shell dress I was making. My distracted thoughts left me making errors in the Hunter pattern as I mentally pulled at the Shell Dress pattern.

The patterns were embedded as memories from their original creators as well as the tailors and seamstresses who had worked on the pattern over the years before I acquired it. But it didn't just come with the memories of how to craft it.

Each memory was touched with the emotions and thoughts of each crafter who'd touched the pattern, imbuing it with a feeling. Switching my mental focus between the layers of memories of the two sets was jarring.

The hunter set struck me with memories of tailors in border towns and dirty shops, images of evening light burning through warped glass onto discolored floors and pressed dirt. The memories seemed to stretch back and back, an entire history book recorded over stitching sessions.

I couldn't tell which memory was the first, but I could feel the change in them as they grew older. From the very beginning, the set was layered with a primal feeling of hunger, a deeper one than I had ever felt, and the longer I worked on the set the more the feeling gnawed on me, leaving an impression on my own mind.

After long enough, it threatened to overwhelm me.

On the other hand, the Shell Dress pattern's memories were completely different. The Hunter pattern felt like something crafted out of necessity, but I could feel the disdain burned into the memories of the first shell dress's crafting, the thoughts and emotions so clear they cut into me.

It had been designed for a Noble, but partially as a vanity project. The few flickering memories of workshops had floors of patterned tiles, towering windows of glass overlooking cities, and seamstresses with dozens of assistants. There were fewer memories of its crafting, which might have been why it was so much harder.

I slumped forward in my chair.

"Something wrong, my light?"

"This pattern kinda sucks," I said.

Mom laughed.

"Some are more… mentally draining than others," she said. "Normally it's not so noticeable until you have a few separate patterns. That's why I don't just spend all day working. More than a few hours can start to grind."

I flicked through the memories of the Shell Dress pattern, still looking for an answer.

"How would you sew chitin together?" I asked.

Mom stared for a second before speaking.

"Chitin is often meant as an armor. It doesn't take well if you approach it directly."

"So?" I asked, fiddling with the leather cut in front of me. I had done a sloppy job stitching it together, frayed seems hanging loose from cut edges.

"You have to stab into it at an angle. Like…think of a bunch of plates on top of each other. Go in directly, it'll crack. And be much harder to pierce, anyway. You have to go between the plates," Mom said, looking away.

I wondered how many patterns she had; how many memories boiled to the surface of her thoughts, imprinted through the system and thousands of lives? Her eyes were distant. She shook her thoughts away and smiled at me. "Why do you ask?"

"Just wondering," I said.

"Working on something with Sandy?" She was still smiling. I considered her.

"Yeah. She got, uh, a shipment in."

"If Henri got seafood in, I'm going to have to go raid his pantry," Mom said.

We wrapped up for the day and cleaned up the workshop, then I headed to the door to repeat my daily routine of working on the shell dress. The memories the two patterns brought to the surface made a strong dichotomy; I felt like I could work on the shell dress forever.

It spun with memories of elaborate workshops and wealth and power. It sung with the future I desired, the one I was reaching for.

I opened the door to find Gerald on the other side. My eyebrows shot up. He was standing there, arm extended like he was going to knock, breathing quickly, hair hanging low over his face.

"Gwen!" he said too quickly, like it had been rehearsed. "I was wondering if you wanted to hang out."

"Sure," I said, stepping past him. "I'm just headed to Sandy's."

"Good…we should get her, too!"

"You make something cool?" I asked, looking over at him.

"Yeah." Gerald was staring forward toward Sandy's house.

We found her and Cinnamon outside before heading to Gerald's house. It was one of the few times I had arrived to find Bob not working the forge.

"Hey!" I said, waving at Bob as we walked through the living room. "Not smithing today?"

"No metal left." Bob smiled. Then he saw Sandy behind me. His smile faded to a frown. "Sandy."

"What?" Sandy asked, stepping into the kitchen and looking around.

Bob was always working, so I understood her confusion. She was looking for something gone wrong. Bob's expression continued to grow harsher. I didn't know why.

"Gave it all to Gerald to practice with. How many patterns you at now, Gerald?"

"Twenty," he said. He didn't sound confident. "At least. Twenty." Gerald was smiling. But his eyes were afraid.

I squinted. Didn't he say he didn't need patterns? That his class worked differently?

Gerald was frozen in the kitchen, staring at his dad, who was staring daggers at Sandy. It was getting awkward. I grabbed Gerald's arm.

We rushed through the living room and upstairs into Gerald's room. They had the privilege of a house unshared; only Gerald's family lived here, but he found a way to make his oversized room feel cramped anyway.

"What is this?" I asked, looking around the room confused.

Weapons hung from every wall. It looked like a medieval torture room. There were weapons of every shape and size, piles of weapons along the floor, half-recycled armor joining it.

"A mess is what it is," Sandy said, pushing past me into the room. She reached down and grabbed the handle of a sword in a pile of blades.

"Don't—" Gerald tried to stop her before she yanked the sword, sending a pile of blades tumbling. Sandy danced backward, dragging the massive blade with her. It gouged the floor. The falling pile of blades left scars. Gerald winced.

"At least your father can afford a carpenter." I patted his shoulder.

"Have you just been making weapons nonstop? This must have taken weeks." Sandy grunted, struggling with all her might to raise the sword she grabbed. "Not that much of this is any use to us."

"Forging is good," Gerald said, reaching out and grabbing the blade from her with one hand. He casually flipped the blade, sliding it into a weapons rack.

"I don't get a bonus for lifting outfits I make," I said, staring at Gerald.

"One of my bonus attributes is strength," Gerald said, the response so automatic it was like it was canned.

"So is Sandy's."

Gerald bit his lip. Then he leaned back against the wall. He stared at the door behind me.

I closed it.

Then I walked up to him, staring at him against the wall.

"What's going on?" I asked, folding my arms and doing my best to look intimidating. I wasn't sure if it was working; even Gerald was a bit taller than me.

"My dad thinks Sandy is clearing the dungeon."

I frowned. Then I stepped back.

"But she is clearing the dungeon."

"Yes. You guys are clearing the dungeon," Gerald said. He didn't meet my eyes.

"Who the hell is this for?" Sandy asked. She was still investigating the dozens of weapons on the wall, and right then she stood in front of a wicked-looking curved dagger with a blade that glinted in the light breaking through Gerald's curtain.

"That one's poisoned!" Gerald said suddenly. "Don't touch it…"

"What the hell do you mean it's poisoned?" Sandy stepped back. "Why would you poison it then put it on your wall?"

"It was an accident. It just came out poisoned," Gerald said.

Sandy stepped left. She reached out to a different weapon—a long, needle-thin rapier. The sword started to glow when she reached for it, and she flinched back.

"What the fuck, Gerald?" She spun on him. "They're enchanted? Did you get your mom's class?" Sandy asked.

"No," Gerald said. He looked like he wanted to say something else, but he didn't.

"But the weapons *are* enchanted," Sandy said, stepping around the room. "Is that why my cleaver is so nice? It's fucking enchanted? You gave me an enchanted weapon? I thought…"

Sandy paced.

I followed her with my eyes, looking at the wall. Gerald stepped past me, reached under his bed, and pulled out another wooden box like the one he had given me when this all started.

"I'm sorry. I meant to tell you guys. It's just…I don't know how you do it. Going off to kill monsters every night. I just want to be a smith," Gerald said, turning around and presenting the box to me.

It popped open, full of needles the size of knives instead of swords.

"I was looking for a good enchantment. One that could work well for these," Gerald said. "After you told me about the one you got stuck in a tree, I figured—"

"What were you going to tell us, Gerald?" Sandy asked, turning around.

"He's Chosen. He's a Noble," I answered for him, staring at his face instead of the needles.

Gerald looked away.

CHAPTER 22

He's a Noble." Sandy said, turning around and staring at him. "No. You were supposed to be the Noble," she said.

"I know," I replied.

Gerald still hadn't confirmed or denied it. He bit his lip.

I was supposed to be a Noble. I didn't know how to feel about it. I was supposed to be a Noble and Gerald was instead, and instead of helping us clear the dungeon he was here forging weapons for hours a day to distract himself from it. He's just a kid and was handed a divine weapon to fight monsters so that we could have a bit more farmland.

I took the box from him.

"Thanks," I said.

"Do your parents know?" Sandy asked.

"No," Gerald said.

"How can they not know? I mean, this…" Sandy said, gesturing at the room.

"They stay out of here," Gerald said.

"That's why you have all the weapons in your room and not the workshop. And why you haven't melted them back down into metal," I said.

Gerald nodded. "The metal's still enchanted after it's broken down."

"Okay, hold on," Sandy said. "If he's a Noble, why isn't—why haven't you been helping us, Gerald?"

"I have been! I made you the swords. What else do you want me to do for you? Die for you?" Gerald snapped suddenly, rounding on Sandy. "Sorry," he said, stepping back.

He was just a kid.

"Thanks," I said, staring at him.

"No, that's bullshit. No *thanks, all good, have a nice day.*"

"He wouldn't have been able to help anyway," I said, stepping between Sandy and Gerald.

"What?" They both spoke at once, each of them offended for a different reason; Gerald, because I was implying he couldn't fight; Sandy, because I was implying he didn't have to.

"Valjean talked to me while in the dungeon."

"Thought he was trying to catch you?" Sandy asked.

"Yeah, well. He was monologuing." I folded my hands. "He thinks it's a Noble who's clearing the dungeon. He wants to send whoever it is to the Academy. So if Gerald was helping and revealed himself, he'd just be sent away anyway."

"Who said anything about revealing himself?" Sandy said. Her voice was still raised.

"Be real, Sandy. Do you think all three of us can run around at night even with stealth? Your dad has caught on. His dad has caught on. How much of the village do you think doesn't know at this point? Valjean practically announced it!"

Sandy started to speak and bit back whatever it was.

The door to Gerald's room swung open. I slammed the lid of the box full of needles shut in a panic, the sound loud in the immediate silence that followed as we exchanged stares with Gerald's mom.

"Girls!" Mari said. She sounded stressed.

We kept staring.

"I figured I'd offer tea?" She said, holding out a pitcher and stack of cups. She stared back at us.

"Thanks," Gerald said, reaching out and grabbing what she offered. Sandy and I continued staring. Gerald slowly closed the door with a foot.

Mari stared toward the box I held as the door shut on her.

"Shit," Sandy said. She folded her arms, stepping back and visibly calming.

"See?" I asked.

"Fuck," Sandy said. "But if so much of the town probably knows, then why…"

"Because they want to live here, too," Gerald said. He set the pitcher down and sat on his bed, holding his head in his hands. "So what's the plan now?" he asked after a moment.

"Valjean will be back." I said.

"We have to clear the third floor before he returns. To open the second set of dungeon entrances. Because he won't be able to guard them all," Sandy said.

"And then what?" Gerald asked. "The town will still be shrinking. If not in size, then in population. We need more."

With another look back at the door, I popped open the box Gerald handed me.

"What do these do?" I asked.

Gerald plucked one from the box and threw it.

It sunk into a wooden mannequin leaning against the wall. His aim was dead accurate, pinning the needle directly into its head. The sudden violence made me stare closer at the mannequin; it was missing an arm and riddled with scars; cuts and burns decorating it.

Gerald gestured and the needle returned to him.

"They return," he said, putting the needle into my hand and taking the box from me.

I stared at it, then at him.

"I don't have a needle-throwing skill," I said.

"They're throwing weapons," Gerald said. "They work on dex. You don't need a skill."

I frowned, but I pulled on the two pieces of the Hunter set I had in my Wardrobe inventory, immediately feeling more able as the cloak flowed into existence around me.

The needle landed in the wall with a thunk.

"Maybe if I had the full set," I said with a frown before copying Gerald's gesture. It floated through the air back toward me, landing in an outstretched hand.

I stared down at Gerald. He could enchant things—like his mother could. His mom would engrave complex sigils and filigree into metal, imbuing it with magical properties. But there were no engravings on Gerald's weapons.

"Could we sell these?" I asked. "I mean, could you sell these? And I could sell clothes made from monsters."

"And out ourselves?" Gerald asked.

"No. We'd need a way to…to smuggle them. And then we can help the town grow in other ways. Invest in it. Bring more people here," I said, plopping down on the bed.

"Start a smuggling ring? Gwen, that's worse than breaking into the dungeon!"

"We'll figure it out," I said.

"So where's my magic weapon?" Sandy asked, arms still folded as she scanned the walls.

"I uh…didn't come up with anything," Gerald said.

"You don't have patterns, do you?" I asked.

"No. My class is divine armorer. When I craft, I do it with Inspirations—it takes mana. And I can't decide what it makes. It's what leaves the metal enchanted…" he said, staring off to a metal ingot on the floor, separated from the pile of goods. Sandy followed his gaze and took a step away from it.

"But they'd have to sell for gold. At least one. Every single piece," I said.

Gerald shrugged noncommittally. Then he turned to me.

"What's the Academy?" he asked.

"You don't *know*?" Sandy replied for me.

"I never wanted to be a Noble. I didn't want anything to do with it," Gerald said.

"It's where they send all new Nobles. To train them. So they don't just die struggling alone in dungeons."

"Okay, but…where is it? Where would they send someone if they were…Chosen?"

"The capitol," I said.

"There are so many people there, aren't there? How do they ever open the dungeon to low-level people?"

"The Academy isn't in the actual city," Sandy said. "It's floors deep in the dungeon."

That night, Sandy and I geared up in silence in her workshop, adorning the stealth outfits in the quiet of the night. I slotted the throwing needles into a belt, tying threads to their ends. I wasn't sure how useful they'd be, but I took them anyway.

Then I finally pulled open my skill shop to spend my accumulated skill.

[Skill Shop]

▶Pattern Mirroring

[UNCOMMON] Mirrors cuts along worked material. Additional levels allow additional simultaneous cuts.

▶Cross Stitching I

[COMMON] Enables system assistance with a new stitch type. Additional levels increase proficiency.

▶Unweaving I

[UNCOMMON] Grants user the ability recycle items into base materials. Additional levels increase the amount recycled.

I dismissed the skill shop, putting another level into Wardrobe to bring it to level three. Something told me I was going to need my entire outfit ready before Valjean returned.

The first floor was almost routine; I used the needles to aggro the wolves, pulling them to Sandy so that she could finish them with the next blow. The wounds they left were shallow; I doubted they'd be useful at all against the spiders. But maybe, if I had some kind of skill for them, they could be.

When the first spider dropped down, I remembered my mom's advice. I didn't stab for the joints of the monster; but I also didn't stab directly through it.

Like I was stitching chitin shell onto a dress, I stabbed at an angle, sheering apart the armored plate of the spider and stabbing into its insides. The spider's legs fell limp while it tried desperately to reach me with its fangs.

I felt a smile growing on my face.

Sandy brought down her sword and the spider died.

We worked together better this time, our practice killing the spiders accumulating. I earned another level and another skill point, and when the sixth spider fell, the forest shook, a thrum of mana running through the floors.

"Yes!" Sandy said, her eyes ablaze as she started forward to the wall at the edge of the dungeon. The shaking subsided.

"How long till it opens, do you think?" I asked, walking up and trying to brush away the vines that blanketed the wall.

"Days," Sandy said.

"Any idea what's on the other side?"

"No," Sandy said, biting her lip. "This is as far as I made it on my own."

"Whatever it is, we'll be ready for it. We barely used any mana today."

I let my hand drop from the wall and turned back to her, the smile on my face matching her own. Clear the dungeon. Expand the town. Our path from here was straight forward.

Mom's advice worked on the chitin dress, too, the replaced scales holding together better as I redecorated the bodice of the dress. It was faster and easier. I selected out the white pieces, making a top of ivory white scales. I was able to finish the dress in a night.

But I found myself frowning still, trying to figure out what was wrong with it. [Embellishment] pulled at me. I crafted a decoration that reached up from the collar, spun from spiderweb and repatterned into their image.

It looked like a spiderweb extending all the way up the neck.

[Cleome I]

▶25% complete

▶Quality +0.2

[PROJECTED SKILLS]

▶Blue Skill II

I still didn't know what Blue Skill was. Maybe it was a category of skill? Like a set bonus? I felt like it would be a bad idea to ask. Then again, most of the town was probably catching on anyway.

Sandy's snoring interrupted my thinking. How long had she been asleep? I had fallen into a fugue while crafting; the moon was already high in the sky. I tried to fold the dress, but its scales resisted. I wrapped the dress in cloth before covering one of Sandy's hooks in a sheathe of leather, hanging the dress from it.

Work done, I yawned and stretched, blowing out Sandy's lamp before heading home. I could pick a new skill point tomorrow.

CHAPTER 23

We didn't see Gerald again for a few days. Sandy was still mad even if she acted civil, taking days to calm down. She took out her frustration on the monsters in the dungeon, swinging with manic ferocity the next day.

When the last wolf was dead, she swung again, splattering blood across the floor before lifting the blade back up.

"Aren't you upset?" she asked. The question caught me off guard.

"No," I replied after too long of a hesitation.

"It should've been you or me. Not someone who squanders it spending all day making…making *toys*." She spat the last word with audible derision.

Sandy calmed down after killing the final spider. In a way, I was glad she wasn't a Noble. She was terrifying enough while angry, without the kind of power Valjean demonstrated; I didn't want to imagine what Sandy would do with the ability to level forests in single swings.

I didn't tell her that, though.

While Sandy calmed, the dungeon only seemed to grow angrier, the wild mana pulsing through more like an earthquake than a heartbeat now. It sent leaves tumbling from the canopy above us.

The door didn't open. But we cleared the entire floor using only two mana between us, becoming more and more proficient. Most of the spiders died in a single hit, my needle sheering through the side. The easier it became, the more the rewarded experience diminished. Across the clear, I only leveled twice, the reward diminishing to a single point per spider. I upgraded my Wardrobe inventory piece by piece, crossing my fingers that the Thread Mastery skill I had skipped would reappear.

It didn't.

The days flew by, the pulsing of the dungeon louder and louder as we got closer to opening the next portal. The set was almost done, and I was burning with the desire to find out what skills it would give.

On the third day, I leveled again, stopping in my tracks on the second floor. "Two skill points?" I asked aloud.

"Just hit level ten?" Sandy asked.

My system had rewarded me two points instead of one. Now I could start splitting my points between upgrading my own skills and gaining new ones, if I ever rolled anything worth picking again.

I leveled Embellishment and Wardrobe.

On the fourth day, the dungeon gate half opened. It was a window; not a door. We could see the next floor. It was a forest, too, channels of crystal-clear water cutting through a canopy in a rainbow of colors. Trees with leaves in purple and red and yellow and green coexisted, a menagerie of colors. All this nested within a circular pit, a straight cliff surrounding the forest. A waterfall poured a slow current into the channels of water.

I pressed my hand to the window, feeling the cold, transparent wall that blocked us from going further, the vines of the second floor curled around the emerging gateway.

Then we saw the monster inside. It just looked like a hill at first, covered in decaying leaves with a back of mottled orange and brown. When it stood, I realized it was fur, colored to camouflage it against the forest floor. It was a bear as tall as one of the trees. It rose from where it drank at the river, lumbering backward and away, the image soft and fuzzy.

"We need to bring some rope," I said, staring at the cliff face.

That night, I finished the shell dress. We had stolen one of Gerald's mannequins, decorating it kindly. The head had been broken off at some point—I couldn't remember if it came that way or if Sandy had beheaded it at some point—so it sat on top of the body tilted at an angle.

The dress was made entirely of scales. Despite its shape, it was armor, lined with hard chitin that caught the light. The left side of it hung below the shoulder; the right side stretched to the elbow, covered in armor. I had stuck to white for the bodice and used metallic red chitin for the right arm. The matching red chitin bracelets rested on the floor, carved into complex patterns of web.

The earrings took days to carve. The standard pattern called for little more than hanging loops made from chitin. [Embellishment] sent me the extra mile, carving spiderwebs out of metallic red.

That the earrings contributed as much as the boots seemed illogical, but then again, magic. Another class probably wouldn't gain anything from earrings even if they were made from monsters of apocalyptic proportion.

I reached out and activated [Quick Change]. It had a limit for how fast it could change clothes; not more than once a second. I swapped my mundane outfit one piece at a time.

"I feel like it'd be faster to just change normally at this point," Sandy said, lazing on her bed. The stack of books she had already read piled up. Three books claimed a haphazard place on the crooked table that served as Sandy's nightstand.

"I paid for the whole spell."

I rolled my shoulders. The seamstress-crafted goods magically expanded here or contracted there, making a perfect fit. I stared down at the earrings with uncertainty.

My ears weren't pierced.

Screw it.

I activated [Quick Change] and brought the full set together for the first time.

There was no pain. I reached up and touched the earrings before sighing with relief. I was ready for the next floor of the dungeon to open. With the set unified, it finally began the process of generating its skill, practically burning with power. The more I raised the quality, the more skill shards the outfit gained.

[Cleome I]

▸100% complete

▸Quality +1.1

[Generating Skills…][14 Skill Shards]

▸Thread Sensing II

▸Thread Mastery I

[4 shards left over…] [Enhancing Skills]

I watched as the skills glowed inside my vision. [Thread Sensing] and [Thread Mastery] both leveled another time.

Thread Sensing from an outfit. My mind shook a little as the ability washed over me; memories rolled unsteadily in my mind, trying to find footing somewhere. They were hazy images still, vignetted with fog and confusion. They were images of a dungeon. They couldn't have been anything else; a hundred monsters crawled across a ceiling in the memory. Then it was gone, slipping out of my hands like a dream and leaving behind still images I could barely recall.

"Gwen? Are you alright?" Sandy asked.

"Yeah," I said. I was doubled over, leaning against the wall. I hadn't even realized. I leaned my back against the wall, the boots stiff and pressing into my legs, and pulled open my system.

[Gwendolyn Tailor][Human, Lv10][Seamstress]

[Health: 52/52][Mana: 9/10][XP: 6/10]

[ATTRIBUTES]

▶SPD: 10
▶WIL: 5
▶STR: 19
▶DEX: 10
▶CON: 26
▶PER: 9
[SKILLS]
▶Crafting I
▶Running Stitch I
▶Hand Spinning I
▶Thread Mastery IV
▶Wardrobe V
▶Quick Change I
▶Embellishment II
[PATTERNS]
▶Hunter Pattern
▶Shell Dress Pattern
[RESISTANCES]
▶Light: 10
[TEMPORARY SKILLS]
▶Thread Sensing III
▶Thread Mastery II

Thread Sensing from an outfit. Fifty-two health. What did that even mean?

The system raised my health to its cap instantly. Could I abuse that to heal? My gut told me no.

I poked at my arm. My skin felt normal, not like it was made of steel or anything. I let out a nervous laugh.

"So?" Sandy asked.

"Does my skin feel like it's made of steel?" I asked her.

"What?" she asked, walking over to me. I held out an arm. She grabbed it, fingers dimpling my skin. She frowned. "No. Are you going crazy?"

"We have to be a little crazy to do this, right?" I pulled my hand back and spun in the dress. The chitin scales clicked as I turned, lamplight dancing off shining surfaces.

"Yeah. You've always been crazy."

There was pounding on the door. I panicked, reaching up and shuffling my clothes into my inventory, swapping them out.

My hunter set was in my inventory, which didn't help. My mundane clothes hung on a rack. I didn't feel any pain from suddenly losing this much constitution, but my focus was on who was pounding on the door. I crept back to the corner of the room, preparing to activate stealth.

Sandy raised an eyebrow at me.

"Gwen? Sandy?" Gerald called, voice muffled by the door. "It's me!"

Sandy's expression soured. I relaxed, though adrenaline still made my heart pound against my chest. I was emotionally on edge. Getting caught in the hunter outfit was something I could explain; showing up in a dress made of spider scales was something else entirely.

Sandy's expression was begrudging when she opened the door. She grabbed Gerald's shoulder and dragged him in.

"What do you want?" Sandy asked Gerald.

Gerald looked between me and Sandy, confused for a moment. I stepped forward from the wall, pulling open my system for just an instant to see my health total.

[Health: 52/10]

"I'm out of metal," Gerald said, sounding anxious.

"So go buy some more? Sell one of your toys. You can afford it, Sandy said.

"I'd have to explain why my weapons are enchanted. And I'd have to explain why I can't break them down." Gerald shook his head no.

"You mean you haven't told your parents?" Sandy asked.

"No! Who can I trust to tell this to? I told you, and how did you react? How do you think they will?" Gerald asked.

"Guys," I said, stepping forward.

"Sorry," Gerald said. He swung a backpack around and pulled out a piece of paper. As he walked to the table, he bumped into a chain and sent it swinging. He spread the paper on the table. It curled at the edges, threatening to close in on itself. It was thick and covered in markings.

"What is this?" I asked, staring over his shoulder, but I knew what it was. It was a map of the town, showing a ringed city that stretched much farther than it did now.

Sandy begrudgingly crossed the room, looking down over both of us and reading the map.

"Huh," she said. "Didn't know it used to be that big."

"Me neither. I looted this out of old records passed down. But forget the city," Gerald said, pointing at one of the distant markers on the map. It was an image of a stack of ingots with a pickaxe over them, clearly labeled *IRON* beneath.

"Is that supposed to be Gwen's house?" Sandy asked, pointing to a spot in the inner city that was depicted with an icon of a needle and scissors. "And...there's yours..." Gwen said.

The map was covered in symbols of buildings that used to be here. Potion shops, mining guilds, carpenters and architects and crafters of all kinds. The most interesting detail though, by far, was the collapsing circle that showed the town's border and where the next two rings of dungeon entrances would arise.

As I watched, the ink circle slowly moved. I reached out and picked it up.

Two footprints appeared in a cleared section of the map that wasn't marked for any house, showing where I was. Sandy stepped back. Gerald stared.

"It's enchanted?" Sandy asked.

"Uh…yeah," Gerald said.

"So…you want us to go mine raw iron in the Wild," I said, staring at the metal resource node south of the town.

CHAPTER 24

The iron store wasn't the only resource node on the map; nodes were replenishable resources that existed outside the dungeons and scattered the territory around the city.

"Is this even feasible?" I said, looking up at Gerald over the map. "I mean, we would need tools, a way to carry the iron back to town, then you would have to smelt raw iron from the Wild…"

Gerald help up a hand. One moment it was empty. The next there was a pickaxe in it. The pickaxe disappeared and was replaced with an iron bar.

Purple light flowed around the iron.

"Oh, wait—"

The iron bar slipped out of his hand like a piece of soap, floating up to the ceiling. Gerald reached for it, sending it tumbling like there was no gravity attached to it.

"Oh shit!" Gerald said as it rolled away through the air.

Sandy caught it with both hands, lowering it back to Gerald, who stored it back in his inventory sheepishly.

"Does everyone have an inventory skill?" Sandy grumbled.

"You don't have one yet?" Gerald asked, seeming genuinely surprised. Then he turned to me. "Did yours come with your class?"

"What? No. Had to spend a stat point on it," I replied.

Gerald nodded and turned back to the map.

"Tomorrow," he said. His face fixed into a harsh expression as he looked at the map. It was odd to see him so deadly serious. "Let's go scout the node."

I changed back into my mundane clothes, storing my stealth outfit in my inventory, and headed home. I spent the morning working with my mom. I had been making slow but steady progress on a null hunter outfit, the materials so basic that they imbued no magical properties onto the finished product.

"Do you want to try it on?" Mom asked. "It's all yours."

I tried to offer her a genuine smile. The outfit gave a bonus to my stats—a pitiful one, even after being boosted twenty percent by my seamstress bonus.

"It's great," I said, folding my arms and feeling the rougher sleeves. The work wasn't my best. It was still something we could sell with the next shipment out, but my focus was on what I made at night. "It feels good to have something that's mine."

"Do you want to start on the next one right away?" she asked.

"No. I have plans for tonight. This is good. Actually…can I borrow you to help me make a mining pattern?"

Mom leveled at me, staring without comment.

"What?" I asked. There was something wrong.

"What did you see?" she asked.

"I…didn't see anything." Was she asking about the memories from the patterns? The ones that were supposed to tell us how to sew? What would I have seen from them?

"You don't have the Miner pattern," she said.

I nodded no to confirm.

"Sit down, please."

My mind set on fire. She knew. She *knew*. How could she not know? What gave it away? Did my lack of reaction to the stats confirm something for her? Was my smile not genuine enough?

I sat. It was fine. It wasn't like I was doing anything wrong. I was doing what I always told her I would growing up. I would kill the monsters. I would save the town. The walls of the room were pressing in on me. This workshop used to be gigantic.

She kept staring.

"I—" I started to speak and didn't know what to say.

"It's okay," Mom said, dragging a chair to sit in front of me. "I know you're helping Sandy clear the dungeon. But I…don't want you to get any ideas. Not from anything you see."

"Anything I see in the patterns?" I asked, the question rushing past my thoughts and escaping my mouth before I finished processing it. What had she thought I saw?

"Yes." She nodded once, curtly. "Some of those patterns are old. Very old. Before our way of life. They don't show the way things are anymore. There comes a time for every crafter to have this talk. You cannot trust the memories imbued in the patterns."

She stared at me as if she was trying to read my thoughts.

"It's fine that you're supporting Sandy. It's great. Your crafting will help keep her safe. But you don't need to kill anything yourself. Seamstresses shouldn't have to fight."

Shouldn't have to.

I nodded, feeling my face flush. She thought it was just Sandy actually clearing the dungeon.

She didn't know I was. Why would she think so? She knew that Sandy's mom had cleared the dungeon. She probably even knew that Sandy had been doing it a year ago. I picked my words carefully, slotting them into a sentence that wouldn't reveal anything.

"So…you'll help me make a mining pattern?"

Mom leaned back. I didn't realize she had gotten so close, leaning across the table. She finally relaxed.

"Yes. And have Sandy bring by something to make it out of," Mom said, tapping her fingers on the table. "Maybe I can help, too."

"What?" I asked, reeling.

"If I had helped her mom, maybe things would be different." Mom stood with a groan. "There's no point obsessing over the past. Run on. You've got lots of work ahead of you still."

Mom left. I sat staring in the workshop, tapping my fingers along the desk.

She didn't know, after all.

I picked up my outfit, changing into the hunter set and meeting Sandy at the edge of the town.

"You're both late." She said, leaning against a tree and staring out. She was wearing her hunter outfit too, staring out into the wild.

"My mom knows you're clearing the dungeon," I said, following her gaze. She didn't say anything for a moment.

"She knows *I'm* clearing the dungeon? What about *you?*"

"She knows you're clearing the dungeon," I repeated, sitting on a large rock. Reality bubbled outside the border of the town. Trying to see past the border was like trying to make out objects underwater. Wind blew the trees above us.

"Okay? So do we need to do something?"

"She said she'd help," I replied.

Sandy choked, pausing for a moment to consider

"Help how?"

"We're going to have to bring her supplies and find out."

Sandy folded her arms, staring hard at the ground and thinking. Gerald arrived a few minutes after, waving excitedly.

"Guys!" he said.

"You ready?" Sandy asked.

Gerald looked to the edge of town. His face said he was unsure.

"Let me just…" he said, then reached out. He must have been activating his inventory skill, because metal started to crawl from his fingertips and up his arm. Heavy gauntlets swirled with green light, the metal clunking together as it covered him. The steel must have been nearly an inch thick.

It continued up his arms, heavy plates glowing purple beyond his gauntleted forearms. Sandy recoiled at the growing sight. Huge pauldrons grew from Gerald's shoulders, then a breastplate decorated with etchings and softly humming. Metal locked into place around Gerald's face, his eyes recessed deep in pitch black.

"Ack—" he said, fumbling around with his helmet. He touched a hand to the side and a blue light glowed between his eyes, complex white lines crisscrossing them.

A shield appeared in his hand, as big as he was, also engraved.

"Ready!" he said, his voice muffled by the metal.

"Can you stop glowing before the whole town sees you?" Sandy asked.

"Oh, yeah." The enchanted glow faded from his armor, the eyes of his helmet dimming again. "Wait, no—" Gerald swiveled, slamming his shield into a tree he was unable to see. Leaves fell loose from the branches.. He dropped the shield with a clunk and tapped his helmet again.

"Alright!" he said.

The tree now featured a massive dent where bark exploded outwards, the metal shield having cut into the side of it. Gerald reached for his shield but struggled to bend at the waist.

"Let's go before someone investigates," Sandy said, reaching for the shield and visibly straining as she tried to lift it for Gerald. "Is this solid steel? No wonder you ran out of metal."

I switched to the scale dress, using my increased strength to help Sandy lift the monstrous shield. We got it just high enough for Gerald to grab the edge of it, and he stored it away.

Panting, I switched back to my mundane clothes. Sandy stared out toward the town. Most of the view was blocked by dense foliage.

"Hello?" someone asked, walking closer to the clearing. "Someone out here?"

"Shit," Sandy said. Then she turned and ran, slamming through into the Wild.

I looked at Gerald, eyes wide, then followed.

The kids in the town used to play chicken at the border. We would jump in and out of the Wild, stepping beyond the border of what was safe and what was out *there*, and then our parents would yell at us when we came back with new holes growing in our clothes and shoes.

We didn't have a system then. I don't know if I just forgot what it felt like a single step beyond the border of the town, or if gaining the system made me aware of it; the constant pressure etching at the edge of my awareness, the furious rage of the world itself encroaching on me. It hated me. It hated us.

We ran.

Gerald edged past me, each of his steps landing with a thump, the sound of metal slamming onto the earth.

We stopped where the forest opened beyond the trees, Sandy having turned around to wait for us there.

There was a shadow in the clearing, a foundation of brick covered in moss and grass. The shadow of a building. A house, maybe. I stopped next to her, staring up at the opening in the sky.

Gerald failed to stop in time. He tried to slow and slammed face-first into the ground, shattering brick in a loose impression of himself.

"Are you alright?" I asked, leaning down next to him. He pushed himself up off the ground.

"I'm fine," he said.

"How heavy is all of that?" I asked.

"I didn't weigh it," Gerald said.

Sandy pulled out the wooden tube containing the map and unfolded it.

"Is it safe to bring that out here?" I asked.

"It's survived a few generations. It'll survive a few minutes out here," she said, orienting herself in the woods before stowing it again. "This way."

Sandy pointed a direction that led off through the woods, a straight line toward the iron mine.

CHAPTER 25

I took a final look back toward the town. It was completely obscured by the tree line; the bubble around it left no trace this far into the Wild. Besides the ever-present minor discomfort, it wasn't any different than a regular forest.

Birds sang and insects crawled, the whole world alive and covered in dancing shadows from the light through the shifting canopy above. Sandy walked hurriedly.

"How long will these outfits last out here?" Sandy asked, turning back toward me.

"Not sure," I said, shrugging my shoulders and scanning the forest around us. "I'd guess a lot longer than regular clothes, though."

The tree line broke, exposed forest floor stretching in either direction around us. The three of us stopped.

Sandy whistled.

I bent down, scraping at the moss that covered the ground, revealing a stone foundation.

"There used to be a wall here," I said.

Sandy pulled the map out again, nodding and folding it back up. Then she broke off in a new direction, following along the wall without a word.

"Where are you going?" I asked while standing to follow. Gerald trailed behind.

Just around the bend, an edifice of white stone brick rose out of the ground. I recognized it immediately; it was a nearly exact match of the one that rose in the center of town, save for the wild randomness of the creeping vines that choked out the brick.

Sandy reached a hand out and dragged a finger down the brick of the dungeon entrance before pulling it back and inspecting her fingers.

The southeast dungeon entrance was dead and inert. Outside of the range of the magic bubble that held the town, it was little more than a brick edifice.

"This is far away from the town," I said, leaning over to inspect it myself. "Will we be able to push the border far enough to activate this?"

"I don't know," Sandy said. "We have to see how far the border stretches when we kill the boss."

We turned about, Sandy reorienting before storing the map and leading us toward the resource node. The terrain grew rougher, rocky ground replacing the softer earth. The tree cover grew sparse and the terrain uneven. I noticed the smoke first.

"What is that?" I asked, grabbing Sandy's shoulder and pointing ahead. Towers of black smoke rose into the air.

"There shouldn't be anything out here," Sandy said, squinting at the horizon.

"I'll scout it," I said.

"We should go together," Sandy replied.

"We need to save mana. We still have to clear the dungeon tonight." I turned to Gerald. "Unless you have a way to scout it?"

He shook his head no, filling the air with the sound of metal clashing together.

I activated [Shadow Cloak], feeling the darkness wrap around me, and walked forward. The rough terrain was slow to navigate, but only thirty yards away I came upon the resource node.

Furnaces poured black smoke into the air, the tree line cut to stumps in all directions.

Tiny crystal monsters roamed around the mines. They were only a few feet tall, their bodies nearly round, transparent, and shimmering, split into dozens of faceted edges that caught sunlight and threw it around the clearing. Their entire worksite looked like it was under a stained glass window, brilliant colors dancing on the ground.

Each one was brilliant and distinct in color, ranging from pastel lavenders and cyan to deep red crimsons and even black.

There were monsters here, right at the edge of our town. Why hadn't Valjean killed them? The town's border prevented them from entering, but what if a kid walked into the Wild? Almost all monsters were instantly hostile.

Maybe they just weren't considered enough of a threat. I counted them as they meandered about. They were loading furnaces of packed earth full of metal. They were *mining*. They had makeshift tools, crude implements that fell apart even as I watched.

I wasn't sure how much of that was due to the influence of the Wild and how much of it was shoddy crafting.

Counting the monsters carefully as they moved about the work site, I mentally tallied twenty-three. I couldn't have been sure there weren't more deeper in, but they weren't coming out…and I wasn't going in alone.

One of them took metal that was still burning hot and poured it out on the ground. It picked it up with its bare hands, its jaw detaching to hang low, and bit the metal, chewing on hot iron like a snack. I did not want to get bit by one of these.

The mining seemed to be little more than a programmed instinct. They had no other signs of intelligence, no communication. They fought over the same tools, over the same iron, and tripped over their feet often.

I turned back, finding Sandy and Gerald where I left them. Sandy continued her devotion to ignoring Gerald, looking anywhere else.

Gerald snapped to attention as I approached.

"Gwen?" he asked.

"Yeah. It's me. There's a whole monster infestation at the cave."

"How many?" Sandy asked.

"I counted twenty-three. But there might be more inside. They look like little…rock golems. Moving crystals. I'm not sure if we'll even be able to cut them."

"You gonna fix my blade if I chip it?" Sandy asked, looking at Gerald.

"If we get any metal out of this," Gerald said, staring dubiously at the pillars of smoke.

We walked to the edge of the mine site, Sandy holding her cleaver free from its sheath the whole time. Gerald was practically jumping at his own shadow, summoning and stowing the shield nonstop.

Sandy looked down into the divot and whistled in surprise.

"Industrious little things, aren't they?"

"What *are* they?" Gerald asked.

"Dunno, but they can't be that strong if they're that small."

The shadow cloak still clung to me, making me practically invisible as I looked over the small slide down into their worksite.

One of them raised an arm and pointed at us, making an alarmed noise. It sounded like a windchime as it spun about and pointed.

"Guess that's our sign. Get down there," Sandy said.

"What? Me?" Gerald asked.

"You're the one with a full suit of armor!"

"But you have…stealth skills…" Gerald said. The monsters were picking up tools. "Okay. I got this. I *got* this."

Gerald charged down the hill shouting. The dusty earth slid loose under him, sending him gliding forward until he stopped by braking with his tower shield, slamming it into the ground.

Then the monsters were on him. Sandy strolled down the hill, humming a tune as a dozen tiny golems wailed on Gerald's armor, the musical tick, tick, tick, tick of dozens of impacts of crude iron on metal resounding through the little clearing.

The monsters let out little tinkling noises in alarm. Some others rushed back into the cave entrance.

Gerald held his shield with both hands.

"Guys?" he said, nearly yelling to be heard through the muffling of the metal helmet. "Little help?"

Sandy swung her sword.

A purple golem went flying with a crack, the body rolling. A line was rent directly into it, and it didn't get back up.

The monsters swinging at Gerald accumulated chipping damage every time they hit him, new cracks and cuts appearing on their own bodies, but that only caused them to intensify their efforts to crack him open.

I circled around the back, stabbing at the exposed back of one of the monsters. The needle sent it tumbling to the ground, but didn't break through the hard crystal shell of its body.

The monster rose with offended tickling noises. I heard Sandy's next swing crack another monster open. A pink golem turned to look at me.

[Running Stitch I] [Mana: 8/10] [Cancel]

[+1 XP]

Gerald flinched in his armor as I was ripped out of stealth with the sound of crystal exploding. My sewing needle tore through the crystalline body of the golem, sending shrapnel flying. It collapsed to the ground. The rest of the golems stopped, paused, and then collectively ran away.

Sandy laughed gleefully as she chased them, swinging left and right with her gigantic cleaver. Each successful cut sounded out with an explosion of force.

"You okay in there?" I asked Gerald.

"Yeah, I'm fine," Gerald said. He still held his shield interposed between the two of us, unwilling to set it down. "Did you get 'em all?"

I looked down at the half-exploded corpse of the one I had killed. The rest were being chased into the cave by Sandy, who was still swinging maniacally.

"Oh fuck—" Sandy said, then scrambled backward, dropping her cleaver and nearly falling on her ass. She grabbed the blade and booked it toward me.

A monster chased her out of the cave. It had a body of burnished copper striped with shiny metallic black, a dozen wires hanging from its face, and claws as long as Sandy's cleaver.

"Oh," I said, staring at the monster for too long.

Three crystal golems rode on its back, the one in front grabbing the wires that hung from the monster's nose, whipping them around like reins to guide it. It tore over the ground with six limbs, making a cacophony of terrible, grinding noises as it rumbled forward.

"Fuck fuck fuck fuck!" Sandy said.

"It's gonna catch up!" I shouted, about to run forward to try to figure out a way to help. Maybe I could kill it mid-stride?

Sandy activated [Shadow Cloak] only a dozen feet away of us.

"What's happening?" Gerald asked.

"Oh no. How much can you block with that?"

"It's enchanted, so, a lot. What's happening?"

"Hold on tight!" I said, jumping behind Gerald as the monster's charge grew to a thunderous crescendo.

It sounded like a bomb went off.

CHAPTER 26

There was an ear-splitting cry. Then the copper mole shot backward, tearing apart earth as it rolled end over end. The clearing lit up as if illuminated by a firework as dozens of Gerald's enchantments erupted simultaneously. The glowing translucent projection of a shield flared around Gerald's tower shield.

The monster landed in a heap in the dirt, stunned. The crystal golems were sent flying across the clearing.

I rushed forward, passing Gerald as I dashed toward the gigantic, copper mole, and stabbed down.

[Running Stitch I] [Mana: 7/10] [Cancel]

The needle made a sheering noise of metal on metal as it passed through the creature's head and out the other side. I sat there for a moment, needle stuck in its head, wondering what was missing.

There was no experience pop-up.

I yanked on the needle, trying to pull it out, but it held firm in the monster's head. Instead, I pulled the monster's head up off the ground, bending its neck toward me. It gnashed sharp, dirty, metal teeth at me, its face eyeless, a featureless plate of metal.

Sandy appeared out of the shadow, her cleaver flashing unnaturally, separating the monster down its spine. That was normally enough to drop the wolves to pieces. But now, it just left a gouge a hand's length deep. Blood like oil seeped from the wound.

I let go of the needle and jumped backward, the monster biting the air where I had been a second ago. It whipped its head back and forth, the thin wires that hung from its face searching the ground.

The needle pierced clean through its head from one side to the other, iridescent black blood seeping from the wound. The system kept it alive by force.

It still had health points left.

I tripped on a rock and fell backward right as the monster's jaw lunged for the ground. It chewed through dirt and rock, swallowing a chunk of earth.

Sandy's blade sent sparks flying as she hacked at its side, the blade scratching down the beast but not finding any purchase to split its side open.

"Gerald? You going to help?" Sandy asked.

"Help how? I only have a shield!" Gerald shouted from the other side of the clearing.

I didn't turn back to look at him. Instead, I activated [Quick Change], replacing my clothing piece by piece while the monster turned to Sandy. The strength stat made my limbs feel like they were full of power.

The monster bit down toward her. She held out her knife with both hands as the monster's mouth closed around it, yanking like a dog with a chew toy.

[Running Stitch I] [Mana: 6/10] [Cancel]

[+5 XP] [Excess discarded]

My second needle exploded through the side of its head, sending chunks of metal flying. The needle clattered to the ground of the dusty clearing, the monster's collapse bringing Sandy down with it. She pushed its mouth open with a boot, pulling her sword free.

"Really?" Sandy asked, calling out to Gerald. "It's dead now!"

"What about the little monsters?" Gerald asked from behind his tower shield.

"They're gone too," I said, looking around in the clearing. The tiny crystal golems had run away as soon as the monster was knocked back by Gerald's enchantments.

Sandy stared thoughtfully at the mouth of the cave. There wasn't even a shadow of human industry here, the Wild having erased any trace of it. In the mouth of the cave, however, were gouges in the stone, presumably from where support beams once stood.

"What're you gonna make out of this?" Sandy asked. She kicked the side of the monster, then turned back toward me.

"Dunno. Feels like a waste to make a mining outfit." I said, leaning down at the monster's side. "Doesn't quite fit the shell dress either."

Sandy looked around the clearing then down at the monster.

"We're not going to be able to carry it home like this," I said.

Sandy grunted in affirmation and then pulled a knife from her belt. She looked between it and the monster. Gerald slowly sidled up, every footstep a tremendous hulking noise.

Sandy put the small knife away, picking her cleaver back up. She kicked the monster onto its belly and stabbed down into the hole she had cut open earlier.

"You guys check out the cave. I'll get to work on this," Sandy said. She grunted, pushing down on the blade. When it didn't budge, she leaned into it with her knee, standing on the monster to press down.

"Let me get the lantern," I said, staring back off to the cave. I really needed a set of armor with a light enchantment.

"Oh! I can get the light," Gerald said, raising a hand to his helmet again. The glow coming from the armor's sockets intensified until it hurt to look at, rays of light pouring out of his helmet. Sandy and I turned to look to each other.

"You know that means you'll be walking into the—potentially *monster-infested*—cave, right?" Sandy asked.

"Oh," Gerald said. "Yeah!"

He stared for a moment at the cave before stepping forward.

"Lead the way, then." I followed behind Gerald, the sound of Sandy's grunts as she cut the monster apart fading.

"I'll yell if anything is trying to kill me!" Sandy shouted behind us.

Gerald stopped at the mouth of the cave, eyes sweeping wall to wall. The light moved with his gaze. With a gesture, one of his iron gauntlets disappeared and returned to his inventory. He ran a finger over the wall streaked with orange veins.

"How does your inventory work? Can you just store the iron right out of the wall?" I asked, following behind him.

Gerald pressed a hand to the wall and grunted.

"No luck."

The mouth of the cave was a single, long path, leading deep inside. We found remnants of the crystal golems' camp.

There, the cave split into four directions, one of them collapsed in and filled with rubble. Sections of the wall were mined clean, mounds of stone and unrefined metal littering the floor. Tools in varying states of disrepair were piled in the corners. It looked like they had hurried to grab what remained of their belongings before running deeper into the cave.

Gerald dove into the rubble instantly, storing some of the pieces according to some unknown logic. The other doorways hung thick with darkness while his light was affixed on the ground.

"Where did the monsters go? Is there another exit to the cave?" I asked.

Gerald looked up, then around.

I gripped the needle in my hand before forcing myself to relax a little. If the golems had another monster like that, they wouldn't have run.

"Let's check all the passages."

We turned down the right passage first. It curved about before ending abruptly at a wall, the veins of iron disappearing where the next passage was carved open.

We turned back. The crystal goblin camp was still undisturbed. There was only one route left. The tunnel at the back of the room slanted downward ever so slightly, a degree or two into the earth. A soft breeze flowed up the mine shaft intermittently, the air smelling progressively more damp.

Branches in the tunnel led to collapsed pathways or dead ends, reaching deeper and deeper until the tunnel changed in a subtle but noticeable way. The walls gained new texture and grew wider, not a shape that could be achieved by pickaxes. It looked like they were clawed open from below.

The cave ended not at a wall, but in a pile of rubble. There was a small clearance at the top, big enough for the crystal golems to climb through, but not big enough for a human. The monsters had retreated into the earth.

"How deep does this place go?" Gerald asked.

"It looks like something dug its way up here," I said, looking around at the walls. "So…probably…very deep."

We turned around and climbed out of the mine, mentally noting where the iron veins ran thick as we crossed.

"You think those monsters are going to come back?" Gerald asked, his voice nervous.

"There's no place in the Wild that doesn't carry the threat of monsters," I replied. Uncleared and unoccupied dungeons poured monsters into the world. The powerful ones typically ranged far from human territory, chased away or hunted by the Nobles. The only real safety, though, was within the bubble that surrounded a well-maintained town.

I activated my system to spend the one skill point I received. I could only buy one new skill from the shop; I was forced to spend the other point on either a pattern or leveling up a skill. With Wardrobe sufficient to hold my entire current outfit, I didn't have to level it.

[Skill Shop]

▶Cross Stitching I

[COMMON] Enables system assistance with a new stitch type. Additional levels increase proficiency.

▶Pattern Projection I

[COMMON] Seamstress Vision skill. Grants user access to a pattern overlay on fabric.

▶Pattern Mirroring I

[UNCOMMON] Mirrors cuts along worked material. Additional levels allow additional simultaneous cuts.

I frowned as I looked over the skills, thinking. Sandy was able to use her butcher skill on live monsters. I wondered if I could do the same with Pattern Mirroring.

What was the difference between an unprocessed bolt of cloth and an unprocessed body of leather? One was alive, sure.

"Hey Gerald…" I asked, walking behind him. "Do you think you could craft a giant pair of scissors?"

[Gwendolyn Tailor][Human, Lv11][Seamstress]
[Health: 52/52][Mana: 7/10][XP: 0/10]
[ATTRIBUTES]
▶SPD: 10
▶WIL: 5
▶STR: 19
▶DEX: 10
▶CON: 26
▶PER: 9
[SKILLS]
▶Crafting I
▶Running Stitch I
▶Hand Spinning I
▶Thread Mastery IV
▶Wardrobe V
▶Quick Change I
▶Embellishment III
▶Pattern Mirroring I
[PATTERNS]
▶Hunter Pattern
▶Shell Dress Pattern
[RESISTANCES]
▶Light: 10
[TEMPORARY SKILLS]
▶Thread Sensing III
▶Thread Mastery II

CHAPTER 27

Scissors…" Gerald whispered to himself. "Giant scissors. They're basically two big blades with a flat edge. How does that…screw in the middle work?" Gerald asked, his muttering becoming faster and more incessant as he thought.

"I think it just holds the blades together?" I said.

We stepped from the darkened mineshaft into the midday light. Sandy had separated the copper monster into pieces, plates of square metal lying to the side, still draining black blood.

"Hey guys!" she said, awfully excited for once.

"Ah no, Gwen! I can feel an Inspiration coming on," Gerald complained.

"Is that bad?" I asked, eyeing him.

"Doesn't go away until I craft. I can barely sleep while Inspired," he replied glumly, his eyes still glowing.

"Good thing we got plenty of metal, then," I said.

"There's hardly enough to make anything," he said, summoning a piece of raw material into his hands.

"Can't you craft new things with the old enchanted metal?" I asked. "Like if you have a sword that swings faster and craft the scissors out of those…?"

"What do you think I made this armor out of?" Gerald asked. "I tried crafting out of some of the trickier pieces. The metal that damages whoever hits it wounded *my* hand. The piece enchanted with antigravity caught the roof of the forge on fire."

"Gerald? How did you do all that without your parents noticing?" I asked, turning to him with shock. Sandy and I were bad at hiding what we were up to, but we weren't that bad!

He only shrugged.

"There's more metal at the furnaces," I said, gesturing with my head to the stacked brick and mud forges the tiny golems had built outside of the dungeon.

"Oh yeah!" he said, rushing past me despite the heavier armor. He leaned down to inspect the metal that was left inside of them. With a casual swing, he blew the bricks apart, inspecting the burning hot metal inside.

Sandy grunted as she pulled at the copper monster's insides, pulling out an organ that looked like a pipe before throwing it on the ground. It made a hollow ringing noise, oil-like fluid bubbling out of the side of it.

"How's it going?" I asked Sandy.

"Good." She smiled, a maniacal look on her face. Black blood ran from her fingers to her elbows, smeared across her face and all over per pants. "I finally gained a level!"

I blinked at that.

"You hadn't leveled all this time?" I asked. She waved a hand.

"I'm already level nineteen. The corpses my dad bought for me to butcher raised my level a lot. This has to be the first time leveled from butchering in like, a year, though! Dad stopped buying the good stuff after we fought."

"You get a good skill?" I asked. It must have been for her to be this happy.

"A rare one!" she said. "A bonus to all materials that I butcher. Look how much I pulled off the thing!" Sandy waved at the stack of copper leather.

"How are we going to carry all these home?" I grimaced at the pile.

"Oh," Sandy said, looking it over. Then she looked me up and down. "You got a strength bonus from that outfit, right?"

I sighed, resigning myself to my fate.

Our return trip took extra time since I moved slowly, my vision blocked by the absolute pile of monster parts I was carrying. We didn't want to leave much of the corpse behind, afraid that it might attract something even bigger and hungrier to investigate. Between the three of us, we were able to carry most of the body. Gerald balanced a pile of metal flesh on his tower shield, holding out the behemoth piece of metal in front of him. How much of his family's storehouse had he used on that piece alone? We weren't brazen enough to bring the entire pile of goods to Sandy's warehouse at once. There was no way we wouldn't raise more questions in the daylight than we had answers for. Instead, we dumped what we had into the little clearing where Sandy had monitored the town's decay.

Now it was a staging ground for our progress in revitalizing it. I switched outfits twice, removing the blood that had accumulated on the outfit's arms, but I was still covered in the sticky, black, tar-like blood of the monster.

"I'm going to take a bath," I said, lying in the clearing. We still had to clear the dungeon again tonight.

"You're just going to get dirty again later," Sandy said.

"I don't care." I sat up with a groan.

I had to scrub for ages to get the monster blood off.

We met up again later at Sandy's house. With the mana we'd spent today, we had to save every last bit we could, which meant waiting until night to sneak into the dungeon.

I stopped right before we entered, glancing around the town square. I hadn't noticed it, but there were more houses awake at night than before.

How many of the town's residents knew what was happening and simply chose to say nothing? It was more than zero, that was certain. We slipped inside.

Immediately, I began to change into the scale dress. It was time to test my strength properly.

"Let me have the wolves," I said, flipping the needle in my hand.

"Thought they didn't give you any experience?" Sandy asked.

"They don't. I just want to…practice," I said. The fight with the copper mole earlier in the day had highlighted my need to find my limits. I had plenty of tools; I had to learn how to use them better.

We turned the corner on the first wolf, and I readied to kill it. With the shell dress, my dexterity was lower, but my strength was higher. My lowered perception made seeing in the dark even harder, and I had to rely on lamps.

I leaned forward and kicked off the ground, using my enhanced strength to throw myself forward, burying the giant needle into the wolf's head. It died ignobly, collapsing in a heap, the sudden weight on my needle hand threatening to topple me.

The needle slipped free with what felt like minimal resistance, despite the same act previously requiring so much effort. Its body collapsed in a heap.

"Satisfied?" Sandy asked.

I stared down at the needle in my hand.

"No."

Strength and speed were separate stats, but I could feel the ability to push my body harder and faster, despite there being no visible changes, just like raising constitution didn't turn my skin to steel. I ran down the hall, gaining speed until I slammed into the next wolf, the stab taking it off the ground and into the air, where it hung limp for a moment before I dropped it.

Exhilaration filled me. The first time we came here I had to take it slow and warily, watching for threats in every corner. Now I was hunting the monsters like it was a game, fighting them for practice when weeks before they were a threat to my life. I cleared the floor in a few minutes, letting out half a laugh as the stealth wolf collapsed to the ground.

Sandy clapped, and I immediately flushed, embarrassed at my behavior.

"Gwen the battle junkie. Wait till your mom finds out."

"Shhh. Don't joke like that. She would be worried sick. Probably throw up. And cry."

Sandy laughed.

"Still better than my dad."

I pulled out the throwing needles from my belt. They still weren't very useful, yet, but maybe with the enhanced strength I could inflict real damage with them.

We stepped into the forest. The alternating day-night cycle of the dungeon meant that it was daytime here, the sun assaulting us from the canopy. I looked to Sandy.

"You want to rush at them still?" she asked.

"No. Draw their aggro. I wanna give these another try." I pulled the throwing needles from my belt. They still weren't very useful, yet, but maybe with the enhanced strength I could inflict real damage with them.

Sandy pushed through the forest, eyes flicking up as the first spider fell toward her. I threw one of the needles, trying to catch it in midair. Without the dex to enhance my aim, my shot went wide, flying off into the canopy. Sandy's blade snapped to the side of the spider, batting it across the forest floor. Then she stepped forward and brought the blade down, cutting the monster open and splattering its insides across the ground.

I sighed as I recalled the needle. This was going to take some practice. I worked on my aim as we fought the spiders, eventually landing enough of the needles to make a difference—though they weren't enough to kill the spiders, even if they landed in their head, and they often returned to me covered in gore. There had to be a use for them still.

"Hold on," I said, stopping in the forest. We had a few more spiders to kill. I pulled out a spool of spiderweb-thread and knotted it to the edge of a needle. I reached out with [Thread Mastery].

The wire-thin thread twisted as I practiced working with the skill.

"But will the enchantment work if I..." I muttered to myself as Sandy stood over me, staring. Then the needle went flying as I sent it into a tree. It stabbed in with a heavy thunk. With a mental pull, I reached out to the enchantment. It flew back to me. "Magic is so cool."

"What are you going to use that for?" Sandy asked.

"I...am not sure yet," I admitted. "Honestly, I can't throw it that much harder with [Thread Mastery] than with my strength. Let's give it a try."

When the next spider fell out of the tree, I sent the dark forward, throwing it and reaching out with [Thread Mastery] to control the string.

It landed in a falling spider, and with a tug, I sent it veering off course, crashing into the ground. Sandy blinked for a moment before bringing her sword down. She cleaved the monster apart.

"Alright. Your strings are good for something other than fancy magic dresses," Sandy said, kicking the dead spider.

The next diving spider, my throw went wide, but I tugged at it with [Thread Mastery], sending the string wrapping around the spider, the thin thread cutting into the leg. I tugged at it, the string sliding down the chitin leg of the spider and into the soft sinew of its joints.

It made a horrifying noise as its leg popped off below the joint. Sandy finished that one, too. Now she looked at the needle in my hand warily.

"It probably can't do that to a human," I said. "Not yet. Spiders just don't have bones."

When we killed the last spider, the world shook.

[Gwendolyn Tailor][Human, Lv11][Seamstress]
[Health: 52/52][Mana: 7/10][XP: 6/10]

CHAPTER 28

We rushed to the vine choked-wall at the edge of the dungeon. It was dark on the next floor, but it was still bright enough to see.

Moonlight shimmered over the rivers, its reflection dancing under a canopy of rainbow-colored trees, leaves whipping about in a storm below.

There was a great, terrible cracking noise, and the glass-like wall that had separated us from the next floor split. Violent wind shoved through the crack, blowing back my hair. I covered my face as the transparent pane cracked apart, turning into sand that stung against my skin.

Then the wind was gone and the way to the next floor was open. I turned to Sandy to see she was already staring at me. We exchanged an entire conversation in a single glance.

"Do you have the rope?" she asked.

I nodded.

Sandy stepped through the portal and I followed closely behind. The boss arena—there was nothing else it could be—was just bigger than a sports arena, but there were no stands. Instead, the ground fell away to a cliff that circled the forest below.

Beyond the rocky cliff was a barren wasteland that stretched on as far as I could see. I turned around to take in the portal gate behind us. It looked the same as the entrance to the dungeon in the center of town; a raised archway of white stone bricks that opened to another reality.

"Nothing to tie a rope to out here," Sandy said, surveying the dungeon below us.

"Just a sec," I said, stabbing one of the needles into the ground before pulling out the much longer rope from my bag. I knotted it through the eye of the needle, then tugged, feeling it shift loosely. I stomped it down until I was satisfied it wouldn't budge, throwing the rope down off the side of the cliff below.

Sandy leaned over the edge, whistling as she looked down. Rocks tumbled from the barren edge and fell below. The whole world looked off, somehow, like it was all slightly…purple. I looked up and learned why.

Multiple moons hung in the sky, a disorganized trio of celestial bodies. The largest of them blazed with purple light, enough to force me to blink. Was there a big purple sun below us? How wide was each floor of the dungeon? How much of it was real?

I'd probably never know.

I walked next to Sandy, holding the rope in my hands and debating whether dex or strength would make it easier to climb down. After a moment, I switched outfits.

"I can't see the boss. Let's activate stealth," I said.

Sandy nodded, then disappeared. I felt the rope tug as she descended, waiting until it was slack again.

[Shadow Cloak I] [Mana: 6/10]

On a whim, I switched out of the hunter outfit. The skill stayed active, my hands disconcertingly invisible as I gripped the rope and descended from the cliff face, sinking below. The forest that had seemed so small from the top now loomed above me, a thousand shapes dancing in the shadows where purple light reflected in the bodies of water that snaked through the forest. It washed over the trees, flickering to highlight the trunks and skipping over the deep, deep shadows between the foliage.

"Sandy?" I asked, my voice a whisper.

"Right here," she said. "I'll follow you. I can see through the stealth, mostly."

"How can you…?" Her Butcher Vision skill? I shivered. "Never mind. I don't want to know."

We crept through the forest, the deepest either of us had ever been in the dungeon. It was just the two of us and the monster. Every minute we spent without finding it made me more paranoid, more restless. The wind blowing through the canopy above filled the forest with the sound of cracking wood and rustling leaves.

Finally, I heard something that wasn't just the noise of the artificial forest. Great halting snores. I looked back to try to find Sandy. Her steadying hand landed on my shoulder, though the surprise nearly made me jump.

"Sounds like our guy," she said, still whispering. "Lead the way." The monster was nestled away in a dark copse of trees, free from the body of water that reflected light through the forest. It looked like a pile of leaves. I observed from a distance, staring into the dark clearing it haunted. Then I crept forward.

Quickly. Quietly. It was asleep; how quickly could I end this fight? Would one attack while it was sleeping be enough? My mind went back to that copper mole, picturing the way the system kept it alive even as it was impaled directly through the head.

We still had to try. If we killed this monster, the border would expand. The other dungeon entrances would open. Valjean wouldn't be able to stop us.

I snuck toward the monster, freezing as I heard sticks crack beneath my feet. For a moment, I thought it stopped snoring, but then it continued.

My hands were practically shaking. The monster was the size of a car; it was bigger than the space that qualified as my bedroom. It was a bear; bigger than a bear. I had never seen a polar bear, but I knew that it was even bigger than that. It had to be more than ten feet long. I didn't whisper to Sandy for fear of waking the monster.

Instead, I held my giant needle precariously over its head and activated my skill.

[Running Stitch I] [Mana: 5/10] [Cancel]

The [Shadow Cloak] around me dissipated, gone in a moment. I braced myself for the feeling of flesh splitting around the needle. I had even mentally prepared to hit an impenetrable wall. But the needle didn't hit anything. Just air.

The image of the monster below me wobbled in a heat haze before melting, fading away into nothing. I staggered forward, carried by the momentum of my strike, and was left blinking in confusion. Was this a trap? An illusion of the dungeon?

Then the world turned upside down as something hit me with the noise and force of a car crash. *Everything* hurt. The world did flips as I sailed through the forest, bouncing off the ground, unable to even breathe as the repeating impacts sent the air from my lungs.

I landed with a splash.

[Health: 23/52]

My body spasmed, water forcing itself down my throat as I tried to reassert control of myself, my side burning. My arms finally started working, and I dragged myself from the river, throwing myself to the shore and trying to orient myself, choking and throwing up water.

"Gwen!" Sandy shouted, practically slamming into me. She dragged me away from the water. The cloak of shadow around her stretched onto me and then snapped, unable to hold us both.

She looked down at me.

"You alright?" she asked, sighing with relief as she poked at me. Then she whipped around, looking deeper into the forest.

The monster stood on all fours between two trees, its eyes glowing.

"It did...twenty-nine. Damage," I said, pushing myself up and struggling to breathe. The system's health points kept me alive, but they did nothing for the pain. "Can't take...two of those."

I reached for my sewing needle, but it was gone, tossed somewhere within the forest. The other was left behind at the top of the cliff. The monster stared with inhuman intelligence, slowly rising to stand on two feet.

It was gigantic, with shaggy brown fur mottled with clumps of green like camouflage. Its limbs were armored and its claws as long as swords.

Then it split in two, a perfect copy of itself appearing by its side.

"We need to run," I said, scrambling to push myself to my feet before the monster could split again. Four monstrous copies stood between the trees, staring. The monster's roar was distant in my mind as I forced myself forward, Sandy following behind.

The monster seemed to be right behind us the entire time, trees exploding as it crashed into them, its every footfall a terrifying, world-shaking noise. And then its roar was on top of us, echoing all around us. I couldn't stop myself from looking back.

A monster loomed over me, taller than me even on all fours. Rows of jagged teeth closed down around my head—

And then it disappeared into smoke. It was so sudden I fell to the ground, slamming into the dirt and stone.

[Health: 22/52]

I rushed to my feet, staring back. Two monsters chased Sandy, gnashing behind her. But a third sat in the distant tree line, staring. The river below it had grown brighter and brighter, blindingly bright to look at. The monster was still a hundred feet back, where we had found it. With a popping noise, the river went dim, and the monster stepped over it, rushing closer to us.

"Sandy!" I shouted, not looking at her. I heard her shout and fall only a few dozen feet past me.

I kept my eyes on the first monster.

"They're all illusions!" I said.

"Fuuuuck," Sandy said from somewhere behind me. One of the illusions must have remained, because I heard it roar over her. There was a swishing noise as she swung her cleaver and the sound cut off. I heard Sandy approach me.

The next river between us and the bear was growing brighter and brighter.

"They're like barriers. It can't cross running water quickly," I said, staring out at the bear.

"No shit," Sandy said. "You think we can get Gerald to make you a bow? We just..." Sandy mimed shooting an arrow at the monster. It roared again from across the glowing water.

Sandy and I both flinched as more ethereal copies of the monster charged us before exploding away into smoke.

"Light and shadow. Those were the elements of the floors above us."

"Shadow I get," Sandy said. "How do you know the other was light?"

"The spiders gave light resistance to…to this," I said, gesturing at my dress. The next river popped. There were only two between us and the monster now. "Let's come back with a better plan than stabbing that to death."

We jogged back to the wall, climbing the rope one at a time. The bear was still chasing…slowly. I started counting the seconds—it took half a minute for the bear to cross each river. It was set up like a raid, a game mechanic taking precedent over reality, the dungeon chopped into pieces like stages of a boss arena.

We stopped at the top of the arena, pulling up the rope and freeing my sewing needle. I'd left the other behind, somewhere down there in the dungeon. I would have to come back for it eventually.

"Shit," Sandy said as we stared down at the bear.

"All we have to do is kill it," I said, staring seriously and massaging my side. The system kept me alive, but I still felt tender. A single swing from that monster had sent me tumbling through the forest. Not only that, three rows of the dress's scales had been shattered, which would take more time and resources to repair.

We walked back through the floors of the dungeon. I rubbed my side the entire way, idly wondering how long the trek would take as the floors grew larger and deeper. We wouldn't be able to go deeper and continue to hide the fact that we were clearing the dungeon.

The way things were looking, everyone would know by Valjean's return, anyway.

I sunk to the floor of Sandy's workshop, trading out my outfit to place the scale dress on the stolen mannequin against her wall.

"That thing could kill us," I said. "What's your constitution at? We need to upgrade you." I side-eyed Sandy.

"Think I wouldn't last more than a hit. It did twenty-nine health damage? I wonder how much of that was you being scraped along the ground." Sandy bit her lip. She was looking over the parts from the copper mole we killed in the Wild the other day. "Need better weapons, too."

"So we start with the mining outfit. Get metal. Collect spider corpses. Once we can both take a hit without dying, we…what? How many stabs do you think it'll take to kill it?"

"Maybe we can do it with arrows," Sandy said.

I reached down to my belt, playing with a throwing needle idly.

"Or maybe we won't need a bow at all."

CHAPTER 29

Since my mom agreed to help, Sandy moved most of our finished supplies to our workshop. The location was more convenient for me now that I didn't have to avoid working around her. Not to mention the workshop was much, much bigger. We would have to repair more of the furniture to a usable state.

Now that we had a guest in our workshop for the first time since Valjean, Mom was making me clean it.

We wiped down every window, leaving the glass a spotless and shiny yellow-brown. I sighed, regretting I couldn't call out a set of clothes to make cleaning easier.

"Do you have a cleaning pattern to give us cleaning skills?" I asked my mom. She was wringing a wet towel out in a bucket.

"No." She snorted, then smiled. "There's enough people with cleaning classes around." We turned to look at Maritha.

She grunted as she cleaned off the mop in her hands, putting it to the floor and pressing forward. She was short and stocky, but her arms bulged with muscles revealed by rolled-up sleeves.

She mushed forward and swiped the floor like a soldier charging into a battle against dirt, though she only made it a few steps before stopping. Even so, she was still faster than us. Four identical clean spots appeared every time she swiped the mop across the floor, letting her clean the entire width of the room at once. The floor shined after just a moment. In exchange, the mop accumulated five times the dirt, staining it black. Maritha frowned at it.

Water dripped from the pile of furniture along the wall.

"You really ought to clean this place more," Maritha said.

"We don't get guests very often," Mom replied, gesturing with her arms.

"No excuse for cobwebs on the ceiling!"

"Well…my daughter hasn't been keeping up with her chore list." Mom swiveled and frowned at me.

"Don't put the blame on me!" I replied, grabbing my own bucket to clean the next window. "We haven't cleaned the place in years."

"I didn't think we'd be keeping it," Mom replied. "We would've moved out… god, this month, if…"

"What's going on with that?" Maritha asked. "Sandy clearing the dungeon again? She's going at it faster than before. You helping? I thought you stopped making fightin' sets."

"Fighting sets?" I asked, turning to Mom.

"Oh, nothing I make anymore. Not like I used to." Mom grinned evilly. "But I seem to have passed down my enormous talent. The curse of greatness falls firmly to my daughter. This town doesn't have anything that could match one of my patterns."

"Where did you work before?" I asked my mom. After diving deeper into crafting myself, I started to realize that parts of the story she gave me through childhood didn't add up. It seemed obvious in hindsight that she couldn't have always lived in this village.

Mom opened her mouth, then paused.

"Glittering City," Mari answered before Mom could.

"Glittering City?" I asked. "You lived in one of the capitals?"

Mari only grunted, sloshing her broom back into the bucket before continuing up the room. Water slid forward all around her, sweeping the floor clean before mostly disappearing, leaving behind only a wet sheen.

"One of the academies is there, right?" I asked, turning to my mom. "How far away is it?"

"A few days by wagon," Mom said. "Wasn't like I worked in the academies, though. Just a sewing shop. Whole teams work together for every single outfit there, combining all our skills to raise the quality level of each piece."

Mom smiled at memories of a long-gone past. Then our conversation was interrupted by a pounding knock at the door. I took one last look at her, and then she nodded, and I rushed to throw the door open.

Sandy scrunched her nose.

"Smells like lemon in here."

"Yeah," I said, turning back. "That's Maritha's skill."

"Better than how it usually smells, I guess."

"Hey! It's not that bad…" Sandy pushed past me, carrying a cart covered in leathers wrapped in paper.

"Those look like normal clothes." Maritha stared at Sandy over her mop, leaning on it as she stood up. She was shorter than Sandy—almost as short as I was, but she still managed to look intimidating.

"What?" Sandy asked, visibly confused.

"Did you make those?" Maritha asked me. Then she continued sweeping the floor, reaching the door and sending water cascading over both mine and Sandy's boots. It quickly retreated away.

Sandy sent a confused look at me.

"Um…" I said, turning back and closing the door. "Maritha knows, too."

"Does everyone know?" Sandy asked, looking between me and my mom.

"Probably," Mom said, shrugging and smiling consolingly. "Would you girls help me pull out some more furniture?"

Sandy sighed, but we got to work dragging out a few more tables from the walls. The pile threatened to fall as we pulled out individual pieces, searching for one or two that were usable enough. Finally, we pulled down a table that only suffered from a bent leg, resting uneven on the ground.

It scraped loudly across the tile as Sandy dragged it. Mom was already looking into the work cart Sandy had brought.

"Hmmm. Is this all you have?" she asked.

"The good stuff is on the bottom," Sandy said, pulling out a chair and wiping her hand along it. A layer of dust covered her hand. She turned to Maritha. "Could you…?"

Maritha pushed her mop in Sandy's direction, sending water flowing over the chair before dripping to the ground in thick, dirty rivulets that raced back up to the mop. Then she continued cleaning.

Sandy wasn't spared by Maritha's aim, a glob of water having hit her forehead and plastered her hair. She pushed the hair back out of her eyes.

"I'm going to smell like lemon for a week," Sandy said.

"Only lasts seventy-two hours," Maritha replied.

"Thanks again for helping, Mari," Mom said.

"It's not free," Maritha said. She turned to Sandy. "From you…I want more of what your dad made last week. And you…make me a magical outfit that makes my joints feel better." She pointed the last bit at me.

"I…don't have anything like that."

"Well. Figure it out or I'll sell you out to Henri," Maritha said before continuing to clean.

Mom laughed.

"Henri already knows," Sandy said.

"You don't say. Can't hide anything from your parents," Maritha replied, almost done sweeping the room.

I laughed nervously. "Could I come talk to Henri soon?" Mom asked.

"Yeah," Sandy replied, frowning. "He's…in the town hall doing paperwork."

Oh shit. Henri knows that Sandy and I are both clearing the dungeon. I sent a panicked look at Sandy.

She raised her eyebrows at me.

"What is this?" Mom asked, having piled the goods out of the cart. She pulled free layers of the metallic armor from the copper mole. "I didn't think the local dungeon had anything like this," she said, frowning.

"I found it outside. In the Wild," Sandy said.

"Is this why you need a mining outfit? The mine south of town?" Mom said, still looking at it. "But you…your class doesn't work with metal, does it? You know what, no. I don't want to know." She waved her hands over it.

"What do you think?" Sandy asked.

Mom looked closer at each of the materials, appraising them. An uncomfortable feeling settled in my gut, a strange nervousness as she closely inspected each piece. Then she grabbed a piece of wolf leather and pulled it out.

"This will do fine," she said. "Gwen, grab the thread…the red one. Seventh shelf." I rushed to comply, opening a well-kept cabinet full of supplies and pulling out spools of fire-red, wire-like thread.

Mom pulled out a pair of scissors seemingly from nowhere, held up the sheet of processed wolf leather, and sliced forward. A few perfect pattern pieces dropped to the table, and she held the remainder. I watched more closely as her scissors easily parted hardened leather, wondering what skills she had that did that.

Mom nodded at her work, staring down before cutting a dozen more pieces in quick succession, leaving them piled on the table.

"Do you still remember the stitches, honey?" she asked, looking back to me. I nodded. "Do you want to work on those while I go talk to Henri?"

That nervousness in my gut got worse.

"I'll go with you." I said.

We walked with Mom to town hall—a luxurious use of our limited space here. Maritha stayed behind to rest after helping clean the workshop.

Mom hummed to herself as she walked.

Sandy and I exchanged terrified glances with each other behind her back, she gesturing between my mom and me with increasing urgency. I didn't know what she meant to signal, but I knew her concern: Henri knew both Sandy and I were clearing the dungeon.

I was still afraid to tell Mom that I was as well. Telling her I wasn't Chosen was bad enough; I couldn't imagine telling her I was clearing the dungeon in secret.

Mom sent a glance back to Sandy.

"You'll have to show me what you've been making soon," she said.

"Oh yeah. Gwen makes all kinds of outfits. Ones that turn us invisible, or grant super strength."

Mom nodded, not commenting further. I elbowed Sandy, gesturing with my eyes, but she shrugged.

We made it to town hall. Mom stopped outside, turning and leveling an eye at us.

"Wait out here, girls," she said.

"Uh—" Sandy started, then stopped. "Okay."

She folded her arms and turned. Mom pushed the door open.

Henri looked up, a rolled cigarette dangling from his mouth. He was pouring over papers spread out in front of him. His eyes jumped to me first, then to Sandy, then to my mom. They grew panicked.

"Henri!" Mom said, her voice cheerful. "Let's talk!"

The door closed and cut off our view.

"You said I made *us* outfits!" I hissed at Sandy. "We should've gone in with her."

"It would've been even more suspicious if we tried to stop her from talking to him alone," Sandy whispered back, looking around and rubbing her arms. The chill of late autumn was starting to set in.

"Do you think he'll tell her?"

"He's not a snitch." Sandy said this last part proudly. "He will support us."

The confidence in her voice flagged at the end.

"What do we do now?" I asked, staring helplessly at the door.

"Finish the mining outfit?" Sandy said.

I rubbed my face.

"She's got to be asking about that, too. That means she knows Gerald is involved. If she…"

I trailed off as I looked behind Sandy.

Marielle strode through town, hands folded gently, walking right toward us. She was practically glaring at Sandy, though her expression softened when she looked at me.

"Girls!" she said.

Gerald looked like a kicked puppy behind her. His only met mine for a second before returning to the ground.

We waved and nodded.

"Is Henri inside?" she asked Sandy. Marielle and Sandy were about the same height. I could feel the electricity exchanged in a single glance.

"He is," Sandy said after a moment.

Marielle nodded, opening the door.

"Why don't you join us?" Marielle asked Sandy. "Since this involves you."

Henri was gesturing wildly on the other side, standing on his side of the table and whispering in an increasingly loud hiss. Mom hadn't sat down. She stared down at Henri across the table, arms folded. Then her eyes locked onto mine.

My heart sank.

She pursed her lips.

I followed Gerald inside. I didn't know how much Henri had told my mom—they had clearly been fighting.

"Henri."

"Mari," he said. His mouth was half-cocked in a smile, but his eyes were tired.

"I'm glad you're here. I wanted to talk," Mari said, looking over her shoulder at Sandy, "about your daughter."

"Mom…" Gerald said.

She just raised a hand to quiet him.

"What about her?" Henri asked.

"About her clearing the dungeon. You're one of the only people with sense in this town. It's time for us to leave." She turned and looked at me. "Now that Gwen isn't—now that we know she's taking after her mother, there's no reason for you to vote for us to stay."

The last part was directed at my mom.

"If my daughter wants to stay in this town, I will stay in this town," my mom said. It was that simple to her.

"Ridiculous. That attitude is bad for all of us," Mari said. "And it's exactly why I'm going to tell Valjean that Sandy has been clearing the dungeon."

"Mom!" Gerald said, but he took a step back.

"Do you have any proof?" Sandy asked nonchalantly.

"We will when he puts you under house arrest and the town continues collapsing," she said, staring down Sandy.

"Sandy's not—stop it," Gerald said. He looked between me and my mom, his face covered in panic and duress.

Henri looked like he was holding back a laugh.

"Of course she is, Gerald. You need to learn not to be so naive. How much can you hang out with these people and not realize?" she asked, waving at Sandy.

"I'm the one clearing the dungeon," he said.

"What?" she asked. "No. You're not."

Henri smiled wider. My mom looked at me, bewildered.

Gerald summoned his shield out of his inventory. It was twice as wide as he was and it slammed into the floor with a crack, shattering a floorboard.

"Gerald..." she said, her voice dangerous as she walked across the room and grabbed the edge of the shield. "You're not a Noble."

Gerald recalled his shield to his inventory.

"I am!" he said. "I'm the one clearing the dungeon. I'm the person killing the monsters. So if you want to tell Valjean someone is clearing the dungeon, you'll have to tell him its me."

Armor grew up his legs as he summoned it out of his inventory. Gerald frowned, upset, and then the leg armor flashed, and he disappeared.

"Well, there you have it," Henri said, blowing smoke. "I'll tell Valjean for you if you'd like."

"No," Mari said, even as she stared at where Gerald had been. She shook her head. "He's not a Noble. He's a crafter. Even if he thinks he is a... No. He can't be."

Her mouth parted slightly, then closed. She side-eyed Henri. Mom looked bewildered.

"Did you know?" she asked me.

"Yes. That's why we need the mining set."

"There's nothing to know. Ignore Gerald. I will talk to him. I...see your point, Henri," Mari said. "None of us need to make haste to talk to Valjean."

Then Mari walked out.

When the door closed behind her, Henri spoke.

"So," he said. "Esme says I should be doing more to support you three."

"Henri is doing plenty!" I said to my mom, trying to end this conversation as soon as possible before suspicions turned to me.

"No, no. She's right," Henri said, ashing his cigarette. "Starting tonight, I can do a bit more for you."

"You're clearing the dungeon tonight?" my mom asked, blinking.

"I clear the dungeon every night," Sandy replied.

CHAPTER 30

Sandy and Gerald stepped into the dungeon ahead of me. With one last look around the darkened town, I followed behind. Gerald froze only a few feet through the gate, holding his shield. I nearly crashed into him as reality twisted around me and I reached the other side.

"Alright," Gerald said. "I'll stay here. You guys go in."

"What if someone takes one step through the gate and crashes into you?" Sandy gestured.

"It's safe Gerald. Just stay behind us," I said, stepping past him. I eyed his armor incredulously. "Nothing is getting through…that."

Gerald stared for a moment, matching my gaze through glowing blue sockets in his armor.

"Alright," he said finally. "No baiting any giant monsters with me this time. Sandy."

"No promises," she replied.

The walk to the Dungeonheart felt slower than ever with Gerald here. He stood on my right, and Sandy on my left. She pointedly avoided looking at him.

Gerald walked slowly, scanning the land around him. The wheat was slowly being cut down, leaving the fields half-worked. Farming skills enabled a single farmer to manage acres and acres of land, and the accelerated time and permanently temperate climate meant that this village could produce literal tons of food very quickly to ship throughout Valjean's domain.

"There's no monsters out here," Sandy said after Gerald stopped for the fifth time. "They're all in the cave. Hurry up."

"You're the one who dragged me out here," Gerald complained.

"You told your parents you were the one clearing the dungeon!" Sandy said. "Do you think they're not going to check now?"

She walked ahead of us. I shrugged. She could take care of the wolves herself. Though Gerald moved with less pauses after that.

He froze at the entrance to the cave, his eyes glowing brighter to see in the dark.

There was a cut-off whimper and the sound of flesh separating that caused Gerald to raise his shield, practically blocking off the entire entrance. He peered around the side, looking at Sandy. She looked unamused.

The next two wolves fell methodically, none coming close to Gerald.

"Alright, through the portal," Sandy said.

"Sandy!" I said, stopping Gerald in his tracks.

"It wouldn't have hurt him. Think they can bite through metal?" Sandy asked, rolling her eyes and stepping forward. The last wolf jumped out of stealth and she cut it down, causing Gerald to step backward.

I shot him an apologetic look.

"There are six spiders on the next floor. Stay way behind us."

We carved through the spiders with ease, cutting them down left and right. It felt as simple as killing with skills had.

Gerald paused nervously over one of the spider's corpses. He leaned down and poked at it.

"I can't believe you guys have been doing this by yourselves all this time. What are your stats?" Sandy scoffed. "I was doing it alone for a while. No fancy magic armor or cleaver, either."

"That…sounds like a good way to get killed," Gerald said.

Sandy frowned.

"Almost did," she replied after a moment. There was a long pause between them.

"Sorry," Gerald said.

"Yeah. Whatever. Just…help out." She raised her hands to stall me. "You don't have to fight. I get it. Most people wouldn't want to."

Gerald looked away.

"What now?" he asked.

"The third floor," I replied. "And the boss."

We crossed the dawn-lit forest to the next floor, stepping onto the third floor. The view was no less stunning than before.

Around us a barren wasteland stretched into infinity, the boss arena below.

"Did you bring the stake?" I asked Gerald.

He nodded, stepping to the edge nervously before pulling a solid metal rod out and slamming it into the ground with ease.

I couldn't leave my other sewing needle behind, and my first was down there somewhere, hidden in the forest. Luckily, there was hardly any foliage, unlike the second floor. Less lucky was that the floor was illuminated only by moonlight.

I tied the rope to the stake and threw it over the edge.

"You'll have to stay up here," I told him.

Gerald looked around, swiveling his metal-covered head.

"Alone?" he asked.

"We're both going down," Sandy said. "So yeah. Alone. Unless you want to fight the giant monster with us?"

As she replied, she squinted at the edge, trying to see the monster below.

I walked to the edge and joined her looking over. I didn't see the monster anywhere.

"It starts out invisible," I said, thinking aloud. "Once it attacks, it loses its stealth."

"Just like us," Sandy said.

"How many hits to take it down, you think?"

Sandy shrugged.

"Two needles to the face killed the mole."

"How much damage did you do to the mole?" I turned and asked Gerald.

"What? Oh, uh. A lot."

"Three needles to the face," Sandy said.

"Don't know I can reach it," I replied. "We also have to not let it hit us."

Sandy nodded.

"It can only cross the rivers one at a time, right? So that's handled."

I checked everything I carried.

The rope tied to my sewing needle had been replaced by a braided spiderweb rope. I called it a rope, but it wasn't nearly as large as the other ones we used; it was more like a piece of yarn. Long, long strings wrapped around the throwing needles.

And my scale dress was still functional.

Sandy grabbed the rope and looked at me. I nodded and she started to descend, kicking down off the cliff face.

I followed once she touched down at the bottom. With another nod from me, Sandy entered stealth, disappearing into the forest.

Between the two of us, it was easier for me to survive a hit. At least until I got her scale dress completed. Once the boss revealed itself, Sandy would attack it. In theory.

My heart raced as I trailed deeper and deeper into the dungeon. I knew Sandy was next to me, but my eyes told me she wasn't. My logical brain could track the truth, but it didn't stop the animal part of me from screaming at me to run.

My predominant memory of this forest was being thrown across my mind. The monster hit like a truck.

We went deeper and deeper into the forest until we found the snoring monster. From far away you could mistake its mottled colors as fallen foliage.

"Over there," Sandy whispered, tapping my shoulder to try to direct me.

She must have been using her butcher skill, because I couldn't see anything.

"Where?"

"A few feet to the left of the sleeping one," Sandy whispered.

I lifted a needle and threw it. There was no skill involved; just strength and practice. As I threw, I mentally tugged at the string with [Thread Mastery].

The wire-like string unraveled as it flew. Then, with a thunk, it landed in a tree. The needle missed.

But the string fell like a net, hanging in midair and just barely highlighting an invisible shape.

The next needle didn't miss, landing in the thing's chest with a noise that was similar to that of the tree. It leapt out of invisibility and swung toward me, claws scraping against an invisible barrier that held it back across the river.

I stumbled back anyway, the sheer size of the monster and suddenness of its appearance catching me off guard.

Sandy appeared behind the monster, her stealth falling away as she activated a skill that gave her preternatural accuracy at cutting apart a monster. Red light flared around the monster's leg where she swung, her sword bending through the air to cut apart the flesh of the monster.

It screamed and staggered forward just in time for Sandy to reactivate stealth.

Copies of the monster appeared around it, ephemeral clones charging across the clearing. One of them exploded to dust on something invisible—Sandy's stealthed form. Her stealth dissipated, and the monster charged toward her.

My eyes widened.

I threw forward two more needles, this time aiming for the monster's leg. One I tugged at with [Thread Mastery], tying the thread around it and pulling. Blood poured instantly, but the monster's hardened muscle stopped it.

The other landed in its thigh. I grabbed the rope and pulled.

It was a stupid decision that sent me splashing into the water.

I gasped and spat fresh water, recalling the needles.

There was a tearing noise before the monster stumbled to the ground. Then the needles shot back into my hand.

What was *that*? A quick look told me: the returning needle had tightened the thread against the monster's leg, causing it to trip.

"Gwen?" Gerald asked behind me. "Are you guys okay?"

The monster turned on me.

"I thought you were staying on the cliff!" I shouted as I threw myself out of the water and scrambled toward Gerald.

"Oh—oh shit!" he said, summoning his shield. "I said no baiting giant monsters at me!"

He was shouting, but the monster was stuck on the other side of the river. I recalled the needles again, stuffing them into my belt.

"Run, idiot!" Sandy yelled as she reappeared on the other side of the river, this time going for a leg. The monster stumbled down again as she cut at its leg, our stacked wounds growing deeper.

Then the monster shifted. It was subtle, but the entire floor shifted. More illusions of it appeared, all roaring simultaneously. I blinked, and the first monster was gone.

"Oh fuck," Sandy said. Then she ran, jumping over another river. The rivers around the monster all glowed at once, delineating an arena he couldn't escape—at least not quickly.

"Gerald!" I said. "Run!"

He recalled his shield and ran with me, jumping over the next river. The copies of the bear spread out. Sandy was nowhere to be seen, having reactivated stealth and disappeared into the forest.

"What's going on?" Gerald asked, looking over the forest.

"I don't know! It turned invisible," I said.

"It made copies of itself!"

"They're just illusions!" I said. Then I followed up, "I hope. They were just illusions before. But it could've switched places with one while invisible. That means we have to treat them like they're all real..."

I started throwing needles, popping the monsters like balloons and causing them to drift away into smoke. They reformed a few seconds later.

Out of paranoia, I threw another needle into one of the freshly reformed bears.

It landed it its chest. The monster roared.

All the illusions grew the same wound.

"Sandy!" I shouted. "SANDY!"

"Here," she said, panting.

"I've got a needle in the real one's chest," I said.

Then, as if to spite me, the same needle slowly grew out of each of the illusions.

"Nope," Sandy said. "We need a new plan." "Run," I said.

Halfway back, I almost tripped on my lost sewing needle. I scooped it up and then ran to catch up. The bears spread out around us, a wall of semi-corporeal monster flesh chasing us to the boundary of the forest.

Sandy threw herself at the rope, climbing.

Gerald dug his fingers into the cliff and climbed at her side. The sight made me stop for just a breath before I grabbed the rope and climbed myself.

The monster roared angrily below us, still fifty feet away but catching up. The illusions of it spread out to light up the rivers around us, a wall closing us in. If we were still stuck down there, we would have to guess which one was real and try to avoid it, or risk being pinned to a wall.

Sandy pulled the rope up while I recalled the thrown needle. The monster roared as it tore out of its chest.

Then Sandy lay on the ground, staring down.

"Aw fuck. How low do you think we got it?"

"Dunno."

"It's about half," Gerald said. "Another fifty health points or so."

"Wait, you can see that?" Sandy asked.

"Yeah." Gerald said. "Can't you?"

"No!" she replied. "I thought you were too afraid of monsters to come down."

"Well…" Gerald said. "I was leaning over and I fell. Then I heard the fight start and ran to you."

"You…fell?" I asked, leaning over the edge of the cliff. Sure enough, there was an impression of Gerald's silhouette stamped into the ground. I turned to him. "Are you okay? Are both of you guys okay?"

"Huh? Oh yeah, I'm fine. Physically. I'll never be able to look at a bear the same again, though," Gerald said, staring down below.

"How did you fall?" Sandy asked.

"I was worried!" Gerald said.

I sighed.

"Maybe it'll be easier tomorrow. We have to see what your dad has planned." Sandy grunted an affirmative.

"Got anything to dispel invisibility?" Sandy asked Gerald.

He shook his head.

"Don't have the metal to make anything."

"We will after tomorrow," I replied. "Let's go."

"Gwen?" Gerald asked.

"Yeah?"

"Can I crash in your workshop?"

I blinked at that. I supposed it made enough sense if he was trying to avoid his parents.

"We don't have a bed in it."

"That's fine." He said.

I turned to Sandy, who just shrugged at me. Then we snuck out of the dungeon. Going from the near dark of the third floor to the now midday sun of the second stung my eyes. I dipped back into the dark.

"Does it always take you this long?" Gerald asked. "You might get stuck like this."

"Got stuck before," I said with a shrug. We split up with Sandy at the exit to the dungeon and looped around town to my workshop. We paused outside.

The light was still on.

"Wait here," I said. "I'll go check who's in there."

I crept up to the door, pushing it open slowly. My mom's eyes jumped to me instantly.

"Gwen!" she said.

She was sitting at a table. More of the furniture had been pulled from the wall, some of it now mid-repair. Tea steamed in front of her.

Behind her, a mannequin was covered in a finished miner outfit.

She followed my gaze to it, then smiled.

"That's for Gerald," she said nonchalantly before returning to stitching something else together.

"Oh yeah, speaking of, uh," I started.

"You called?" Gerald asked. Mom's eyes widened a little. I resisted the urge to slap my own face.

"I didn't," I said.

"Oh," he replied, staring awkwardly.

"He was wondering if he could sleep here in the workshop for a…night or two," I said.

Mom smiled.

"Sure, dear. I'll get you a blanket…though we don't have a soft pillow to spare."

Gerald slunk into a chair near the mining outfit and reached out to touch it. He smiled madly at it.

After staying to chat for a bit, I left Mom and Gerald behind in the workshop and headed to bed. We had a busy day tomorrow.

The breakfast conversation was awkward.

"Pass the salt," Maritha said.

Terry nodded, sliding it over. Her eyes glanced toward Gerald and away from him.

I eyed this morning's meat with suspicion. It was definitely some kind of monster meat—a lesser gift from Henri that had been saved for a few days.

"So," Maritha said. "When are you going to the Academy?"

"Mari!" Mom said, pushing her shoulder, but all three of them stared Gerald down like hawks.

Gerald choked on his food, stopping for a second to clear his throat.

"I'm…not," he said. The table erupted, each of them asking a different question simultaneously. Gerald flinched back, an armored gauntlet appearing on his hand for a second before he dismissed it. That reflex was going to get him in trouble.

The conversation went quiet at it.

"Excuse me," he said, stepping back from the chair and walking out of the house.

Maritha ever so slowly grabbed his plate and scraped it onto her own before continuing to eat as if nothing had happened.

"Is he not coming back?" Terry asked.

I shook my head no, feeling my face flush.

Then I continued eating breakfast. I needed the energy for later.

"How long till Valjean finds out?" Maritha asked.

"Oh, next time he's here, maybe days, maybe weeks," Terry replied.

"I'll run a bet on it."

"Mari!" Mom admonished her.

"Do you think he'd pose for a portrait?" Terry asked.

I shrugged noncommittally and dumped my plate.

"Ask him for me!" Terry said.

"Tell him to bring a pillow if he's going to sleep in the workshop to-night," Mom said.

"And to take a bath," Mari joined in.

I ran out of the house and into the workshop, finding the miner suit mannequin already empty. Where was Gerald?

Probably at Sandy's if he didn't want to go home. With a sigh, I started heading that way. We had some more metal to mine.

CHAPTER 31

The next day we ate breakfast without Mom. I didn't find her in her room either. Mari and Terry gossiped about the news in town, about who knew Sandy was clearing the dungeon and who they thought didn't. They had restrained themselves before.

I found Mom in the workshop after.

"Gwen!" she said, excited, turning to face me.

Behind her, one of the wooden mannequins was covered in a half-finished suit of armor. I bit my lip. She had used the copper mole leather. But she could probably make better use of it than I could. She looked happy; proud, even, putting her hands on her hips and standing beside it. Mom also looked very tired.

"How long have you been out here?"

"Since a while before sunrise," she said, turning to face the armor. "I'd be finished already, but I figured I'd wait for you so you can get contribution points."

It was less an outfit than actual plated armor, sections of the leather embossed with symbols of lightning. It was also separated into more than five pieces; it was one of the largest sets I had ever seen, something that would befit a knight.

The arms and gloves hung in midair; presumably from one of Mom's skills. Tiny metal plates covered leather gloves for each finger, while metal gauntlets covered the forearms and reached back to actual pauldrons. The armor stretched from the chest to the feet; it would cover almost every inch of whoever wore it.

"This looks like something a blacksmith would make," I said, walking up and sliding my fingers down the side of it. It was cold to the touch. Still, despite the amount of material that had been used to create it, there should have been more left over. "Where's the rest of it?"

"The line between blacksmith and tailor isn't so wide. You need both for some things." Mom shrugged. "The half-finished helmet is over there." She gestured to a workstation where lamellar plates of the copper-like leather were stacked.

"No, I mean the rest of the monster. There should be some left over, no?" I asked. The wagon that had carried it over was completely empty of the leather goods that Sandy brought. Instead, there was a mining outfit there under a few pieces of paper and leather.

"Oh," Mom said, thumbing her chin. "Some patterns call for…more resources than are visible. This is a much higher level design than you've seen. Something I hadn't made in a long, long time."

"Something you used to make in the capital?"

Mom smiled and nodded.

I ran my hands along the inside, trying to study the design of the pattern. I could see seams in the leather Mom had cut through, threads that pierced into the armor and held it together, and I followed them with my fingers to where they just…disappeared. Not like they ended; like they were still taught and stabbed into something invisible, but my fingers didn't find any more armor there. It was like the material stretched into a direction I couldn't interact with. Tracing the patterns was giving me a headache; I let my hand fall away with a frown.

"I don't have to do that for the helmet?" I asked, turning the little plates over.

"That part is already done," she said. "I'll guide you through the rest."

I picked up one of the tiny plates. It was heavier than it should have been. The same erratic designs were embossed on its side.

"Is this Embellishment?" I asked.

"Yes!" Mom said. "After ten levels, you can use Embellishment to influence the pattern skills. I tried to redirect its electrical skill to a defensive skill. We won't know how it works until you finish it, though." Mom smiled.

"Where do I start?" I asked, pulling out a sewing needle from the desk.

"Start with putting that away," she said, folding her hands for a second before reaching into the box that carried her own supplies. Even into adulthood, she never let me touch her sewing supplies.

Now she was going to loan me a piece of her kit. My eyes widened a bit at the sight. Even the single potion the house kept was less guarded than this; though that made me belatedly wonder if she had let me take it on purpose.

Mom pulled out a tiny, pocket-sized sewing kit engraved with nearly invisible, glowing patterns in the metal. They were a shining silver. My eyes grew wider, mentally tallying the cost in gold of a single piece of enchanted metal, and the entire kit was probably more than our entire city made in a year.

"Enchanted?" It was the only thing that came to mind, escaping my mouth before anything else.

"And yours now." Mom smiled proudly.

"How can we afford this?" I asked.

"Oh, we can't. I stole a few before I left."

"You *stole* them? Don't they know? Hasn't anyone..." I trailed off seeing my mom's wry smile.

"They're valuable here, but for the workshop I worked at? Not so much."

I inspected the pattern we were working on again. When I was younger, I hadn't put together the pieces to appreciate the full scope of what my mom worked on. Valjean, a minor Noble, could tear down a forest with a single swing. What could the highest-level Nobles at the center of the continent do?

What could I do if I reached that level?

"Aren't you going to ask what they do?" Mom asked. "No, you're probably too excited to get started! They're enchanted with Edge, of course, for sharpness...and Safety, to prevent them from harming their user. Especially since that needle will cut almost anything. Don't drop it."

Her face became serious at that last part.

"Have you dropped these before?"

She nodded grimly. "Straight through a floor."

"They're enchanted not to harm people, though?" I asked, appraising them again. They were in a tiny, leather case. Now that I looked at it, I could see that it was enchanted, too.

"They're enchanted not to harm their *user*," she said.

I grimaced.

"No one was hurt or anything," Mom said, then stepped over next to me at the workstation. "Now..." She leaned in, and I saw her [Pattern Projection] skill activate, highlighting and animating exactly what I had to sew. That must have been a higher-level version of the skill.

I stabbed the needle in, feeling it part the metal-like material as if it were made of butter, then I stopped.

"Is there any way to see how a skill will change at level ten?" I asked.

Mom shook her head.

"The variations and evolutions of every skill's level are only really fully known by the craft guilds. And the guilds can only exist in the capitals. Out here...there isn't enough material to reach high level. Also, you poked a hole in the table."

Oops.

Mom walked me through the rest of it, slowly bringing the helmet all the way together. It was made of layers of plates with gaps for the eyes, hanging down loosely from where the top of the helmet covered the head, dipping low enough to cover the neck. The pieces fit together perfectly.

A couple times, I stretched the hole too wide, but Mom was able to repair the leather without reducing the quality.

I lifted the helmet up, the loose pieces jangling. This was going to mess Sandy's hair up so bad.

"Should I put the sewing kit back?" I asked, looking over.

"No." Mom shook her head. "You keep hold of it. But if you get any more exciting materials, you'd better show me before you use them." Her eyes were nearly manic now, lit up as she lifted the helmet and added it to the armor.

[+10 XP] [Level up]

[Storm Curtain Helmet (Rare, Lightning) completed!]

[Quality Assessment: (Good)]

"Perfect," Mom said behind me, absolutely beaming at the set of armor she had created.

"What skill did it get?" I asked, squinting at it. It wasn't my outfit; I didn't get an interface for it.

"A Noble skill," Mom said. "Parry. Help me throw it in the cart."

We pulled off the pieces and threw them into the cart before covering it with a layer of cloth. I had to take the cart to Sandy's and then head into the Wild. But first, I had to pick a new skill.

[Skill Shop]

▶Thread Reinforcement I

[COMMON] Grants user the ability to reinforce common threads with mana.

▶Mending I

[COMMON] Allows user to repair clothing from patterns they are unfamiliar with. Additional levels increase quality of final product.

▶Always Prepared I

[EPIC] Seamstress Inventory skill. Grants users access to a small, extra-dimensional tool chest. Additional levels allow additional storage.

Thread Reinforcement would allow me to create stronger threads from what I had available...which was currently super-reinforced spiderweb thread. I mentally filed it away, though, betting that evolving it to level ten would give at least a point of Thread Mastery.

Mending would let me repair patterns other people made. But now that my mom was in on the game—or at least part of it—she could repair her own outfits. She would probably love to do so, judging by her enthusiasm for making an actual, terrifying murder-dress for Sandy.

And Always Prepared was epic rarity.

I grabbed the skill, then looked around my skill sheet to figure out what to assign the last skill point to. I needed to test Always Prepared first. What would upgrading the skill do, exactly? It mentioned creating a tool chest. With a simple mental command, I reached out to it.

A finely lacquered chest of dark wood popped into existence an inch above the table before clattering down into it. It looked…almost exactly like Mom's accordion-fold chest.

It was probably only a little more than a foot across, and I quickly pulled it open.

"What is that?" Mom asked, shock evident in her voice. She turned from the cart and quickly stepped up to me.

The box folded open into dozens of smaller compartments fit for tools to punch leather or spots to place reels of thread. There were also two much longer compartments that stretched from one side to the other, almost fit for two giant sewing needles, and an open bottom compartment. Like it was sizing them just for what I needed. If I leveled the skill more, I'd probably be able to fit them.

"Always Prepared," I replied. "A new inventory skill?"

"You got a—a *new* inventory skill? You already have Wardrobe?"

"Yeah," I said, staring down at the box. "I've made a few outfits for the dungeon clearing."

Mom nodded politely, as if what I said made sense. She also stared intently into it.

"What can you store in it?" she asked.

"It says tools, but…" It was big enough to fit more than that.

Mom threw me a spool of thread without comment.

I set it inside and dismissed the storage. The wooden chest disappeared. I half expected the spool of thread to fall through where the chest was and clatter against the table, but it disappeared as well.

I looked up at mom, who nodded, then I brought the chest back. The thread was still sitting inside.

"So it can fit more than tools," she said, then reached back to her table, where she had a mostly empty cup of tea. She raised an eyebrow.

"There's no way it stores just anything," I said, grabbing the cup and carefully lowering it into the box before dismissing and recalling it. Again, I expected the liquid to just freely splash out, if not the cup as well. To my surprise, the tea and its cup was stored and recalled perfectly.

"Guess you got a really expensive lunchbox, Mom replied.

I laughed. It was a really expensive lunchbox; if only my Mom knew how much work it really took to get this skill.

"I wonder how far I can recall it from."

"It would be a good thing to find out," Mom shrugged. "Maybe you can store it in the cold until you need it." We said our goodbyes as she headed upstairs and I left for Sandy's, pushing the cart with the outfits on the bottom. I left the box behind on the table, intending to experiment with exactly how far I could recall it from.

I spent the second skill point upgrading my Wardrobe skill. Every day, more and more people became involved. Which meant more to hide. Mostly in the form of clothes.

Like this cart, for instance. Some people nodded and waved as I walked down the street. I gladly returned the smiles and nods, wondering what they thought I was up to. Their eyes lingered on it. I wondered if they thought it was full of monster corpses.

It was an easy thing to imagine, what with a butcher clearing the dungeon and working with a number of the town's most prolific crafters.

Also, it technically was a wagon full of dead monsters. They were just already processed.

Gerald was already waiting for me at Sandy's workshop. I was surprised to see she hadn't made him wait outside. She was still ignoring him and reading inside, but it was a massive improvement. She dog-eared the page and threw the book on her makeshift nightstand before kicking her legs off the bed and standing up.

"So?" Sandy asked.

"Mom went crazy making this," I said, pulling off the makeshift tarp atop the wagon and revealing the outfits and leftover material underneath. There was nothing left of the copper mole; there was plenty other leather left, though.

Sandy whistled as she lifted the storm curtain helmet.

"It's heavy," she said.

"Got the mining outfit, too." I turned to Gerald, who was looking dejected in the corner.

He sighed and pushed himself to his feet, leaning over the wagon to look down at the mining outfit before blinking tiredness out of his eyes.

"You okay?" I asked.

"He's been sulking all day," Sandy replied.

"Just tired," he said. Gerald rubbed at his eyes, pushing his bowl-cut long hair out of his face, before reaching down and grabbing a piece of the mining outfit. Then he stopped and looked around.

"You can change in there." Sandy pointed to the barricaded door that led to Henri's side of the house.

Gerald sighed, gathered the outfit, and stepped through. That involved pushing aside the stack of furniture. It clattered to the floor.

"Is he doing okay?" I asked Sandy almost conspiratorially.

"He went home to his parents' last night, remember? Probably fought. Or maybe he slept out on the street," Sandy replied, looking thoughtfully at the door before turning back to me.

I bit my lip and nodded. There wasn't anything I could really do for Gerald. Letting him sleep in our workroom wasn't a long-term solution, and I couldn't resolve his family trauma for him.

"Should I change, too?" Sandy asked, holding up the storm curtain helmet between us. She was already wearing the stealth hunting outfit.

"On the one hand…half the town knows." I said. "On the other…"

"It's a secret everyone else is pretending to keep," Sandy said. "I normally play along with those." She threw the helmet back onto the cart and pulled the cloth over it.

"I'm leveling wardrobe to be able to carry the outfit for you. We need it to kill the boss, not to go mining," I said, and she nodded, looking contemplatively at the armor.

"I wonder what it does," she said.

Gerald stepped back into the workshop after a short time wearing the mining outfit. It looked like what a regular miner would wear, except that the coveralls were made of thick, black wolf fur. Almost every part of it was, save the layers underneath. Even the boiled leather helmet was covered in fur.

Sandy laughed.

"What skills does it have?" I asked. Gerald frowned as he opened his system, his eyes tracing back and forth to read something I couldn't see.

"Shadow Cloak," he replied.

"Then…we're good to go?" I asked.

Gerald nodded, then turned invisible. Sandy followed, disappearing.

"Hey guys, if we're all invisible, how are we going to know if we're together?" I groaned.

"We could make bird noises at each other," Sandy said, her voice coming from the direction of the door as it swung open.

"I'll just…stay visible." I said, walking out the door.

It shut behind me.

CHAPTER 32

I felt like I was talking to imaginary friends as I walked through the woods with Gerald and Sandy both invisible. I could hear their footsteps breaking branches and crunching through foliage as we walked.

"You guys really don't have to be invisible for this," I said.

"You could've joined us!" Sandy said.

I groaned.

"Gerald would've gotten lost."

"No I wouldn't," he replied, sullen and not at all in the mood for joking.

We came onto the clearing in no time, rushing through the Wild and the ever-present vague discomfort I felt at it.

"Will you guys go check for monsters?" Gerald asked.

"Sure," Sandy said. There was a rush of dust as she slid into the clearing. The furnaces of the crystal golems had all but melted away into the ground, nothing more than a few lumps remained to show that the terrain had changed. Even monsters weren't spared from the Wild's constant degradation.

I slid down the hill next, needle in hand, though the clearing was dead and silent. It was extremely eerie, especially with my friends both invisible. My eyes scanned the tree line, but I saw nothing but small animals and waving leaves.

"All clear!" Sandy shouted.

I flinched back.

Then she grunted, and the entire suit of armor fell out of her hands and onto the ground.

"I thought we agreed not to bring that!" I said.

"Yeah, well, walking out of town wearing it would be stupid," Sandy said. "So I just carried it. It must weigh, like, forty pounds by the way. Where is it even hiding all that? Your mom must have used everything I saved."

I rubbed my temples.

"Come on. You can't wait to see what it does either, right? What skill does it give? Have you checked yet?" Sandy asked.

"No. Mom said it gave a Noble skill but she didn't say what."

"And you didn't immediately check? You're nuts. I'm putting this on."

"Guess we'll get mining then?" I asked Gerald, looking in the general direction I last heard his voice.

He popped into existence with a frown, a pickaxe now in his hands. Then he slowly disappeared again. I wasn't sure if he reactivated [Shadow Cloak] or if summoning the pickaxe didn't cancel it; bringing stuff out of my own inventory didn't cancel my stealth, even with [Quick Change].

I lit another oil lamp before heading toward the cave, trusting Gerald to follow me. Light caught on the edges of metal veins, practically glittering in the dark. As the outside world and sunlight fell away, it was replaced by the burning orange of the lamp.

"Here is fine," Gerald said, stopping me only a few dozen feet in. He appeared visible next to me, walking farther into the cave before summoning his shield. It stuck into the earth and walls, blocking the passage off almost entirely.

Gerald sucked in a breath. Then he swung.

At that moment, I was harshly reminded of the difference between Nobility and regular people. They gained stats every level, not just from equipment. I hadn't seen Gerald fight. Not properly. He had shields, not weapons.

But that pickaxe shattered the wall, stone crumbling away in a small avalanche. The pickaxe sunk deeper into the stone, stuck inside. Gerald grunted.

The mining outfit's skills must surely have been what made the ore separate itself from the falling stone. Rubble rose to his shins, still tumbling downward, and I stepped back. The shield flickered with its enchantments as stone bumped against it, filling the tunnel.

Gerald left the pickaxe buried in the wall, then sank down and ran his hands through the stone, the metal disappearing as his fingers easily parted what must have been a hundred pounds of rubble. Not all of that was skills.

My grip on my sewing needle was tight.

"I...I think that's enough," Gerald said, turning back toward me.

I nodded. It definitely was. He'd knocked loose most of the wall. He gripped his pickaxe and tugged, but it didn't come loose. He grunted, and it disappeared into his inventory. He crushed rubble underfoot as he turned to leave.

"Oh," he said, turning back and swiping at his shield to recover it before walking out into the field.

Sandy was only just pulling on the last pieces of the armor. She rushed to pull on the gloves.

"The hell was that noise?" Sandy asked.

"Gerald...mined," I said, looking over at him. He nodded.

"I'm done for today. I got all the metal I need for tonight."

"What do you mean—did he collapse the whole cave? Because it sounded like it."

"Just a wall." Gerald scratched his chin.

"A wall? He mined a wall?" Sandy looked at me.

"He collapsed a wall. Blew the whole thing down."

"Sounded like an explosion out here," Sandy replied. "No monsters, right?"

I shook my head no. Then Sandy pulled her helmet on.

Her eyes were visible through the holes in the cascading plates. She whistled, reading through her system. Then flexed.

"So?" I asked. I would be lying if I said I wasn't excited about what skill the outfit had, though it wouldn't be my skill.

"Lightning resistance...twenty strength attribute...and...Gwen, hit me with your skill!" Sandy said.

"What? No. I don't want to damage the armor."

"Trust me!" Sandy said.

"I'll hit you," Gerald said with a shrug, re-summoning his pickaxe.

"Gerald!" I shouted.

"Do it!" Sandy said, voice excited.

Gerald swung. There was a ringing noise of metal on metal as Sandy caught the blow with a wild swing of her arm. The ground beneath them exploded up, peppering them both with dirt. Gerald closed his eyes and stepped back as it fell onto him.

"What was that?" he asked.

"Oh shit, that took three mana," Sandy said. "I can only do two more of those today. The skill it gives is called Parry."

"It...deflects attacks?" I guessed.

"Yes!" Sandy said, lifting her helmet off. "Now I can finally fight that damn bear."

"How high is your health?" I asked.

"One hundred," Sandy said. "Hundred ten."

"Fifty points in constitution? That's ridiculous." I said after doing the math in my head. How much of that was due to the quality of the material and how much of it was my mother's crafting skills? Compared to that, what I made really did qualify as Ragged. I needed to level up my sewing skills; I had been focusing too much on fighting. A wide grin covered Sandy's whole face, fixed in a manic expression.

"We're going to kill that damn monster tonight," she said.

I stood next to Sandy above the boss arena on the third floor of the dungeon. She only had six mana left; she'd used four earlier. One to turn invisible and drag the armor out of town; three to test her Parry skill.

We'd left Gerald behind. He was still trying to convince his parents he wasn't lying and that he was a Noble, but that didn't mean he had to come with us to clear the dungeon every night. As strong as he was, he was still more of a liability than an asset in a fight.

He did loan us the metal stake that we tied the rope around the night before. He failed to mention the metal was recycled from something enchanted.

Half of it glowed with a purple light, while the bottom flickered blue. It kept bouncing as I tried to stab it into the ground, stinging my fingers, but not enough to damage my health.

"What the hell is it enchanted with?" I asked Sandy.

"Dunno. Maybe that rebound that's on his armor?"

Gerald's equipment was almost entirely enchanted with a buff called Reflection. He had detailed it to us. He failed to mention this stake was, too.

"Maybe?" I asked, pushing the rod slowly into the ground instead of stabbing it in. It worked perfectly. I sighed with relief before pulling the rope from my bag. "Any sign of the boss yet?"

Sandy walked over and peered over the edge.

"I don't see him."

I finished tying off the knot and threw the rope over the edge. Then I crawled over and scanned the forest myself.

There was nothing obvious below us.

I did one final check of my gear. My throwing needles were threaded with spiderweb and stuck in my belt; I had forgotten the enchanted scissors my mom had given me.

Stepping back from the edge, I activated [Always Prepared].

Nothing happened.

"What's up?" Sandy asked.

"Forgot my scissors at home," I said. I had forgotten to recall the chest to check its range. With a frown, I reached out to the skill to store the chest. There was no confirmation at all. Then I resummoned it, and it fell down in front of me.

"Whoa," Sandy said as the chest landed in front of me.

I opened it and pulled out the enchanted scissors, stuffing them into my belt before dismissing the chest again. It disappeared with an audible pop as air rushed to fill the space it had been.

It was good to know I could recall it from any distance. I was sure I'd find a way to exploit that…eventually. I wonder if I could store a person in it…maybe if I spent enough points leveling it up.

I pulled one of Sandy's tiny knives from my belt to share her Butcher Vision.

"Okay. Let's do this." I said, grabbing the rope and descending the cliff side.

Sandy followed behind. The forest was lit by moonlight, and I found myself nearly jumping at every noise. We came upon the place we had found the bear last time; it wasn't there.

"Nothing invisible?" I asked Sandy.

"Nope," she said.

We circled around through the trees until we found the monster drinking from one of the rivers. I didn't approach it, instead analyzing the monster carefully. Last time we fought, it had projected an illusion of itself, pretending to be defenseless and sleeping. This time didn't look any different.

Even though it ducked its mouth into the river, the water was undisturbed beneath it. It wasn't real.

I touched the edge of the knife, sharing the vision from Sandy's skill to see the invisible monster.

It was standing behind a tree, lifted onto two of its massive paws, half its red line hidden behind the tree as it presumably leaned against it to stare down at us.

With the flick of my wrist and through an effort of practiced aim, I buried a sewing needle in its face. The string was wrapped around my fingers, controlled with [Thread Mastery]. I turned and ran. The monster roared, leaving stealth, its illusion charging at us.

As I ran, Sandy ahead and to my right, I threw a wire sideways. It buried itself in a tree, creating a tight tripwire.

Sandy stepped between me and the monster as I jumped over the next river, landing with a huff and pulling the two strings.

"Come on, bastard!" Sandy shouted at the bear, holding up her giant cleaver. It bored down on her, wildly swinging a paw, and I saw Sandy's skill activate as her cleaver met it.

Fur and skin sloughed off the side of the bear's arm, earning another monstrous roar from the creature and revealing muscle like bound cables beneath. The real force of [Parry] was directed at the monster's chest, which exploded inward like a cannonball had hit it. Sandy turned and ran. A half dozen copies of the bear followed in an instant, chasing her, as the boss itself turned invisible. She landed next to me, falling to her knees under the weight of her armor. The river glowed between us and the monsters.

The dozen copies of the bear exploded into ephemeral smoke as they encountered the tripwire. The still-invisible boss activated my [Thread Sensing] as it touched the line, allowing me to perceive it fully. I threw another needle. It landed in its neck instead of its other eye. It screamed, charging forward again. The needle popped free of the tree as the monster slammed into whatever ephemeral force held it back from the river.

"It's going to die," Sandy said, looking toward the bear and holding up the cleaver.

"We can't know that," I said, even as I whipped at [Thread Mastery]. The loose wire on the ground pulled back toward me, then whipped around with the needle at the end acting as a weight. Lines of thread glittered in the moonlight along the monster's leg fur. I reached out with [Thread Mastery] and pulled.

Blood flowed down the monster's leg as it roared again.

"We can barely damage it otherwise!" Sandy said, standing like a batter at the ready. "One more and I'll be straight through its chest."

"You only have one [Parry] left in you," I cautioned, trying to pull the thread tighter. It refused to cut through the monster's muscle.

There was a popping noise as the glowing light emerging from the river dimmed and the monster crossed to the other side, swinging down on Sandy instantly.

CHAPTER 33

There was an explosion as Sandy's skill met the bear's attack. At first it was a noise like thunder as the skill magically gathered all of the bear's attacking force. Then her [Parry] redirected it and the sound turned to tearing flesh and creaking bone.

Blood splattered her as the monster's chest caved in, muscle parting as easily as anything else. The bear staggered backward.

And stayed standing.

"Oh shi—" Sandy didn't get time to finish her sentence as the monster swung at her again. She tried to block with her cleaver, which just led to the broken edge of the cleaver cutting her as it flew into the air. Then Sandy went flying.

I dropped the strings I was holding, pulled out the giant sewing needle, and activated my skill.

[Running Stitch I] [Mana: 9/10] [Cancel]

The needle parted flesh like butter, sliding through the monster's skull and into its gray matter.

It collapsed to the ground in a heap, ripping the needle from my hand. I took two quick steps back.

The entire fight had happened so quick. It was almost anticlimactic. I turned to look for Sandy. She had already risen to her feet, brushing dirt and blood from her armor. The shoulder had been cut open, and half of her cleaver was broken off. It was still a cleaver…just a lot shorter.

"Sandy!" I said. "Are you alright?"

Sandy looked up at me, then back toward the monster.

"Did you get an XP notice?" Sandy said, reaching down slowly and grabbing the cleaver.

"What? I…" I felt my eyes widen. I tried to throw myself forward.

The world turned upside down as force hit me like a car crash, shock and pain erupting on my side. Then it was dirt, rocks, and plants scraping me as I tore apart the foliage. I tasted earth in my mouth, twitching on the ground as I struggled to move.

The monster had played dead. My thoughts raced as I struggled to process the sudden disorientation, choking and spitting up dirt. By the time the world started making sense again the bear was crawling toward me. Moonlight glinted off the needle stabbed into its head. Blood and ichor seeped from the open wound in its chest.

Both of its eyes were destroyed.

But it continued sniffing at the ground, coming closer and closer. I tried to breathe, but my lungs refused. I felt weak. I tried to push myself off the ground as the monster slowed then stopped only feet from me.

It rose on its hind legs, lifting up a single paw to crush me. I wouldn't survive two hits in one night.

Then Sandy's cleaver slammed around the back of the monster, quickly buried halfway into its neck.

The bear staggered backward. Sandy grunted.

Then the blade was ripped free, blood pouring out from the fresh, deep wound in the monster's flesh. She brought the cleaver down again, and again, until the bear's head rolled off its neck and its body collapsed on the ground.

[+10 XP] [Level up]

"Holy shit." I said, finally pushing myself up off the ground. I was shaky, but I was alive.

And I was afraid to check how much health I had left. That next hit the monster was preparing for would've killed me.

Sandy stepped around the monster, lifting the helmet off her face. It was splattered with blood—not hers. Red spilled down the chest of her outfit and dripped to the ground. Sandy was panting.

Another notification popped up.

[Tier 0 dungeon cleared]

[Weekly clears: 1/1]

[Opening sub-dungeons]

[Opening return portal]

A shimmering gate opened, showing a distorted image of the town center.

"That easy, huh?" she asked, lifting up the broken cleaver.

"We almost died," I replied, pushing myself to my feet again and circling the monster. The camouflage patterns of its fur were marred and matted by the blood drying on it. "How the hell are we going to drag this thing out of here?"

Sandy grunted, reaching into her helmet and trying her best to wipe away the blood that stuck to the inside of it. After a moment of thought, she leaned down and dipped it into the river, leaving it clean but soaking wet. She shoved it back on.

Then she reached down, throwing her arms around the monster. She pulled as hard as she could. It moved a few inches.

"Nope," she said. "We're not getting this out in one piece."

I reached for the needle jammed into the monster's head and tried to pull it free.

It was stuck hard, buried in the bear's skull. I put a boot to it and pulled, stumbling backward when it came free. Then I began the arduous process of recalling the thrown needles one at a time, bundling the wire back up and shoving them into my belt. The wires and needles were covered with crusting blood.

I wondered if my new inventory would clean them like Wardrobe did with my clothes.

Sandy got to work without comment, pulling out sheathed knives from her own much smaller pack and carving into the monster. She gave up on using the smaller knives after only a minute or two, switching to the broken remains of the weapon Gerald had made her.

"Seems like he saves all the good magic for himself," Sandy said, grunting as she struggled to slice open the monster's back, working the cleaver into it like a saw. Without her mana, she had no skills to help her cut it.

It hit me then, as I stared at her cleaving the monster apart.

"We did it," I said, my voice an overpowering whisper in the dungeon's quiet.

"Yeah," Sandy said, stopping cutting and looking up. She leveled an even stare at me. "This will keep the town going. Indefinitely. We could expand it a lot, even. We'd have to find a way to get someone here to build more houses…unless we just want to build them by hand. But we still need to go farther."

I nodded.

"I haven't forgotten. Now we need to…find her," I said, unsure how to broach the subject. "Valjean can't stop us if he comes now. We can keep the town expanding by clearing the side dungeons…"

Sandy looked up and out over the forest, staring at nothing. Then she stabbed back down with her knife, cutting the monster apart. I looked at her storm curtain armor. I would have to level Wardrobe all the way to ten to be able to carry that for her. I wondered what the upgrade for the skill would be. One of my points from the level-up were going to that without a doubt.

As for the other…I opened my skill menu.

[Skill Shop]

▶Unweaving I

[UNCOMMON] Grants user the ability recycle items into base materials. Additional levels increase the amount recycled.

▶Alteration I

[COMMON] Aids user in retrofitting clothing to increase its quality level and repair it. Additional levels allow user to upgrade old equipment to higher levels.

▶Mending I

[COMMON] Allows user to repair clothing from patterns they are unfamiliar with. Additional levels increase quality of final product. Now that Mom was working with us, I didn't need the Mending skill yet. Getting outfits from others was a non-issue. Alteration would be great... once I had more skills to raise the quality of an outfit. For now, I only had low levels of Embellishment—I would be better off leveling that skill and improving my future outfits.

And as for Unweaving, I'd have a practically limitless amount of material to work with. With that in mind...I put another point into Wardrobe, bringing it to eight. Then I loaded my arms full of still-bleeding chunks of monster flesh, as much as I could carry, and followed Sandy out of the dungeon. Luckily we didn't have to climb the rope out while carrying these.

We washed what we could in the still rivers before bringing them to Sandy's workshop to be stripped and tanned.

I found the workshop's light on when I got home.

"Mom?" I asked, pushing the door open to find her inside. She looked up in surprise. She was taking apart a piece of the long-abandoned furniture, nails and hammers out to repair it. There had been no point to do so before, when it was just the two of us working here.

"You're back!" she said, standing and wiping her hands against the leather apron she was wearing. "How is it going?"

I stepped in and shut the door behind me.

"Sandy cleared the dungeon tonight."

Mom blinked in surprise. Then she smiled.

"Good. Good! I'm glad. Did the... did it help?" she asked conspiratorially, a hushed whisper.

"Yes. The skill on that armor was...crazy," I replied. "What was that designed to do?"

"Eh." Mom waved her hands. Her eyes trailed up like she was remembering something; probably memories from inside a dungeon. "Sort of a...lightning rod, for dungeons with adverse conditions. My Embellishment reworked the lightning redirection skill into something hopefully more useful."

I nodded. I needed to learn to do that. If I could control the outcome of skills like that...

"What skill is that?" I asked.

"Embellishment ten," she said.

"Ah. Of course." I frowned. Everything came down to levels and power, as always. How many more levels would I need to gain Embellishment ten? I had to raise Wardrobe to ten as well.

Mom smiled knowingly.

"You'll get there, my light. Especially when Sandy starts bringing back materials from the sub-dungeons."

I nodded at that.

"You need help?" I asked, waving at the furniture.

Mom paused for a moment.

"No," she said, taking off the leather apron and throwing it aside. "I was just getting ready for bed."

When I lay down, I found myself staring at the ceiling, unable to sleep for more than an hour.

We had done it. We'd won. For the most part. Now we had to find and bury Sandy's mom. That dark thought hung over me.

The dungeon's four ancillary gates had opened, each one providing entrance to a new environment. I stayed up imagining what would await me inside of them. Would the first floor of each new dungeon be as difficult as the third floor of the first?

Or would they be even worse?

CHAPTER 34

wen!" Terry shouted.

I stepped from the hallway into her workshop. I hadn't visited in a few days. And things here were different.

The tables that before had been scattered around the room and decorated with bottles were now gathered in the center to create a single workstation. Terry had indeed dried spider blood as pigment. But there was also a bottle of concentrated green sitting in the center of the desk; there couldn't have been more than a few ounces in it. I stared at it. It was glowing.

It was a *potion*.

"You…" I said, still struck staring at it. Terry had rarely ever pulled out the full set of her glass equipment. This was one of the first times in years I had seen it all in one place.

"I leveled up," Terry said. Her hands were folded over her knee, and she was staring at the center of her table nonchalantly. "It's a shame that Sandy can't bring me more of this," she said, waving toward a few much darker bottles, filled with a deep green color.

"We…could," I said, stepping into the room hesitantly, like the alchemical fixtures of glass in front of me might explode at any moment. It didn't look like a very safe laboratory. There were smudges of paint on the sides of bottles, as if Terry was painting and brewing at the same time.

"Oh. Right. You said…Sandy got it. You didn't say from where. Is this…?"

"Yes. It's from here," I said, lifting up the tiny bottle. "So what is it?"

"A draught of acid resistance," Terry said.

I held the bottle up to my face and looked at it before setting it back down on the table.

"You should sell it," I said.

"Give it to Sandy as a gift. You never know when you'll need it."

I whittled away a few hours waiting for Sandy to be ready, anxiety filling me the entire time. I painted for a bit, and spent some time working on a null hunter outfit, though now that Mom knew we had a ready supply of monster materials she didn't pressure me to work on it at all. I still just needed something to do, some way to feel useful.

It worked.

Afternoon came before I knew it and I found myself in Sandy's workshop. I sat on her bed and ate her snacks while she pinned the bear leather for tanning.

"I didn't think we carried that much out," I said, watching Sandy work.

She grunted, attaching the last corner of the leather to the rack. She lifted it off her desk to bring it outside.

"Finally leveled up. Got a skill to get more monster per monster."

"More monster per monster?" I asked.

"More monster per monster," she nodded. "When I carve off the leather it... stretches. I get more of it."

"Huh," I said. "Neat."

There was a pounding on the door that led into the house.

"Sandy!" Henri yelled through the door.

It was still barricaded. I ate another piece of jerky and made eye contact with Sandy. She opened the other door and stepped outside, closing it behind her. I sighed, standing up and freeing the furniture from the door where her dad waited. It swung inward toward me.

"Henri," I said, looking up at him.

"Gwen. Is Sandy here?" he asked, peeking around the room. "I didn't meet you two in time last night."

"We went mining."

"You went mining?" Henri asked. "So is Gerald really a Noble? Smithing?"

I nodded.

"What's up?" I asked.

"I told you I would help you with the dungeons. A more...complete set of buffs," he said, sighing at his absent daughter and staring at the door.

I followed his gaze.

"I think she's still just mad at Gerald," I said. "I don't blame him for not wanting to fight monsters."

I turned back to find Henri searching my face. He sighed, running his hands back and through his hair.

"I think it might be the other way around. She is taking her anger at me out on Gerald." Henri sighed. "Step inside."

I followed him to the kitchen. It was much cleaner than the last time I was here, the sink cleaned to empty and every surface swept to a shining polish. The tile floor caught sunlight and threw it back up, while the granite counters made the room feel clean and polished. Much of it must have been imported from other towns; Henri was born with one of the more valuable class professions.

In a city, he could enhance dozens of other people.

In the center of the kitchen on the table that was functioning as an island were a set of four meals. Two of them were older, probably from last night. Another held a bowl of still-steaming stew.

"I know that—mana is probably one of your biggest issues, yes?"

"Yes," I said, leaning over one of the stews. I took a spoonful and ate it.

Henri's cooking was, quite literally, magic.

"So this is food for mana regeneration?" I asked after a moment. There was no pop-up to confirm it.

Henri shook his head no. I cocked an eyebrow.

"That is…prohibitively expensive," he said, running his hands through his hair again. "This will replenish your mana plus give you extra over your maximum while you eat it. The higher above your mana cap it's raising, the less effective it is, so it's better if you spend your mana first."

"Wait," I said. "You're telling me this soup is a straight-up mana potion?"

Henri just nodded.

"Well, we're going to need something other than bowls to carry it," I said, looking around the kitchen.

"I don't have any Thermoses," Henri said.

"Bottles or flasks, then. A flask full of soup."

"I do have those." Henri said, touching a hand to his face.

"Ready?" I asked Sandy.

We were standing outside the southernmost dungeon; it was the one closest to the iron mine we were exploiting.

We each had flasks hung around our neck, tied together with little leather strips Sandy pulled out of her storage. She stood out in the Storm curtain armor.

"As ever," Sandy said.

The southern dungeon entrance emerged from the ground like a stone ruin in the middle of nowhere, the image inside dim from here. I wondered what would be inside, staring at the portal, but it didn't reveal any secrets to me.

Maybe a mine or a cave, since it was close to those resource nodes in the Wild. My skin itched standing here, still slightly outside the radius of the town's domain.

I was wearing the scale dress, prepared for whatever we would have to fight inside. We still weren't sure what level of monster it would open to. I was practically shivering with anticipation.

Sandy stepped through forest, the portal flickering. Though it was afternoon, we had no need to obscure our movements when the gate was so far away from town. It was night inside the dungeon, and Sandy's lantern on the other side gave me warped images of a barren landscape.

I stepped through after her.

The first thing I noticed was that I no longer felt the itch of the Wild eating away at me. There was practically no perceptible difference between stepping through this portal and the one in town.

But it stood out here. The persistent itch of the Wild, the constant feeling of the world trying to destroy me disappeared, replaced instantly by the comforting feeling of belonging that I felt in town. The dungeon providing that same feeling was creepy.

The second thing I noticed was the pervading cold, a chill immediately assaulting me. I gasped as the vertigo from moving between a dungeon entrance washed over me and sent me stumbling forward. My breath was visible in front of my face.

Around us, a blanket of snow choked the world. Snow fell all around us.

"Shit it's cold," Sandy said.

I rubbed my arms. My right arm was covered in leather, but my left was exposed, and my boots didn't reach all the way up my legs. With a thought, I activated [Quick Change] and switched into the stealthy leather hunter armor, suppressing a shiver.

"No kidding," I said, looking around. "This is…different."

At least light poured out of the dungeon entrance behind us. Besides that, there was nothing to differentiate the world around us, falling into darkness in every direction.

My eyes slowly adjusted to the much darker world. In each direction there was a shape moving in the dark. It was sparkling, glowing blue.

Sandy stepped closer to me, staring out into the dark.

"I'm guessing we have to hunt those down," I said, looking at the shape moving directly ahead of us. It must've been very far away. Or very small. It looked about the size of my hand from here, obscured by the falling snow that suffocated all sound from the world.

A chilling wind hit us, sending snow drifts rolling below us.

Sandy nodded and stepped forward, her feet crunching on the fresh snow.

I gripped my needle, wishing this outfit had gloves. I was going to have to craft something just for this cold.

The terrain dipped before rising again, our footing uneven in the snow. It rose halfway up my leg as we approached, the snow attacking my body heat. I half expected to receive a [Frostbite] debuff by the end of the night.

We reached the source of the glow, getting close enough to make out the shape of a monster crawling over it. A massive rock rose from the ground, glowing blue, made of repeating crystalline shapes.

"Is that… crystal?" Sandy asked, looking up at it. The monster seemed gigantic up close, even though it wasn't much bigger than anything we had fought before. It was symmetrical, made of dozens of three-dimensional diamond shapes with identical legs stabbing out from each side. As we watched, it pulsed with icy blue light. The crystal below it resonated, glowing back. Then the monster seemed to suck the energy out of it, causing it to dim before crumbling apart.

Almost imperceptibly, the monster grew.

"I think the rock is crystal. But I think the monster's…ice." I said, staring at it. It wasn't even close to anything biological. Instead, it was a transparent mass of bluish ice with legs that ended in spikes.

Sandy looked down at her broken cleaver, then back up at the monster.

"How are we supposed to fight these things?"

"I could probably pull it off the rock…" I said, reaching for one of the throwing needles in my belt. Even as we spoke, the monster glowed again, siphoning more power from the stone beneath it.

I wondered how valuable that giant rock was.

Then I wondered how many times we would have to clear the monsters in this frozen hellscape to open the next floor.

"Do it," Sandy said.

I threw the needle, trying and failing to use [Thread Mastery] to wrap around the creature's leg. I was in the wrong outfit.

Recalling the needle, I changed and tried again. The cold biting into me redoubled.

This time I threw two needles, grabbing opposite legs with thread and pulling as hard as I could. The monster didn't have articulated fingers or any real way to grip the crystal; it was just sort of sitting on it at an angle, propped up by gravity. So when I pulled, it slid across the surface and dropped to the ground.

Sandy dashed forward, swinging her cleaver into it and chopping violently into its side. Ice exploded up out of it.

The monster made a noise that sounded like wind rushing in the snow; or maybe it was the wind. Then it glowed blue. Alarmed, I stepped back. Sandy did the same, but not fast enough.

A pulse of blue light shot out in all directions.

"Fuck! Ouch," Sandy said, stumbling back and falling into the snow.

[Running Stitch I] [Mana: 9/10] [Cancel]

The monster lived, even as my needle split into it. Because it wasn't made of flesh, the wound wasn't clean or even. It exploded into jagged pieces of ice as my needle ripped it apart, the crystalline structure fracturing where the pattern repeated instead of at the point of the wound.

I attacked again.

[Running Stitch I] [Mana: 8/10] [Cancel]

[+2 XP]

CHAPTER 35

Sandy cursed, fumbling to remove the gauntlets covering her arms. She was steaming—literally. Steam wafted off her under the armor. Her skin was red, as if it had been burned.

"You alright?" I asked, grabbing her arms and turning them over.

"Yeah. Damn. Not a good match up for a butcher," Sandy said.

The damage was only skin deep, probably entirely thanks to health points acting as a shield between us and the monsters.

The cold was setting in quickly.

"We have to move," I said, kicking the corpse of the monster. It was made of ice. There was absolutely nothing I could make out of it.

"Hold on," Sandy said, stepping up and around me. She looked around, her expression unknowable beneath her helmet, before she suddenly shoved a hand into the snow beneath the monster.

She pulled out a glowing blue crystal the size of a marble.

"What is that?" I asked with a frown.

"Not sure," Sandy said. I could hear consideration in her voice. "Butchering skill led me to it."

She rolled the marble between her fingers before passing it to me. I took it and inspected it. It was cold to the touch like a piece of ice but more solid; it didn't melt as I held it.

"Wonder if its usable? Some kind of…elemental core. Alright. Maybe we can gain something here. Let's hurry." I shoved the core into a pocket and started trekking toward the next light.

There were trees fighting back the cold here, husks stripped of leaves and life, dead and black in the dark. They were thin enough that a copse didn't block our view to the next monster. Snow piled at their roots, creating tripping hazards for us to navigate.

I turned to Sandy as we came into view of the next monster.

"Hold on," she said. "Let me try something."

"You have enough health left?" I asked, staring her down.

"Yeah," she said, nonchalant as she stepped up to the monster. This monster sat among a pile of bones. It was curvy, its body a miss-mash of circular shapes like a bundle of grapes with legs like sharp ribs hanging from the side of them.

Sandy kicked it.

I stepped back, waiting for its attack.

It stumbled over on its side, catching itself on its half dozen malformed legs. Then it pulsed blue.

Sandy activated [Parry].

The wave of blue disappeared instantly, reappearing on the edge of Sandy's blade and shooting out around her. It passed over me harmlessly. In the other direction, it slammed into the monster, which listed to its side before recovering. There was a harsh crunching noise coming from the monster, but it seemed undamaged.

Sandy leapt forward and hacked at it, snapping her blade down on the segments of its body. They crunched and cracked before falling apart, the light of the monster slowly dying. Once again, she reached down and plucked free a core from the icy body.

"Parry told me the name of the skill when I used it." Sandy said, pushing the core over to me.

"Didn't look like it damaged it?" I asked, shoving the core in my pocket. "What was the skill?"

"Frost Nova" Sandy replied.

"Go figure—a frost skill doesn't damage…an ice elemental?" I asked.

Sandy shrugged. Things had changed from mundane to magical so quickly. She pulled her helmet off and started drinking from the flask of soup around her neck.

"I wish I hadn't eaten so much today," She said, stoppering the flask as we headed to the next monster.

"Too bad we can't just get mana potions. Oh, yeah, that spider blood you gave me?" I said.

"For the paint, or whatever?" Sandy asked.

"Yeah. Terry made a potion out of it. Leveled up. Acid resistance. Speaking of leveling up…" I said. "Let me get a hit in before you kill the monster this time. I didn't get any experience from the last one."

"Sure thing," Sandy said.

We came upon the next monster.

This one sat atop another crystal, its body jagged, squarish shapes. I popped it once with [Running Stitch] and Sandy swung onto the damaged portion I created, breaking the monster to pieces.

The forth monster died just as easily. I felt the small thrum of mana as the dungeon built toward opening its next door, but I didn't wait around to see where it would be. I headed right for the exit to the dungeon. I was freezing.

"Need a damn fire to warm up," Sandy said, exiting the dungeon after me.

I rubbed my arms and stretched my legs, trying desperately to warm up. At least it was still sunny; the last light of the day was slowly falling below the tree line.

I plucked open the flask at my neck, drinking the hot soup. Was it still hot because of one of Henri's skills? Or was the metal insulated? I looked down at the flask in my hands. Who insulated a flask?

"At least we did it, though," I said, leaning down with my back to a tree and rubbing my hands together.

Sandy grunted, sitting next to me on the dirty forest floor.

We sat there drinking soup until we were warm, basking in the last rays of sunlight as it fell below the horizon.

I played with the tiny marbles Sandy had pulled from the monsters. They were completely useless to me.

"Maybe the bear monster could make us warmer clothes," I said.

"You in a rush to fight it again?" Sandy asked.

"Not particularly," I replied.

Sandy threw her head back, looking up through the leaves.

"I hope the next floor has something we can use," Sandy said after a minute.

"Where to after this? East?" I asked.

The dungeon's entrances were in the cardinal directions of the town. Killing the first floor of the center dungeon had maintained the town's domain; maybe killing these four monsters was enough for that as well. But the domain had slowly grown as we cleared the second floor.

It might take more to maintain it there, now.

"East." Sandy shoved herself to her feet.

We were starting with the two closest to the mining node at the south end of town. If they had what we were looking for, we could keep our focus there.

Like a cobblestone path, a circular route free of trees connected the four dungeon entrances. It was overgrown with moss, clumps of dirt sporting grass from the months and years of the town's dungeon slowly decaying or being unmaintained. The path between the dungeons showed the shadow of where the town's wall would have been. For now, it was buried beneath the ground.

It was easy to see where it would rise.

Like a cobblestone path, a circular route free of trees connected the four tertiary dungeon entrances. It was overgrown with moss, clumps of dirt sporting grass from the months and years of the town's dungeon slowly decaying or being unmaintained.

The forest was calm and quiet here, the area so close to town free of monsters. Or animals, for that matter. Almost everything larger than a squirrel or small bird avoided the area around the town.

Come to think of it, animals rarely entered the town at all. It was a detail I had overlooked, slowly filtering out of my mind from years of living here. We didn't have problems with rats. Nor did anyone have bird feeders.

So there were practically no distractions as we came upon the next dungeon entrance.

"Hopefully this one will be warmer," I said, standing outside. I used [Quick Change] to return to the scale dress.

The buffer of health reassured me more than stealth could.

"Ready?" I asked Sandy.

"As ever," she said, hefting the broken cleaver.

"How's your mana?" I asked, looking over. Mine had slowly refilled as I drank down the stew. I estimated that there was probably enough to refill my mana twice over.

"Full. Ready to go. I don't think I can eat any more, though," Sandy said.

"Just one more clear. We can check out the north and west dungeons tomorrow."

"Hope this one isn't cold as balls."

We stepped through the portal.

"I think you jinxed us," I said, staring around.

The sun was slowly rising over an arid hellscape. The terrain was obsidian glass and porous lava stone; streams crisscrossed the distance, glowing red. Shrubbery sparingly dotted the landscape; strange, alien plants that seemed to glow and bloomed with red and orange fruits and flowers.

The flat landscape hid nothing, allowing me to see the monsters we were up against. Gigantic lizards chewed at the shrubbery where they could find it or rolled on their backs across the landscape. They were almost alligators, but their bodies were thicker. Like Komodo dragons, maybe.

"Those look much better," Sandy said. I heard excitement in her voice.

"For leather?" I asked. Sandy took a step forward. "For leather, right? You're not planning on eating lizards."

She didn't reply.

CHAPTER 36

Sandy walked up to the monster, her footsteps full of a confidence I didn't feel. Above us, the sky was red-orange. Gigantic black roots crisscrossed the landscape, some kind of strange, alien plant that I had to be careful to step over while following her.

Sandy swung on one of the monsters.

It was almost lazy and almost too easy. Her blade sunk halfway into it, cutting apart scales and flesh. Then she jumped back.

I rushed forward at that, but it didn't appear there was anything wrong. It was just a big, dumb lizard, rolling around in pain.

"You want your experience?" Sandy asked, looking over at me.

[Running Stitch I] [Mana: 9/10] [Cancel]

[+1 XP]

The lizards were worth less than the frost elementals. I doubted they'd be worth anything at a higher level, despite how relatively terrifying this floor was.

"Why are you so confident about these?" I asked as we swept the dungeon, cleaning the first three lizards out.

Each of them were low to the ground, giant ugly things with shiny black scales. They were stupid, and slow.

"I remember eating them," Sandy replied. "They taste great, by the way."

I stopped following Sandy and stood still in my tracks.

"Do you think this is the place?" I asked. She kept walking forward, and she turned around now at me. A river of lava in the distance bubbled and popped, liquid stone pouring out then rapidly cooling and solidifying.

"No," Sandy said, turning around. "The night she…the last night I saw her, she had been bringing home seafood all week." Sandy started walking forward again.

"Seafood?" I asked, walking after her. I doubted the lava dungeon was going to open to some kind of grotto or water dungeon. "Hey, you don't think the next level is going to bring us underground do you?"

"Don't see why it would," Sandy said.

"Isn't that what most dungeons do? Head deeper underground?"

"What? No. The center dungeon took us to different forests."

"So this one will…take us to different volcanos?" I asked.

Sandy grunted. We arrived at the next monster.

[Running Stitch I] [Mana: 8/10] [Cancel]

[+1 XP]

"Oops," I said. I had killed it instantly before Sandy got a chance to get experience. "Sorry."

"It's fine." She shrugged. "I'll get experience carving it up."

We cleaned out the fourth monster easily. At the fifth, we stopped and stared at it a few feet away. It lounged on the hot ground near the rivers of lava. Its scales were bright red.

"Miniboss?" I asked.

"The frozen dungeon didn't have one."

"The monsters in there didn't need one," I said.

The red lizard looked up at us, tasting the air with its tongue. It turned away from where it was bathing in the heat of the lava river and walked toward us, dragging its stomach on the lava field.

The miniboss among the wolves was black and hid in shadow, the floors of the dungeon seeming to revolve around darkness, light, and illusions. Or maybe illusions were part of light? The bear had both stealth skills and light illusion skills, though the spiders had none.

So logically, the red lizard should be—

Sandy tackled me out of the way as a stream of fire leapt out of the lizards mouth.

I pushed her off me and inspected her quickly.

"You gotta stop diving in the way of damage for me," I said. This time, at least, she didn't get hit.

Sandy scrambled forward and swung her sword. There was another wave of heat as I turned back to her in time to see her [Parry] the monster's stream of fire, swinging a now red hot blade to instantly bisect the monster.

[+1 XP] [Level up]

"Shit," Sandy said, waving her blade. The heat had stuck to it, leaving it nearly glowing. It cooled into a lumpy, misshapen form.

I brushed porous lava-stone off myself.

"Gerald should have a replacement for us by now," I said, consoling Sandy. She was still frowning at the misshapen cleaver.

"Yeah," she replied. "Do you have the rope on you?"

"Of course—" I flinched back as a bubble of lava popped in the river nearby, splattering on the stone. "Yeah. It's in my bag."

I fumbled to bring the rope out as Sandy dragged the corpse of the lizard away from the lava. She took the rope a handful at a time, wrapping it under and around the lizard to drag it forward. Sandy tied quick, proficient knots, then grunted as she pulled the lizard around.

She collected two more of the bodies, leaking blood as she dragged them through the lava planes and back toward the portal. I grabbed the other end of the rope, helping her pull. It must have been a few hundred pounds of meat.

If this had been the central dungeon and not a sub-dungeon, we probably wouldn't have been able to loot it all, not without being spotted dragging it through the middle of town. We stepped out into night falling over the forest. Chill winds whipped through the trees. I grunted and reoriented myself, looking toward the town.

"So what's the plan? Wait for it to be fully dark?" I asked, gesturing with my head to the bodies we were dragging.

"Screw it. Let's just pull them in," Sandy said.

Might as well. Most of the town already knew.

It was a pain in the ass to drag the bodies over the uneven terrain, and the uncomfortable press of the Wild pushed in on us the entire time. The scalding heat of the lava plains was more comfortable in some ways than the irritating and constant itch of the area outside the town's domain.

We left a trail of broken foliage dragging a stack of three lizard bodies back to Sandy's house and up to the workshop. I ducked inside and changed back into my mundane clothes before stepping back out.

Cinnamon barked over the fence. I squinted, then dropped the rope and walked over to pet him.

At first I had thought he was leaning against the fence, raised up on his back legs to stand taller than it. Then I realized he was just that tall. The fenced area was designed for pigs or small animals, and Henri had never replaced the ones he used to have.

Cinnamon bumped his nose into my hand as I pet him.

"Sandy?" I asked. "Are you feeding him like, stat-raising food or something?"

Sandy pulled out a tanning rack and supplies from a shed next to the house. She was still wearing the storm curtain armor, though her helmet was under her arm. I hadn't even thought about that as we walked into town. Killing monsters was becoming mundane; a new, seriously messed-up normal.

Cinnamon whined as I stopped petting him. Then he stepped back from the fence and barked.

Sandy walked up next to me, holding a hand out for Cinnamon.

"All of Dad's food is stat enhancing," she said, implying it was obvious. It kind of was. "I gotta change; you wanna untie the lizards?"

"I got it," I said, eyeing Cinnamon. His tail was wagging at speed.

I turned about and started undoing Sandy's knots. I struggled with them at first before managing to tug them free, sending a few hundred pounds of lizard bodies falling sideways to the ground.

There was a thump behind me. I turned around slowly.

Cinnamon slowly padded passed me, leaning down and sniffing at the corpses. He reached out and scratched one of them with his foot. Then he barked again.

"What is it?" I asked. The dog swirled and looked at me. He was named after the patterning of his fur, great swirls of white through creamy orange, and his eyes matched, staring down into mine with uncanny intelligence.

He looked from me to one of the corpses, scratched at it, and barked again.

"You can't eat that," I said.

Cinnamon barked.

"What have they been feeding you? Do they even have enough food… I guess all the leftover monster meat, maybe? There's no way we can use all this material…" I said, mumbling to myself.

Cinnamon stepped past, scratched the other lizard, looked at me, and barked. Was he asking if he could have one of the other bodies instead of the mini-boss corpse? I squinted at the dog. How intelligent was he?

"You can't have that one, either," I said. I felt crazy talking to a dog.

Then he moved to the third corpse, put his mouth around it, and started dragging it away.

"Hey!" I said, but he ignored me, dragging it right up to the gate.

Sandy popped out of her house, and to my surprise, Henri was behind her in the doorway.

"Remember these?" she asked, turning around.

Henri looked down, saying nothing. He slowly reached into a front pocket on his jacket, pulled out a rolled cigarette, and lit it.

"Hey! Don't do that in my room," Sandy said, frowning.

Henri looked at her, took a step forward, and lit his cigarette. He took a long drag before replying.

"Yeah," he said, looking down at them.

"Where'd the third go?" Sandy asked.

"Uh…I said, stepping up to Cinnamon's fence and looking over.

"Cinnamon!" Sandy said, following me to where he was currently tearing it apart in the pen. "Ugh. That one's ruined. How did he get out?"

"Sandy, he's taller than the fence," I replied. She blinked, looking between the fence and back to her dad. Henri stared at the lizards still.

"It's fine. There's more than we can eat anyway. We should throw a dinner party," Henri said. "Our pantry is practically full at this point."

"You could sell it," Sandy said.

"To Valjean. The Noble. Who will be able to identify it as monster meat," Henri said. Then he took another drag, still staring at the corpses. "Bring them inside," he said before turning around to leave.

"Cinnamon! You're supposed to ask before taking things! Do I not feed you enough?" Sandy said. She started walking around the fence to step inside.

"Sandy? The lizards?" I asked.

She sighed and turned around.

We brought the lizards inside.

"Help me hang these," she said.

I changed into my strength-enhancing dress, helping her lift the corpses onto her hooks.

"Ow," she said, recoiling her hand from pulling up the red lizard.

"What's up?" I asked, leaning around, hoping she hadn't stabbed her hand.

"Damn thing's blood burned me," Sandy said, inspecting her hand. The monster's blood sizzled as it hit the floor.

I stared at it for a moment. There's no way it was completely valueless. If spider blood could be refined into something, then this blood must have been equivalent to an alchemical product. I wondered if every part of the monster was more valuable than we were giving credit for.

Working on our own, we could just barely pull out a few corpses a night.

But there was value to gain beyond crafting patterns.

"Sandy, can you…" I trailed off as she'd already put a bucket down to catch the blood draining from the monster. It was a shame how much of it had already been lost dragging it through the forest.

Sandy stared at the steaming blood worriedly, as if she was afraid it would start a fire in her bucket. After a minute or two, she shook her head. Then she easily picked up the remaining black lizard corpse and hung it one-handed.

Right. She had a skill to help her handle bodies. But it seemed to be less effective on the more magical corpses.

This lizard's blood was cold, black, and oily.

Sandy got to work immediately, ripping into the red lizard before stepping back, the blood flowing faster as it was opened.

I plopped onto her bed and opened my skill shop.

[Skill Shop]

▶Mending I

[COMMON] Allows user to repair clothing from patterns they are unfamiliar with. Additional levels increase quality of final product.

▶Unweaving I

[UNCOMMON] Grants user the ability to recycle items into base materials. Additional levels increase the amount recycled.

▶Pattern Projection I

[COMMON] Seamstress Vision skill. Grants user access to a pattern overlay on fabric.

The system seemed to really want me to have Mending. I sighed. I still had two points. I could look at patterns…or I could push Wardrobe to level ten. Honestly, it wasn't a valuable skill for most seamstresses unless you had multiple outfits to show to different clients.

But I had no idea what it would do at level ten. My mom's wasn't even at level ten. It wasn't something you needed, really. I could use it to swap between three outfits…but I wasn't sure that would be worth it on its own. I did my due diligence and opened my pattern store too.

▶Fisherman's Coverall Pattern (Intermediate)

[COMMON] Grants minor bonus to Constitution and Dexterity. Grants bonus to Fishing.

▶Harvester's Coverall (Basic)

[COMMON] Grants bonus to Constitution and Will. Grants Scythe Proficiency skill level based on craft quality and materials used.

▶Seeder's Uniform (Basic)

[COMMON] Grants bonus to Constitution and Will. Grants set bonus skill based on craft quality and materials used.

[Wardrobe: level X] Seamstress Inventory Skill. Grants user access to a storage inventory for 10 sets of clothing. Users gain 10% of stats from all stored sets and any active skills.

"What?" I asked aloud.

"Hm?" Sandy asked, turning over her shoulder.

But I was too busy to reply. My heart was racing with excitement as I pulled open my system, mentally pulling at my [Wardrobe] skill.

The upgraded version showed that all my stored clothes had been shoved away into a single slot. I had spent two points to upgrade the skill to level ten, hoping to store at least the two additional pieces of gear needed to fit Sandy's storm curtain armor.

Instead, I could store everything we had made.

"Gwen?" Sandy asked again.

I ignored her, racing through my menus to look at my stats. Then I pulled open my interface. I was in my mundane clothes currently, but I was inheriting ten percent of the stats from my stored hunter outfit, as well as its skills. Not only that, but I was boosting those inherited stats by thirty-eight percent at level fourteen.

[Gwendolyn Tailor][Human, Lv14][Seamstress]
[Health: 52/10][Mana: 8/10][XP: 0/10]
[ATTRIBUTES]
▶SPD: 10
▶WIL: 5
▶STR: 5
▶DEX: 11
▶CON: 5
▶PER: 6
[SKILLS]
▶Crafting I
▶Running Stitch I
▶Hand Spinning I
▶Thread Mastery IV
▶Wardrobe X
▶Quick Change I
▶Embellishment III
▶Pattern Mirroring I
▶Always Prepared I
[PATTERNS]
▶Hunter Pattern
▶Shell Dress Pattern
[TEMPORARY SKILLS]
▶Bow Proficiency I
▶Shadow Cloak I

"I upgraded one of my skills to ten!" I said, rocking forward. This meant I could enhance my baseline—I could craft faster and better if I crafted more dextrous outfits, or I could stack different skills. I wondered if Shadow Cloak would reach tier two if I stacked it? Of course it would. It had to.

"Nice. What did you get?" Sandy turned around now, paying slightly closer attention and looking away from the bleeding corpse of a lizard.

Instead of answering, I pulled on the [Shadow Cloak] skill, eager to test my ability to turn invisible on a whim, and I felt the darkness around me answer.

"The hell?" Sandy said. She blinked at where I'd been, then over to the scale dress hanging on the broken mannequin. "Instant outfit change...?" she guessed.

"Nope," I said, returning to visibility.

"Hmmm," she said, putting the knife in her hand down at her table and crossing her arms before guessing again. "Permanent skills of anything you craft."

"God. That would be sick," I replied, frowning. Of course Sandy would guess something even better than what I had. "No. I can use all the skills from outfits I have stored!" I replied.

"Damn. That *is* nice. Two outfits' worth of skills?"

"*Ten* outfits' worth of skills, and ten percent of the attribute points on them."

"*Damn*," Sandy said. "I need to get a skill like that."

She continued cutting apart the lizard. I frowned. If I could grow this fast, once I had ten outfits, it would be practically impossible to keep up. But our classes didn't gain attributes from leveling.

"I'll have to give the best outfits to you so you can keep up," I said.

Sandy scoffed.

"I'll need a set of Gerald's armor if you keep that up."

"Damn. I need to craft more sets." I briefly regretted not spending more points on different patterns. I could probably acquire a wider range of skills with different sets. Then again, if I had spent my points any other way, I wouldn't have the ability to use them.

"The bear leather is still in the stacks. Got more than we can use at this point," Sandy said.

I looked over. There were piles of monster leather on the floor at the foot of her bed. But it wasn't everything we had collected; we had more stored outside in the shed, including the stranger bits and the remnants of the boss monster. I rose to my feet and grabbed a lamp before stepping outside, heading to one of the dilapidated sheds by Sandy's house.

The roof was in better condition than the rest of the shed, slouching boards leaving gaps where rain could slip in, but nothing was stored here for terribly long anyway. The remnants of the bear boss lay on top.

What kind of skill would it give if I crafted a hunter set out of it? Would the stats be higher with my raised Embellishment skill? More invisibility? Or maybe I would be able to project copies of myself like the bear had?

So far, every outfit I'd crafted had granted abilities the monsters had themselves.

They were strange squares of tanned leather with the fur still on them. Some sections had the bear's mottled camouflage that had matched the bottom of the leaf-covered forest floor, while others were just a lavender fur.

I brought a whole armful back inside and was setting them down before clapping my hands.

"Alright. Just need the thread, the mannequin…" I walked over and stored the scale dress in my newly expanded inventory. Then I stored the storm curtain armor, too. I had a Noble skill in my menu now. I smiled stupidly at that. It felt like a dream half fulfilled. Or maybe more than fulfilled. I could keep my mother's legacy and gain the power to protect it, too.

"Isn't your thread at your mom's workshop?" Sandy asked. She looked like she was done with the lizard.

"What?" I asked. "Oh. Yeah. We moved everything over, didn't we?"

"Probably a better work area anyway."

I looked around Sandy's room. There were giant dead lizards hanging from the ceiling.

"Let's move to my mom's workshop."

We found the lamps on but the workshop empty. I piled up the materials on the table, pulling free my tools to start cutting the pattern, then stopped.

I had mana left over after clearing two dungeons. I even had more soup. Sure, cold soup, but it was cold soup that could replenish my mana. And my scissors were enchanted.

I activated [Pattern Mirroring], consuming one of my remaining points of mana. I still had six. I cut through the leather easily, a perfectly cut copy popping out of the leather on the other side of me. Then I continued working. It halved the time necessary to prepare the pieces of leather for the patterns.

Humming to myself, I tore apart and rearranged the outfit, using my mana liberally and forcing myself to drink cold soup. [Embellishment] pulled at me and activated as I cut apart the leather to create camouflage from the mottled pattern for the cloak and front sections of the clothes.

This outfit would be so warm for the ice dungeon.

Without the need to cancel [Running Stitch], the magic made me practically a sewing machine, especially with my practice crafting this outfit. My fourth Hunter pattern was almost complete in a single night.

Sandy yawned on the other side of the room.

"Think I'm going to turn in for the night. See you tomorrow," Sandy said with a stretch. She paused halfway to the door. "Oh, do you wanna harass Gerald with me tomorrow?"

"Sure thing," I replied. I had returned to stitching almost unconsciously, excited to fill each of the slots in my stats. I shoved away the three pieces of the set that were already finished. "Maybe he'll have your weapon ready for you? He hasn't asked us to go mining again yet."

"I'm not counting on it," Sandy replied, swinging the door open. "Good night, Gwen."

CHAPTER 37

I met Sandy in the morning after breakfast. Then we headed to meet Gerald. His forge was running. We hadn't seen him in a couple days—I knew he mentioned off-hand that his skill made him obsessive until he finished working on something. I thought he had undersold what exactly that meant. His family's forge was open air, letting the heat of the fires out. It had a roof to block the rain, but today was windy, and nothing stopped it from blowing through the forge around Gerald.

Gerald was muttering incessantly. Bob was nowhere to be found. The colder weather and overcast sky drove most people inside for the day. Except for Gerald, who was pounding at a metal rod.

"No…no, that's wrong…" he said. One of his hands was wrapped around the burning hot metal, completely unfazed, while the other hit it with a hammer.

I looked at Sandy. She looked back at me, one eyebrow raised.

The forge was in utter disarray.

Half-slagged metal sat on the ground around Gerald, along with a half dozen imperfect halves of gigantic scissors. They featured a dozen different decorations; reliefs in the metal decorated the dark rods along the ground.

Piles of leather and leather scrap decorated a table in one corner, along with a half dozen knives and cleavers stabbed into its wood.

"Gerald?" I asked, walking into the workshop. He was in a fugue state, focused so completely on his work that he didn't even seem to notice me calling his name.

I stepped over lumps of half-shaped metal to approach him. I saw one blade of a gigantic scissor just past him on his right, leaning up against a wall. It was polished to a sheen, impressions of flowery filigree decorating it, leather wrapped shoddily around the handle. The blade seemed to cut into the stone beneath it.

I wondered what it was enchanted with.

"You okay, buddy?" I asked Gerald, returning my attention to him.

He still didn't seem to notice me. I reached out and put a hand on his shoulder.

Gerald flinched, turning around and making eye contact with me. The burning hot rod he was carrying swung with him, and I flinched when it stopped in midair a few feet to my right.

I blinked.

The room was burning hot, the heat of the furnace radiating and overcoming the chill of the wind.

"Gwen," Gerald said, blinking. "Gwen!" He shouted this time, eyes sparkling, the gleam behind them partially manic.

"Gerald," I said, taking a step back.

"I didn't expect to see you so soon! I…" He swung the metal rod as he spoke, turning around to look at the half of the scissor he had made. "That wasn't ready for you to see yet! Oh!" He said the last word as he noticed the metal rod in his hand, stepping back to dunk it into a bucket of water. Steam boiled up around it, filling a quarter of the room and clinging to Gerald's skin.

He blinked the water out of his eyes. Scalding-hot droplets clung to his skin, his head steaming.

"Are you…alright?" I asked.

Sandy stepped out from behind me.

"I'm amazing! This is the best I've felt in weeks!"

I flinched as Gerald put his hands on my shoulders. They were wet from the steam. I gently removed his hands and he pulled them away, leaving a soot stain on my shoulders.

"Oops. Sorry," he said. "I, uh—don't touch that!"

Gerald suddenly turned and shouted behind me to Sandy. I heard a scream and whipped around, ready to activate [Quick Change].

Sandy's hand was on a blade, a gigantic cleaver that screamed as it sunk deeper into the wooden table. She flinched back and the blade stopped vibrating and screaming, though she shook her hand as if the blade had bit her.

"You alright?" I asked, stepping toward Sandy.

"Yeah, but the damn thing took a point of mana. Gerald, what the hell are… all of these?"

There must have been a dozen blades on the table, including the gigantic cleaver. Sandy had reached for the biggest. Gerald made a noncommittal grunt and stepped toward the table, grabbing and flinging the screaming sword away. It split the stone floor where it landed, sinking just an inch into the ground to remain upright.

"I…made a few knives for you. You can see some of them didn't quite work out. That one ended up having a…side effect. It's called Buzzing Blade. Vibrates really fast. Also makes a horrible sound if you don't optimize the shape of the blade. I have to figure out how to restructure that one so it doesn't scream…"

As he spoke, he looked over the blades.

"Only one of them is worthwhile. But which one...? This one?" he asked, grabbing a cleaver that was half embedded into the table. "Oh oops. Oh shit."

The cleaver went from dull gray to red hot in a few seconds.

"Oh shit oh shit oh shit—" Gerald pushed past me, flinging the knife into the bucket of water just as it started to vibrate and hum. There was a splash and then an even bigger explosion of steam.

Gerald stepped back from the steaming bucket.

"What was that?" I asked. "A heat enchantment?"

"Yes! But I couldn't find a way to turn it off."

"Gerald, how long have you been crafting?" Sandy asked.

"Huh? Oh. Is that the sun?" He was staring past us and outside the little outdoor forge. "What day is it?"

Gerald had been at this for multiple days. My jaw was slackened.

"Are the rest of these fucking bombs, too?" Sandy asked.

"No! None of them are explosive. I tried, though. An enchantment to stab something and make it explode. Sounds helpful, right?" Gerald said, walking back to the table.

"No! It doesn't! We need the monsters in one piece. We can't build armor out of scraps!"

Gerald ignored her, grabbing an axe from the table.

"I tried to enchant this one with Gravity Resistance but it..." He pulled the blade out of where it was sunken into the wood. Immediately, it started to float up, until he was holding it above his head. He had to grab it with both hands to stab it back into the table, which bounced when he slapped it down. "Yeah."

"Floating metal seems to be a recurring theme for you," Sandy said.

"Well...yeah. But now, the good stuff!" Gerald said, lifting a chef's knife from the table. The blade was a bright, shining silver, polished to a shining edge. Gerald gestured with it as he talked. "This one is enchanted with a—oops."

His casual flick of the wrist projected a visible aura of light that shot out and sliced the table in half. One half of it clattered to the floor with the weapons on it. The other half floated toward the ceiling with the axe embedded in it.

"Uh..." Gerald said.

"Gerald? You alright, dear?" His mom asked, slowly pushing open the door that led into the house. She looked at Gerald, who was still steaming, then at the floating table. Then she made eye contact with me. Finally, the door slowly swung closed as she retreated back inside.

"Hey don't point that at me, Sandy said, stepping back as Gerald started to talk again.

"Right. Right," he said, stepping across to the table covered in leather scraps, where he pulled out a boiled-leather sheathe embellished with complex designs and put the blade inside it. Then he looked at the table currently scraping the roof of the forge, considering it. "Did you bring any rope with you?" he asked.

It took a combined effort between the three of us and a few minutes to get the table back to the ground. Gerald tied the axe to one of the pillars holding the roof up, leaving it floating and bobbing in the wind like a balloon. It looked more than a little dangerous.

"So…is this for me?" I asked, reaching out to grab the handle of the giant scissor blade before thinking better of it. Who knew if this one would really explode or not?

"Yes! But it's no good without its other half," Gerald said. "And I haven't been able to forge another half with the right enchantment."

"Do you attach the enchantment before you finish forging it?"

Gerald shrugged.

"They both kinda happen at once."

"Gerald?" Sandy asked. She was holding the sheathed chef's knife in her hand. "What does this knife do?"

"It's a Windblade!" Gerald said unhelpfully. "You just…swing it."

He made a whooshing noise and gestured with his hands at the remains of the table.

"And it takes a mana point?"

"Huh? Oh yeah. You have plenty, right?" Gerald turned toward Sandy. The wind picked up and blew hair out of his face. He had to push it out of the way; the water from the steam earlier made it cling to him.

"I have NINE now!" Sandy said.

"What did you use it all on?" Gerald asked, nonplussed.

I rubbed my face.

"When do you think you'll finish the other half of the scissors?" I asked.

"Dunno. I've been at it all night…" Gerald paused, looked out into the empty village, and squinted. "And morning."

"You should sleep," I said.

"I've got to put out the forge," Gerald replied. He grabbed a shovel and started pouring sand into the furnace.

"Should we start on the north dungeon?" Sandy asked, nodding the direction with her head.

"Nah. Your dad is making dinner for us, right? We should wait until our mana soup is ready," I replied.

"Then what are we doing until then?"

I pursed my lips.

"Let me finish off that outfit. I should be able to do it before dinnertime. Then we can head to the north dungeon."

Sandy shrugged.

"I'm gonna take Cinnamon for a walk, then."

"You don't wanna come hang out?" I asked, turning around to walk toward the workshop.

"Naw. I'm gonna try this out," Sandy said, gesturing with the knife in its boiled leather sheathe. It was the size of a regular chef's knife; tiny compared to her cleaver.

I wondered if it would even activate with her skills. It wasn't a butchering knife, after all.

"If it doesn't work, you could always give it to your dad. I'm sure it will help his cooking."

"Or destroy the kitchen." Sandy scoffed. "It's enough of a mess already."

We split up down the road, Sandy circling back to her workshop as I headed to my own.

The half-finished pieces of my third Hunter pattern sat on the table.

I hadn't figured out how the system decided to name sets in progress; the first two had been randomly assigned the name Tacca, and this one took a new, weirdly Latin-looking name.

[Ophrys I]

▶77% complete

▶Quality +1

[PROJECTED SKILLS]

▶Light Cloak III

▶Random Hunter Proficiency III

I'd probably never figure it out. I wasn't even sure if Latin existed in this world or if it was some older, archaic language that the system decided not to translate.

I burned a little bit of my remaining mana, bringing myself down to five as I worked through the afternoon to complete the outfit. But it was worth it.

[Hunter's Cloak (Common, Light) completed!]

[Quality Assessment: (Fine)]

[Generating Skills...]

▶Projection III

▶Trapping III

[+2 XP]

Neat. All in all, I had gained twelve experience points from the bear. *And* I could probably craft an entire second outfit from it. Or I could let my mom do it…but that would slow down my leveling.

I pulled away the remaining pieces of the outfit by sweeping my arm over them, burying them in [Wardrobe]. I could feel the smallest twinge as my stats increased.

[Gwendolyn Tailor][Human, Lv14][Seamstress]

[Health: 28/28][Mana: 5/10][XP: 2/10]

[ATTRIBUTES]

▶SPD: 10

▶WIL: 5

▶STR: 11

▶DEX: 14

▶CON: 14

▶PER: 10

[SKILLS]

▶Crafting I

▶Running Stitch I

▶Hand Spinning I

▶Thread Mastery IV

▶Wardrobe X

▶Quick Change I

▶Embellishment III

▶Pattern Mirroring I

▶Always Prepared I

[PATTERNS]

▶Hunter Pattern

▶Shell Dress Pattern

[TEMPORARY SKILLS]

▶Bow Proficiency I

▶Shadow Cloak II

▶Tracking Proficiency I

▶Thread Sensing III

▶Thread Mastery II

▶Parry V

▶Projection III

▶Trapping III

The sum of all the skills I had crafted was plainly listed. It was a mouthful. I would hate to have this read aloud to me all the time; it was a good thing I could see the system entirely in my head.

I debated starting another outfit. I had four slots filled in my inventory right now, but I was going to have to give Sandy the storm curtain set back later. But my overall stats would be higher with the minute bonuses while wearing a set; not to mention the additional skills. The latest hunter set even boasted fifty percent higher stats from the raised quality.

Eventually I decided against it, heading out to meet Sandy at her workshop.

Cinnamon was chewing on…something in their yard. Lizard meat, most likely, the cuts of it that weren't any good for humans. He crunched through bone and all.

Sandy stared out distractedly, petting the dog.

It was still afternoon, the sun shining.

"Hey," I said, walking up with my hands in my pocket.

Cinnamon's tail sped up, though he kept eating.

"Gwen." Sandy nodded. "You ready?"

"Yeah. How's the knife?"

"Better fit for a lumberjack. Cut down a tree trying it out." She pushed herself to her feet, brushing dog fur off herself.

Cinnamon barked.

Sandy directed him back to the pen—he jumped over the fence as she walked around to open the gate—and then we headed off north.

It still wasn't late enough for Henri to have made dinner, so we were going to clear a dungeon and then circle back.

"How much mana do you have left?" I asked Sandy. We stopped in the woods north of town to gear up. I dropped her storm curtain armor for her while switching into the scale dress myself.

I felt more comfortable with a larger buffer of health in a way that was hard to describe, though it wasn't enough to counteract the uncomfortable presence of the Wild.

The forest paths outside of town were becoming more familiar to me. Now I could observe where the trees were younger, where paths had once stretched in front of houses beyond the tiny remains of our town.

Not for the first time, I wondered how large our town actually was. At some point long ago it must have been much, much bigger than most people now would believe.

It was like seeing the fossilized remains of the town. As we walked along a tiny, hard-packed road with the shadows of buildings on either side of us, I imagined what the town must have been like. Was this a shopping center? Maybe once there were wares on display behind fine glass windows, magical goods and potions for sale. In my entire time in this fantasy life I hadn't once seen a city; they told us that travel was dangerous.

It didn't seem that dangerous now. But we still hadn't ventured beyond the destroyed edges of our own town.

We came upon the north entrance, a wobbling hole in reality.

"You ready?" Sandy asked. I nodded, and she stepped inside. I followed only a second behind.

At once the itch of the Wild shifted, the comforting atmosphere of the monster-filled dungeon displacing it.

I took a long, deep breath of thin air, taking in the horizon. We were high, high up. Mountains rose around us, thin patches of trees clinging desperately to the stone faces of cliffs. I took a step and rocks tumbled down the steep incline beside me. Caves opened like mouths in the side of mountains.

There was no glow or indication of where to go from here. Sandy seemed pensive as she looked around.

"Well?" I asked, turning about to take everything in. "Where to?"

CHAPTER 38

Narrow walkways of packed earth and loose stone wound around the mountainous dungeon. We moved slowly to keep our footing, climbing higher to try to find a direction that would lead us to the dungeon's monsters.

The icy dungeon was mostly flat and the enemies within it glowed, making them practically beacons at night. Here, the dungeon's environment was obscured by the uneven terrain.

"I hope we're not going to have to climb a different mountain," Sandy said, staring out toward different mountain peaks reaching up from the forest floor.

"Let's just get up high and look around first," I replied.

We ended up having to scramble over rocks to reach the top of the nearest mountain.

When we crested the top, I was glad we had scouted the area before making any decisions. Pillars of smoke rose from out of the tree line.

"Well, looks like we found what we're hunting."

We climbed across the mountaintop, chasing the smoke in the dungeon's dawn light. I hoped we hadn't found something intelligent.

Even though the smoke was only a few hundred feet away, it took time to scramble over the rocks and rough paths on the mountain. We finally saw the monsters when we passed a final copse of trees. I stopped, staring in disbelief.

There must have been almost twenty of them.

They were tiny little golems made of translucent crystal in a dozen colors. The smoke rose from furnaces that they refueled even as we watched. They were the exact same monsters we had encountered at the mine on the south end of town. Were they burning furnaces to cook metal too?

But what did that mean? This dungeon gate hate been closed for years. No one could have let them out. So the monsters either escaped their dungeon somehow or someone freed them. Unless they reproduced in the Wild. Were there more colonies of the things scattered somewhere?

"Gwen," Sandy said. I had gotten lost in my thoughts. One of the tiny golems was marching toward us.

It stopped suddenly, staring at us, and I could feel the tension in its tiny, glowing eyes as it stared up at us. Then it started to make an alarm noise like birdsong. The rest of the monsters charged at us, holding rudimentary wooden tools. They all screamed as they ran, a mix of tinkling noises and birdsong.

"Oh shit," Sandy said, turning to run back.

There were at least a dozen of them. Using my ability to attack one would just open me up for the others to stab me. So I turned and ran with Sandy.

"Do you think you can Parry them?" I asked as we followed our path back. Rock slid under our feet.

"Only one at a time. The rest will just stab me!" Sandy said.

"Same problem as me, then." We slowed to a stop at a rock face. The monsters were small, their stubby legs unable to keep up with us, which left them farther behind, but only barely. We didn't have time to scramble up the wall.

Sandy pulled out her new knife and swung it just as the monsters closed in on us. There was a cracking noise as a burst of wind cut a thin gouge in the stone.

The closest of the monsters exploded.

The rest stumbled backward.

"Okay," I said, stepping forward and holding the needle.

"I can't swing this with you that close," Sandy said.

The monsters were spreading out around us, pinning us back to the wall.

"I have a new skill. Projection. Same one the bear had, I think. Light cloak skill. I'm gonna—"

The monsters closed in, holding their tiny spears out. I didn't waste time on any more words.

A perfect copy of me appeared in front of me, my mana dipping by a point. Then…it stood there. The monsters paused at that.

Sandy swung again. Three more of them exploded. It was like their bodies were under pressure; they shattered like glass when damaged, even more so than the crystal golems we found in the mines outside of town. I activated [Running Stitch], destroying one of the monsters myself using the longer reach of my arms to stab forward before leaning back. Sandy swung again and another group of them exploded. The rest charged us.

I activated [Projection] again, this time mentally willing the illusion to charge at them as I summoned it. The monsters ducked out of the way as the second copy of me ran at them, giving Sandy enough time to swing again.

I finished the last one with a [Running Stitch]. The dungeon shuttered.

No more monsters came.

Sandy and I were quiet for a moment. I only had one mana left.

No more monsters came.

"Well," I said, stepping forward and digging into their bodies—the chunks of them that remained. Just like the ice elementals of the frost dungeon, these had tiny cores that glowed a bit brighter than the rest of them. Now that I knew to look for them, they were obvious. I wondered if I could use them in embellishments.

"Didn't expect a swarm of them," Sandy said. She sheathed her knife and leaned down to pick apart the monsters with me.

I looked between her and the distant columns of smoke.

"Better than rats or something," I replied.

Once we peeled free the last of the tiny, ugly crystals, we moved back to their camp. This gave me some hint at what the crystal golems were; some kind of earth elemental. I bet we would find a copper mole if we reached the next level of the dungeon. Maybe a few of them.

A copper mole was much stronger than a spider. But monster strength wasn't linear. These tiny elementals were an example; they were theoretically less dangerous than the wolves. At least to a Noble.

To us—who didn't really have combat skills for dealing with hordes of monsters—they were *more* dangerous.

A floor of six copper moles, though? Definitely more dangerous than the floor of spiders.

The monsters' camp was much like the mine we visited for Gerald. Tiny, hand-made furnaces burned, the behavior baked right into the monsters. There were no metal tools, though. Instead they were stone and wood. And unlike the mining golems, who had attacked using tactics, these had charged us in a more direct fashion.

Their camp was more rudimentary too. Maybe the ones we met outside were higher level. Or maybe they'd adapted.

Whatever the case, we found nothing of value in the camp.

"This dungeon is awful," I said as we scrambled back over rocks toward the exit.

"You should make us climbing outfits," Sandy replied after climbing the wall behind me.

Uneven footholds became ladders to push us up and over the terrain.

"This is my new least favorite dungeon. At least we don't have to constantly clear it."

"You would rather dive the ice dungeon?" I asked.

I slid down to the rocky path through the exit and stepped out into the night.

It was still windy even after the sun had set.

We passed through the forest and made it back to Sandy's house. Henri opened the door for us.

"Girls," he said, stepping aside to allow us through.

We ducked into the hallway and chased the smell of food.

"You look…" Henri stopped himself mid-sentence as he trailed behind us.

"Hungry?" Sandy offered, shouting over her shoulder as she dodged into the kitchen. There was food set out. Solid food. I pulled up a chair, sat down, and started scarfing.

There were also flasks ready for us.

"No. Like you've been rolling around in dirt," Henri said, pausing at the entrance to the kitchen.

"We climbed a mountain," I said, talking between bites of a giant, soft steak. The meat fell apart in my mouth. "What is this?"

"Spider," Henri said.

I spat it onto the table.

"What?" I asked.

He leaned against the doorway.

"Nah. It's lizard."

"Spider's good, too," Sandy said with a shrug. She was eating at a much slower pace.

"It's early," Henri said.

"We're not done yet," Sandy said.

He raised his eyebrows.

"Out of mana?"

Sandy nodded, not bothering to talk while eating. Instead, she pulled out Gerald's knife and set it on the table.

Henri squinted and stepped forward, reaching for it. Sandy slapped a hand on it.

"Uses mana. Don't touch it," she said.

The meal was all meat and vegetables. No bread.

"Does your class affect things you bake?" I asked.

"No. Only cooking," Henri replied. "So…the dungeon had a mountain?"

I nodded with a mouth full of food. Henri's expression was pensive.

"The lizards…the mountain…" Henri listed off some of the dungeons we had previous cleared.

"The snow," Sandy said. She stopped eating. She was tapping the table. "There's one more."

Henri nodded. Then he turned around and left us to eat.

I stared at Sandy, trying to figure out what that was about. She shrugged.

We ate.

Then we headed to explore the contents of the last dungeon.

We stood outside the entrance. The wind was still strong tonight. And now it was sprinkling rain down on us. I rubbed my arms as I stood outside.

My mana was full, but I felt like my stomach would explode.

"Ready?" I asked.

Sandy was pensive this time, seemingly unwilling to enter the dungeon.

"No," she replied.

"What's up?" I asked.

"It's—my mom has to be in this dungeon. They all might've changed a bit, but there should be enough to…she couldn't have been in any of the other dungeons."

"There's nothing to do but move forward," I said. Then I stepped past her and into the dungeon.

The world tilted. The discomfort of the Wild left. And the smell of the sea met my nose.

Birds chirped above us. The dungeon felt alive.

It was beautiful.

A blue sea stretched over the horizon while sand gave way under my feet. Clouds decorated the sky in thin strips and the sun beat down on the beach.

A crab of monstrous proportions skittered along the shore. It was hot pink.

I heard the sucking noise of the dungeon behind me as Sandy stepped through and displaced the air.

I was glad to have the scale dress. For once, it was a fitting environment: hot, but not as hot as the lava fields. There was no fear of lava splashing on my exposed legs. And no frostbite.

It took me a moment to realize Sandy was unusually silent.

"Sandy?" I asked, turning around. She was staring out over the sea, her expression haunted.

I turned back and walked toward her.

"You good?" I asked, the sand giving way beneath my feet.

"Yeah. This is the place," Sandy said.

"The place," I replied, looking over the beach. It was nicer than the other dungeons. But that wasn't what she meant. She meant this is the place her mom died. "How do you know?"

"Seafood," Sandy replied.

"Seafood," I said, thinking aloud. Sandy had told me her mom brought home seafood the last time she saw her. Thus, the dungeon she was clearing had to have been one that could provide seafood. Her mom was a butcher like her—it made sense that she would bring the bodies home to practice her skills. And why wouldn't Henri make food out of them?

Sandy nodded.

"Do you need a second?" I asked, scanning the dungeon. There was only a gigantic crab scuttling up and down along the beach. A river split the beach, washing away sand as it rolled into the sea. Farther inland, clumps of grass held the sand together, sparse trees dotting the horizon.

Sandy shook her head.

"It's ridiculous that we're here."

"Killing monsters with our classes?" I asked, pulling out my giant sewing needle.

"No. Clearing the dungeon ourselves. It's Valjean's job, and yet my mom is dead and he's alive, letting the dungeon decay."

We approached the crab together. It spun around, staring at us before skittering back and forth on its legs. Each of its claws was half as large as I was, and it snapped them together to create a clicking sound.

[Running Stitch I] [Mana: 9/10] [Cancel]

[+4 XP]

The crab died instantly, my needle splitting apart its chitin with ease and piercing directly into its brain. It slumped, nearly ripping the needle out of my hand despite my enhanced strength.

"I felt like that was worth more experience that it should've been," I said, pulling my needle free. Blue blood spilled into the sand.

I bet I could make another version of the shell dress out of this. This was closer to what the dress was made for; something more for a beach party than hunting monsters. Though maybe the Nobility needed it for both.

Turning left and right, I couldn't see another crab as far as the horizon stretched.

"Where are the rest?" Sandy asked, a near mirror of my thoughts.

"Buried under the sand?" I ventured.

The ocean's water splashed at my ankles.

"Let's get this crab out of here," Sandy said.

We pulled the corpse up to the portal, dropping it off outside of it, before heading back down the beach to search for more. I looked for deformities in the sand or bubbles under the water but I couldn't see anything of the sort.

Instead, we found the monster as we walked over the river that fed into the sea.

It leaped out at us.

By now, our paranoia in the dungeons was extremely high. As were our reaction times, even accounting for the effect of superhuman perception and dexterity levels. We threw ourselves out of the way as a vicious flying fish shot out of the water.

Sunlight bounced off its iridescent scales, sending light scattering over the sand in a rainbow of colors. Its small, bat-like wings beat against the sand as it tried to right itself.

So many of these dungeon monsters were just…stupid.

"Is that second monster for this dungeon?" I asked, tense. I was looking between the fish and the water. Were there more of them hiding somewhere? None of the other dungeons we'd cleared had two different types of monsters. It seemed the farther we delved into the dungeons, the stranger they got. Luckily, I would be able to rely on my expanded Wardrobe to cover new skills and patch weaknesses in the set of abilities I had.

[Running Stitch I] [Mana: 8/10] [Cancel]

[+4 XP] [Level up]

The fish went silent as the sewing needle pierced through its head and into the sand.

I waited for Sandy to make a quip about fish scale armor or how bad it would smell, but nothing of the sort came. My needle slid out of the fish with ease, and Sandy grabbed it by its tail, dragging it back to the gate.

Sandy looked back out over the dungeon, scanning for something. Then she walked back to where the fish had jumped out of the river, pulling out her knife.

Her head shifted left and right as she searched the river.

"It's not here," she said suddenly, turning around.

"What isn't?" I asked.

Sandy grunted, leading us forward down the beach toward a group of boulders rising from tide pools.

"There it is," she said, stopping suddenly and pulling out her knife.

I looked about the rocks…and saw nothing.

"Sandy?" I asked.

"It's blending in," she replied. Oh. A monster is here. I squinted harder at the rocks, trying to see anything abnormal.

"Does it have a stealth skill?"

"I don't think so."

She swung the knife. There was a crack as it cut apart rock, sending up a puff of dust where the rock exploded.

Then part of the rock started bleeding.

An octopus had half-crawled out of the water, its tentacles the color and shape of the rock around it, allowing it to blend in perfectly. Now it fell into the tide pool with a splash. The dungeon vibrated under our feet, signaling that all the monsters had died.

Sandy stepped carefully over corals, tiny fish ducking out of her way as she splashed into the water. She pulled out the octopus corpse and raised it up with a hand.

"This is the dungeon," she said. "We're clearing this one."

We dragged the octopus to the gate. Three mismatched monster bodies made an odd pile. Sandy sat down by the gate, looking out over the beach with her arms folded. I didn't comment. I just sat down next to her, waiting for her to be ready.

I knew she wouldn't want to talk.

Instead, I poked around my system to see what was available. I almost skipped right over my pattern section before the last one caught my eye.

[Skill Shop]

▶Cross Stitching I

[COMMON] Enables system assistance with a new stitch type. Additional levels increase proficiency.

▶Pattern Projection I

[COMMON] Seamstress Vision skill. Grants user access to a pattern overlay on fabric.

▶Mending I

[COMMON] Allows user to repair clothing from patterns they are unfamiliar with. Additional levels increase quality of final product.

I almost skipped right over my pattern shop before the last one caught my eye.

[Pattern Shop]

▶Fisherman's Coverall Pattern (Intermediate)

[COMMON] Grants minor bonus to Constitution and Dexterity. Grants bonus to Fishing.

▶Sailor's Uniform (Intermediate)

[RARE] Grants bonus to Speed and Dexterity. Grants bonus to Sailor skills depending on craft quality and materials used.

▶Houndsmaster's Uniform (Intermediate)

[RARE] Grants bonus to Speed and Constitution. Grants bonus to Tamer skills depending on craft quality and materials used.

CHAPTER 39

Terry labored over the table, carefully measuring the hot blood from a lizard. She was wearing goggles and gloves.

I was working in her workshop for a change of scenery. Her window was open, and the whole room smelled like rain and wet earth. I was stitching together a Houndsmaster's Uniform pattern out of what remained of the boss. I knew I was going to run out of material before the job was done; I was going to finish the rest with shadow wolf material.

The other point I had went into leveling up my Always Prepared skill. The extra-spatial storage still wasn't big enough to fit my sewing needles. But it was heading that way.

Terry brought something to boil on her side of the room. I leaned over to look past her. Fumes poured from the top of the bottle and seeped out the window.

"Is it safe to be in here while you do that?" I asked.

She turned around and looked at me. I noticed that she had covered her paintings in progress with drop cloths.

"Completely!" Terry nodded, giving a big thumbs up. The bottle behind her hissed. "Oop."

Terry turned around, fiddling with the device she was using to boil.

I continued working on my set. With the mana to spare and the proficiency at crafting, I could turn around most sets in just two days. I was estimating the houndsmaster set would take me three. It was a more complex set, ranking at intermediate and completely unfamiliar to me.

There was also the fact that its memories pulled at me even more intensely than the other patterns' had. The hunter outfits were filled with so many memories from so many people working on them that they came out as fully mundane. The shell dress had been made in a high-end noble parlor; the memories it conveyed were refreshing, if anything.

The memories of the houndsmaster outfit stung. They were alien, full of landscapes that only half made sense. They provided visions of workcamps filled with animals, clearly deep within dungeons. But I wouldn't know where. The seamstresses and tailors in the memories still worked in groups, four to a dozen working together in open air "workshops" set up in camps, surrounded by dozens more groups. The camp was probably full of Nobles with tamer classes. I saw flashes of giant monsters stomping between tents in the background, through the peripheral vision of the crafters in the memory. Friendly monsters. Tamed monsters. Still, it was unnerving to see how many workers were deep inside the dungeon. I had seen firsthand exactly how loyal Nobles were when it came down to it. I'd hate to be a peasant if a camp got over run.

Then again, maybe it was some kind of safe floor.

After an hour, Terry turned around with a tiny bottle, the red liquid inside glowing. She shook me from my thoughts as she held it out.

"How'd it turn out?" I asked, still snipping cloth into its pattern.

"Lesser draught of heat resistance," Terry said. "I think I can make three!"

I nodded at that.

"How much experience?" I asked, setting the houndsmaster outfit down. The smell of smoke in the camp from the memories was giving me a headache.

"Almost a level," Terry said, setting the draught down before stretching.

"You going to make more now?" I asked.

"I think I'll continue my painting," Terry said, already taking her safety gear off. She set the remaining materials by the window for ventilation.

I stopped sewing as Terry started dragging furniture around, pulling out an easel and a chair and mixing paints. I decided to leave her to her painting. That was as much work as I was going to get done realistically anyway; I had spent three mana, and it was early into afternoon. Henri agreed to make dinner earlier for us after last night.

And I was hungry.

No more feeling overstuffed as I made myself drink soup for my mana. Instead, I was absolutely ravenous and excited as I headed toward Sandy's workshop. I shoved the scattered pieces of the houndsmaster outfit into my Wardrobe, and the leftover materials and tools fit nicely into the Always Prepared chest.

Sandy wasn't outside this time, which made Cinnamon all the more excited to say hi to me.

"Hey, boy," I said, stretching a hand over the fence for him to smell. Then I violently recoiled as he licked my hand. "Hey!"

He barked playfully, running in a circle. Then Cinnamon ran in and out of the small shack working as a makeshift doghouse. He whined at me expectantly as he came out, as if he wanted me to follow.

"What is it?" I asked, leaning over the fence.

He ducked back in, and came back out with a gigantic spider in his mouth. I winced.

It wasn't big-like-a-hand big. It was big-like-a-monster big, and he dragged it along the ground.

"Did Sandy give you that?" I asked.

Cinnamon brought it close to me. I inspected it, making sure it was dead before reaching out.

Cinnamon pulled back, playing keep-away.

The spider was unbutchered, mostly eaten, and completely dead.

Sandy's door shook as she stepped out.

"Gwen?" she asked, walking up to me.

"Did you give your dog a full spider?" I asked.

Sandy turned to look at Cinnamon, who was still holding the spider in his mouth, tail wagging earnestly.

"Did you get into the storehouse again— Hey!"

Cinnamon leapt over the fence and ran.

"I'm not playing right now!" Sandy said, taking a step toward him. He ran away. Sandy sighed, exasperated. "How's your day going?" Sandy asked, giving up on Cinnamon and leaning her back against the fence to look at me.

"Good. Good. Got most of a new outfit done. Or a third of it," I said, leaning over the fence. Cinnamon was outside another house, still dragging the spider corpse with him. "Are you going to let him do that? He's going to scare the crap out of someone."

Sandy shrugged.

"Can't catch him unless you've got a set geared for speed for me."

I pushed off the fence and headed for the door.

"What's the route today?"

"Let's start with the ocean dungeon. We'll see how we feel after. The lizards are easy, but I feel like the air there is terrible for my hair."

"We gotta clear what, two a day?" I asked.

"Yeah. The border's holding steady," she replied as we swept through her workshop and then into her house. Her room was phenomenally clean for once, invaded by the smell of food from the kitchen on the other side.

Henri turned from the pantry.

"Girls," he said. "How do you feel about hunting more lizards for me?"

"Guess we're going to the volcano after all." I said, pulling the flask off the table. "You need it for this?" I asked, uncapping the soup and drinking it as I let myself fall into one of the chairs.

Henri only nodded. My daily routine of killing almost a dozen monsters was becoming more and more comfortable. Of course we had to go kill some giant lizards for him to make us some delicious, mana-replenishing soup. Just like a grocery list. *"I'm going out for milk. Need anything?"* *"Yeah, go ahead and kill some giant monsters and bring back their corpses."*

"East first, then?" Sandy asked, not sitting down.

"Yeah." I set down the flask.

We made our way toward the lava fields on the east side of town. Sandy turned around only a stone's throw into the Wild, frowning as she looked back into the bubble of warped air surrounding the town's domain.

"Cinnamon! Go home! We aren't going for a walk right now!" she yelled.

I blinked back. Her dog had been quietly following us. He came out from his hiding place and ran excitedly back toward Sandy's house. Sandy made a *tch*ing noise before we spun about and headed for the dungeon.

The lizards were almost disappointingly weak. There was a rush of excitement in many of the dungeon clears; the moments where a horde of golems backed you against a wall or a half dozen shapes hid in the shadows above you. Here, there were no surprises. Wide, flat land that allowed you to see all your enemies and the environment's hazards. The only part that brought any excitement was the fire-breathing elemental miniboss.

Sandy cut it down with a [Parry]. Then we cleaned up the rest of the dungeon, the mobs falling to single strikes of my needle despite theoretically being a higher level. It only took us a few minutes to clear the dungeon now that we knew we didn't have to look out for pitfall traps. Or traps of any sort, really. The dungeons were less like dungeons and more like miniature snapshots of ecosystems.

This left me with even more questions for the origin of the earth elementals that we had found at the mines south of town. I wondered if those had escaped from the dungeon. The thought bugged me as we circled around the north side of town, Sandy opting to walk farther rather than change back out of the storm curtain armor.

I insisted she not just stride through the middle of town wearing it. Monsters must be able to escape their dungeons somehow. Could they reproduce in the Wild? Were elementals natural creatures, or were they born from mana or on some other plane?

They must have been able to reproduce. But monsters had never escaped the dungeon at the center of town.

A theory formed in my head. The domain around the town kept monsters out. Maybe it also kept monsters in the dungeon. The only time a portal could be open outside the domain would be the edge gates in the Wild.

Maybe those dungeons could break. What happened when the dungeon shrank and the gate closed? Did the floors inside just stop existing? Or did they continue resetting, somewhere outside of time and space?

Maybe they popped out of existence, spitting their monsters out.

The cities needed dungeons to exist to spread their domain. The dungeons, though, needed no such thing, as far as I knew. The dungeon would remain even if the rest of the town collapsed. I would never have to find out if that meant letting the boss out, because I wasn't going to let the town collapse.

"Ready?" Sandy asked.

We had already come to the western gate, standing outside in the golden afternoon light.

"Yeah. Are you?" I asked.

Last night, Sandy had taken a while to calm down in this dungeon. The sight of it clearly brought up emotions for her. Which was fair. Her mom had died in this dungeon. Probably not on this floor, but still.

Not to mention the last several meals she shared with her were probably made of the monsters inside.

I followed up when Sandy didn't reply.

"I could probably just take care of the monsters here if you want."

"No," she said. The response was almost instant. I heard her suck in a breath as she stepped into the dungeon, and I followed a breath after, the world warping as we walked onto the beach.

Each of the dungeons was a hellscape, except this one. It would be an amazing place to come just to relax, if Sandy didn't have the memories attached to it. I had the tact to refrain from saying that aloud. We got to work right away, the floor's three unique monsters presenting practically no challenge.

I paid extra attention to each of them anyway, after my experience with the first dungeon's boss. The mechanics of that fight were an evolution from the mechanics before it; stealth and ambush. So what would the lower floor of this place be like?

I wasn't sure.

The lava dungeon seemed obvious; more and more fire, demanding heat re-sistance. Large, strong, but dumb mods. The north dungeon…probably grew into a bigger and bigger horde as you went deeper. Useless for experience and crafting, though the dungeon had provided me tons of hints for the monster ecosystem outside of civilization.

But how did a beach dungeon get more intense? It would be too stupid for it to just be stealth again.

I dodged out of the way of the flying fish throwing itself out of the water.

"Hey, Sandy," I said casually as I stepped up and impaled the monster. "What do you think the second floor here is like?"

"Hmmm," she said noncommittally, grabbing the gross, slimy fish. "The monsters all seem to want to fight in the water."

"What?" I asked, looking between her and the fish. "That fish seems to want anything but."

"Dungeon mobs are stupid." Sandy shrugged. "They just throw themselves at you. But the monsters…they can all go underwater."

"Do you think the second floor is underwater?" I asked.

Sandy looked down at the fish then back up to me.

"I hope not."

The dungeon rumbled under our feet when we killed the last monster, already growing in intensity, and we dragged our prize home. The night was still early.

"Should we clear another?" I asked Sandy. She wasn't herself today. Level headed enough in the dungeon, but not talkative while clearing it.

She took a moment to reply.

"No. Let's go home." She took a swing of her soup flask before tossing me her storm curtain helmet without warning. "Clothes?" she asked.

I pulled out her mundane clothing and we changed in the woods, walking directly through the middle of town. I stared toward the blacksmith's shop. Gerald's forge was cold and dark. Hopefully he was getting some much-needed sleep.

In a way, the dungeon had become more comfortable than walking through the too-quiet town. None of the other adults had confronted us except for Gerald's mom. Hell, Henri ended up being supportive. Which made me paranoid as I looked through the windows lit in the early night.

But there was no confrontation—just a slow walk to Sandy's house.

Henri met us outside, giving us small talk before getting to the point.

"I made you dinner," he said.

"You already gave it to us." I held up the flask in my hand.

"No. I made something special. Come in."

The surprise was revealed a bit early by the smell of crab, but I didn't mind.

Inside the kitchen, laid out on the table were segments of gigantic crab legs, cooked open. I felt my stomach rumble. Maybe I'd eaten too little today. And besides, eating mostly stew couldn't be good for me.

I plopped into a seat and picked up a crab leg before looking up at Henri. He took a seat across from me, starting to eat without waiting.

The dinner was painfully quiet, silence hanging between us. Sandy stared at the table for a long time before starting to slowly eat.

"This was our favorite," Sandy said, her voice almost a whisper.

Henri just nodded.

I deliberated on what to say. This must have been bittersweet for Sandy. If it was just bitter, she probably would've stormed out. After eating a gigantic crab leg, Sandy stopped and looked up at Henri.

"Would you like to come?" she asked. "I'm going to…find whatever I can and bury it."

There was another awkward pause.

"Yes," Henri said.

"Thanks," Sandy said. Then she followed up with, "…Dad."

I sat very awkwardly, caught in the emotional crossfire.

"Should we…hug?" Henri asked.

Sandy broke the tension with half a laugh.

"No," she said.

"Okay," Henri said. "Do you…want to smoke?"

"You can't offer your daughter a cigarette," I said, breaking into the conversation. "She doesn't even smoke. Maybe we could just help with the dishes."

"Okay," Henri said, visibly relaxing.

We ate a bit longer. Then, when we were done, we helped clean up, soaking dishes in the sink before wiping them down.

Mom wasn't awake in the workshop when I went home. I crept up the stairs and collapsed into my bed.

In the morning I continued my progress on the houndsmaster suit, pushing closer and closer to completion. I was starting to see the final shape of it through my memories. It came with a thick leather cloak not unlike the hunting outfit, but this one wasn't made for the weather. It was designed to be only loosely attached and easily discarded, so that if something grabbed the cloak, they would rip it off rather than pull down the wearer.

The sleeves were huge, bulky and padded with leather, as were the legs. As I crafted, I couldn't help but think how miserable this would be to wear in the lava dungeon. The storm curtain armor couldn't have been much better, though. The thick leather of the houndsmaster suit was designed to resist the biting of small, untrained dogs and monsters long enough for someone to train them.

I could feel the designer's intentions imbued along with their memories in the design. And as I focused more, I could see those thoughts and memories moving like a real, tangible thing, flowing from my hands into the conception of the design. The act of stitching it together, combined with my class, was enchanting the material. The deeper I reached into the memories, the more I saw—

I felt a headache behind my eyes as a very different image flashed.

It wasn't someone crafting. It was someone *fighting*. A seamstress fighting, ducking back, their cloak exploding into shreds as a monstrous jaw the size of a house nearly closed on them. I watched as they pulled their weapon up. A pair of scissors. An absolutely gigantic pair of scissors, blade open and extended. The monster slammed into the exposed edge of the blade, flesh parting as easily as snipping cloth.

The pattern the seamstress was cutting was overlaid on the monster and reflected a dozen times as [Pattern Mirroring] activated. The reptilian giant screamed as blood and viscera erupted from every side of it, the basso roar shaking the ground beneath her—

The memory shattered as my hands stopped moving.

CHAPTER 40

I came back to myself breathing hard, fighting for air as if I had been drowning a second earlier. Sweat beaded on my back.

"What the hell was that?" I said aloud, despite the fact that I was alone. I looked over to the door to my house. For a second, I thought about asking my mom. Then the memory of a conversation floated to the surface.

"*The story ends with him dying, so.*"

Alex the tailor. A story about a tailor who beheaded a monster with a thread. My mom seemed really excited about it for an instant, then it was as if she didn't want to talk about it.

My heart still raced from what I saw in the vision of that memory. It was like I was a passenger in the seamstress's head as she tore apart a monster, equal parts fear and exhilaration. In that instant, I knew with absolute certainty that the story of a tailor killing monsters was something similar. It wasn't a story at all. It was a memory.

How much could I learn from each of these patterns? No, that wasn't the right question. The right question was: what did this mean? It meant that there had been a time when it was normal for the crafting classes to kill monsters."

I looked down at the unfinished houndsmaster set and winced. Even looking at the parts caused me physical pain, a lance running through my head.

Trying to work through it and continue crafting made the headache intensify until it was debilitating. I laid my head across the cool workshop table for half an hour until it receded again.

I wouldn't be getting any more work done today. Stealing casual glances at the pieces of unfinished armor drove another spike of pain into my head.

So I tracked down Sandy.

It wasn't very hard. Our town wasn't very big. And she was always more or less near her house. Today she was working in her front yard.

"Gwen?" Sandy said my name like a question, a note of anxiety in her voice. It was abnormal for me to track her down this early in the morning. Especially if nothing was wrong.

"Sandy!" I walked up and leaned over her fence. I frowned when I saw Cinnamon wasn't inside it.

"Done crafting for the day?" She asked, pulling a scale-leather sheet out of the tub it was soaking in. She turned to hang it on a rack.

"Sort of," I said. I looked around. "Where's..."

Sandy whistled. Cinnamon came running, sliding along the ground as he nearly slammed into Sandy. He was holding a—stick was the wrong word. It was a small tree, roots and all, a sapling that he had clearly pulled out of the ground. He set it down in front of Sandy, drool dripping.

"Did you teach him keep-away?" Sandy asked. She took a single step toward Cinnamon.

He whipped up the sapling and ran.

"Anyway. What's up?" she asked, turning back to look at me as Cinnamon sprinted into the middle of town.

"I wanted to ask you something about your crafting," I said, pausing to consider how to word it. "When you...use a skill, do you see a memory?"

Sandy paused, then continued pinning the piece of leather up.

"Sometimes... Not for this, though." She waved at what she was working on before slapping her hand on her thigh.

"But for...?" I asked the leading question.

"For butchering." Sandy nodded. Then she wrinkled her nose. "But I don't get it. The memories make it look much easier than..." Sandy stopped. She turned to look at me, her eyes widened with an unasked question. "You have memories of people fighting with seamstress skills? How does that work?"

"I only get memories from the patterns. Feelings. But they're not all of crafting. And I just had one today of a seamstress fighting. With a giant pair of scissors," I said.

Sandy just nodded. When she didn't say anything else, I asked another question.

"Is that...normal for you?"

"As far as I know, it's normal for all classes. Even dad's."

I blinked.

"And how does a cook fight monsters?" I asked, stepping closer and almost whispering.

"Dunno. Maybe a seamstress makes them clothes with Bow Proficiency or something," Sandy said. Then she paused. "Actually, that would make a lot of sense.

Like, all our classes can boost the shit out of one Valjean. Or you could boost like a hundred people a little bit."

"Okay wait. Go back. The butchers in your memories make it look easy?" I asked.

"Yeah. They have to have higher stats. Even cutting into my first corpse when I unlocked the class, half the memories were of people cutting into live monsters, learning the best way to cut them."

"How many people have worked to clear the dungeons? If every class and every skill has memories like this, then somewhere or sometime this must have been the norm," I said, biting my lip.

"Can't get my stats as high as the memories seem." Sandy shrugged. "Maybe things were just really different at some point. Maybe we used to get points like Nobles did."

"Maybe there's a skill you have to raise to ten for your class to gain more stats. Like when I raised Wardrobe to ten."

Sandy finally finished pinning the leather.

"Wanna steal lunch? There's leftovers from last night," she asked. "Then you can tell me whatever memory has you freaking out."

"Sure," I replied.

We ate a lunch of cold, but cooked, crab meat while I relayed the memory and the headache to Sandy.

"That's weird, though," she said referring to the headache. "Hasn't happened to me yet."

"I still feel like my head hurts," I complained, leaning back in the chair. I was stuffed.

"Should we harass Gerald?" Sandy asked.

"I don't want to see any more sunlight." I groaned.

Sandy let out half a laugh.

We burned the morning relaxing until my headache started to recede. Then we swept into the dungeons. It was still early afternoon; we had plenty of time and plenty of mana, so we resolved to clear all four of the dungeons. We started with the north and south.

Now that we knew what to expect with the horde of little golems, we approached with stealth. Sandy and I crept up to the monsters from the bushes, moving around the edge of their encampment.

I practiced [Thread Mastery] throwing needles and wrapping them around the golems' legs before using the enchantment to rip them into the bushes. We crushed the first four of the little monsters without the rest catching on. Then they began to search the area in little groups. The tiny monsters only reached to my shin.

Sandy cut them down with waves of her wind blade. We plucked out their tiny elemental cores, pocketing them until we could figure out what they were good for.

We reached the south dungeon with mana to spare.

"You really need to make me a warmer outfit for this one," Sandy said, decked out in the Hunter pattern rather than Storm Curtain. She was still rubbing her arms as we jogged to the first of the elementals, breath visible in front of her. We didn't want to spend any longer than necessary in here.

Killing all four of the elementals brought my experience up to four. At this rate, we could level again tonight.

We were sore, cold, and tired by the time we returned home, now in the waning hours of the evening, golden light hovering through the town.

Henri met us with a tentative smile and actual plates of food along with the flasks. I felt like I was eating double as much since I started clearing the dungeons.

"Does having higher stats raise your metabolism?" I asked between bites. Then, before Henri could answer, I asked another question. "Do cooks enchant their food?"

Henri shrugged, waving his hand in a universal "sort of" gesture.

"What are the cooking memories like? Do you have to spend points on recipes?"

"Yes." Henri smiled ruefully. "Though you can get a skill to learn recipes by eating them. Most chefs get that one early. As for the memories…they're full of yelling. Kitchens can be as intense as dungeons. Ah, at least that's how the saying goes. I haven't actually…" He trailed off.

"Okay wait, you literally get to earn skills by *eating?* That's so unfair," I said. Then I took another bite.

Henri smiled again.

We joked and ate, and when my plate was empty I slowly drank soup until my mana was full, and then we left to clear the dungeons again. First the lizards, which we dragged back to Sandy's house.

They only gave me a single experience each now, but in total the dungeon had pushed me eighty percent to my next level. I would level tonight in the beach dungeon.

It was a shame the golems—the earth elementals—didn't give any experience. I could've leveled already.

Finally, with trepidation, we headed to the beach dungeon. We passed through the town without incidence, but there was an air of nervousness. Neither Sandy nor I had commented on it, but the quake that followed as the dungeon's floors were cleared was slowly growing more and more intense, to the point it was no-ticeable over today.

We stopped outside, stretching before entering. My legs were sore from how much running around we had done today, but only barely. It probably would've been worse without my boosted stats.

"Are you ready?" I asked.

"Not really," Sandy said, looking through the portal. She stared at the entrance for a long moment. "I leveled up."

"Just now?" I asked.

"Yeah. In the last dungeon. But I just spent the points. Okay. It's kind of dumb, but, I had Butchering at level nine. I raised it to ten. Because of what you said earlier."

"And?" I asked.

Sandy made a *tch* noise.

"If I'm reading it right, I can gain attributes while butchering."

"No," I said. "Permanently?"

Wind whistled through the trees. It was proper nighttime now, blue light spilling down the canopy and highlighting Sandy's face. She was frowning.

"Permanently," came the reply. "I could've grown so much more if I had known…but it's limited. I can only pull a point from most monsters. A few from some." Sandy groaned.

"This is great!" I said. "No point in worrying about losses that haven't happened yet."

"It's not that. It's that we're going to have to kill that giant bear again to pull points from it." Sandy sighed.

"Then we will kill it as many times as it takes."

Sandy choked on a laugh. Then she laughed a bit harder.

"Have I told you you're crazy?" she asked.

"All the time," I said. Then, without waiting, I stepped into the beach dungeon. The amount of mana in the air made the hair on my arms stand on end. The feeling was familiar. The gate to the next floor was going to open. A look back at Sandy told me she felt it too.

We hunted down the monsters one at a time, but we didn't see any sign of the gate, even as we killed the octopus creature and the ground started to rumble. It definitely wasn't in the tide pool.

I had leveled up once, too, and now I deliberated over my options as we stood over the tide pool. The sun was rising and beating down on the back of my neck. I wondered if my constitution helped me resist sunburn.

[Skill Shop]

▶Alteration I

[COMMON] Aids user in retrofitting clothing to repair it and increase its quality level. Additional levels allow user to upgrade old equipment to higher levels.

▸Pattern Projection I

[COMMON] Seamstress Vision skill. Grants user access to a pattern overlay on fabric.

▸Efficiency I

[RARE] 10% chance to not cost mana when using a skill.

I paused at Efficiency. That skill was good. *Really* good. Maybe not the most helpful thing right now, not while I had Henri's soup potions to restore my mana. But it was rare… I bit my lip. I didn't want to choose it. Not in light of the memory I had seen while crafting the houndsmaster set—the explosion of gore and viscera as the seamstress's scissors tore open the monster, like the lines dividing the pieces of a bloody puzzle.

The headache started to build behind my eyes again, so I grabbed onto a different thought to distract myself. The one that came to mind was the giant half-finished scissors Gerald had made.

I dumped both points into Pattern Mirroring.

"Tomorrow, definitely," I said to Sandy. She was looking down at her knife. "You good?" I asked. She couldn't have just leveled up again. "You good?" I asked.

I had been too absorbed in my own system to notice.

"Yes," Sandy practically growled the reply, looking down. "I just got a point in constitution."

"That's great!" I said.

"It would've been better if I had this skill forever ago." Sandy sighed.

We walked back to the gate to go home. It stood out, a white stone archway jutting out of the sand. The wind blew drifts against it, piling up miniature dunes on the side of the gate.

I took another look at the horizon. Before I could process what I was seeing, I felt Sandy's hand gripping me.

Out in the water was a second archway.

It opened tonight after all.

Cinnamon sniffed at the ground.

Sandy had been out all night. It was safe now, he thought and leaped over the fence.

There was a shuffle inside. He flattened himself to the ground now, following his instincts, his ears pressed back on his head. The old man, the mean man who wouldn't share his good-smelling food, shuffled about inside the house.

Cinnamon thought he was approaching the window…but maybe not. He heard the grumpy man splashing around in the water. When the mean man didn't approach the window, Cinnamon kept going.

Cinnamon was a growing boy. He couldn't live on just the snacks Sandy gave him. No, he had to supplement his diet at night. And he loved to hunt.

He was dragging his belly along the ground, being *sneaky* like Sandy was. She would be so proud of him if she saw him!

He followed his nose. There were so many strange smells, good smells, delicious food! Nothing as good as what Sandy brought home. That tasted better. It made Cinnamon grow! So full of life.

But the food here was good, too! Once Cinnamon was far from the town, far enough that he wouldn't be hurt, he burst into full run. The earth zoomed by under his feet. He shot through the trees, passing the most hospitable land around the town until the foliage grew thick. Plants were torn apart as he shot through the woods.

Then he brought himself to a stop, gouging the ground as he used his paws like gigantic brakes.

He sniffed the ground. He smelled something delicious. It was above him, hiding in the thick foliage of the greater forest outside the town. Cinnamon leaned up against a tree, scratching at the bark and peeling free layers. He wasn't any good at climbing yet. He only managed to get a few feet up before falling.

He spun around, lowered himself to get ready to pounce, and barked up the tree.

His snack jumped down voluntarily.

There was a woomph as Cinnamon bit it out of the air, his tail running at full speed. It was one of his favorite snacks; it was crunchy, and it helped him level up. He loved them ever since Sandy had given him some.

Not to mention how many legs it had! The legs were the best part. Ever since he had started hunting them, though, less and less stayed around the town. He had to go a little bit farther every time to find one.

It was like they were running away from him.

A long, white string hung from the end of the monster, connecting it up to the nest of the sting above. As Cinnamon ate the one on the ground, he pulled at the rope, hoping there would be more. He would need more than this for food tonight.

He was a growing boy!

That's why he ate his whole meal. By the time he finished, there was nothing left but splotches on the ground. His tail waggled as he sniffed, trying to find more. None came down on him.

Then he smelled something strange. There were people. And animals! Ones he had smelled before.

His tongue lolled out of his mouth as he chased the smell. He stopped a few dozen feet away, crashing into the bushes. He scooted along the ground as he tried to see them.

They were tense.

Three of them stood atop their wagons, covered in armor and blood. One of the wagons had a patch applied to it, tears in the wood that looked like claw marks.

Cinnamon very slowly pulled himself back through the bushes, staying low. That was the Noble!

They were not very nice.

And Sandy didn't like them.

Cinnamon had to tell her.

But she wouldn't be back for hours!

Cinnamon sniffed at the ground. Then he shot back toward the town until he found Sandy's trail and started following it. His Tracking skill kicked on, a red line in his vision showing him where to go.

He had to tell her!

CHAPTER 41

"We're going in," Sandy said, before I could even ask.

I was quiet. I didn't say anything.

The waves lapped up the beach with a crash of seafoam before receding. Sandy walked forward. I wasn't sure if she was conscious of it. The expression on her face was a mix of manic aggression and fear, like she was staring down a monster.

But there were no monsters. Just us and the beach. Just us and the breeze. Just us and the dungeon.

"Alright," I said.

We stepped down the beach and up to the portal, stopping again outside of it. I wasn't sure if I was imagining it, but it felt like the tide was getting higher, each wave rising up the beach. The water splashed around my ankles as waves came in. My boots were already soaked.

"Ready?" I asked.

Sandy didn't say anything. She nodded, fixed her face in a determined forward stare, and stepped through.

I followed after.

The warping effect of the dungeon was the most intense it had felt since that first time, the world shifting violently. It was bright inside, and it took my eyes a moment to catch up to what they were seeing.

We were in a cave system. It was the most stereotypical dungeon-like floor we had entered so far. My eyes scanned for threats, paying attention to every odd and irregular shape in the rocks that might give away monsters blending in along the walls. When I wasn't looking for monsters, I was filled with a sense of wondrous awe.

I knew that we were performing magic. Killing monsters, using spells. It was all very real. But so many pieces of it became mundane over a lifetime. Stepping into this place was different. Yellow and orange plants glowed along the walls, tiny stems retracting and extending over and over, creating a rippling pattern of light.

It was reflected on the surface of the water below. Wind whistled through the cavern, making the surface of the water ripple. When the reflection broke, glowing red coral could be seen in the shallow pools.

It was a grotto. A cave system filled with ocean water. It was at low tide, for now, and there wasn't a sign of a monster. The plants filled the cave with artificial, luminescent light.

"Holy fuck," Sandy said, audibly sucking in a breath next to me.

This was the most dangerous environment we had ever been in. And the most beautiful. I took a look over at her.

"Yeah," I said.

Her eyes followed a path up the walls, along the lines of glowing flora. I didn't know if she was looking for monsters or still taking it all in. She bit her lip.

"So…which way?" I asked, spinning around. The exit to this floor sat against the wall. To my surprise, water splashed in through the gate, running over my shoes and into the shallow pool behind me.

The caves still smelled like the beach.

Sandy stepped forward, splashing through the ankle-high, salty ocean water. She looked left, then right, staring into the two largest openings that led away from this room.

Then there was a huge splash from our left.

"That way, then?" I asked, meeting Sandy's eyes. She gave me a calculating look. Then she nodded, knife in her hand as she stepped through the water and beyond. The water level dropped to only a centimeter, but I looked at the pond in the center of the cave with worry.

It was still low tide.

Did the dungeon have tides? Did it have moons? Was it even round? Was I procrastinating?

I shook off the thoughts and followed behind Sandy, needle at the ready. The plants sent waves of movement up and down the walls, causing my eyes to jump side to side. But no monsters appeared.

My eyes tracked the water. The seaweed that grew in the shallow tide pools looked like the silhouettes of dark tendrils crisscrossing the glowing red coral. I was still searching the moving shadows of the depths when Sandy gasped.

My head flicked up.

Sandy charged into the water.

"Sandy?" I half asked, half shouted lifting the needle in my hand and looking between her and the water. That red coral didn't look safe to touch.

I followed her through the water. It was only thigh deep, splashing around us. Sandy charged through it. I stepped carefully around the coral, not willing to risk touching it. At least nothing ambushed us as we crossed the water.

"Sandy?" I asked again. She stopped on the other side of the water. Then she shuddered and leaned down.

I felt my heart drop.

"Are you alright?" I asked, reaching her side. She was blocking whatever she was leaning over, up against the wall. When I placed a hand on her shoulder, she flinched. Then I saw what she was looking at.

Depressed against the rocky ground of the cave, soaked in saltwater and tattered to shreds was a pile of clothing. Or the imprint of a pile of clothing.

Time had pressed it flat against the wall and floor. There was no body; not anymore. We were two floors deep in a dungeon; six days passed here for every day on the surface. Six years for every year above.

Sandy was wracked with silent sobs as she turned over a rusted piece of metal in her hands. A comparatively tiny butcher knife. An outfit that didn't impart any skills.

This was as far as her mother had made it. But she had been alone. I leaned down and put a hand on Sandy's back.

She sobbed.

I opened my mouth to say something, but I didn't know what. There was a lump in my throat. I just sat there and supported her weight, letting her lean on me.

There was a splash in the water behind us. I turned, looking over my shoulder.

A monster loomed behind our backs, seawater dripping from its side. The top of it glowed with red coral, its body a looming silhouette of a crab. We might have walked over its body to get here.

"Sandy," I said quietly. The crab wasn't moving yet. Instead it was clicking, its luminescent yellow eyes scanning the room. I shook Sandy's shoulder. She was clutching the little rusted remains of the knife in her hand so hard it was shaking.

The monster took a step forward. I couldn't wait any longer. I charged at it.

[Running Stitch I] [Mana: 5/10] [Cancel]

My needle sheared against the chitin, sparking as if it was made of metal, the light illuminating in the dark. It didn't pierce it. I fell forward along the outer edge of the monster's shell, splashing face-first into the water. I pressed my hands down on red coral, and exactly as I expected, it burned. My health ticked away a point at a time as I shoved myself out of the water, momentarily disoriented, throwing my head back and forth to find the monster.

"Sandy!" I shouted, spinning around, but the monster was still bearing down on me. I threw my needle up between us as if I was going to block its massive claw.

The pincer bit down on the needle and ripped it out of my hands, sending me tumbling back into the water.

I scrambled back out, reaching for the second needle behind me. The crab flung the first needle away; it clattered against the wall, the sound of metal on stone ringing through the cave.

This thing was dangerous. Beyond dangerous.

[Running Stitch I] [Mana: 4/10] [Cancel]

I stabbed it in the mouth this time, blood and gore gushing out and splashing into the water around me. The monster staggered back, taking my needle with it. I reached for the throwing needles on my hip.

The monster's mandibles opened, more of its insides spilling out as it aggravated the wound. Then it leaned down toward me. I fumbled to pull one of the needles free.

The crab fell sideways as Sandy cut off two of its legs in one strike. It made a low, terrible noise, like a hiss of pain as it stumbled backward. The insides of its legs poured out of the clean-cut wound like liquid slop.

My hands burned.

Sandy swung again, and the monster collapsed into the water.

Then she stepped on top of it. I wasn't sure if her armor's gloves stopped the coral from burning her or if she just didn't care.

She stabbed into the water over and over, the Windblade enchantment sending splashes of water and blood up around us as she cut into the monster. It died on the third stab.

[+4 XP]

She kept going even as the dungeon started to rumble with the indication that we'd cleared it.

When she ran out of mana and the water stopped splashing around her, she kept stabbing down, easily piercing the chitin of the crab with her knife, staining the water as blue blood poured out of the wound.

Sandy screamed with every stab until her voice guttered out. Then she stopped stabbing, sitting in the water on top of the crab as the mana in the dungeon roiled over us.

Normally, by now, it would've dissipated or slammed into place to open the gate to the next floor. Instead, though, it boiled around us. I looked uneasily at the cavern's walls, where the water level was rising.

"We should go," I said to Sandy. My voice was quieter than I expected. She just nodded, lifting herself off the crab slowly. The water parted around her as she walked back to the wall.

"Take these," she said, looking back at me.

I nodded, walking up and activating [Wardrobe], pulling the tattered scraps into my inventory. Then we trudged back to the entrance. Sandy held the rusted remains of her mother's knife in her hands like it was the most precious artifact she owned.

The mana in the dungeon didn't dissipate as we reached the exit. I stopped and looked back, taking everything in.

"Was that it?" I asked.

Sandy just looked at me, confused.

"Just the one monster? The mana is…tingling."

"I'm not sure," Sandy said, her voice quiet and restrained.

With a shrug, I stepped through to the beach.

I found myself somewhere else entirely. For just a fleeting second, I felt something look down on me. More than one something. It was the same experience as when I awakened my system for the first time. But it was also slightly different.

The last time, I felt a single gaze weighing down on me. Just the weight of that perception felt like it would tear me apart. This time, I could count the things looking at me. I could feel the weight of their perception as a physical thing. One. Three. Six. Nine. Ten of them, all shuffling about, looking at me like they hadn't expected to see me.

There was a high-pitched ringing in my ears as an eleventh perception weighed down on me, somehow closer to me than the others. This one was…deformed. It was upside down and sideways, barely awake, and the weight of its gaze was familiar. This is the one that had looked at me when my system was awakened. My skin was burning hot.

I collapsed to the ground, trying not to vomit as I was shoved through the portal. I was half afraid I was going to float off the beach. I tasted seawater.

"Gwen?" Sandy said. She was shouting. I was in the ocean. I tried to push myself to my feet, but spat out ocean water, retching instead.

There was an alert in my interface.

I ignored it, nausea rolling through me as I crawled away from the seawater. I couldn't stand. My limbs felt weak. When I felt hot sand between my fingers instead of the cold, soul-draining wetness of the ocean, I blinked the stinging water from my eyes.

And I read the pending alert.

[Tier 0 dungeon alert]

[Title contest quest generated]

[Deepest Clear updated: Gwen Tailor, Sandy Butcher]

[Notice: Previous Deepest Clear was greater than 12 months ago.]

[Previous Deepest Clear: HIDDEN]

[Would you like to make your recent clear public? Y\N]

"N…no!" I shouted. Sandy flinched.

"Gwen? Are you alright?" she asked, leaning down next to me.

"Y— I'm fine," I said, making sure I wasn't going to say anything dumb the system would take as an answer to its prompt.

[Confirmed! Title Contest Quest generated.]

[Conditions]

▶Clear all open sub-dungeons to floor two

▶Clear central dungeon fourth floor

▶Timer: 72 hours from next reset

▶Dungeon Reset disabled from start of next reset until quest cleared or failed

[Rewards]

▶Ownership of title: Stitch transferred to Gwendolyn Tailor

[Stitch: Tier 0, Village]

[Current title holder notified.]

CHAPTER 42

I stared, not waving away the system prompt. I was queasy, still on the sand, sick at whatever the system had just done to me. If that was what the church worshiped, then I understood why they would call it a god. Just the weight of that many perceptions made me feel like I was about to black out.

It was like there was a hundred-pound weight around my neck.

Sandy didn't look much better than I felt. She had sat down on the beach and taken off her helmet. Her eyes were puffy and her face was red.

"Are you good?" Sandy asked. "You didn't get, like, poisoned?"

"No. You didn't get…that?" I asked, looking over my shoulder at the gate. The water was definitely rising. It was constantly draining into the gate to the next floor now, higher up the beach. I worried that the dungeon in there would flood eventually.

"Didn't get *what?*" Sandy asked, her voice sharp.

"I got a quest. 'Contested title quest generated,' it said."

"A quest? What do you mean a quest? I thought only Nobles… *Title quest?*" Sandy asked. She scrambled up to me in the sand and squinted like she was trying to see my system.

"For ownership of the town," I said.

Sandy's breathing intensified.

"Let's—let's do it. We start…tomorrow. What do we need?"

I explained the conditions of the quest—clearing the dungeons—and that this was the Deepest Clear in a year. If Sandy had kept going just a little bit farther, she would've generated this quest herself.

If she lived.

But we were only able to do this because we worked together. The more people joined in helping us, the easier it became. First Sandy, then Mom, then Henri. We were stronger together.

"We got plenty of time before Valjean comes back." Sandy said.

"We might only have a few days. The system said it notified the current title holder…which would be Valjean."

"No. We have plenty of time," Sandy said. "We have to be able to do this now. We won't win a head-to-head against Valjean. But tonight…let's just go home."

After a few minutes I had mostly recovered. I stood, albeit without fully trusting my legs, and took the first step toward the exit. I flinched as a monster dove through before I reached it.

I reached for my sewing needle by reflex, holding it out between myself and the monster as it barked. Its wagging tail and bright golden eyes made me drop the needle.

"Cinnamon?" Sandy asked.

The dog tackled her, licking her face before backing off to inspect her.

"Get down!" she said, pushing the dog back, half yelling. Cinnamon whined in concern. "You're supposed to be in your pen!"

"Does he get out a lot?" I asked, staring at the dog. It was one thing for the dog to extend games of fetch across town. It was another for it to track us into a dungeon! What if he got hurt?

"He may…be leaving the town sometimes. I mean, he is obviously a very big dog. A very good boy," Sandy said, leaning forward and scratching Cinnamon behind the ears.

He slipped away, barking again.

"What does he want?"

"More treats, probably." Sandy grunted, tossing the body of the flying fish. It landed with a splat in the sand in front of Cinnamon. His tongue lolled as he panted, mouth open, drooling over the fish. Then he shook his head and barked, running in a circle around Sandy.

"Or not," I said.

Cinnamon ran from Sandy, stood between her and the portal, and whimpered.

"I think he wants us to follow him." Sandy said. Then she picked up her helmet and shoved it on.

We walked out of the dungeon with Cinnamon in front of us. Every three steps, he turned back to look at us. But he had stopped barking. We trailed behind him as he stomped through the forest with ease, the mild discomfort of the Wild itching at us the whole time.

"Where are we going?" I asked. With night having fallen, it was hard to keep our bearings. Cinnamon sniffed the ground. "I'm not sure following your dog blindly into the night is a good idea."

Cinnamon turned and whined.

"Should we head back to town?" Sandy asked.

Cinnamon half barked, then whined more.

"I think…there's no harm in it. We could probably handle anything out here fine." I rubbed my arm as I spoke. This was unnerving.

We followed Cinnamon as he looped through the forest. Sometimes he would stop, turning at a harsh angle to loop around. Finally, he broke through some foliage before spinning around and running back to us.

Cinnamon whined.

We stepped through the last line of foliage…and onto the main, dusty road that led out of town. Tracks were carved in the earth from the wear of hundreds of wagon wheels. Grass and flowers fought to reclaim the edges of the road.

And on the other side of the bubble, in the town's domain, we saw the wagons. Lanterns hung from their sides, making them visible even through the warping air.

"Shit," Sandy said.

"Shit," I agreed.

Then we snuck through the Wild, around the edge of town.

Cinnamon followed distantly behind us, dragging his belly along the ground. When I turned around to look at him he stopped, throwing his paws over his eyes. He was much more intelligent than a puppy…but not more intelligent than a toddler.

In town, the Nobles were already searching house by house again. Another surprise census.

"He wasn't supposed to be back for two weeks," Sandy grumbled.

"I know. I jinxed us." I sighed.

Sandy's house was in sight. We'd almost made it.

Then one of the mage lights turned from the street, visible through the warping haze that separated the city and the Wild.

"Shit!" Sandy said.

I hissed between my teeth.

"We need to get home before we miss being counted. And you need a change of clothes. Let's slink around to my place before they check there."

"Slink around. Like we're hiding!" Sandy whisper-shouted.

"We are hiding!" I replied.

The Wild was visibly expanded beyond where it had been last time Valjean was here. There was no way he hadn't noticed that. Not to mention the alert that someone had cleared deeper than him.

There was no mage light at my house, thankfully.

We sprinted from the Wild to the workshop, threw open the door, and stepped inside. Cinnamon ducked in before we shut the door. He barked before shaking himself off.

"Gwen?" Esmeralda asked.

"Mom!" I said.

"What…are you wearing?" she said, looking me up and down. I felt red creep up my face as I realized that, with everything going on, I hadn't changed back into my mundane clothes.

"Yeah, she's been clearing the dungeon with me. Her stats are way higher than mine," Sandy said, ripping her helmet off. "Do you have a spare set of clothes for me?"

I activated [Quick Change] not replying as Mom stared at me, waiting for me to explain.

"Sandy," I hissed.

"She definitely knows!" Sandy shouted. "Have the Nobles come here yet?"

"No. They haven't come yet," Mom replied, swinging open the cabinet I used to hide my extra clothes in to reveal a spare set of basic clothes in white linen. "You are so grounded," she said to me.

"I'm eighteen!" I replied.

"You've got burns on your hands." Mom threw the clothes to Sandy. "Just don't go out without the potion. Taking that was smart." Mom sighed.

Sandy threw her helmet to me. I caught it, stuffing it away into my inventory.

"She has the skills from every outfit she's crafted. Gwen will be fine. We gotta get presentable." Sandy looked around. "Where are all the…"

Monster parts, she left unsaid. Mom swiveled around in her chair, looking back at the crates of mundane leathers and materials. They were stacked into a pile. Mom had plenty left in reserve.

"Stuffed into the bottom," she said.

Sandy nodded. Then she turned around and started changing.

"So… How was the dungeon?" Mom asked.

Sandy flinched.

"It was a beach." I chose my words carefully, one at a time. It took a little bit of resistance to avoid saying *We got a quest to take control of the town*. I didn't even want to mention that. The less people knew, the better. "The first floor," I said.

"Was it…nice?" Mom asked.

"No. The second floor was a gross, watery cave," I replied.

Mom looked in Sandy's direction for a long moment, then nodded, apparently deciding something for herself.

"How about the other dungeons?" she asked, wisely pivoting. Sandy turned around with her new soft linen shirt on. "There's one that's hot as hell, one that's cold as hell, and one that's high as hell. They all suck," she said.

There was a pounding at the door. We looked at each other. There had been no mage light outside, no signaled approach of the Noble.

"Esmeralda?" Valjean's voice rumbled through the door. He knocked again. At least he didn't kick it open.

Mom looked at us. I nodded at her and stuffed the rest of the storm curtain armor into my Wardrobe. The door clicked and swung open.

"Mayor Valjean!" Mom said. "Pleasure to see you…" Her voice flagged at the end, dropping in enthusiasm, and I turned around to discover why.

Valjean sniffed and pushed his hair back out of his face. It was wet—it had started raining outside. He was holding a set of clothing, and sighed with what was clearly bone-deep exhaustion as he stumbled into the workshop, throwing his bundle onto a table. He was dressed in armor of mixed metal pieces overlapping finely designed clothes.

"Sorry to spring this on you. Do you think you could do a rush repair on these? I didn't have time before…" Valjean paused as he looked at me and Sandy. We were both tense, just staring back at him. The room froze for a moment.

"Hi," I said.

Valjean stared for a moment before coughing and clearing his throat.

"I didn't have time to bring these in for a normal repair. Then we ended up running into a boss on the way to town," Valjean complained.

My eyes scanned his outfit. As I looked closer, I stopped focusing on the elaborate filigrees covering most out of the outfit and the complex niceties of the design. Instead, I saw the scratches in the metal, the gouges at the edges, the clean break in the bracer on his right arm. Something had seriously messed him up.

He was pushed off base, uncomfortable and stumbling.

Good. The thought pushed itself into my head, unprompted.

"Do you pay extra for surprise orders?" I asked. Mom looked over and blinked at me. Sandy slumped into a seat, watching the conversation play out. It'd be suspicious of her to run away whenever Valjean showed up. She fidgeted with her hands on the other side of the room.

"Yes," Valjean said. "Of course, of course… You might need a smith as well. Sandy, are you up for processing a monster? It might be a little beyond your level, but it won't make it all the way back with us."

"How long are you staying?" Sandy asked.

"Three days," Valjean said. His expression darkened for a moment, but he cleared it with a shake of his head.

CHAPTER 43

Valjean and Sandy left with the monster in tow. I hadn't seen it when we circled around the wagons.

Without Mending, I couldn't help my mom repair Valjean's spare outfit. I wasn't emotionally ready to continue working on the houndsmaster set yet. Thinking about it now still gave me a headache. I was starting to worry that I broke the pattern somehow and that the pain would be permanent. Instead, I just watched my mom work. She pulled Valjean's outfit—all boiled leather and enchanted linen—and set it on a mannequin before inspecting it. She touched it with some kind of skill, seemingly pulling more of the outfit out of midair and revealing dozens of stitches.

The crisscrossing patterns of thread looked almost like circuitry rolling away along an axis I struggled to perceive. I followed along as mom snipped away damaged threads and pulled them out one by one before patching the rents in the material, stitching them back together, and sewing the threads back in. Whatever cut through that armor must have cut directly into Valjean.

He looked like he had healed fine.

Eventually, watching my mom work gave me a headache as well. But it was deep into the night now.

I headed out of the workshop and across town. The rain was pouring down, I ran, the ground already squelching underneath my feet. I almost crashed into the Noble who walked into the street, one of my feet sliding as I came to a stop underneath the edge of his umbrella.

He smiled around a lit cigarette.

"Hey," he said, holding the umbrella out.

His eyes glowed bright red. Not like an enchantment; like he was using a class vision skill. A powerful one.

He wore a cloak, but his hood was back. His hair was cut short. The lamplight from a window reflected off the rings on his fingers.

The bow over his back glowed in the dark.

It hit me that his entire outfit looked like the Hunter pattern I had. Just better in every way.

This was a tracker. Valjean brought a tracker. His eyes flicked over my shoulder, still glowing red, and his smile started to turn into a frown. I panicked as I realized I hadn't replied.

"Hi!" I said.

His expression turned back to a smile, the red fading from his eyes. With a snap, a mage light appeared in front of him. With the skill dismissed, I could see the rich brown of his eyes. The light caught on perfect teeth. I wondered if raising your constitution helped with dental health. I hadn't met a dentist class.

"Going for a walk in the rain?" he asked.

"I'm heading to the butcher's," I said, pushing past him.

He followed me, holding the umbrella over me.

"In the middle of the night?" he asked, catching up and walking alongside me. He stood more than a head over me. "What for?"

"I heard she was cutting up something cool."

"Hardly." He frowned. "Damn thing tore up one of the wagons, though. Tried to eat one of the horses. What's your name?"

"Gwen," I said.

"I'm Olivier," he said.

I kept walking. Olivier frowned.

"My house is Briarthorn," he said.

I didn't know if that was meant to impress me. He frowned deeper.

"Do you know who has been clearing the dungeon?" he asked.

"If I knew, would I tell you?" I asked, turning to face him. He had walked with me all the way to Sandy's house.

"I'd hope so. You've a civic duty," Olivier said, his face scrunched up like he had tasted something sour. "Well. Do let me know if you see anything suspicious."

Olivier turned and left. I watched him go, standing in the rain despite the door being a step away. When his mage light grew dim, I swung the door open and stepped inside.

The room was packed.

Sandy threw a glance at me before turning back to her work.

She had broken the monster into pieces—probably to get it through the door. It would have been as large as one of Valjean's wagons, if it was in one piece.

It was a spider the size of a tank. Each of its legs was a different color, and each one must've been a foot thick. They glittered iridescently. The main body was shimmering white. It looked like a much, much more ramped-up version of the tiny spiders we'd fought.

Cinnamon was curled up in one corner of the room, an imprint of mud in the ground around him. He gnawed on one of the massive legs.

"Is it okay to let him have that? Isn't it valuable?" I asked.

"Can't keep most of the damn thing anyway," Sandy said.

"What do you mean?" I stepped toward her, over piles of limbs and huge chunks of bug meat.

Sandy pulled out a knife to demonstrate, popping out a single plate of the monster's shell. She cut into the plate and smoke hissed out. The plate started to dissolve, falling to the ground in a pile of white goop.

"Entire thing's like a puzzle box. Even following my butcher skill, it's like it's designed to sabotage me as it comes apart," Sandy said, her voice rising with frustration.

"We've done plenty for today," I said. "Have you…told your dad?" I asked.

Sandy set her knife down and rubbed her eyes.

"Yeah. Can you meet us tomorrow? Early."

I nodded.

"Just like Valjean to gift us a corpse we can't use," I said, looking over the pile of monster parts. "How much do you think you'll be able to pull out of it?"

Sandy paused.

"Maybe just enough for one outfit," she said.

I stared at the corpse, hungry. Not for the spider—there was no way I was eating any of that. Not even if it gave me mana. But for the skills.

If the little spiders gave me Thread Mastery II, what would an outfit made from this do?

Sandy stepped around the pile of monster parts and pulled the tiny rusted knife from her bed stand. She plopped into her bed and rolled it over in her hands.

"Did you bring it with you?" she asked.

"Yes," I replied, fetching the destroyed set of clothing from my [Wardrobe].

They were basically just strips of fabric and leather at this point, destroyed by wear and saltwater.

Sandy held them like they were precious.

The morning was somber. I had to double back in the rain to sleep. Olivier didn't bother accosting me this time, though, and I fell into my bed and immediately spent what felt like an hour staring at the ceiling.

Every muscle in my body was tense. The next few days would be all or nothing. We had our town to lose or gain on the results of a single quest. My system brought up a clock in the middle of the night when the gate of the dungeon shut. I stared as it started a countdown that moved from seventy something hours to sixty something, ticking down like a doomsday clock.

I couldn't remember falling asleep.

I did remember waking up, though. The morning was somber.

Mom asked where I was going. I told her where and why.

She joined me. We couldn't invite too many people, gathering in one place while the Nobility was here. But we could gather a few. It was a small, quiet occasion. We met Henri out back behind his house. He was smoking and holding a shovel.

There was a tiny hole in the ground, a pile of scrap leather inside of it beneath a rusty knife.

Sandy sat in a chair outside, staring blankly into the forest and scratching behind Cinnamon's ears.

Henri held the shovel out to me. I took it, ceremonially taking a single shovel of dirt and dumping it into the hole. He nodded, and I passed it off to Sandy, who shoveled once as well.

Henri said a few words about his wife. I didn't know her. He told us how they met, about their first date, their favorite activities, how they had moved out to the frontier town. It had been bigger back then. He wiped tears out of his eyes and sat down.

A few other adults from the village came over the course of the day, each one shoveling their own dirt. There was a tension anytime another person approached. Henri sent everyone away with a bag of food. The Nobles never investigated. We all had a hand in burying what remained. It wasn't so much covering over the past as celebrating what was and what is. This was our town. Every single person had as many memories as Henri and Sandy did, entire lives here, simple as they were.

I couldn't let them take this town from us. Not from any of us.

CHAPTER 44

Sandy had bags under her eyes as she led me around to her workshop. It was still morning, before lunch, when she pushed the door open and it swung inside.

The monster was mostly disassembled and already loaded onto two carts at the door. At least, the parts that could be salvaged were loaded. There was a giant mud spot in front of Sandy's bed where Cinnamon had lain. He was currently creating a new giant dirt spot on the other side of the room, chewing apart slagged pieces of the monster.

"It was a pain in the ass to take to task," Sandy said. "I lost more than half of it. It's like its entire body is set up to self-destruct. Still got half of it to go."

"Valjean said they found it in the woods," I said, stepping over a pile of monster parts. "It looks like something that would've come out of the central dungeon."

"So do the spiders that Cinnamon has been eating. I thought he was hunting them from the woods until he found us in the dungeon. Maybe he's been going in," she said.

There was a pounding at the door. I looked at Sandy, who shrugged before stepping to the door to open it.

Olivier looked down as the door swung open. Not at me, but at the ground. His eyes were glowing with his active skill. He scratched at his face, talking without looking up.

"Did a monster come in here?" he asked.

"No. Just Cinnamon," I said.

"Oh! It's you again," Olivier said, making eye contact with me now. He smiled. It was obviously more forced this time than it was last night. "What is…Cinnamon?"

Olivier poked his head into the room, looking left toward the bed.

"Woah!" I said, putting a hand on his chest to push him back. He didn't budge. His head swiveled to the right instead.

He recoiled like someone had hit him.

"By all the gods—do you live in here?" he asked. "With the corpses?"

"Yes! Now get out!" I started closing the door. He caught it on a boot.

"Do all peasants live like this? Are the hooks hanging from the ceiling normal?"

"Have you never been to a village before?" I asked, frowning. The Nobles that Valjean brought had always rotated out. But none had ever been as naive as this one—at least none who bothered talking to us. Valjean must have gone out of his way to hire a tracker. I hoped it was expensive.

Sandy stomped up, pulled the door back, and slammed it. The noble moved his foot out of the way.

I sighed.

"That guy has no sense of privacy," Sandy said. Loudly. He definitely heard it.

"He has tracking skills," I said, stepping back from the door and talking quietly. "Was butchering the monster at least good for experience?"

Sandy nodded vigorously.

"I gained almost two levels from this alone. I hope we don't have to fight anything like this soon."

"Is your dad cooking?" I said. I smelled food. Sandy shrugged.

I pushed my way into the kitchen. It wasn't barricaded anymore. Henri looked almost as tired as Sandy. Dishes lined the table, mismatched pots and bowls as Henri stirred a gigantic pot full of soup.

"This…isn't made of spider, is it?"

I hadn't missed that most of the bug meat was gone from Sandy's work room.

Without replying, Henri pulled a cup of soup and handed it to me. I tasted it with trepidation. It was delicious.

"Going to have enough for tonight. Save your appetite." Henri said. I nodded, but I drank the rest of the soup. I hadn't eaten all morning.

"You're going to have some left over, too," Sandy said, looking at the table.

Henri waved a hand dismissively.

"That's for everyone else." We headed back into the workshop and wheeled the carts outside—only after peering through the window and making sure Olivier had gained some distance. Then we took them to my mom's workshop.

I wasn't going to waste this material on my own pattern.

Mom sat tiredly, organizing the scraps of damaged material she had pulled out of Valjean's pattern into her storage chest. She gave me a weary smile as I brought in the work cart.

I wondered how valuable the scraps of material were if she was sorting them out piece by piece. She had even pulled out broken strings with fraying edges, sorting them like precious stones.

"So," I said, blowing out a puff of air and turning around to wave at the two work carts full of spider parts. "We have…this."

"Should I keep cutting it up?" Sandy asked, standing over the cart.

Mom walked over it, scanning each piece of the material and turning it over in her hands.

"You want me to help you make an outfit to clear the dungeon with?" Mom asked, turning to me.

"Yes," I said, my eyes flicking away from my mom's and to the pile of monster parts.

"You just had to ask." She smiled wryly.

And then she went to work. Mom practically flew around the workshop, using some esoteric skill to fling material onto the extra desks set up. Cloth spun to land in perfect position, chunks of monster landing beside them.

"Can I help with anything?" I asked, stepping forward.

"No," she said. I recoiled. But she smiled, stepping over to me and putting a hand on my shoulder. "Rely on me, light."

Sandy started cutting apart the unprocessed remains of the monster. I wrung my hands for a moment about what I should do before remembering the Houndsmaster pattern.

I pulled it out and set it down on a single table in the corner of the room.

Mom shifted between a half dozen tables, moving like a machine to finish pieces of the outfit she was working on. It took on strange shapes; hard, hollow tubes bent in ways that were hard to look at. I blinked away from it and continued my own work. With any luck, I could finish the houndsmaster set tonight.

I licked my lips and activated [Running Stitch]. The patterns and memories were…normal. Flashes of the stitching and leather punching, memories of warnings where to avoid stabbing my own fingers, and images of people crafting the outfit in a hundred camps and workshops.

It must have been a popular pattern.

The shell dress had only had a few poor memories attached to it.

The houndsmaster outfit, on the other hand, was filled with rich memories, scents and smells, the feeling of a heart pounding inside my chest—

I was standing with an arm extended, the skill already activating in the memory. I was also still in the workshop. The world reeled like I was on a boat in a storm, both memories lilting to the side until I remembered to keep my hands moving, stitching the outfit together with precision informed by memory and controlled by magic.

In the memory, I felt myself activate [Befriend] at a drake. At an actual dragon—a hulking leviathan that poured fire across the ground toward me. Two monsters pinned it to the ground. A completely white ape with glowing blue eyes held its right arm, swinging a gigantic paw and releasing a gust of freezing white. The drake's flames guttered out.

I felt the seamstress in the image switch, calling on a different skill, and for just a flash the memory of what was in her [Wardrobe] passed through me. Ten complete outfits, every one with skills for either surviving the Wild or taming monsters. She had a complete build from outfits alone.

The thought of it caught me so off-guard I stopped sewing, the memory shattering into pieces again.

Blinking it away, I realized that the seconds of remembering had been almost an hour in real time. I had pulled the memory up, piece by piece, like pulling on a thread. The headache wasn't nearly as bad this time.

But more importantly, the outfit was almost complete.

I kept working at it, slowly and carefully. Every few minutes, I stopped and checked my quest's countdown timer.

Cinnamon was a good boy.

He paid attention.

He followed Sandy outside when she carried the cart of good food away. It seemed unfair that she was going to eat the rest herself, but he was an adult now. He could hunt for himself. He wasn't getting lots of time to play lately.

Cinnamon looked to his right, sitting up.

The guy who came over had skills just like Cinnamon. Cinnamon made a bet that he would like to play.

Cinnamon activated his [Tracking] skill and started following the red line left behind by the Noble.

CHAPTER 45

I finished the houndsmaster set before sunset, without the emergence of another memory. I felt conflicted. In a way, I was happy that I had managed to finish it. But I also craved more; I wanted to see inside of the strange world of those seamstresses. I wondered just how far in the distant past those memories really were. I felt them like hundreds of threads pulling away from me.

Were there others out there like me?

There must have been. I had no idea how vast the world was. I stretched the completed outfit over one of the open mannequins in the room.

I had made it from the red scale-leather of the boss lizard. Tightly packed crimson scales shined where they reflected light. Once they were cleaned their surface was dazzlingly bright and smooth. The arms extended into huge, padded leather sleeves made to absorb bites. Hopefully the lizard scale would help it resist cutting as well.

The pants were straight cut, finished with red scale-leather. A huge hood and cloak draped over the back, contrasting starkly with the bright red; it was made from black shadow wolf fur.

I blinked as I looked at it closely. The cloak wasn't entirely black; it featured streaks of red scale that ran from the hood, terminating at a shining red bottom edge. Memories pushed themselves to the forefront of my mind: I had done that, and I had done it mostly while under the influence of the second set of memories.

The quality of the set bumped up.

[Houndsmaster's Uniform (Uncommon, Fire) completed!]

[Quality Assessment: (Good)]

[Generating Skills…]

▸Befriend III

▸Wildspeaker I

[+2 XP]

I brushed a hand over it, activating [Wardrobe] to inventory it. Despite the fact that the set my mom was working was many times more complex, and that I had started mine days ago, she looked done as well.

She was wearing her stitching gloves. My eyes traced the silver filigree on them. Mom sighed contentedly.

"Is it done?" I asked, stepping cautiously behind her. Calling it an outfit would be a misnomer.

"Yes," Mom said, still admiring her own work. Her hands were folded over her lap.

It was a knight's armor. Shining white, embellished with the pattern of a central spiderweb that snaked out from the center of the breastplate. It had a triangular helmet with a neck guard spreading from the chitin, embellishments of spiderweb patterns spread across it. The web was made of the colorful pieces pulled out of the legs; it was a glittering purple that contrasted with the white. Every single section of my skin would be covered by it.

I grabbed one of the gauntlets in my hand. It was made of segments of chitin. There wasn't even any stitching visible. This was stretching the definition of what a seamstress could work on.

"Would you like to try it on?" My mom asked.

I stored the gloves in my inventory first, then the rest. Since I didn't make it, I wouldn't know what skills it would give me until I wore it. So I fit it on piece by piece.

It was simultaneously hot and stuffy and freezing cold. Near the joints, padding pushed in and insulated me, while in other places, sections of cold chitin pressed against me and siphoned heat away.

This was outfit number seven. Seven outfits in my storage. Three more and I'd have the stats of two separate outfits, plus all the skills. I was leveling and improving bit by bit. But not as fast as a Noble, who would have the advantage of finely made, high-level clothes on top of superhuman skill levels.

Even the garbage scraps from Valjean's outfits were valuable enough to keep.

I felt myself make a fist, the chitin covering my right hand clicking as it came together. Then I pulled open my stat menu.

[Gwendolyn Tailor][Human, Lv16][Seamstress]
[Health: 66/66][Mana: 10/10][XP: 0/10]
[ATTRIBUTES]
▶SPD: 25
▶WIL: 5
▶STR: 29
▶DEX: 8

▶CON: 33
▶PER: 11

[SKILLS]
▶Crafting I
▶Running Stitch I
▶Hand Spinning I
▶Thread Mastery IV
▶Wardrobe X
▶Quick Change I
▶Embellishment III
▶Pattern Mirroring I
▶Always Prepared II
[PATTERNS]
▶[Hunter Pattern]
▶[Shell Dress Pattern]
▶[Houndsmaster Pattern]
[TEMPORARY SKILLS]
▶[Bow Proficiency I]
▶[Shadow Cloak II]
▶[Tracking Proficiency I]
▶[Thread Sensing III]
▶[Thread Mastery V]
▶[Parry VII]
▶[Projection III]
▶[Trapping III]
▶[Befriend III]
▶[Wildspeaker I]
I might not be a Noble.

But I was already stepping beyond the human threshold.

"Thread Mastery seven." I practically whispered.

Mom folded her hands together, smiling.

"Well, what are you waiting for?" She asked. "You have a dungeon to clear."

Cinnamon was a very, very stealthy boy. He lay on his belly between two houses, tracking Olivier back to the circle of wagons that had been set up in the middle of town. A third Noble worked to do a hack-dash repair of the wagons, hammering to drive nails in, securing wooden planks to the gashes. Cinnamon's ears popped up as Olivier spoke.

"Probably hurting more than helping, yeah?" he asked, slinging the bow from over his shoulder as he sat on a wooden bench pulled up in front of the fire. Sparks kicked off the flame, the wood crackling.

Cinnamon knew this was his moment.

He charged forward at full speed.

Olivier flinched and cursed as Cinnamon's mouth opened, slobber whipping out as Cinnamon's teeth locked on Olivier's bow like a throwing stick. Then Cinnamon jumped, clearing the wagons and landing hard on the other side.

He whined as the fall hurt his legs, but it only took him a second to recover and keep going. He ran between the houses, ducking and weaving to reach the bubble that kept the town locked in. Then he plunged into the Wild.

Cinnamon jumped as an arrow landed near him.

He spun around, looking back to see Olivier holding a much less ornate bow.

"Bring. That. Back," he said between panted breaths.

Cinnamon's tail waggled. He adjusted the bow in his mouth, shifting it over and covering it in slobber.

Did Olivier think they were playing fetch? Cinnamon was playing his favorite game instead. Keep-away.

He turned and ran into the forest.

Henri had filled multiple flasks with soup. I was already starving after spending most of the day toiling away.

But the results were worth it.

I strapped the flasks to my belt. I'd have to take it off to put it on over the spider armor later.

"Have you seen Valjean?" I asked Henri.

He shook his head.

"Haven't seen him since yesterday."

"Thanks, Henri," I said, touching a flask at my waist.

He nodded.

"Thanks, Dad," Sandy said, leaning against the kitchen counter.

We crossed through town, watching with extreme paranoia. Neither Valjean nor Olivier were anywhere to be seen. The third noble was at the center of town, guarding that dungeon's entrance. But that didn't matter to us. We would slip by later with stealth.

First, we moved toward the ocean dungeon, stepping into the Wild.

Sandy changed beyond the town's edge between the foliage and trees, and only minutes after that we stepped from a forest onto a beach.

"Are you ready?" I asked Sandy. She nodded silently in her armor.

I'd been worried about her after we cleared this dungeon a second time. The timer was at sixty hours. We couldn't afford to mess up.

We were going to clear this in one go.

The wind blew drifts of sand as we stepped up to the crab along the beach. I stabbed into the monster, parting its chitin easily and killing it. Then we killed the fish. We didn't even use a skill. I stabbed the needle down, my enhanced stats allowing me to part its scales and end it.

We weren't taking any corpses home with us tonight though. We left them in the sand.

The octopus monster in the tide pool died as easily as ever. Then the portal, suspended in the ocean water a few feet from the beach, flashed to life.

I looked at Sandy. Her expression couldn't be read, covered up as she was by the storm curtain helmet. I wondered what would be across this sea if I sailed it.

Probably just another wall.

The waves lapped over the edges of the portal to the next floor. As I took a step forward, the dungeon entrance started to warp.

A Noble stepped through.

"Gerald?" Sandy asked.

"Sandy..." he said.

He was dressed in head-to-toe armor; not a single piece of him was showing. He sunk ankle deep into the sand. In his hands he held a gigantic pair of scissors.

"Do you guys have time to go mining soon?" Gerald asked.

I was about to say something. Sandy choked out a laugh. She leaned over and rested her face in her hands.

"Maybe next week, Gerald," she said.

Gerald held the scissors out.

"What do they do?" I asked before taking them. He pulled them back into his chest.

"It's not very impressive. Some stats. Plus they—"

Gerald grunted, and the scissors shrank, flying out of his hands like a loosed balloon before falling onto the beach. His armor creaked as he grunted to pick them up.

"It does take mana, though," he said. "When I heard Valjean was back in town, I rushed to finish the other blade and...this is what happened. The other half of the scissor is just enchanted with sharpness."

He held out the now-tiny pair of scissors. I took them gently, afraid of the general stability of Gerald's productions. But they didn't expand. I willed them to, just like with the throwing needles, and they exploded outward in size with a tiny sting to my finger.

[Mana: 8/10]

"Is that the *ocean*?" Gerald asked, looking out over the beach.

"How did you find us?" I asked, frowning and finally processing as my thoughts recovered.

"Oh, I just followed the pull of my equipment. I can sorta sense you," he said. He wasn't paying attention. He had taken his helmet off. And now he was stepping toward the sandy beach. He was mesmerized.

I put a hand on his shoulder, yanking hard to make him stand still. He flinched.

"We're in a dungeon," I said.

"Ye–yeah," Gerald replied. His helmet reappeared. "Let's go mining again soon, okay?"

"Sure. Do you want to kill a giant crab with us?" I asked.

"No. Not even a little." Gerald rushed out through the exit.

I dragged the giant scissors with me, carving a line in the sand as I moved to the gate to the next floor. Sandy said nothing when I looked over to her.

"I could take this next floor on my own," I offered. "You could stay up here."

"No," Sandy said. She seemed upset at the suggestion. "Let's go."

She unsheathed her wind knife and we stepped from the fresh air of the beach to the hot, humid air of the caves. Sandy put a hand on my shoulder and stepped in front of me, eyes scanning the water as we plunged deeper into the dungeon.

The monster was obvious now.

An irregularity in the burning hot coral at the bottom of the watery pit highlighted the monstrous crab's shape. Sandy held up a hand to me, telling me to wait, before circling around to the other side of the water.

She flicked her knife. A wave of wind cut through the brine, splashing it up and out of the pit. The monster breached the surface, splashing saltwater through the entire cavern.

It circled around, gigantic claws snapping menacingly. I knew that my needles weren't very effective against the crab. So I didn't try. Instead, I activated [Pattern Mirroring], snapping out with the scissors at one of the monster's joints.

[Pattern Mirroring I] [Mana: 7/10]

As the scissor blades closed on one of its legs, a section of the Shell Dress pattern appeared, overlaying my vision. A second one of the crab's legs lit up on my left.

Both were sheared in half.

"Yes!" I said as the crab staggered to the left, clicking its claws angrily. Behind the crab, I heard Sandy swing twice, the mana blades of her knife erupting with cracking noises that sheared through more of the crab's legs. It collapsed back into the water, claws flailing about.

Sandy put a hand up to cover her face from the splashing water as she stepped closer to the monster. Then she thrust her knife down once, stabbing into the water, and the thrashing stopped.

[+3 XP]

CHAPTER 46

One down, four to go, as easy as that. We jogged from the western ocean dungeon entrance to the northern mountain dungeon, drinking mana-restoring soup the whole way. Salt clung to my skin where brine had evaporated, but I counted my blessings that I wasn't covered in coral burns this time.

The late evening chill made the cold of the saltwater all the worse, and I found myself almost wanting to visit the lava dungeon next instead of the mountain dungeon. Almost.

All of that compounded the constant, aggravating itch of the Wild.

Sandy and I both kept throwing nervous glances behind us. But there was no Valjean. No Olivier.

"Do you think the tracker will be on us soon?" Sandy asked.

"No sense in worrying about it," I replied, touching the tiny scissors on my belt and debating activating them. "This first floor is going to be almost all you."

Sandy nodded. Then she stepped through the gate to the mountain dungeon.

We threw ourselves at it. It was warmer here than in the Wild, but still cold. The air felt thin as we scrambled over rocks to get to the little camp of gem-like earth elementals. Dirt managed to sneak through the various joints of my knight's armor, filling up my boots as we scrambled over rocks.

We stopped a bit away from the camp to clean them out.

"We really need a magic shower or something," I said as I pulled my boots back on.

"Maybe you can get a cleaning set," Sandy said.

"Ha. And what? Kill monsters with a maid's uniform?" I pushed my leg down and shifted back and forth to ensure the boot was on tight. Then I pulled out my throwing needles.

I yanked the golems away and isolated them one at a time so that we could pick them off without fighting the full swarm of them at once. They gave no experience, which made this a long toil with very little reward. It was nowhere near as hard as before, though. Thread Mastery six made manipulating the threads attached to the throwing needles heinously easy. I could throw the dagger and control the end of the strings to wrap around the mobs and pull them away with ease.

Eventually, the last few earth elementals realized what was going on and charged us all at once. Though by that point there were only four of them.

The entrance to the next floor was at the back of the camp, looking like the entrance to the mine if not for the swirling nighttime image of the next floor.

"God fuck. We have to fight four unknown monsters, don't we?" Sandy asked, standing outside the portal and looking in. She squinted as if trying hard enough would let her see what was inside.

"Probably just two, right? We know what the next floor's monster might be," I said, looking over to Sandy. She had an eyebrow cocked. "The copper mole?"

"Oh. Ohhh. You think that's what's in there?" She leaned forward. Then she nodded, apparently satisfied.

I followed her into the next floor of the dungeon.

To no one's surprise, it was another cave. This one, though, seemed almost artificial. The walls were marked with claw scratches like a creature had carved through them. They opened in a dozen directions.

Veins of multicolored crystals decorated the walls, pouring down a dozen colors like light through a stained glass window. It made the place look almost holy, bright pinks and purples dancing on the ground below. Veins of crystal flecked through the wall. It looked almost identical to the elementals' bodies.

I tightened my grip on the sewing needle in my hand, praying I was right and that this wasn't another horde room.

We slunk down the nearest tunnel, walking through sporadically illuminated caves. Sandy lit a lamp after the first dark turn, the orange light contrasting with the multicolored veins.

We found the monster after a few turns. Well, found is the wrong word.

First, we heard it.

It scratched and tore at a wall in the distance, then walked, each step loud and ponderous in the quiet dark of the cave. We snuck up to it as it slunk away.

It was a copper mole. But it was fatter than the one we had met at the mine. I looked to Sandy, trying to guess how to approach this monster.

"It mostly sees with those whiskers, right? Do you think you could... cut those off?"

"Not without it attacking me," I said. "But maybe with my new level of Thread Mastery..." I grabbed one of the throwing needles at my belt, letting loose the string and holding onto one end of it, before sneaking up to the monster. It seemed to sense my footsteps in the floor, turning around while I was still ten feet away, shaking its head back and forth to scan with the gigantic, whiplike metallic whiskers.

I did not want to get hit by one of those.

The needle in my right hand flew low below the monster's whiskers before I mentally commanded the thread to fly upward. The needle on the end acted as a weight, and it wrapped around the whiskers on the right side of the monster's face, eliciting a scream. I contracted the threads tight, binding half the monster's apparent sensory organ.

Its complete lack of eyes was disconcerting, even with the metal plate covering its face. With a yank, the mole staggered forward. I winced at the way the monster flinched, but I activated [Running Stitch] all the same.

[Running Stitch I] [Mana: 8/10] [Cancel]

I knew that wouldn't be enough to kill it.

[Running Stitch I] [Mana 7/10] [Cancel]

[+3 XP]

The monster collapsed. I was starving. We didn't have time to eat enough to recover our mana completely, especially while jogging.

"Easy!" I said.

Sandy nodded slowly. We both wore helmets now.

The lava dungeon was going to suck.

I sat on the ground and opened a flask of soup, tipping it back. I was rationing myself to eat only when I needed to recover mana, otherwise I would've drained all the flasks.

Sandy sat cross-legged next to me.

We took a few minutes to recover. I could already tell that I would be sore after today, and we hadn't even delved into the ultra-hot or ultra-cold floors.

"So…where's the exit?" I asked Sandy.

"I thought you were… Oh shit." She sighed. We spent an extra half hour lost in the dungeon's caves. The floor was huge—way bigger than its separate tunnels and rooms made it seem. The patterns of randomly colored glowing veins did nothing to help with our sense of direction. Backtracking didn't help us either.

Eventually we found the gate from the sound of wind whistling through it and into the cave. We made our way back to the main room and exited back to the mountain floor. We still had to scrabble over a few rock faces to get out of the dungeon. At least we were finally dry when we stepped into the windy night of the Wild.

We were working through the dungeons clockwise.

"Bets on the second floor of the lava dungeon? I bet it's a dragon," Sandy said.

"There's no way it's a dragon. That's gotta be way higher level. Right?" The drake from my crafting memories flashed through my head. If it was a drake, we were straight-up screwed. We could give up hope of killing that even if the whole village helped. I felt a frown spread on my face.

"I mean, it's gotta be a big lizard, right?" Sandy asked.

Cinnamon was a good boy. Trees exploded around him.

He thought he might have made Olivier a little too angry.

Arrows pierced through the trunks of trees, turning them into shrapnel that made Cinnamon pivot in order to avoid them. No less than three times he had to climb a falling tree to avoid being under it when it hit the ground.

And he was starting to get tired. Olivier could win this round of keep-away, he guessed.

He dropped the bow. But he kept running.

Eventually, he realized Olivier was no longer chasing him. He looked up to the canopy of the forest above him. Then he realized that he was lost.

Cinnamon whined.

Stepping into the lava field dungeon was almost refreshing after being out in the night. The comfort of the heat just made me dread the upcoming frozen dungeon all the more. Sandy and I split up immediately, each of us tackling one of the slow, stupid, black lizards that roamed the lava fields.

The mundane ones had stopped giving me experience. But they were also pitifully easy to kill. Sandy and I met up near the archway to the next floor of the dungeon. It was visible from where I sat; the bright red fire-breathing lizard stood between us and the gate, painfully close to a lava flow.

Sandy pulled out her wind knife. I threw one of my needles forward, whipping it back to tie the thread around the monster just like I had with the copper mole's whiskers. Instead, I locked the monster's mouth shut. Sand whipped out with her blade, cutting down the monster's side.

[+1 XP] [Level up]

▸Thread Sensing I

[RARE] Grants user a metaphysical sense of threads, allowing them to see where they are through walls and what is in contact with them. Additional levels allow farther sensing

▸Mending I

[COMMON] Allows user to repair clothing from patterns they are unfamiliar with. Additional levels increase quality of final product.

▶Cutting Mastery I

[COMMON] Enables system assistance for cutting patterns from whole material. Additional levels increase proficiency.

My hands were practically shaking when I saw my choices. Everything was coming together. I closed my eyes and sucked in a breath as I selected the skill and felt Thread Mastery move to seven.

"You good?" Sandy asked.

"Leveled up," I said, kicking the corpse of the fire monster. As I freed the thread keeping its mouth shut, hot, napalm-like liquid spilled out. I was glad my threads appeared to be fire resistant. "Ready?" I asked, looking up to the gate.

A bubble of lava popped from the river behind it, splattering the base of the gate with burning-hot liquid stone that slowly cooled before our eyes.

Sandy winced.

"As I'll ever be." She said.

We walked through this one together. Yet another cave.

This one was illuminated by a river of lava that split the cavern down the middle, occasionally broken up by half-complete bridges. Surrounding us were porous rock and slick obsidian stone that held almost no traction for anyone unlucky enough to be diving this room.

We stayed close to the wall, practically hugging it. Slipping here would be a death sentence. I made a note to myself to try to find a pattern that came with boots with traction or cleats.

We both flinched as a lava bubble popped, but we continued deeper into the cave, moving in one direction and on one side to carefully track our path.

This time, the monster found us.

It wasn't a dragon, not exactly. It was a reptile, sure, but—

"Is that an actual *turtle?*" Sandy asked.

The monster was making a horrible, high-pitched squealing noise from the other side of the river. It slapped its feet, waddling back and forth angrily. Its shell was a deep, dark black that seemed to reflect almost no light, its edges flecked with near-glowing red. Its mouth was a beak of monstrous proportion. I didn't want to find out what that monster could do up close. It must have been more than five feet from side to side, as big as the giant underwater crab had been, if not bigger.

The errant thought of how good a soup it would make did cross my mind.

I threw one of my throwing needles, but it bounced off the monster's shell ineffectively. It screeched louder at that.

"No luck that I'll kill it from here," I said.

Sandy nodded.

She flicked her knife.

There was a crack as obsidian glass exploded, a line of damage appearing across the river and along the monster's shell. It retreated inward, losing all traction along the slippery surfaces of the cave.

It slid right into the river.

Lava splashed up around us, causing me to jump back, scrabbling for ground. A rogue drop of lava splattered onto my boot. I flicked my foot repeatedly before remembering that [Quick Change] could clean armor. I switched away the boot and stood on the surprisingly cool obsidian in mundane socks.

When I pulled the boots back, one had a burn mark where the droplet had hit it.

"Sandy? Are you okay?" I asked.

"Fine!" she said. There was a line of fire in front of her.

"Did you...parry the lava drops?"

[+4 XP]

I looked down into the river where the turtle was being carried away, completely cooked.

"Not all of them, looks like," Sandy said, gesturing to the burn on my boot. "Sorry."

"S'fine. Just glad I wasn't wearing a cloak. I'd be on fire," I replied, and then we climbed our way out of the dungeon.

"So...ice monster."

"Dunno what it's gonna be. But I can guarantee it's going to suck." I said.

The lava dungeon was one of the easiest to cross, entirely flat and a clear line of sight from entrance to entrance. We were out in only a few minutes. When I stepped out of the dungeon and back into the Wild, I nearly crashed right into Olivier.

CHAPTER 47

Olivier's face was a grimy mess. His hair was in frayed tangles, and his clothes were covered in mud. He looked like he had been on a mad dash through the forest. He snarled.

"There you are."

His hands glowed.

I didn't wait. A month of clearing monsters kicked in my instincts. I threw a throwing needle just like I had for the monsters, the string circling around him and whipping his arm back. A spell went off, bright white and yellow, a cage appearing on the ground behind him.

Whatever that was, it had misfired.

Sandy punched him in the face.

He didn't even budge.

With a frown, Olivier lifted the arm I had yanked back, overcoming the magical mastery of my threads with a kind of bored ease. His snarl intensified.

"I hate this goddamn place," He said. "To think my brothers and sisters are at home living comfortably while I'm out here in the sticks, covered in mud, fighting lowborn! *Working* for a fucking lowborn! Fuck capturing you."

The next few seconds happened in a flash. Olivier drew his bow to his hands in an instant, knocked an arrow, and drew.

Sandy reacted just as quickly. I watched in near slow motion as she activated [Parry] at the same time the arrow hit her helmet. There was a tiny little dent where the head of the arrow had started to bend the metal.

Olivier rocked backward, slamming into a tree so hard it split the bark.

He slumped against the tree, leaning forward, seemingly unconscious.

"Ohhhhhhhhhhh shit Sandy you just assaulted the hell out of a Noble." The words tumbled out of my mouth in a rush. I was already dashing forward to check his pulse.

"Steal his clothes!" Sandy said.

"What?" I asked. "Sandy, clearing the dungeon is one thing! You just assaulted a Noble!"

"You assaulted him, too! Steal his clothes. They're magic right? Shit, now tie him down!"

"Is he even alive?" I asked, putting my fingers to his neck. He *was* still alive. His pulse was healthy, even. That parry had sounded like a gunshot. "Oh shit."

I pulled out two of my throwing needles, whipping them around the tree and pulling the threads as tight as I could before snipping off the ends and keeping the needles. That left me with just three left with strings attached.

"I don't even think this will hold him," I said.

"Gwen? Your hunter set gives you bow proficiency, right?" Sandy asked.

I turned around slowly, afraid of what I knew I was going to see.

Sandy was holding Olivier's bow.

"Are you *looting* right now?"

"Well, we're super fucked, right?" Sandy said. "So we should take everything we can to win,." Her voice was high pitched.

I looked back at Olivier. Then I pressed a hand to his chest and activated [Quick Change]. I wasn't sure if it would work. I had never tried with another person's clothes.

It activated, but not how I expected. The clothes Olivier wore, I couldn't change at all. However, I could access his inventory.

And he had a second set. I shoveled it away into my [Wardrobe].

I took Olivier's bow from Sandy, holding it in my hands. I felt [Bow Proficiency] activate for the first time, guiding me on how to hold it and knock the arrow.

"We don't have arrows!" I said.

"Can't you steal them from him?" Sandy asked, pointing at Olivier. We were yelling. Olivier groaned in his uncomfortable sleep.

"Oh shit," Sandy said. "Frost dungeon!"

Then she turned and ran.

I made a choked noise before running after her.

We were properly sprinting this time. The dungeons were quite the walk from each other, even following the path along the remains of the town's walls. We made record time, though, stopping and panting at the entrance to the last sub-dungeon.

Sandy kept stealing glances behind us and into the forest.

"Six more floors," Sandy said.

"Let's go," I said.

We plunged into the icy dungeon, speedwalking to the first of the four monsters.

Sandy stared up at it. I reached for one of the needles at my waist, but she grabbed my wrist to stop me.

"Shoot it!" she said.

"I don't have arrows!" I replied.

"Use those!" She said.

"It won't fly straight," I said, looking at the needle. "It's not fletched."

"Use your thread skill," Sandy said.

I pulled the bow from my back and drew it. I pulled on the thread, which under the control of [Thread Master], spun out behind the needle, twirling.

Then I fired.

The arrow shot out with surprising speed and accuracy, landing with a crack in the monster's side. It dimmed as it fell dead.

But I didn't get experience for the elementals anymore.

I recalled the needle-arrow, and the corpse was dragged along with it. We didn't bother harvesting it. We were already onto the next.

I practiced with the bow. The skill made it easy to increase my proficiency, and my superhuman dexterity made aiming much less of a challenge than I suspected it would be. Each of the elementals died in a single shot, and then the other gate opened near the entrance.

Snow clung to our armor as we stepped through into a cave made of solid ice. Walls of blue ice shone with light just as the crystals above had. Bridges crisscrossed a patchwork of rooms that were covered in stalagmites of solid ice, sharpened points gleaming menacingly in the low but constant light of the cave.

It was even more slippery than the obsidian.

I gave one of my two giant needles to Sandy, stabbing it into the ice and using it for stability as we moved at a crawl along one of the walls. There wasn't even powdered snow in here.

We crossed through the mouth of a tunnel on our left and into a gigantic central chamber, our eyes sweeping the room.

I didn't see a monster.

I proceeded carefully, wary of the icy ground. Sandy's lamplight glowed and reflected off the walls in a hundred directions, each faceted surface creating the illusion of movement as we walked deeper in. Then I was swept off my feet with a crack.

The slick surface of the ice kept me sliding away, shooting down the open cave, and the monster roared. I grabbed at the ice to try to stop myself but kept sliding until I slammed into the wall. Olivier's bow skittered across the floor to hit me.

[Health: 89/102]

Whatever it was, it wasn't half as strong as the bear.

I looked up to see an uncoiling serpent of pure ice, eyes glowing. It had blended right in with the cave. It opened its mouth, as if to roar, but the sound of harsh wind blowing echoed out instead. A glowing aura of frost surrounded it.

Sandy [Parried]. The monster's head snapped back as the aura disappeared. Then it bore down on her. I pushed myself to my feet, drawing one of the little needle arrows and firing it into the monster's side.

It landed with a tiny pop, barely damaging the monster. Sandy's wind blade made cuts up its side, but she had already swung three times. She couldn't have more than a few mana left.

I activated the skill from Olivier's looted inventory as I drew my needle.

[Ignite Projectile] [Mana: 5/10]

It cost half my mana. Half of it! But the arrow and the entire length of string attached to it lit up with supernatural flame as I loosed it.

The needle flew out through the air. And it *missed.*

I pulled on the thread, dragging the somehow burning metal needle down and wrapping it around the monster. I gestured out to return the needle to me—then canceled it, pulling on the strings to send the needle up.

The monster screamed in its weird way again, the elemental making the noises of whistling wind as I wrapped the needle around and around its body. Boiling steam poured off the monster, flashed from ice to water. I finally ran out of thread as the last length of it wrapped around the monster's neck. Steam filled the chamber around us, the water making the ice even more slick. I drew another throwing needle.

The monster bore down on Sandy. She [Parried] again.

The monster's half-melted neck snapped, and its head flew clean off.

"Holy shit!" Sandy said, her voice echoing in the cave. "That's way worse than the other floors!"

I rushed over to her as fast I could without slipping.

"You hurt?" I asked, leaning down.

"Am I hurt? Are *you?*" She inspected me up and down. "Damn. Didn't even dent your armor."

I touched my breastplate. Maybe that's the only reason it did less damage than the bear.

"Let's get out of here." I said.

"Just one dungeon to go," Sandy said. "We're definitely looting this one, right? C'mon, you can carry an elemental core."

She stabbed down to split the monster apart, tearing away bricks of ice until she found a round core the size of my fist. It glowed blue. She shoved it into my hands.

I activated [Always Prepared] stuffing the core into the wooden chest.

"Just one more dungeon," I echoed.

CHAPTER 48

We recovered in the forest outside the dungeon. Surprisingly, we were almost out of soup. We weren't out of mana though; we both managed to top off in less than an hour. Sandy switched her storm curtain armor for one of the hunter outfits so we could use stealth at the town's edge.

We were so, so close. There were more lights on than normal at the few houses in the town center. The Noble guard sat at attention beside a campfire a few feet from the center dungeon's entrance.

We had done this before.

I trusted Sandy to fend for herself as I slipped around the guard and into the gate. The world changed from a pitch-black, cloud-covered night to late morning.

I walked down the path inside the farm dungeon before turning back to whisper.

"Sandy?" I asked.

Nothing.

A few seconds later there was a warping noise as the gate activated. I tensed, half expecting that the Noble playing guard had followed me through.

"Sandy?" I hissed again.

She popped into existence, reality warbling where she appeared.

"Switch," she said. I pulled her armor from my inventory, dismissing my stealth. Sandy got changed just inside the entrance to the dungeon, then we walked the path to the wolf den.

Every few seconds we threw nervous looks back to the entrance. But the man was watching the town square. Not the entrance. Surely Valjean had warned them we had stealth skills? Would he really miss something like that?

It didn't matter right now anyway. What mattered was clearing the dungeon. Taking ownership of the town. Why would Valjean care? He didn't even want it. I remembered what Olivier said.

"Olivier sounded pissed about having to…what was it? 'Work for a low-born?'" I asked.

"Yeah." Sandy shrugged. "Go figure the people who look down on everyone else find ways to look down on each other too. Valjean's a Noble, Olivier's a Noble… They're both assholes."

I shrugged. I was the last person who would say she was wrong about that. My hands shook with excitement as we entered the rocky wolf den. I listened for the normal scratching of the fixed wolf.

There was no sound at all. I stepped deeper in, expecting and ready to find the wolf waiting just around the corner of the next tunnel. But I didn't find any. My anxiety rose as we twisted deeper and deeper into the Dungeonheart.

I heard Sandy gasp behind me as the final room came into view.

The gate was open. The floor was clear. All four of the wolves were in barely recognizable piles of flesh, scattered across the floor, swatted like bugs. There was no sign of a fight anywhere except for where the monsters had landed, each and every one ripped to shreds.

I remembered my earlier conversation with Henri. He hadn't seen Valjean at all. A sinking feeling landed in my stomach.

"What the fuck?" Sandy whispered. "Why would he clear the dungeon?"

"I think I know," I said. I turned my head to face Sandy. Then I pointed at the gate. "He's in there. He has to be."

"No sweat. We do the same thing we always have. Clear the dungeon," Sandy said. I didn't have half her confidence. But I followed her to the next floor anyway.

We sat in silence as we took in the next level of the dungeon. The trees were all cut down again. I couldn't even see the spider corpses among the rubble.

We moved slowly and cautiously, inching forward toward the next gate.

The next floor was open too.

There was no second guessing ourselves now. We were already here. I swallowed my fear and stepped through.

The cliff on the third floor was destroyed.

There was a mark where a clean cut sheered the rock face. A pile of rubble had sunk into the ground below.

Valjean hadn't bothered with a rope. He had just broken the world to suit his needs, creating what amounted to a staircase of broken rock and rubble. Sandy grunted and walked past me. The rubble slid under her feet, the ground unsteady. I followed to her right, climbing down to the forest floor. There was a quiet wind. I looked at Sandy before following her to the center.

The final floor was open, the bear's corpse next to the open gate.

The bear was split in two. Bisected almost perfectly down the middle, and left to rot in the field. The wind blew over it, sending ripples through the standing puddle of blood beneath it.

Sandy and I looked at each other again. I couldn't see her face behind the helmet. I took a tentative step forward. This was our chance, tonight. All we had to do was defeat whatever we found on the other side of this door.

Just one more step. Then we were through.

The monster inside bore down on us instantly. I didn't see it; I just heard the rush of air and threw myself to the side, my armor breaking foliage as I dove out of the way.

"Sandy?!" I asked, shouting as I rose to my feet. A gigantic spider had crashed directly down on us out of the gate. No monster had sat outside the gate before this. The spider made a terrible hissing noise from where it stood atop the dungeon gate, its legs seeming to burn as it touched the exit.

"I'm alive! You?!" she asked, shouting from the other side of the monster.

This was the thing Valjean had killed in the woods, the thing that had damaged his wagons and Sandy had cut apart. Almost. Instead of white, this one was black. And far, far bigger. Spikes rose from its chitin carapace, nets of web connecting them together.

I swallowed hard as it turned around, looking at me. Each of its eight eyes was another color, shining in the dark of the forest. But it wasn't nighttime, even though we'd switched floors; the canopy of the forest was choked out.

And not by leaves.

Layers upon layers of webs stretched above us.

"How the hell do we kill this?" Sandy shouted.

"Just like any other spider!" I said, dashing forward.

[Running Stitch I] [Mana: 9/10]

The needle scraped along the edge of the spider, sending up sparks. Just like the crab, its carapace was as hard as metal. The spider flipped a leg out and sent me and my needle tumbling separately to the ground.

[Health: 59/102]

I grunted as I pushed myself to my feet, scanning the ground for my needle as I analyzed what the monster was doing. Then I stopped, choking.

"This is an interesting weapon. Are you the blacksmith, then…? No, he has a son." Valjean said, holding the giant sewing needle in one hand and a necklace in another. He let it drop to his chest.

His back was turned to the monster. I stared, wide-eyed with horror. Why was Valjean here? He sighed.

"I didn't expect two Nobles. Nor the blacksmith for helping you." Valjean frowned. He kept walking forward until he was no longer standing between us and the monster. He must not have recognized us under the armor.

I grabbed the second throwing needle from my belt, but before I could free it, Valjean threw my giant needle at me. It buried itself in the ground.

The monster took a step toward me.

I ripped the needle out of the ground and held it out in front of me. My eyes jumped between the monster and Valjean. He walked with an almost casual indifference.

"Do you know the reason why Nobles are legally required to attend the Academy?" Valjean asked. "It's funny. The unchosen treat it as an affront." He swiveled to look at the spider.

"No," I said to Valjean, still looking between him and the spider. The bug seemed to have no inclination to move.

"One percent of the population will always be Nobles. Chosen, unchosen. Did you know that fifty percent of Chosen Nobles die within three years?" Valjean said.

Then he activated a skill, disappearing and then reappearing fifteen feet away.

The spider charged me.

There was a crack behind it as Sandy swung with her knife, gore erupting from where she cut one of the monster's legs. The monster stumbled, spinning around with a hiss. It rushed at Sandy. I tried to dash forward, but the monster was just too fast.

I stopped myself short when Valjean reappeared between the monster and Sandy. It stopped attacking. Why had it stopped attacking? Valjean wasn't taking the monster's aggro. Did he have this thing tamed? A hundred thoughts raced through my head.

"Why are you giving us a lecture?" I shouted the last word, staring at the monster as it spun around, moving away from Valjean.

"Many new Nobles, like you, charge straight into the dungeon. Almost all of you die. Do you know what that means? It means there will be another Chosen. And then that Chosen will charge into a dungeon and die. How do you think this ends for you? There's no winning here." Valjean spat. "You can't steal the title from me. Trust me, if there was a Noble who could maintain this town, they would have the title. You can't even kill this monster."

Valjean waved behind himself.

"We killed all the others!" I said. Sandy was still holding her knife. I looked at her. She looked ready to run.

"The monsters in the central dungeon don't get stronger linearly—they get stronger exponentially. Do you—do they have math classes here? This monster isn't…it's not like fighting two of the monsters from the previous floor. It's like fighting four of them. Look—it's already healing."

Valjean, and the scowl stuck on his face, both disappeared.

Sandy [Parried]. The sound of the clash rang out through the forest.

A single parry from the bear had blown it inward, tearing the thing apart.

This time, Sandy's parry just made the spider monster flinch. She paused for a second. Then she ran, circling around the monster to stand next to me. The spider spun with her. There was a tiny crack in its face.

I pulled out the scissors and activated them, wincing as my mana dropped to eight out of ten.

Then I shot forward, snipping at one of the monster's rotating legs. I felt the scissors bite into the monster and stop hard. It made a hissing noise. I pulled the scissors back, scoring a deep cut in the monster's leg.

I stumbled back. Valjean appeared next to me, crouching over.

"Giant scissors?" he asked. "You know, with two Nobles, one of you has a better than zero chance of earning land. If you move through the right channels, operate correctly, you could take this land yourself."

"Fuck you!" Sandy said. She was pointing her knife at Valjean now. "Neither of us are Nobles!"

There was a pause. Valjean blinked, stood to his full height, and pushed his hair back.

"What?" he asked.

"Neither of us are Nobles," I repeated, my voice practically a hiss. "Is this some kind of sick game? Do you just like showing people how weak they are?" My voice rose in volume as I spoke.

"I—no. The only way that Nobles accept that— By seeing how strong the monsters actually get, I… I was trying to convince you to go to the Academy. Not to—" Valjean looked down at Sandy's knife. Then at my scissors. "You're not Nobles. You're…Gwen? You're not a Noble."

"If you can clear every floor of this dungeon, why are you letting our town rot?" I asked, stepping toward Valjean. I watched the spider take a step on my left.

"Do you know how many people die in tier zero cities?" Valjean said.

"We *do*," Sandy spat. "But you're the one trying to take away the entire life we've lived here."

"No access to running water, sewage, quality of life—and the local council won't agree to be moved. *What life?*" Valjean asked. "You're… This is crazy. The two of you are suicidal. You actually killed all the monsters before this one?"

"Yes! Are you going to help or not?" I asked, pulling out a needle. Valjean squinted at it. I pulled it back on the bow and fired it, the magic assisting me.

Then it lit on fire as I activated [Ignite Projectile].

[Mana: 3/10]

I wrapped the wire around the burning spider, the thin thread finding the gaps in the chitin at its joins, cutting in, and igniting. The monster's blood seemed to be flammable, dripping and lighting the forest floor on fire. The webs on its back erupted in flame and smoke.

Sandy whipped her knife down into the monster over and over, parrying as she did, metal and blades of wind cracking over the monster's carapace. Finally, its chitin split open.

The spider hissed as it rushed toward us. I grabbed my needle, activating [Running Stitch] until my mana hit zero.

I wasn't sure when the monster had actually died. Its head was a gory mess. I had scrambled the front of its body. Its legs kept twitching.

I panted. Sandy panted.

[+10 XP]

[Level up]

[Title Contest Quest complete! Title of Tier 0 Village, Stitch, transferred to Gwendolyn Tailor.]

[Congratulations! Mayoral interface will be enabled after 24 hours' residence in Stitch.]

[Notice: Quest completed in under 24 hours from reset. Bonus: +10 XP]

[Level up]

I turned to Valjean.

"What now?" I said, the momentary excitement getting to me. "Guess it's not your town anymore, is it?" I shouted.

Valjean nodded.

"Fuck you." Sandy said, again.

Valjean nodded again. He opened his mouth to speak, turned, stopped, and looked at the monster. Then he turned back to me.

"Was that Olivier's skill?" Valjean asked.

"I—" Oh shit. He saw that. "No."

Valjean nodded again.

"I'm arresting the both of you."

CHAPTER 49

Give Olivier's clothing back," Valjean said, exasperated. I had changed back into my own mundane clothes—though I quickly stored my armor, as much as it irritated him.

"Don't have it. You saw me store the armor. I only have room for one," I said.

My wrists were in gigantic metal cuffs presumably meant to contain Nobles. They were like giant weights to me. Sandy sat across from me in the middle of town, wearing her own set of cuffs.

Without any mana left, I couldn't use [Shadow Cloak] to run away. Sandy currently sat across from me in the middle of town. And Valjean wouldn't let me eat my soup.

"You had his skill," Valjean said. "Do you have it?" he asked, turning to Sandy. She spit in his face.

"Okay," he said, wiping it away. "That was gross." Then he sighed.

The third Noble returned, dragging a still-unconscious Olivier with him. The man flopped Olivier onto a bench.

"Go fetch me the blacksmith," Valjean said. The Noble nodded and spun back around. Gerald's house was visible from here.

"No! No." I said. "You don't have to—I threatened them into helping!" I said. Valjean raised his eyes.

"Alright. I'm sure that's what they'll testify, then."

I sent a panicked look to Sandy, who shrugged. She had changed into a set of plain linens as well.

But there was nothing either of us could do except wait.

A few minutes later, Gerald walked out of his house. He shook as he walked up to us. He stared at me, looking as if he was about to cry.

"I said the blacksmith, not his—" Valjean was interrupted.

"I'm a Noble!" Gerald said. I'm the one who's been clearing the dungeon. I made their weapons!"

"Huh," Valjean said, lifting up the scissors. "You made these?" He spun his finger and the scissors shrunk.

Gerald nodded.

"Prove it," Valjean said.

"Gerald, no—" I started.

"It's alright, Gwen. I'm done hiding. Arrest me instead of them!" Gerald said.

"You idiot—" Sandy started.

Gerald summoned his shield. I groaned.

"He really is a Noble," Valjean said. His voice sounded almost bored. "Arrest him."

The Noble guard pulled out a set of handcuffs and slapped them on Gerald. He looked back and forth expectantly.

"So?" Gerald asked. "Let them go."

Valjean took a drink from a flask.

"God, what the hell? Do you guys have broth in these? I need alcohol." Valjean sighed. "They're arrested for assaulting and robbing a Noble, Gerald."

"What?" Gerald asked, stunned.

"Throw them in the wagon. We've wasted enough time here already."

We were unceremoniously ushered inside one of the wagons.

I was pressed onto a little bench between Sandy and Gerald. The guard took our handcuffs off before stepping out, the door locking from the outside. The seat was plush, but the space was cramped. It wasn't magical like the priest's had been.

I stared at the floor. I didn't even get a chance to talk to my mom.

We sat in silence for a few minutes. Then we felt the prickling sensation of the Wild on our skin.

"You're an idiot, Gerald." Sandy whispered.

"What did I do? You guys attacked a Noble?" Gerald asked, looking up. He was in immense distress, the lines of his face wrinkled. His eyes were red and puffy.

"You didn't have to turn yourself in! We were already arrested! What did you think would happen?" Sandy said, slowly getting louder.

"I'm not the one who decided to clear the dungeon!" Gerald said.

"Guys! Will you sit the hell down!" I said. Then I leaned back, rubbing my temples, trying to stave off a headache. "We are so screwed."

"Did you complete the quest?"

"What quest?" Gerald asked.

"Yeah. It's completed. I have the title. But that doesn't seem to matter now." New determination filled me. "We just have to get to the city. Then I can give you the hunter outfit and we can stealth away." I said, looking over at Sandy.

She nodded her head, thinking about it.

"Okay," she said. "Then what?"

"We'll have to hike back through the Wild…" I said.

"Uh, where am I in this? Do you have three stealth outfits?"

"We'll leave you there. Don't worry," Sandy said, "I'm sure Nobles are treated better."

We lapsed back into silence.

Then there was scrambling on the roof, followed by a bark.

"Olivier, no!" Valjean shouted.

There was a twang, whistle, and crash as Olivier knocked and loosed his bow in half a second.

I leaned forward on the bench.

"The fuck is happening?" I asked.

The door swung open, the latch unlocked from the outside.

"Cinnamon!" Sandy said, leaning forward. The dog rolled over immediately, filling almost half the wagon.

I dashed for the door just as Valjean blocked the exit. He shook his head with disappointment, looking down at Sandy's dog. The door shut in my face. The wagons started forward again with a hitch. Cinnamon was covered in dirt and mud. He started licking Sandy's face.

"Stop!" she said.

Cinnamon twirled around, covering all of us in hair before pressing his face to the wagon's window.

I sighed. Now we were stuck in a wagon with Sandy's dog, too.

"How long is the wagon ride to the city?"

"Just over a day," Gerald said.

We both turned to stare at him.

"What? You know my mom has to go sometimes."

"Uh… no, I didn't, but okay," Sandy said. She sighed.

We spent basically an hour in silence after that, just processing.

I'd just been arrested. I'D JUST BEEN ARRESTED! And Sandy made it worse by assaulting a Noble.

Right before I had a panic attack, the door rattled, and Valjean stepped in. Cinnamon growled.

Valjean petted him casually. Cinnamon's tongue lolled out of his mouth as Valjean scratched behind his ears. He pulled the door shut and sat down on the less comfortable-looking seats on the other side of the wagon. Valjean sighed.

"My bed is going to be covered in dog hair, isn't it?" Valjean asked.

"Your…bed?" Gerald asked.

Valjean gestured at us.

I looked behind us, seeing that the cushion on this side of the wagon was indeed a mattress bent at ninety degrees.

"Yes. It is," I said.

Valjean rubbed his eyes.

"You've created a massive headache for me. I've talked to Olivier; he's willing to let this go if you return the outfit you *looted* from him."

"I already told you, I don't—"

Valjean held up a hand to forestall me.

"Yeah, okay. If Olivier's outfit is returned, I've convinced him not to charge you," Valjean said before rubbing his eyes again.

"You said you would give this town up if there was a Noble who would take it. We can clear the monsters. Why don't you just leave? Let us run it."

"Only graduates of the Noble Academy can earn land, Legally speaking." Valjean shook his head.

"I'm a Noble!" Gerald said. "You could give the land to me...then we could run the town."

"Shut up, Gerald," Sandy said.

Gerald frowned.

"That's actually what I want to talk to you about," Valjean said. "You can kill the monsters. Hell, Gwen proved you can even have the title transferred to a peasant. Which I didn't know." Valjean frowned. "That's not what they teach at the Academy. But letting peasants into the dungeon at all is..." He waved his hand.

"So you're going to give us the town?" Sandy asked.

"No," Valjean said. "It's not that easy. I want to...I grew up in a border town, did you know? I'm a Chosen. A lowborn. We're looked down on by the other Nobility...it's not important." Valjean waved the line of thought away.

"You're...Chosen? What were your parents' classes?" I asked.

Valjean frowned.

"I never found out."

"Oh."

"What?" Gerald asked.

"His parents died," Sandy said.

I elbowed her.

"If you have an alternative—if you can give the people of Stitch a better life than the one they have now. Then I have no problem with it. But to do it legally—in the eyes of the law—you must be a graduate from the Academy. Just because the system lets you take the title doesn't mean the nation will let you keep it."

"We're not Nobles," I said.

"Do you have to be?" Valjean leaned forward. "You killed a fourth-floor boss."

I blinked, leaning back.

"Only members of the clergy can inspect status." Valjean looked down at me. "If you have an alternative…something better than the system that's in place, I want to see it. Do you know there's no way to certify another person's class and the Church doesn't work with the state? Legally, the status of Nobility is only officially conferred on graduation from the Academy. So if you were to attend as you are now, and if you were to graduate, you'd then be legally allowed to hold the title."

"So…you want to send us to the Academy?" I asked.

Valjean nodded.

AUTHOR'S NOTE

Hello! I'm Crown Fall! Thanks for reading *Dressed to Kill*. If you're reading this, you're out of chapters. You can find more of my work at http://linktr.ee/coteh as well as work from other amazing authors. You might even find more chapters of *Dressed to Kill*.

Please leave a review and come join us on Discord for shenanigans: https://discord.com/invite/jHJP9RB.

Information on my writers circle can be found at http://card.hiatus.city.
Check out Slifer's work at http://slifer.hiatus.city.
Check out Jess's amazing work at https://thisambiguous.one/.
Another book I really enjoyed listening to the audiobook of was a LitRPG called *The Daily Grind on Audible* by Argus: https://podiumaudio.com/audio-book/the-daily-grind-a-slice-of-life-litrpg/

If discord isn't your thing, check out these LitRPG Facebook groups:
LitRPG Books: https://www.facebook.com/groups/1069684616388207
GameLit Society: https://www.facebook.com/groups/LitRPGsociety
LitRPG Forum: https://www.facebook.com/groups/litrpgforum

If you're wondering what I mean in Monster Hunter, it's Gunlance/Longsword.

ABOUT THE AUTHOR

Crown Fall is the son of a lonely orc and an adventurer. He grew up in the drag-on-infested countryside. Dragon makes for good steak.

9 781039 448438